"L......y and appealing first mystery...a promising debut, deftly juggling a cozy modern suspense story with an up-to-date romance."

—*Publishers Weekly* on **Larkspur**

"A second adventure for California bookdealer Lark Dodge… Always literate, intriguing… add a plus for readers planning a trip to London and environs."

—*Kirkus Reviews* on **Skylark**

"Sharp characterization—particularly of the marvelously wry Lark—and a mystery that is skillfully intertwined with Lark and Jay's life as they try to start a family grip the reader's interest up to a resolution that puts an intriguing twist on the standard sleuth-in-danger finale."

—*Publishers Weekly* on **Mudlark**

"The delight of the Lark Dodge series is that you can read them as satires or as straightforward murder mysteries. But you should read them."

—*The Oregonian* on **Meadowlark**

"A deceptively stately pace, accompanied by interesting subplots and vivid jaunts in the country."

—*Library Journal* on **Malarkey**

 *Buffalo Bill's*
Defunct

Also by Sheila Simonson:

Buffalo Bill's Defunct

A LATOUCHE COUNTY MYSTERY

 Sheila Simonson

2008 / PERSEVERANCE PRESS / JOHN DANIEL & COMPANY
PALO ALTO / MCKINLEYVILLE, CALIFORNIA

A Perseverance Press Book
Published by John Daniel & Company
A division of Daniel & Daniel, Publishers, Inc.
Post Office Box 2790
McKinleyville, California 95519
www.danielpublishing.com/perseverance

Distributed by SCB Distributors (800) 729-6423

Book design by Eric Larson, Studio E Books, Santa Barbara, www.studio-e-books.com

Cover image: Monotype by Lillian Pitt, from the "Ancestors" series. Collaborative Master Printer: Frank Janzen, TMP. Printed at Crow's Shadow Institute of the Arts, Pendleton, Oregon. Photographed by Studio 421, Pendleton, Oregon.

"Buffalo Bill's". Copyright 1923, 1951, © 1991 by the Trustees for the E.E. Cummings Trust. Copyright © 1976 by George James Firmage, from COMPLETE POEMS: 1904–1962 by E.E. Cummings, edited by George J. Firmage. Used by permission of Liveright Publishing Corporation.

10 9 8 7 6 5 4 3 2 1

LIBRARY OF CONGRESS CATALOGING-IN-PUBLICATION DATA
Simonson, Sheila, (date)
  Buffalo Bill's defunct : a Latouche County mystery / by Sheila Simonson.
    p. cm.
  ISBN-13: 978-1-880284-96-4 (pbk. : alk. paper)
  ISBN-10: 1-880284-96-0 (pbk. : alk. paper)
  1. Indians of North America—Fiction. 2. Sheriffs—Fiction. 3. Librarians—Fiction.
  4. Petroglyphs—Fiction. 5. Columbia River Gorge (Or. and Wash.)—Fiction. I. Title.
PS3569.I48766B84 2008
  813'.54—dc22
      2008000709

My thanks to Meredith Phillips,
the kind of editor writers dream of.

This book is for my sweet husband, Mickey,
who is very very patient.

AUTHOR'S NOTE

It would be foolish to insist that the Columbia River Gorge is fictional. It is spectacularly real, a National Scenic Area that adjoins two National Forests, with Mount Adams and Mount St. Helens on the north in Washington State, and Mount Hood on the south in Oregon. On the north side, it is sparsely populated.

For the purposes of the story, I rearranged the scenery and political geography of the western end of the Gorge, subtracting Skamania and part of Klickitat counties from Washington and combining them into fictional Latouche County. Latouche County does not exist outside my imagination. There is no Tyee Lake. Klalo, the county seat, resembles at least four small towns in western Washington, but is its own imaginary place. I hope there are real toads in it.

I changed the demography of the local tribes as well as the geography, though I tried to make the ethnic variation plausible. The Klalo tribe is Chinookian in language and in some of its customs, but it is as much a product of my imagination as Latouche County. Its principal chief, Madeline Thomas, doesn't exist, but I wish she did.

Buffalo Bill's Defunct takes place in October 2004.

Buffalo Bill's
        defunct
                who used to
                ride a watersmooth-silver
                            stallion
and break onetwothreefourfive pigeonsjustlikethat
                                            Jesus
he was a handsome man
                and what i want to know is
how do you like your blueeyed boy
Mister Death

                                —e.e. cummings

 *Buffalo Bill's*
Defunct

 *Chapter 1*

THE twenty-five-foot moving van shifted down. Meg McLean clenched her hands on its steering wheel. She kept her foot on the accelerator and her eyes on the double center line. No passing? No kidding.

To her left, a parade of cars sped toward her in the oncoming lane of the narrow highway. To her right, past the graveled shoulder, the scenery dropped two hundred feet straight down to the Columbia River.

Meg was driving Washington State Highway 14 east from Vancouver, the last stretch of a long haul from Southern California. Ahead of her, a logging truck laden with splintery cedars wound upward. Behind her, a bronze Lexus hung just far enough back to be visible in the van's side-view mirrors. The Lexus had its lights on "bright." The driver had been looking for a chance to pass for five miles.

The van held all of Meg's possessions, forty-two years' worth, with her '97 Honda Accord clamped to the tow-bar. The truck's maximum speed was an unwise sixty-five downhill. On long upward grades like this one, the speedometer hovered at thirty-five, dropped, then surged a bit as the truck shifted down again. The drivers behind her were entitled to impatience. She hoped one of them wouldn't shoot her. She hoped her daughter wouldn't phone. Lucy had called every day of the trip at precisely three o'clock. It was one minute to three.

The truck's CD player held only one disc at a time. It was recycling George Gershwin's piano-roll pieces. Meg had listened to all of them twice but she didn't dare take her right hand off the wheel long enough to change discs.

The honky-tonk accompaniment made her feel like a character

in a silent film who was being victimized by technology—Harold Lloyd on a girder. She glanced right and drew a shaky breath. The river glinted in the afternoon sun, now three hundred feet down.

The highway twisted into a stretch of evergreen forest splotched with the intense yellow of maple leaves on the verge of falling. Falling down. Down.

Her cell phone beeped. Meg touched the Talk button with a sweaty finger. "Can't talk now, honey."

"Mom!"

"I'll call you back," Meg shouted at the phone. Both fists gripped the wheel like death as the parade of vehicles emerged at the edge of another cliff.

Her daughter's grumbles cut off. The dial tone hummed beneath the tinkle of Gershwin's manic piano.

Half a jaw-clenching hour later, the landscape flattened. Signs of human habitation began to appear in the dense, rock-strewn forest—a shed here, a mobile home there, a dirt road trickling into the brush. The Lexus passed and inserted itself between Meg's van and the log truck.

At the first turn-out, she pulled over onto loose gravel, shoved the gearshift into Park, and set the emergency brake. She popped the Eject button on the CD player and leaned back in the blessed silence, eyes closed.

Cars flashed past. She heard them but she didn't look at the drivers' reproachful faces. Finally she hit the speed dial and connected with Lucy.

"Are you still on the road?"

"You got it, kid."

"I thought you were supposed to be in Klalo by now."

"I'm doing my best. Highway 14 is a goat track."

"You should have hired a professional mover. It couldn't cost that much more." Lucy was calling from Stanford University, one of the more expensive institutions of higher learning in the nation. She knew very well why her mother was economizing.

I will not quarrel with my only child. Meg fumbled in her nylon CD holder for soothing sound. The discs adhered to their tight transparent slots. Beethoven? Too dramatic. Vivaldi? Too jumpy.

"Mom, are you sure you're making the right move?"

"It's a crap shoot."

"Mother? Are you all right?" Fear, confusion, honest concern. Lucy was a good daughter.

Meg sighed. "I'm fine, Luce, just not used to this kind of road." She glanced at her watch. Three-thirty. She was only two hours behind her AAA TripTik schedule. "So how was the test?" She closed her eyes again and drifted as Lucy swung into an account of her first math exam. Math was important. Lucy wanted to be a physicist.

It was four-fifteen before Meg reached the city limits of Klalo, seat of Latouche County, and four-thirty before she pulled onto the driveway in front of her one-car garage. Driveway was a dignified term for two strips of grass-infested gravel. The garage, an afterthought of the 1920s, stood well back beside the two-story frame house she had bought in a burst of summer optimism. In the chilly light of mid-October, it didn't look like home.

Maybe that was too harsh. What it looked like was a nineteenth-century farmhouse, though it faced a quiet tree-lined street near the library she was going to run. Head Librarian, Latouche County Regional Library. Sounded good.

The van fit neatly onto Meg's period driveway, but the rear end of the Accord stuck out into the street.

"The hell with it," she muttered. She set the brake and killed the engine. Because she was a short woman, she had to rappel down the side of the truck and reach up to slam the door. She fumbled the house keys from her purse, opened the side door that led into the kitchen, and sprinted for the bathroom. Bladder.

She washed her hands at the salmon pink retro basin and avoided looking in the mirror. There was no soap and no towel. She rubbed her hands dry on her jeans and picked up her purse from the cat-barf–patterned linoleum—original, the realtor had assured her with a straight face. When Lucy graduated from Stanford, Meg would replace the bathrooms, both of them. At least the one upstairs had a shower.

She drifted back into the kitchen. It was empty of appliances except for a propane range and a water heater. There was no dishwasher. The whole house was empty, in fact. That was as it should be, but the blank volumes of space made her uneasy. When the *ding-dong* of the doorbell echoed on the chilly air, she shivered.

She moved the thermostat up to seventy-five as she plodded down the hall to the front door. The propane furnace whooped on. She drew back the bolt and wrestled the door open. It took both hands.

"Hi, I'm Darcy Wheeler. You must be Miz McLeen." Darcy was plump, taller than Meg, and dressed in jeans. Her sweatshirt logo promoted Washington State University.

"McLean, like Shirley MacLaine, different spelling." Meg forced a smile. "Call me Meg. Come in. Are you a neighbor?"

"Next door. The Craftsman with blue trim." Darcy stepped over the threshold, two Styrofoam cups with plastic lids thrust before her. "I brought you a cup of coffee."

"Uh, thanks." Meg was wired from the drive.

"One's decaf and one's not," Darcy said brightly. "Hey, no place to sit."

"It's pretty bare. I'll take the decaf, thanks."

Darcy, who looked fifteen but could be thirty, strode across the dusty oak floor of the living room and set her cup on the mantel. "Lots of room. Are you going to unload that humungous truck all by yourself?"

Meg followed her. "I thought I'd call a temp agency."

"A what?"

Panic grabbed. "Where do I hire casual labor?"

"You mean guys to help you move the furniture? Gosh, we just get our friends to do that... Oh."

"Oh," Meg echoed. "Wow." A little problem she hadn't antici-pated. The thought of heaving her refrigerator off the van all by herself made her want to hop on the first plane to LA—were it not that she'd have to drive the van to Portland Airport on High-way 14.

"Let me think." Darcy sipped coffee and brooded.

Meg sipped, too. Not Starbuck's but okay, a latte from the espresso stand on the corner, probably.

"I could go see if Rob's home. His truck's there."

"Rob?"

"Your neighbor on the other side. He'll think of something."

The other side. Meg had coveted the Victorian gingerbread, though the house was too big for a single woman and not for sale.

"Yeah," Darcy said. "I'll talk to Rob." She abandoned her coffee and disappeared out the side door. She knew her way around. Meg followed on leaden feet.

ROB Neill was painting the interior of the house after two years of procrastination. In the week of comp time he had taken, because otherwise he'd lose it, he had painted his daughter's bedroom and the kitchen, and torn off a lot of wallpaper elsewhere. He had just reached the annoying alcove between the kitchen and the formal dining room. Like much of the house, the alcove had been done up in beige with cream trim. Rob's grandmother had been an admirable woman, but he suspected her of color-blindness.

He had scrubbed the space with TSP, covered the oak floor with a tarp, and slathered everything with sealant. Now, at last, the moment of truth. Was the Mediterranean Blue his daughter selected in August going to be too dark? He squished the roller in its pan until the fleece cover dripped paint, rolled off the excess, and laid down a long, perfect stroke. Aha.

He set the roller on the pan and backed off a step, squinting. He could never remember whether latex dried lighter or darker. If darker, he was in trouble. The woodwork would be Circassian White, or whatever the paint company called it, and the old lace curtains had washed up well enough to lighten the gloom. Dark or not, the blue would do.

Grunting with satisfaction, he filled the roller again and set to work. As he lost himself in the rolling rhythm, his mind drifted. He was going to have to defend his budget. Again. He should be up at the computer crunching numbers. The sheriff liked numbers. How To Lie with Statistics. It was an election year. Mack always got nervous in election years, though he had been kept in office four times by the voters of Latouche County and had no serious rivals.

Rob laid down the last stroke on the north wall and set the roller back in the pan. Three-dimensional pie charts could be diddled. He soaked the edger in blue paint. Maybe a PowerPoint presentation with pie charts. Mack was susceptible to the Wonders of Computers, but Rob didn't like PowerPoint graphics. I could just wing it, he mused, though he knew he wouldn't.

The trouble with public service was that the public wanted it, even demanded it, and didn't want to pay for it. A lot of new housing, all of it taxable, had gone in since the last budget battle. As far as Rob could tell, these new voters would spend half a million dollars on a house without blinking twice but a half-mil levy to support the library or the fire districts would go down in flames. "Ever git my hands on a dollar agin," he sang in his unmelodious baritone, "I'm gonna squeeze it till the eagle grin." The blue paint on the alcove wall looked pretty damned good.

He had finished with the edger and picked up the roller again when the doorbell rang.

MEG was standing behind the van, staring blankly and trying to remember how to unhook the Accord, when Darcy materialized on the far side of the car with the neighbor. She performed introductions and pronounced Meg's surname correctly.

The man's name was Rob Neill—a spondee, *boom-boom*. Robert, Meg supposed, or Robin Hood, or Robinson Crusoe. He was fortyish, thin, medium tall, with straight sandy hair turning gray, and he looked at her from unsmiling gray eyes.

"Hi. I'd shake hands but..." He held out a palm splotched with blue paint for her inspection. His clothes—jeans and a sweatshirt that told her Guinness was good for her—were pied with paint: blue, white, and lemon yellow.

"Sorry to interrupt you. Do you know how to unhook these things?" Meg gestured to the Accord on its little metal ramp.

He scowled. "Didn't they give you instructions when you hired the truck?"

"They did, but my brain died about ten miles back."

His mouth twitched. "Highway 14's a slow drive. At least it wasn't raining."

The horror of driving that road in wet weather struck Meg dumb. She stared at him. It could have been worse.

He bent to look at the chain mechanism. "Hmm, yeah. Front-wheel drive car... Combination?"

There was a padlock. After a blank moment she came up with the code.

He removed the lock and fiddled with the hitch and the cables. "Okay."

"That's it?" Relieved, Meg fished in her purse for the car keys.

She had three sets of keys so it took awhile. Docking her car neatly in front of the house, Meg returned to find Neill removing the towing contraption from the back of the truck.

He grunted and gave a heave. The mini-trailer dropped onto the gravel in a little puff of dust. He pulled it onto her patchy unmowed lawn, clear of the van. "I hear you need help unloading."

Meg took a long breath. "I do. Two people, preferably. I budgeted two hundred dollars."

He straightened and smiled at her for the first time. "More than beer and pizza."

"Beer and pizza, too, if necessary," Meg conceded.

"What time?"

Meg almost said "now," but the thought was too horrible. Every bone in her body ached. She wanted a hot shower and bed. "Is there a motel in town?" She had stayed at a cheap hotel near Portland Airport when she came for the job interview last spring and later that summer when she was house-hunting.

"The Red Hat Inn," Darcy piped.

"Sounds like a refuge for deer-slayers."

Darcy blinked.

Neill grinned through the paint blotches. One of his incisors was crooked. "A respectable establishment, Ms. McLean. The restaurant does great chicken-fried steak."

Meg shuddered.

"Venison steak."

"I think you're rattling my chain. I'll take any help I can get, but eight tomorrow morning would be ideal."

"Okay," Neill said. "Beer and pizza at eight o'clock. See you. I have to get back to work. Blue latex is drying on my paint roller as we speak." And he turned and walked off, disappearing through a rose arbor that, incredibly, still showed a few pink blossoms.

"That's settled," Darcy said cheerfully. "Welcome to Klalo. I have to run now, Meg. My son's Cub Scout meeting lets out in five minutes." She trotted off.

Surely she wasn't old enough to have given birth to a Cub Scout. "Thanks," Meg called after her. Darcy waved.

Alone and glad to be alone, Meg wandered back into the house. She remembered to lower the temperature on the thermostat to a respectable sixty-eight degrees. Then she locked up, fetched her carry-on, cell phone, and laptop from the cab of the van, locked *it* up, and stumbled over to the Accord. She supposed she ought to stow the tow trailer out of sight but she didn't remember being given a key to the garage. A puzzle. Her brain whirred in place. That key wasn't with the others. She'd have to stop by the real estate office, but it would be closed by now.

She threw her belongings into the trunk. Dragging the balky trailer around to the back yard involved bumping it over flagstones and hummocks of grass and through a derelict gate. The trailer nudged the gatepost. With a creak, the remains of the gate declined against an anonymous bush. Lots of yard work. Lots of yard *to* work. Grass and fruit trees and beds of dead irises.

She parked the trailer in a hollow behind the garage and tried to peer through the building's single window, a cloudy square on the back door. The door didn't give when she shook it. She couldn't see anything but the sheet of stained plywood someone had leaned against it. She hoped that didn't mean the garage was full of junk. The house was empty. Had she inspected the garage? She couldn't remember. She'd looked at a lot of houses in three days.

Fatigue dragged at her shoulders and knees. Time to find the motel. She looked the Red Hat Inn up in her handy AAA Guide. She had passed the motel on her way into town and hadn't seen it, because she had been busy not looking at the Columbia River. It flowed right at the city limits with a municipal marina for fishing boats and pleasure craft.

The river was very, very big. She thought of the sad trickle of water through the concrete channels of Los Angeles. It would take some time to get used to this much fresh water moving past.

The town itself was pleasantly quaint, a well-preserved jumble of housing in most of the architectural styles of the nineteenth and twentieth centuries. She had expected the dearth of pseudo-haciendas. What had surprised her was the relative lack of strip malls and fast-food franchises, and the trees, lots and lots of trees.

Klalo sat at the edge of a major national forest. To the north stretched ridge after rising ridge of blue-green firs and spruces, but the homeowners had not been content with native timber. They appeared to have imported all the deciduous species of northern

Europe and the American Midwest, and all those trees were still leafed out. Each house had at least one huge tree in its front yard, and not one of those trees was a eucalyptus or an olive or a palm. Even the bushes were different. Meg did not see oleander. Who would have thought she'd miss oleander?

The Red Hat turned out to be pricier and better than she had expected. A tourist resort, why not? The Columbia Gorge was a National Scenic Area. She put the room on her overloaded Visa. Then she took a long shower, sat in the jacuzzi, dried herself on the vast bath sheet, and took a two-hour nap. When she rose, she was ready for chicken-fried venison.

 *Chapter 2*

W HERE?" The shorter of the two movers—Jake, his name was—shifted his grip on Meg's queen-sized mattress. The other, Todd, steadied his end against the wall.

"Upstairs, front bedroom."

Both men groaned. They had only been working an hour, but they had already moved all the smaller boxes and other clutter into the designated rooms. Meg watched them as they trundled the wobbly mattress up the stairway.

They had told her they were off-duty sheriff's deputies looking for a little cash. They were young, fit as tigers, and fast. The boss said she was willing to pay them a hundred apiece to unload, no shit?

"No shit," Meg had murmured, bemused. "Is Mr. Neill the sheriff?"

Jake snorted.

Todd said, "He's just head of Investigation, not our supervisor, really. We're uniforms. Drive a patrol car."

Meg groped through flashbacks of a thousand TV dramas. "Partners?"

Jake nodded. "We have Wednesday and Thursday off. Rob thought we might want to pick up beer money."

"Rent money," Todd corrected, rueful.

Jake frowned at him. "You blew the rent again?"

"Not all of it," Todd said meekly.

"I'm delighted to meet you both," Meg interposed. "You're saving my life." She took them inside the house and showed them around the ground floor. She would make them coffee, she decided, as soon as she found the pot.

The two young men had been waiting on her front porch when she drove up at 7:52. They introduced themselves, shook hands, and amiably directed nonexistent traffic as she backed the truck around and inched the rear end across the sidewalk. At the right moment Jake stopped her. By the time she jumped down from the truck they had pulled out the built-in metal ramp. It reached smoothly over the front steps and settled with a light clank onto the porch.

"Front door's narrow, but we can take it off the hinges and roll the heavy stuff through on the handcart, no sweat." Todd squinted at the door. He was twenty-five, at most, with a round, rosy face, black hair, and dark eyes.

"Except the refrigerator," Jake muttered. He looked to be a few years older than his partner/roommate—squatter, uglier, less optimistic.

"Well, great," Meg said faintly. "Go for it." And they did. They finished before noon, refrigerator and all, and even helped her lift the car trailer into the back of the van. Meg never did find the coffeepot.

She bought them lunch at the nearest drive-in, paid them in crisp fifties, and almost cried when they volunteered to follow her in the Honda all the way to Vancouver. She had to return the van to the rental agency before five P.M. and she would have had to take a taxi for the fifty-mile ride back to Klalo.

SHE owed the two deputies a lot more than $200, she reflected, strapped into the back seat of the Accord. They whisked east past Camas, retracing her route of the previous day. Todd drove. He was a cowboy but Meg didn't care. Maybe she would never drive again. She could walk to work.

"You're the new librarian, right?" Jake, making conversation.

"Not for another ten days," Meg said.

"My sister drives the bookmobile."

"Annie Baldwin?" Meg visualized the stocky aide she had met last spring. There wasn't much resemblance, and the woman had to be ten years older than her brother.

Jake craned around the headrest and gave her an approving smile. "Yeah, Annie, my big sister. She says that old truck's gonna need a new transmission."

Meg's groan was only half-theatrical. The library budget, like all library budgets, was tight.

"Annie's old man can baby it along for a while."

"Her husband's a mechanic?"

"Works for the Forest Service planting trees, but he can fix anything, fixed my ex-wife's Datsun when it died last winter. Saved me a bundle."

"Cheapskate." Todd passed a pickup. An oncoming car let out a long, moaning honk.

"Hey, slow down, guy." Jake returned his attention to the road briefly.

Meg breathed again. "So you're deputies. How did you get into law enforcement?" She eased back against the seat and listened to their lives.

Jake Sorenson was thirty, divorced, a former MP. Todd Welch had a certificate in administration of justice from Clark College. He was single and a rookie. Jake had been on the county payroll for five years. They were underpaid and overworked but cheerful about it.

They had shared an apartment in town for six months, an arrangement that probably wouldn't last long, from the sound of things. They took verbal jabs at each other—most, but not all, good-natured. Jake was neat, Todd a slob. Neither liked to cook, so they mostly lived on pizza and Chinese food from the Safeway deli. Jake worked out at a local gym. Todd ran when the spirit moved him. His girlfriend taught second grade, owned her own double-wide mobile home, and they were both Republicans. Obviously a match made in heaven. Jake didn't express a political preference. Neither of the two deputies used the library, but Todd's girlfriend checked out lots of historical romances.

When they reached Klalo, Meg remembered to ask Todd to stop at the real estate office for the key to the garage. The harried agent eventually found it. The guys decanted Meg at her front door and waved good-bye as they chugged off in Jake's old pickup, set for a night on the town. Nice kids. Meg peered up Rob Neill's driveway but didn't see his truck. She'd thank him tomorrow. Meanwhile, the house.

At that moment, she felt a return of the zest with which she had begun the journey north. This was it, a new beginning,

McLean, Stage Three. Stage One had been Feckless Meg. Stage Two, of course, Mom. Stage Three would be different. Margaret the Magnificent.

First things first. She made up her bed and tacked a sheet across the window until she could find the box of curtains she'd salvaged from her condo. She also located bathroom furnishings and supplied the upstairs john with towels, toothpaste, soap, and shampoo.

The towels led her down to the ground-floor bathroom and from there into the kitchen. Although the refrigerator hummed, the stove ignited, and rusty water whooshed from the tap when she turned it on, the table and counters were still covered with movers' cartons. The cupboard shelves were bare. She had made a grocery list and was about to go out to the local supermarket when her cell phone rang: Lucy at the appointed hour. Lucy seemed relieved to find her mother coherent and cheerful.

One call led to another. Meg rang the library and announced her safe arrival. Marybeth Jackman, the woman who was going to be her assistant, sounded cool but warmed up a little when Meg assured her she didn't need help.

Jackman had been appointed temporary head on the death of the previous chief librarian. She had been an unsuccessful candidate for Meg's new job. Fences to mend there. Ah, well, there was plenty of time left before that problem had to be faced.

Meg drove through the almost deserted streets to the supermarket, racked up $150 worth of groceries, and even remembered to stop by the liquor store on the way back—demon rum was not for sale in ordinary Washington food stores though there was wine and beer in abundance.

When Meg had stowed her purchases and unpacked china, cutlery, and basic cookware, she poured herself a Scotch and started a pot of vegetable soup. At that point she remembered the garage-door key.

She sipped Red Label and meditated. There was no great hurry. She could investigate the garage in the morning. On the other hand, it might be a good idea to park the car under cover. Klalo had a low crime rate, but years of living in Greater Los Angeles had taught Meg caution. The Honda Accord was vehicle of choice for car thieves.

The lid of her stockpot rattled. She turned the gas down, nipped at the whisky, and dug the key out of her coin purse. It was an undistinguished object; if she hadn't stuck it in the purse it might have been lost forever.

Wandering out the side door, she made a mental note to have all the keys copied. She could leave the extra set with Darcy in case of emergency.

The key didn't work on the rear door of the garage, so she trailed back through the collapsed gate and across the uneven flagstones to the drive. The front doors, which opened out like shutters rather than rolling up like the usual garage door, fastened with a padlock. The lock opened on her second try and the doors on her third. Grass had grown up along the bottom edges of the doors.

Dark and dank but empty. That was her first, relieved impression of the interior. She had been afraid she would find floor-to-ceiling junk. The garage had a dirt floor—dirt and gravel like the driveway. Memory was returning. She *had* inspected the garage.

After a moment, her eyes adjusted to the gloom and her nose quivered. It was dark, all right, and worse than dank. Somebody's cat must have died.

Annoyed, she edged along the wall, feeling for a light switch. At the back of the building she groped near the door and dislodged the sheet of plywood. It fell inward with a swish of compressed air. Meg blinked grit from her vision and found the switch. An overhead job-light, not very bright, dangled from the cross beam. It shed a dim pool of illumination over the space, which looked rough, as if someone had stirred it.

The fallen plywood reached about a third of the way toward the churned spot. An image returned. When she'd viewed the house at the end of July, the gravel had been raked as smooth as a Zen garden. The real estate agent told her the owner had held a series of garage sales before the final clean-up. The house had only been on the market three days when Meg first saw it. She wished she hadn't missed the garage sales.

She squatted at the edge of her plywood raft and touched the gravel. It was dry but a little greasy on her fingers. Maybe a confused mole had surfaced in the middle of the garage, then ducked back down in disappointment. No, the surface wasn't mounded—

not moles or gophers. A few shards of black pottery lay scattered over dirt and rock. One shard was palm-sized. Meg turned it over, surprised to find it heavy. Not ceramic. Stone.

She picked it up and straightened, holding it under the light. A stick figure had been chipped into the surface. Garage-sale detritus?

Uneasy, Meg carried the shard out into direct sunlight. Brown and gray blotches on the black surface almost obscured the partial drawing of a flute player with an odd, rayed headdress. The musician curled over his instrument, but the tip of the flute was missing. The figure looked like a petroglyph but surely wasn't. Before she applied for the library job, Meg had read up on the attractions of the National Scenic Area. Petroglyphs featured large in the prehistory—upstream, she thought, near The Dalles on the Oregon side.

Leaving the doors open to air the garage out, she went back into the kitchen. She set the rock fragment on the counter, washed her sticky hands, and returned to her Scotch. Should she call someone? Not 911—there was no emergency, probably no crime, though she had read that looting was a problem at Native American sites throughout the West. She thought of Neill. She owed him a thank-you. She could mention her "find" to him, ask his advice.

Conscience eased, she stirred the soup and went back to unpacking kitchen goods. One thing led to another. By nine o'clock she had eaten soup and artisan bread, rearranged her grandmother's china in the glass-fronted dish cupboard, and was off in what had been the ground-floor bedroom setting up her office. The sun had long gone down. Apart from a passing motorcycle and the barking of an occasional dog, the silence of the neighborhood was absolute. When the brisk knocking came it startled her. She dropped a handful of paperbacks.

Another knock resounded. Kitchen door. She straightened, creaking a little, walked into the kitchen, and peered out.

It was Rob Neill.

She glanced at her watch. Nine-fifteen. Late to be paying a friendly visit.

"Hi," she said, opening the door. "Come in. I want to thank you for Todd and Jake. They did a great job."

"Good." He stepped past her. He was paint-free, wearing a sports jacket and polo shirt over pressed levis. Formal attire after yesterday's paint-speckled jeans and sweatshirt. "Are you aware your garage doors are open with the light on?"

She smacked her forehead. "I forgot. I was carried away by the thrill of unpacking. Have a chair." She waved vaguely at the kitchen table. "Can I get you a drink?"

"No, thanks." He remained standing. "I chased the county commissioner's dog out of your garage. He was digging at something."

She stared at him, frowning. "That's strange."

"The commissioner's dog is worse than strange. One of these days he's going to eat a baby."

"Don't you have a leash law in Klalo?"

He sighed. "We do. The commissioner is a Libertarian. He does not believe in leash laws. Towser was Born Free."

Her memory conjured up a fat, truculent face and high-pitched voice. "Ah…Commissioner Brandstetter? I met him."

"Right."

"When I said strange I didn't mean the pit bull."

"Rhodesian Ridgeback. A hundred pounds of playful pooch."

"Whatever. I meant the garage. Is the smell gone?"

"I didn't sniff."

Meg saw the shard on the end of the counter by the cell phone. She'd put both items there out of reach of dishwater. "I found this." She handed the shard to him and described her venture into the garage, the area of disturbed surface, the dead-cat odor.

Frowning, he took the piece by the edges. He seemed to frown a lot. He didn't say anything for a long time.

"It couldn't be anything important…. I thought about calling the sheriff's office…." She shut up.

"Do you have something I could put this in, an envelope or a baggie?"

The ghost of Feckless Meg, teenaged rebel, rose in her, and she almost denied possessing anything as incriminating as a baggie. He *was* a cop. Reason triumphed. She yanked open the drawer to the left of the sink and found a self-sealing plastic bag.

He slipped the shard into it and laid the bag on the counter. "Shall we have a look?"

"Not if I'm going to be jumped by a Libertarian hound." She dug in a lower drawer. "Here's a flashlight. The garage light's not very bright."

He took the big flashlight from her, hefting it as if it were a weapon. "Let's go."

The dog had slunk back. It was huge, beautiful, and terrifying. A strip of sleek hair grew backwards along the ridge of its spine. When the dog saw Neill it crouched in the driveway and woofed. Neill squatted down, eyeball to eyeball, and grabbed it by its collar. "Towser, go *home*!" He released the collar and gave the beast a swat.

It loped off with another sweet woof.

"I'm impressed."

"Experience." He shone the light into the interior of the garage. Something scuttled away. "A rat."

"Ew."

The beam of light shifted, steadied. He didn't enter the garage. "Shall I turn the overhead light off?"

"I think we have a problem," he interrupted.

"We?"

He turned to her, face serious. "Something is buried there in the center of your garage. Animals have been at it, probably for some time. I'm going to call Dispatch."

Meg opened her mouth to protest, shut it, and stared.

His eyes were grave, frowning. "Did you walk around much in there, touch anything?"

She pointed. "I walked along that edge to the back door." She described her actions of the afternoon.

"Where did you find the petroglyph?"

"There." She jabbed a finger toward the center.

"Pity you picked it up."

"I wouldn't deliberately mess with evidence." Evidence of what? "You haven't even gone in to look."

"No, and I won't. It's city business, not my jurisdiction unless the chief calls on us."

"For God's sake."

He sighed. "There are procedures, Ms. McLean."

"As I live and breathe."

A smile touched his lips. He took a cell phone from his jacket pocket and poked out the emergency number. Coded conversation ensued. Neill seemed to know the dispatcher. A patrol car was on its way.

They stood looking at each other in the dim light. After a moment he sighed. "Why don't you go in and wait where it's warm?"

Meg felt the nip in the air. She rubbed her arms. "I'll go in when I know what's happening."

"That could take awhile. I'll come for the rock fragment when the officer gets here. Will you sign a consent-to-search form? He'll need it before he goes in."

"To search the garage? Sure."

He cleared his throat. "He'll need to search the house, too."

Constitutional protests rose in Meg's throat. "But I just unpacked," she wailed.

"I'm sorry." His smile was rueful. "Very sorry. It's a cinch to search an empty house. Too bad you didn't spot the rock before the guys unloaded your truck."

"Had I but known," Meg snarled.

"Is that a quote?"

"It's what all gothic heroines say as they plunge into catastrophe."

 *Chapter 3*

COMMISSIONER Brandstetter's dog hung around. Rob saw him bounce behind the patrol car as it drew up with its lights flashing. Towser lifted his leg on the left rear tire, sniffed Rob's ankles, and gave a soft woof. All along the street, front doors opened and citizens peered out.

The window of the patrol car slid down. "Hiya, Neill." Dave Meuler, bald, fifty, and steady. "Teresa said you called." Teresa Morales was the 911 night dispatcher. "I ain't getting out of this car with that hound on the loose."

"Sit." When the ridgeback squatted obediently on its haunches, Rob grabbed its collar. He peered down the block. A rectangle of light shone from the house at the end.

"Commissioner!" he roared, projecting his voice like a ham actor. "Get your butt down here or the dog dies!"

Dave chuckled. "Bastard's too damned lazy to take his dog walkies."

Rob scratched Towser's big, square head. The dog licked his free hand. "It's a matter of principle."

"My ass."

It took Harold Brandstetter five minutes to walk the short distance. He was about Rob's height, five-ten, but he had to weigh close to three hundred pounds. Rob thought the man's knees were going. He wore sneakers, sweat pants, a T-shirt that said GOD, GUNS, AND GUTS, and a red brocade robe that looked like something from a 1940s movie about high society. He toed out as he walked.

Rob said, "Evening."

"You got a fucking nerve threatening to shoot my dog." The voice was high and harsh like a buzz saw.

"Just describing natural consequences," Rob drawled. "Dave's armed. I hear his mother was bitten by a Doberman."

Brandstetter snorted. "What's going on here anyway?" His bright little eyes darted back and forth, taking everything in. He was sweating.

"Ms. McLean reported property damage—kids messing around in her garage, I guess. Dave will check it out when your dog's elsewhere."

Brandstetter's eyes narrowed. "McLean? That's the new librarian, right?" He had voted against giving her a contract. He voted no a lot.

"Right." Rob released Towser's collar. The dog bounced four feet straight up, placed his front paws on his master's shoulders, and licked Brandstetter's face."Down, goddammit," Brandstetter shouted, staggering back. "Sit!"

Towser sat with the air of one expecting a kibble.

Rob steadied the other man, then let his hand drop. "Put him in the house, Hal."

After a moment the commissioner shrugged. "C'mon, dog. Heel." He strutted off toward the streetlight where two or three of the curious had gathered. The dog trailed behind.

When they were out of earshot, Rob said quietly, "Remember the Lauder Point case?" Shortly after he joined the department, he had been assigned to investigate the theft of Native American artifacts from Lauder Point County Park.

Dave opened the door and slid out. He arched his back, as if he'd been sitting in the car for several hours, and rubbed the side of his neck. "Sure, I remember. Tribal council sued the county."

Rob described the damaged petroglyph.

"Part of the loot?"

"Maybe."

Dave whistled. "And you think they stored the things next to your grandma's house?" It was Rob's house, and had been for more than two years, but everybody would go on thinking of it as Hazel Guthrie's house. He watched Dave meditate. "Lauder Point? After all this time?"

"Yeah." Lauder Point, ten years before, had been Rob's first big case. He had not covered himself with glory. "I'll have egg on my face. Again."

"If that's what the whatchacallit drawing is."

"Right. Uh, there's something else buried in that garage. It stinks."

Dave had taken a step along the drive. He froze. "Somebody's picnic debris?"

"Could be. Or a dead cat." Neither wanted to say it might be a human corpse. Rob cleared his throat. "Let's do it by the book. Got a consent-to-search form?"

Dave turned back to the car. "Right. I'll call in while you're getting the signature. D'you want your forensics crew? The chief'll throw a fit if he has to use 'em. He's over budget." In criminal cases, the city of Klalo contracted control and evaluation of physical evidence to the county.

Rob smiled. "I just spent two good hours arm-wrestling the sheriff over *my* budget."

"Election coming up." Dave rummaged in the glove box.

No kidding. Sheriff McCormick was a competent manager, and he backed his men up when the occasion called for it. Come election time, though, he always talked fiscal accountability, and he talked a good ballgame. Canceling overtime two weeks before Hallowe'en was counterproductive, though, or so Rob had argued. The sheriff had finally agreed. He would look without joy on an expensive investigation—as this would be if the rock shard turned out to be part of the Lauder Point loot. So much the better, then, if the chief of police picked up part of the tab.

Rob talked the situation over with Dave and remembered to ask him for a small evidence bag. By 10:30 most of the gawkers had gone back inside their warm houses. Margaret McLean took her time coming when Rob got around to knocking on her kitchen door. She looked rumpled and exasperated.

She sat at the kitchen table and read the form while he transferred the broken petroglyph to the evidence bag, which was paper. Organic matter was apt to rot if it was stored in plastic. The brown blotch on the surface of the petroglyph could be dirt but looked like dried blood. Rob labeled the bag and dated it, then tore a sheet from the small notebook he always carried and wrote out a receipt.

He handed it to her. "Okay to do the search?"

"Do they have to go through the house tonight?"

"It's a little pedantic to search the house at all," Rob said, "but the courts like us to be thorough."

A search of the house was probably pointless as well as pedantic, but he didn't say that. When Old Strohmeyer died, the place had been cleaned and repainted. However, if a crime had been committed afterwards, whatever the crime might be... Rob's mind chased the thought.

It had to be afterwards, he decided. Before the house came on the market, the garage had been cluttered with so much junk the old man had parked his truck out on the drive.

It bothered Rob that *he* hadn't noticed anything suspicious in the weeks since the house sold, but he hadn't. He'd racked his memory. Living next door to the crime scene was going to be embarrassing.

Ms. McLean expressed her feelings about the search in some detail, but her heart wasn't into venting. She yawned. "Could you do my bedroom first? Then I can go to bed while your crew paws through the rest of the house."

That seemed reasonable. "I'll see what I can do to hurry them up, but it'll be a couple of hours at least." Longer, if the dead cat turned out to be a dead man. He didn't say that. No need to alarm her.

She groaned, but she signed the form. "I'll be in the living room taking things out of boxes."

"I'd rather you didn't."

Another groan.

"You could read a book."

She looked at him. Her eyes—hazel and expressive—had a speculative gleam. "My computer's up. I think I'll go online and look up petroglyphs. There's a site on rock art, and one on the Columbia Gorge Scenic Area."

"Check out Lauder Point Park," he said wryly and regretted the indiscretion.

Her eyes narrowed. "State park or county?"

"County," he admitted. "There's a website for tourists." He'd helped design it. It needed updating.

"Do you want printouts?"

"Anything specific to the area in the last two or three months. Otherwise I think I'm current."

"Okay." The idea of an Internet search energized her. "There's fresh coffee on the counter. Mugs in the cupboard." She whisked from the room, a trim woman of about his own age, short, with her brown hair cropped so it curled around her face. She reminded him of his grandmother, but he didn't think he'd share that thought with her. Smiling, he went out to talk to Dave and await the evidence team.

There wasn't much occasion to smile after that. Dave shone his flashlight on the disturbed area of the floor and agreed with Rob that they were seeing a human hand, or rather, the remains of a badly decomposed hand with much of the flesh and some bones missing. An edge of filthy cloth, the cuff of the shirt, blended with dirt and other debris. The hand was barely visible from the drive.

Dave called Wade Hug, the chief of police, who showed up within fifteen minutes looking like a bear rousted from hibernation. Rob explained what he thought they had. When the chief heard about the possible Lauder Point context, he cheered up and offered to transfer jurisdiction on the spot.

"If there's a homicide, Wade, it's yours."

Hug advanced several contrary arguments. Rob dug his heels in. It was all a matter of budget, who would pay, the city or the county. The city had only two experienced officers and two rookies, no detective on the staff, and the chief routinely handed serious cases over either to Rob or to the state patrol. After twenty minutes of argumentation, Hug drove off to consult the sheriff. He had agreed to call in the county Crime Scene Unit.

While Dave and Rob waited for the crew, Dave retraced Margaret McLean's footsteps of the afternoon. Rob considered objecting, but decided tact was in order. Though Dave was a good ally, he could be a master of obstruction when he was offended.

From the plywood sheet, Dave reported that he could see the hand clearly. He inched back out to the driveway, careful not to contaminate the site further.

It bothered both of them that Ms. McLean hadn't spotted the hand, but the doors had stood wide for hours after she opened them, and Rob had seen the dog digging away.

"Hand probably wasn't exposed when she opened up," Dave said.

"She did notice the smell."

"I hope so." Dave made a face. "Let me guess what's on your mind. You're going to want me to investigate old Towser's fecal output."

"We could make Brandstetter do it." Gallows humor. The thought of the dog violating the corpse made Rob queasy.

By midnight, with the crime scene lights blazing away and the photographer's strobe pulsing, the crew had unearthed the body of a man, badly decomposed.

Rob sent Deputy Linda Ramos, the team's photographer, into the house to tell Ms. McLean the news, and to let her know she could go to bed. That was a judgment call on Rob's part, but they wouldn't get around to searching the house before morning anyway.

He would need to take the librarian's statement, too, and he'd have better questions to ask her when he had some idea of the time-frame. She had bought the house in mid-summer, August, he thought. Exactly when she made the offer might be crucial, and when the sale closed.

Rob had spent a lot of time and grant money training his people. They operated almost like archaeologists, lifting the dirt away, slow and careful, with trowels and even small paintbrushes. They kept good records, triangulated important objects, measured everything. From siftings of the nearby soil, they discovered two finger bones and a button from the cuff of the victim's shirt, but only a few small flakes of basalt that might have come from the broken petroglyph.

The medical examiner, who had to drive from Vancouver, showed up around one-fifteen, pronounced the man dead, and made a lot of preliminary rumblings as he probed the corpse.

Beneath the fog of medical jargon, Rob read that the victim had probably been dead for some weeks, maybe a couple of months, and that he was either Hispanic or Indian, though that wasn't a certainty.

"Could be Asian," the examiner grumbled. "Could be a square-headed Caucasian. Younger than forty, older than twelve. Cause of death probably one of the head wounds." He made a fist and whacked the back of his own skull by way of illustration. They were standing in the street. "Can't tell you more at this point, and don't quote me."

"Me, quote you?"

The medical examiner grinned. "I'll do the autopsy for you here, if you'll spring for a night at the Red Hat."

"Sorry. No money."

"Tomorrow, then. Eleven A.M. in Vancouver."

"I'll send Minetti to observe. Thanks, Doc." Earl Minetti was Rob's sergeant, the deputy in charge of the evidence team.

"No problem." The ME cleared his throat. "The guy's watch is still running."

It was, too. Rob verified that, breathing through his mouth as the paramedics bagged the body, placing separate bags on the hands and feet. A battery-operated Swatch sagged from the wrist the animals hadn't got to. For some reason the watch brought the tragedy home. As the ambulance pulled away and headed west toward Vancouver, the forensics team watched it leave in unbidden silence. Then they went on with their chores.

Rob felt a familiar wave of grief and depression. He supposed he would never understand how anybody could snuff out another human being's life and then shove the body into a hole like a sack of garbage. Not for the first time he wondered whether he should give up the job and go back to Silicon Valley. Except that option was no longer open.

The victim's face was in bad shape, and they had found no obvious identification on the body, no wallet with a handy driver's license, no letters from home, no unpaid bills. Minetti would have the task of doing a thorough examination of the man's effects—after the autopsy.

Meanwhile, there was enough to go on. And one further, peculiar discovery—the body lay in a square cavity that looked as if it had been dug many years before the murder.

Rob had hoped to find indisputable evidence that the artifacts from Lauder Point had been stored in the garage. That remained debatable. What was odd was that the body had been crammed into a cavity in the center of the garage floor, the walls of which were lined with railroad ties. The space was shorter and somewhat shallower than a real grave, the ideal cache for stolen loot, but only two more chips from the basalt petroglyph had showed up there.

They examined the heavy plywood sheet for everything from

fingerprints and footprints to bloodstains and soil types, and sent samples off to the state lab. At some point in its past, the plywood had been given creosote treatment. It covered the cavity exactly. Nevertheless, dirt and gravel had been shoveled or raked over the victim, and the lid had been left unused, propped against the back door. A rake and a rusty shovel hung from the far wall of the garage. Rob pointed them out, and they were bagged and labeled.

He brooded about the lid. If the perpetrators had put it back in place with dirt spread over it, the body might not have been discovered for months—not until Margaret McLean's Accord broke through the plywood. Maybe they hadn't been able to close the lid over the victim's arm, if rigor had already set in. Without the lid, they would have had to import soil to fill the cavity—from the backyard?

He made himself a note to have the crew investigate the ground behind the garage for signs of digging—and to interview the neighbors, who must have seen something. Himself included. He racked his memory. Nothing. He needed a time line.

The old man who had owned the house was a contemporary of Rob's formidable grandmother. A retired contractor, Emil Strohmeyer had been reclusive, notable as a fly fisherman. Rob had bought two antique bamboo rods at the estate sale. He wished he could consult his grandmother about Strohmeyer. She had known everything about everybody in Latouche County over the age of fifty.

By half past four, when it started to rain, the crew had completed a workmanlike survey of the floor of the garage. Their feet in the little booties designed to protect the scene began to churn up mud in the drive, so Rob sent them off to sift through their notes and secure the bagged evidence. He would meet with the team at 8:00 in the courthouse annex, along with as many other deputies as McCormick would authorize, to map out the investigation.

Meanwhile, he needed a shower. The stench of human corruption is pervasive. He left Dave, now the city's official liaison, to guard the site for the rest of his shift. Dave sat in his car with the heater on. Yellow crime scene tape gleamed in the rain.

*

"WANT a muffin?"

Rob started. It was not quite seven A.M. He was on his way back from the espresso stand. Hot coffee slopped through the hole in the plastic lid onto his right hand. He was also holding a cup of double-shot espresso in his left. He looked around. The librarian.

"Morning, Ms. McLean. Dave."

Dave Meuler swore and sat up. He'd fallen asleep over the wheel of the patrol car. The window was down and Rob could smell wet wool.

Rob handed Dave his coffee. He took it with a nod and a sheepish grin.

Margaret McLean stood at the edge of her yard, peering through the rain. She had thrown a jacket over her head.

"Muffin?" she repeated.

"Uh, sure. Dave?"

Dave shook his head no. Steam from his coffee cup clouded the window in front of him. "I'll pass. In sixty-three minutes I'm gonna sit myself down to the Hungry Logger breakfast at Mona's." He sounded pleased with himself. He had been excused from the eight o'clock briefing. "Thanks."

She nodded and turned back to the house, rainwater spraying from her wet jacket.

"Rob?"

"Yeah?"

Dave held up an evidence bag. "Towser."

Rob grinned. "Good man. See you later." He took a companionable sip of coffee, which burned his lip, raised the cup in salute, and walked to the house.

He had showered, shaved, and dressed in clean clothes from the skin out. He'd even poked Mentholatum up his nose, but he could still smell the odor of death. He'd also tried to think things through without much result. At least he'd made a list of questions.

The kitchen smelled of baking, a definite improvement over eau de corpse.

When he was outside his second muffin—bran, moist with raisins—and had drunk his coffee, Ms. McLean laid a stack of printouts beside him on the table.

"What's this?"

"Kokopelli. The flute player."

"Kokopelli is Southwestern. This one's different."

Meg digested that. "The fragment I picked up was small for a petroglyph."

He sighed. "Yes, I know. That's what made me think it might be a piece taken from Lauder Point when the artifacts in the park were stolen ten years ago."

"You spotted it right away?" Incredulity and disappointment vied on her expressive face.

"I was the klutz who fumbled that investigation. Believe it, I now know every missing piece in photographic detail. The flute player stone came from a bluff inundated when the Corps of Engineers built Bonneville Dam in the 'Thirties. They split off the rock face in order to rescue the figures. What you found was a piece from the right-hand side of the basalt slab."

"What's the rest like?"

"There were two other figures facing him, to the left. They were larger, looked as if they were twins dancing side by side to the music. Twins occur a lot in the rock art of this area, but the musician is unusual. The other two petroglyphs are less distinctive. There's a version of Tsagiglalal, She Who Watches."

"Isn't that the logo for the Scenic Area?"

He nodded. "This one has googly eyes, concentric circles rather than spirals. The other stone drawing is an animal figure called Running Elk."

"I see."

"The Klalo people called your stone The Dancers." He finished the last morsel of muffin and rose. "I have to go now—a meeting with my deputies in half an hour. Todd Welch will replace Officer Meuler when we're not here, so don't be alarmed if a county car shows up. We'll be back to conduct the search of the house and grounds by ten, if that's okay."

She sighed and nodded.

"I'll take your statement then. One question. When she showed you the house, did the real estate agent point out the storage space in the floor of the garage?"

She blinked. "The what?"

He explained about the lined cavity.

"Good God." She sounded blank. "I didn't see the sheet of plywood then, either. You say it was a lid?"

He nodded.

She frowned as if concentrating on visual memory. "The surface of the garage was raked smooth. It looked as if it had been newly graveled."

"Thanks. That helps. I'll talk to the agent before I call Charlotte Tichnor."

"That's the woman I bought the place from, right?"

"Yeah," he said. "Emil Strohmeyer's heir. He had others but he left her the house because she took care of his medical bills. At least, that's what people were saying when she put the house on the market." He glanced at his watch. "I have to run. Thanks for fixing breakfast. Under the circumstances, it was generous-minded of you."

She murmured something polite.

Sheriff McCormick's conference room was overheated. Rob's team, smaller than he liked but adequate, looked sleepy. Minetti wasn't happy with his projected trip to Vancouver. He didn't like autopsies, for one thing, and, for another, he was an anxious supervisor. He wanted to be on top of the house search.

Rob said, "I'll stay with them, Earl."

Minetti's eyes dropped and he shrugged. He was ten years younger than Rob, ambitious, something of a hotshot. "Okay. It's yours, Linda."

Behind her fashionable wire-rimmed glasses, Linda Ramos's dark eyes sparkled, but she had the wit not to gloat. There were other egos involved. Minetti usually seconded Thayer Jones, who was experienced but slow. Rob decided to give Thayer the backyard while Linda and Jake Sorenson did the house.

"How long is this going to take, Neill?" The sheriff sounded belligerent, and, under the belligerence, plaintive.

Rob said soothing things about overtime, and noted the relief among team members that they weren't going to be working another full shift. They had to be as tired as he was after the all-nighter.

"I need to secure the site and make sure the house isn't part of the crime scene," Rob concluded with a deliberately vague gesture because he had no idea how long that would take. "Then we'll stand down until Earl can bring us something definite about the victim. I'll take Ms. McLean's statement and do some telephoning. The former owner of the house, the feds, and that new officer the intertribal fisheries people have hired to look into looting." He would also check the FBI's NCIC database before he left his office in the courthouse annex, but that went without saying.

Sheriff McCormick slapped his hands on the conference table and rose. "Right. Let's get on it. And keep your lips zipped. We don't want a lot of speculation out there in the community. Refer the press to me."

Rob cleared his throat. "What about Maddie Thomas?"

Mack winced. "Not yet."

"I want to talk to her." Madeline Thomas was principal chief of the Klalos, a formidable and articulate woman. She was not a fan of the Latouche County Sheriff's Department.

"Let's wait until we have more definite information. You aren't sure there's a link with Lauder Point yet."

Rob was sure, but he didn't insist. He would have to talk to Maddie eventually, but maybe Mack was right to wait. No reason to stir the chief up sooner than he had to.

"MESSY process," Margaret McLean muttered, scrubbing her hands under the kitchen faucet. Linda had fingerprinted her first thing. "For purposes of elimination, right?" No flies on Ms. McLean.

Linda grinned and stowed her gear. Jake Sorenson was finishing a cup of coffee.

Good coffee, Rob reflected, sipping his. What it was to have a cooperative suspect. He cleared his throat ostentatiously and fingered the tape recorder, though it didn't need adjusting.

The librarian dried her hands and sat opposite him with an air of resignation. "Okay. Have at me. I suppose I'm the prime suspect."

"As a matter of fact, you're down near the bottom of the list." He sent Linda and Jake off to inspect the house, both of them grinning.

"They're not going to read my data files, are they?"

"Nope."

A small smile warmed her face. "Good. Jake should know my computer just got here. He carried it in."

Jake had been instructed to point out everything he and Todd had brought into the house for the record. Rob didn't say that. He turned the tape player on, gave his name and the date, and asked her to identify herself.

"Margaret McLean, spinster of this parish."

Rob frowned. Some people had to make jokes. Defense mechanism.

"Sorry." She didn't look remorseful. "I'm Margaret McLean, 404 Old Cedar Street. I own the house."

"When did you buy it?"

"I put earnest money down July 25th. The deal closed August 13th. I flew up and signed all the tax documents on the 15th."

"Fast."

"I thought so. I paid cash, used a certified check." She named a Wells Fargo branch in Santa Monica.

Cash. With no mortgage involved—and no bank inspectors to nose around—the process would have gone faster than usual. "Did you return to Klalo at any time after you signed the papers?"

"No, and I was only in town for about an hour on the fifteenth." Her face darkened. "I had to take a day off work to sign."

"You received the keys at that time?"

"Yes, but not the key to the garage. I picked it up yesterday. Apparently they forgot to give it to me."

"That's the key to the padlock on the garage's front doors. What about the back door?"

She shrugged. "No key to that."

"There *is* no key, or you don't know where it is?"

"Don't know."

Neither lock had showed signs of being forced. The real estate agent had some explaining to do.

She had pulled her capacious purse to her lap and was rooting in it. "Aha!" She brandished a small manila envelope. "If you want to document my drive north, I have receipts from a significant number of service stations between here and Los Angeles. The van was a gas hog."

"I'll take your word. So you decided to buy the house, paid the earnest money, and left here the 25th of July?"

"I flew out of Portland Airport July 26th at six-thirty in the morning and didn't return until I came to sign the papers. I flew back to LAX immediately because I was moving my daughter to

Stanford early. She's a freshman and attended a science orientation. She wanted to look for a part-time job, too."

"Big transition."

"For Lucy and for me." She had a fetching smile, expressive of untrammeled delight.

He cleared his throat.

The smile faded. "I can probably document where I was throughout August, lots of receipts."

He said, "It won't be necessary, Ms. McLean. You were working after that?"

"During and after." She gave the name and address of the library she had worked at, and the name and a telephone number of a colleague. She had been deputy head of a consortium of public libraries, much larger than the Latouche County Regional Library.

He wondered why she had chosen to move to a rural system. "Do you have connections in Latouche County?"

She looked blank.

"Friends, relatives…"

"Just Hazel Guthrie."

"What?" He gaped.

"She's my hero. I think she died a couple of years ago but she was a legendary librarian. She worked out a procedure for dealing with attempts at censorship from community groups. It's a national model."

When he didn't speak, she leaned forward, eyes sparkling. "What's wonderful about it is that it's nonconfrontational. It keeps the books on the shelves, but it gives people who have grievances a way to express their feelings, too, and even to become part of the selection process. She also computerized the library, both catalogue and circulation, years ahead of everybody else, and before that she made interlibrary loans available to ordinary patrons, not just university professors. I could go on." In her enthusiasm she jiggled the purse and it began to slide off her lap. She grabbed it and swung it up on the table. "Don't tell me you never heard of her."

"Paused at eleven-eighteen." He shut the machine off and smiled at her. "I wouldn't dream of it. Hazel Guthrie was my grandmother."

Margaret McLean blushed charmingly for a forty-something woman.

"I live in her house."

Her eyes narrowed. "You're fixing it up. I hope you don't mean to sell it. It should be a national shrine."

"I'll keep that in mind." He spoke drily but he was moved. His grandmother had died at eighty-seven, about fifteen years before her time, as far as Rob was concerned. He still missed her intelligence and humor. His grandparents had raised him after his mother's death the year he turned ten.

Hazel Guthrie had not been a demonstrative woman, but he had never been in doubt of her affection. After a few years of post-adolescent revolt, he hadn't doubted his affection for her, either. They had drawn closer in the last ten years of her life, when he came back to Klalo.

He fiddled with the recorder, then turned it on. "Resuming at eleven-twenty." He took Ms. McLean through her arrival in Klalo, her retrieval of the garage key, and her discovery of the rock drawing, with attention to the state of the garage floor and the position of the plywood lid.

"The victim's hand was partially exposed when I saw the open doors," he added. "Weren't you aware of it earlier?"

She shuddered. "No. I thought moles had been digging, or rats, but I didn't know why. There was a bad smell, like a dead animal. My God, how awful." Tears came to her eyes, and she blinked hard. "I thought there might be a dead cat, something like that." She sniffed and dug in her purse for a tissue. "Sorry."

He waited for her to compose herself. "Okay, thanks, Ms. McLean. Interview ended." He glanced at the kitchen clock and added the time.

She blew her nose. "You're very formal."

"I was being official. Thanks, Meg." He rose and stretched. "And thanks for the coffee."

"That's it?"

"For the time being." He slipped the recorder into his jacket pocket and gestured toward the living room where Linda and Jake were moving around audibly. "They'll be at it awhile yet, and Deputy Jones is checking out the backyard." He explained why.

"I guess that makes sense." She sighed. "This is going to be a

nightmare, isn't it? And to think I just wanted to settle in peacefully and get acquainted before I start work. 'The best-laid plans...'"

He dipped into memory. "'Of all sad words of tongue or pen,
the saddest are, it might have been.'"

She laughed and he found himself laughing, too. "Gran and I
used to do that, cap each other's clichés."

"The last bastion against Alzheimer's."

"That, at least, was a problem she never had."

She said ruefully, "I was thinking of my own descent into
oblivion."

 *Chapter 4*

"MAY I speak to Charlotte Tichnor?" Rob identified himself, leaned back in the chair, and wriggled his stiff shoulders. He was phoning from home so he'd be handy if something turned up in the search next door.

The woman at the Seattle end of the line said, "She's at Harrison Hot Springs for the rest of the week. This is her daughter, Carol Tichnor. Are you calling about my grandfather's house?"

"What makes you say that?"

"The house is our only connection with Latouche County these days. We sold it in August."

The royal *we* irritated Rob. "Your mother sold it, certainly."

"She's out of town," she repeated.

"I talked to the realtor who handled the sale. She told me someone borrowed the key to the garage after Ms. McLean's offer was accepted." Rob took a sip of cold coffee and his stomach roiled. He supposed he should eat lunch, though the idea wasn't appealing.

"That was before the sale closed. We thought some family things might be left in there, so I asked the office to mail us the key. I dropped by, but the garage was empty, so I gave the key back."

"There should have been two keys, padlock in front, regular lock in back."

She hesitated. "Just one key."

"Did you mail it back?" He fiddled with his ballpoint, clicking the nib in and out.

"I put it into an envelope and slipped it through the agency mail slot on my way out of town."

He jotted a note, probably illegible. "I see. Did you enter the garage?"

"No, I just stuck my head in the back."

Meg had said the key didn't work in that door. Rob noted the discrepancy. "When was that?"

"Oh, I don't know. First week of August. Must have been a Friday."

"You entered the back door?"

She gave a short laugh. "Okay, okay, I confess. After going to the trouble of getting the key, I just peeked through the window. The garage was empty. I didn't bother to go in."

Rob wondered whether she was telling the truth. If she was, the back-door window had not been blocked by the plywood lid at that point. "You could see clearly?"

"It was dim," she admitted, "but I was looking for a big piece of furniture, an oak chiffonier. It wasn't there. The place was empty," she repeated, sounding peevish.

He allowed his skepticism to enter his voice. "Are you sure you didn't go into the garage and open the storage compartment in the floor?"

To his surprise, she gave a gurgle of laughter. "Great-grandpa's hidey-hole?"

"What?" He sat up straight.

"I can tell you don't know our scandalous history. My great-grandfather, Otto Strohmeyer, was a notorious bootlegger. He had a still up near Tyee Lake. He used to stow the hooch in his garage until it was time to distribute it to his clients."

Rob swore under his breath. The garage had obviously been built in the 1920s. Why hadn't he thought of bootlegging? It was the kind of thing Gran would have left unsaid. She would have known about it, of course, but she wouldn't have wanted Rob-the-child to judge Emil Strohmeyer for the sins of his father. Not that she would have considered bathtub gin much of a sin, nor did Rob. It was the scofflaw mentality that bothered him. That and the violence. A Clark County sheriff had been killed in a shoot-out with bootleggers.

"Did everyone in your family know about the cache?"

"Mother did, of course. We—my brothers and I—used to spend a month with the grandparents every summer. Grandpa showed it to me one day when I got bored and wanted to go home to Seattle. I was thirteen. He'd probably already showed it to the boys." She hesitated, then gave another giggle. She had to be pushing fifty. "Mother would not have approved. She's always been the soul of propriety."

"So she might not have discussed the space with the real estate people?"

"Probably not. It's like cancer."

"What?"

"The C-word. Her generation never mentioned it, like it was shameful or something. Same with bootlegging. Never mind that the old man's illicit sales kept the family off the soup line during the Depression."

"Wasn't the Volstead Amendment repealed by then?"

"It took years," she said coolly, "and meanwhile the sale of moonshine flourished. Grandpa had some good stories. His dad used to take him along for the ride when it was time to go out on the delivery route. The sight of Grandpa's innocent face probably disarmed the revenuers."

Rob stared at the wallpaper pattern in Hazel Guthrie's home office, cabbage roses in sad need of replacement. "I see. Well, Ms. Tichnor, I'm sorry to be the one to break the news, but we found human remains in that compartment, very likely a murder victim. I'm afraid your mother is in for a little embarrassment."

There was silence on the line. Finally, Carol Tichnor said, her voice high and tight, "A murder victim? Who?"

"No idea, ma'am. Male, dark hair."

"Oh, God, oh, uh, excuse me. This is awful. I need to think...." The line went dead.

Rob hit Redial and after six rings got an answering machine. He left his phone numbers, home, cell, and office, but he had the feeling Carol Tichnor was not going to return his call until she'd talked to someone—her mother? And a lawyer, or the family insurance agent. People like the Tichnors were apt to worry about liability.

He set the receiver back in its cradle and rose, yawning in spite of the stimulus of new information. His eyes kept going out of focus from lack of sleep. Not the sharpest knife in the drawer, Roberto.

The second-story window overlooked his backyard and a generous portion of the Strohmeyer yard. He corrected himself. The McLean yard. Thayer Jones was pacing behind the garage, head bent. Good luck to him. He would need it.

Just how upset was Carol Tichnor, and why? And what about the old lady? The soul of propriety. He'd known women like that, older women mostly. There are two kinds of social constraint, guilt and shame. Some people worry about their souls, and others worry about what the neighbors will think. Charlotte Tichnor was apparently the second type.

Rob made a mental note to get the King County Sheriff's Department to talk to the Tichnor ladies. A patrol car parked in front of the house with its lights flashing would be just the thing in a super-respectable neighborhood. As he recalled, Charlotte Tichnor was the widow of a surgeon. What would the neighbors think?

Neighbors. His tired brain slid back to Klalo. Commissioner Brandstetter and the egregious ridgeback. The Wheelers: wholesome couple, nice little boy. Dennis Wheeler was a sports bore and proudly red-neck. Darcy was into crafts and good deeds. Rob liked her but thought she needed a job, something with a lot of office intrigue. As it was, she came across as intrusive sometimes, even downright nosy.

After Hazel's death, Darcy had kept bringing him pies and cookies and casseroles with orange cheese melted over them. She'd told him he should replace Hazel's furniture with country kitsch. He wondered how much she knew about the Tichnors. She had hung out at their garage sales.

All of the neighbors would have to be interrogated. The hell of it was, he wasn't sure of the time line. It would be unfortunate if the crucial month was August, and it probably was. People took their vacations in August. He had. He'd driven his daughter, Willow, up to Tyee Lake for two solid weeks of fishing and bonding. A good time.

He forced his mind back to the case. Had the Wheelers gone away, too? And what about the folks across the street? Three houses, two with elderly couples who went to bed early, one with three girls who didn't and a red Mustang in cherry condition.

Two of those young women were wind surfers. They supported their passion with jobs in the tourist trade. The third, Kayla, the nurse, was a pistol. Their older neighbors had gossiped about drugs, but he thought it was mostly talk. The surfers paid their rent and mowed their lawn. One of them had a Lhasa Apso.

Towser. Something would have to be done about that dog. He was well trained and amiable but he needed scope—twenty square miles of African veldt, ideally. Towser was Tammy Brandstetter's, and she was too lethargic to give him the exercise he needed. Hal didn't care. The dog had become a nuisance after the Brandstetter son left home.

There was something about Brandstetter's son. What? A pot bust, Rob thought: possession, not a serious charge. Tom was a quiet boy, into black T-shirts and nose rings, but polite enough the few times Rob had spoken to him. Rob thought Tom had moved to Portland. He wondered if the Brandstetters heard from the kid these days, or if he'd dropped out of sight. Tom had dark hair when it wasn't purple or green. Maybe he'd given up nose rings. The corpse had no studs or rings or tattoos Rob had noticed.

He thought about Earl Minetti off in Vancouver. What if the victim the ME cut open was Tom Brandstetter? Better Earl than me, Rob thought wearily. He hated autopsies almost as much as Earl did.

He walked back to the desk, bent down, and wrote "Bootlegger's cache, how many knew where it was?" on his notepad. It would be great if nobody did outside the family. Somehow he didn't think that would be the case.

He sat down and picked up the phone. Time to get on to the agencies that might have information on looting and looters—the Bureau of Indian Affairs, Land Management, and the Inter-tribal Fish Commission. He thought he was looking for a collector as well as a thief or thieves.

During the ten years since the Lauder Point theft, Rob had kept track of the sale of native artifacts, or tried to. It was a flourishing trade with an international dimension. In that time, none of the distinctive pieces from the heist had surfaced in area antiques shops, at swap meets, or on eBay, nor was there anything on the NCIC database. There was no way of checking on the less remarkable arrowheads, baskets, and blankets. If the thieves hadn't shipped their booty off the first day—to Germany, or Japan, or New York— somebody here was hoarding it, gloating over the petroglyphs and the beautiful ceremonial knife with the obsidian blade.

*

THE doorbell rang. Linda and Jake had given Meg the go-ahead, so she was unpacking lamps in the living room. I'll have to teach Darcy to use the back door, she reflected, dusting Santa Ana grit from her hands. It was amazing how much topsoil she had brought north. The caller had to be Darcy Wheeler. Or the Avon lady.

Darcy beamed at her, confident of welcome. "Hi, Meg, I hear you had a little excitement last night."

"Come in," Meg said with resignation. "I owe you a cup of coffee." Not for a second did she doubt that Darcy knew everything the other neighbors knew.

She did, of course, but she hadn't seen the police activity herself.

Meg poured coffee, gave Darcy a terse account of the previous evening, and listened to her almost apologetic reason for missing the excitement. It turned out that Darcy's son went to bed early. Around 8:30 she had begun their nighttime ritual. He had read her *Green Eggs and Ham* and, for the umpteenth time, she had read him *The Poky Little Puppy*. Meg remembered that book. Lucy had been mightily fond of it, well past the age of reason.

Meg's heart warmed to Darcy. Anyone willing to read and re-read *The Poky Little Puppy* was a Good Parent.

Mother and son had fallen asleep together before nine out of sheer boredom. The boy's name was Cody. After Buffalo Bill? Not a prepossessing role model. Meg restrained herself from reciting e.e. cummings's subversive poem about William Cody to the mother of Cody Wheeler, but she thought of Rob Neill and wondered if he knew it. She decided to save it up for him. How do you like your blue-eyed boy, Mr. Death?

"So who's the stiff?"

"I beg your pardon?" Meg warmed Darcy's coffee.

Darcy giggled. "I watch too much TV. Do they know who was buried in your garage?"

Meg said, "I don't think so, but it's not the sort of thing the police tell innocent bystanders. Such as myself."

Darcy craned around, looking. "Didn't the cops make a mess? I thought fingerprint powder was black?"

"They used something called an iodine fuming gun. The iodine fades after awhile." Meg wanted Darcy out of her kitchen but curiosity intervened. "Did you or your husband notice anything odd going on in the garage after the FOR SALE sign came down this summer?"

"Is that when they think the murder happened? No, we didn't, but we wouldn't have. We took Cody to Disneyland the first week in August and took our time coming home. Dennis's dad and his wife live down in Valencia. We drove through the redwoods on the way back."

"Lots of traffic on 101 that time of year."

"There sure was. The car overheated in Ukiah. We had to stay overnight. Dennis was pissed."

Meg wondered whether Dennis had been angry or drunk, or both. "What does Dennis do?"

"He's a machinist. Makes good money when he's working. A lot of the jobs are in Portland or The Dalles or Vancouver, though. Sometimes Cody and me go with him."

And what do *you* do? Meg caught herself before she asked. "Tell me about the neighbors."

Darcy made a face. "They're pretty dull except for the lesbos across the street."

"Lesbos?"

"Oh, that's just Dennis. He doesn't like gays. There's these three women, all muscle. They wind-surf up at Cascade Locks when the weather's right. I think they've packed it in for the season now, though."

The Gorge was prime wind-surfing territory, according to the tourist information site. Meg tried to look encouraging.

Darcy bit a hangnail. "Tiffany and Lisa staff the shop on Main Street that carries wet suits and boards. Kayla works at the nursing home on the River Road. She's an RN."

Solid citizens, in other words.

Perhaps Darcy read disapproval in Meg's face. "I kind of like them myself," she offered, "and they're probably not lesbians." She gave an uneasy laugh. "Never came on to *me*. Guys hang out with them in the summer, real party animals. The old folks don't like the noise."

"I get the picture." And I wouldn't like the noise either, Meg reflected, rueful. Old folks.

"Mrs. Iverson's deaf." Darcy giggled again. "That doesn't stop her from complaining about the music. Her husband's sort of past it. The other old couple, the Brownings, are snowbirds. They spend half the year here and winter in Arizona. He's retired military. They're leaving for Flagstaff next week."

"What about the Brandstetters?"

Darcy scowled. "If that damned dog gets loose again I'm going to complain, I don't care if Hal *is* a county commissioner. Towser knocked Cody down twice this summer, scared the pants off him." She glanced at Meg as if for reassurance. "Cody's not a chicken, whatever Dennis says, but that animal's bigger than a little boy. It scares *me*."

"Me, too. What's Mrs. Brandstetter like?"

Darcy shrugged. "Nice enough. She's a bookkeeper. I don't see much of her. Their son gave me the creeps, but he's been gone now more than a year."

"No youngsters around for Cody to play with."

"Not on this block. There's plenty farther along the street, past Rob's house. *He's* okay, I guess—quiet, not very friendly—but then he's a cop. I liked the old lady."

"Hazel Guthrie?"

"Yeah, she started me reading to Cody when he was real little. I was never very good at school, but I want him to be educated. He reads like crazy, loves books."

And what does Dennis think about that? Meg left her question unvoiced and gave silent thanks, first that her child was a daughter, and second, that Lucy's father was out of the picture. *I'm* subversive, she thought guiltily. "Well, Darcy, I'd better get back to work. Thanks for telling me about the neighborhood."

"I guess you got a bad first impression. Give us a chance." Darcy rose.

"I won't jump to conclusions." Meg moved to the hall. "Did you know the woman I bought the house from?"

"Her with the Mercedes? She wouldn't give me the time of day. Her daughter runs an antiques shop in Port Townsend during the tourist season—divorced, took her maiden name back. Lives up in Seattle with Madam Charlotte when she's not at Port Townsend or off on a buying trip."

Darcy took a good look at Meg's china and drifted into the hall. "Carol and me talked a lot in July. Carol's the daughter. She came down to help run the estate sale. Sales, I should say. They held two. She must have closed her shop up north or left somebody else in charge. July's prime tourist time. I like Carol but she drinks a lot."

"Interesting." A lot compared to what?

Darcy stopped to gawk at the living room again. Meg's furniture was fairly decrepit and she hadn't hung any of her watercolors yet.

"I like the love seat," Darcy said generously.

Meg shepherded her guest to the door. "Drop by again."

"Okay. See you later."

Meg thought she probably would.

EARL Minetti's phone call woke Rob from a nap. Though he was expecting it, the ring jolted him awake with his heart racing.

"What have you got?" he asked when Minetti had identified himself.

"You know Doc. He doesn't like to commit himself." The phone crackled. "Here's what I picked up. We got a male Amerind, early twenties, dead about ten weeks." Earl cleared his throat. "His head was bashed in. Skull fracture, multiple blunt-force trauma. Doc will fax the details. Oh, and he thinks the guy was moved after death, maybe as much as twelve or fourteen hours."

Time for rigor to set in. "You okay?"

"I threw up. Par for the course."

"Have you had a look at his effects?" Rob kept his tone matter-of-fact. Earl rarely admitted a weakness.

"The lab's running tests on his clothes. I'm bringing the rest with me. There wasn't much." A horn sounded and a whooshing noise. "I'm in the car, just passing Washougal."

"Okay." It wasn't. Earl should have used a secure line. He had to be upset. "Put the stuff in the evidence locker and go home. We can look at it tomorrow." When Earl squawked a protest, Rob said firmly, "Go home. Remember what Our Leader said about overtime."

Earl laughed. The phone crackled again.

"I sent your team home at three," Rob added. "Thayer found signs that the ground behind the garage was disturbed, but Ms. McLean parked her tow trailer back there, so the area's mucked up. Nothing in the house." They'd found Meg's fingerprints, Jake's and Todd's, and a few that were probably the realtor's or another viewer's. No traces of blood at all. "Linda did a thorough job."

Earl grunted. "So our guy stumbled on the perps out behind the garage, and they hit him with a shovel?"

"Something like that."

"Maybe he was in on it." Earl's voice sounded easier.

"A falling out among thieves? Maybe."

"I could come in this evening."

"Go home, Earl. See you tomorrow bright and early." Rob hung up and took a swallow of very old coffee. He intended to put in some unpaid overtime himself that evening, but his people had been on the job for upwards of eighteen hours. Enough was enough.

It always bothered Rob on cop shows when the police worked twenty-four hours a day, seven days a week, without sleeping or eating anything except doughnuts. In this case, the petroglyph had been missing for ten years and the homicide victim had been in the ground over two months. No point in rushing things and doing a bad job. Still, it wouldn't hurt to take a look at the man's effects.

The phone rang.

"Robert Neill." He fiddled with the notebook. Something Earl had said...

"Lieutenant Neill, this is Madeline Thomas." Maddie was probably the only county resident who bothered to use the department's quasi-military ranking system.

Rob drew a long breath and laid his pen down. "Afternoon, Chief Thomas. What can I do for you?"

"Communicate," Maddie growled. "You found sacred objects that belong to my people yesterday, and I haven't had a word from you."

Rob said carefully, "We found something that *may* be a fragment of one of the petroglyphs...."

"Which one?"

"The Dancers."

She groaned. The sound was dramatic but not theatrical. Maddie didn't fake emotion. Her pain was real, but she was willing to use it.

He let her express her indignation. When she wound down, he said, "We have a homicide."

"So I heard."

"I need to ask how you found out about the petroglyph."

"I have my sources."

Rob took an educated guess. Jake Sorenson had been brought in to work with the evidence team. Jake had a roommate who had also been at the scene. "Did Todd Welch tell you our victim is probably an Indian?" He used the term Indian with confidence born of despair. Madeline held "Indian" and "Native American" in equal distaste. He didn't want to hear what she'd say about "Amerind."

She was silent.

Todd's mother was Maddie's younger sister. Rob waited. So did Chief Thomas. She was both stubborn and intelligent.

Rob sighed. "Are any of your people missing?"

"You know what the job situation is like. The kids leave for college, or they go off to find work. They don't always keep in touch."

How did she know the victim was young? He started to ask her, then decided to let it ride. "He would have disappeared early in August, first or second week."

Silence.

"Think about it, ma'am."

"I'll ask around," she said heavily.

Rob thought she wouldn't have to. She would know. "About the petroglyph…"

"What do you care?" That was a meaningless jab and both of them knew it.

"Have you heard anything about the missing objects?"

"I'll get back to you." She hung up on him, the second hang-up that day.

Must be something in the air.

 *Chapter 5*

ROB, Dave Meuler, and Earl Minetti met in Rob's uninspiring office in the courthouse annex before eight-thirty Friday morning and talked strategy. They had had a look at the contents of the evidence locker, which were not inspiring either. The Swatch still kept time.

Dave stood up. "I'll get on the interviews right now—the retired folks and Darcy Wheeler." They had thrashed out a list of questions and Dave was raring to go.

Rob envied his enthusiasm, which was understandable. Interviewing witnesses had to be less monotonous than driving around placid Klalo in a patrol car. "You can catch the other neighbors after they get off work, but leave the Brandstetters to me."

Dave grinned. "My pleasure." He gave a one-finger salute and left.

Rob turned to Minetti, who was still sitting across the desk from him, upright as always. Earl sat like a Marine. "No fingerprint matches?"

Earl shook his head, no.

Rob shifted the greasy sheets of fax paper so as not to lose the ME's report and the preliminary lab results in the general clutter of paperwork from pending cases. Forensics had been able to lift prints from the victim's left hand, though not, unfortunately, from the Swatch. The national database showed the man had never been booked for a serious crime nor served in the military.

Rob shoved himself to his feet. "He wasn't a felon, not a convicted one anyway. He was young. He was probably an Indian. Can they do anything with teeth?"

"He had good teeth," Earl said gloomily.

Rob walked to the window. "No dental work at all?"

"Two small porcelain fillings. I sent out a request to the dentists."

"And Vancouver's doing a portrait from the corpse?"

"Right."

An artist's reconstruction was necessary because the body had been savagely damaged by the beating, by rats, and by the action of insects after death.

Remembering the gargoyle face, Rob shivered. It was raining and had been since they'd found the victim. Sympathetic magic. A gust of wind shook yellow leaves from the maples that rimmed the parking lot—spindly vine maples, weeds from the point of view of gardeners like his grandmother, but beautiful in October.

"Uh, Rob?"

"Sorry. What were you saying?"

Earl gave a super-patient sigh. "I was saying, maybe the Lauder Point connection isn't really there."

Rob turned and looked at him.

Earl flushed red and stuck his jaw out. "I gotta say it, Rob. You have Lauder Point on the brain. Maybe the chunk of rock art isn't connected to the killing at all."

"Maybe not. A whole series of unconnected felonies occurred in that garage. Bootlegging. Looting. Murder. God knows what we've missed. God knows what my grandmother missed, living there all that time."

"No need to get sarcastic." Earl gave a righteous sniff. "I was just hypothesizing. And you told me she—Hazel, I mean—didn't mention the bootlegging."

"No." Rob turned back to the autumn scene outside.

Carol Tichnor had not returned his call. He'd talked to King County and a car was on its way to her. So far he hadn't found anyone local who remembered Otto Strohmeyer's free enterprise. Rob had sent Thayer Jones to the *Progressive* to see what was in the weekly newspaper's morgue. In the 'Twenties it had been a daily. Now it was a step above *Nickel Ads*, but there were archives.

Not that they'd say much. If Otto Strohmeyer had never been caught peddling moonshine, there would be nothing useful in the newspaper, even from those golden days of yellow journalism. Emil Strohmeyer's obituary would list next of kin, though.

Charlotte Tichnor had brothers and sons. There was Carol. Emil's grandchildren were of an age to have grown children themselves. Lots of folks knew about Strohmeyer's hidey-hole.

The wind had picked up. Leaves whirled and settled on the windshields of cars in the lot.

Without identification of the victim, Rob's mind was whirling in circles like the leaves. No missing persons in a six-county area met the man's description, now that fingerprints had eliminated three possibles.

Earl made a noise, not quite impatient.

Rob turned from the window. "Okay, let's focus on the killing. *I* think it happened in the course of a felony—moving stolen goods."

"Which would make it homicide."

"Right. If he was beaten in a brawl unconnected with the petroglyph…"

"He might have been."

"Then it may be manslaughter. In either case, we need to know whether the man was killed there in the garage or elsewhere. He was definitely moved post-mortem. It's going to take time for the lab to give us results on soil traces from his clothes and so on, so let's have another, closer look at the garage."

"Bloodstains?"

"Spatter patterns on the walls, for example. You're the expert, Earl."

"Thanks." His lip curled.

Asshole. Rob said, with malice, "Don't forget to look outside—on the back wall of the garage. I'm sending Linda for a heart-to-heart with that realtor. We need to find the key to the back door, if there is one, and if there isn't, we need to know why not."

"I think it's against normal practice to mail a key to the former owner."

"Probably, but Carol Tichnor made a point of saying the sale hadn't closed when she asked for the key."

"Still, if it was a multiple listing there were several sets of keys available."

"Good point," Rob conceded. "Talk to Linda before she leaves for the agency office." The keys were interesting only because neither lock had been forced.

Earl rose. "D'you think the shovel was the weapon?"

"It's being tested." Rob tapped the faxes. "But the wounds sound to me as if they were made with a thin metal cylinder. You should look for a crowbar or a tire iron, but I bet bucks the weapon's at the bottom of the river."

"Probably." Earl left with minimal ceremony, still miffed and still self-righteous. Rob wished he'd shave off his mustache.

Rob was confused. He needed to talk to Maddie Thomas face to face. The Lauder Point connection *was* questionable. It depended on Rob's identification of the petroglyph, from memory and from photographs in the files he had salvaged from county park brochures. The photographs were not very good, and he was beginning to doubt his memory.

Well, there were good photos of the fragment Meg McLean had found—Rob had seen to that. As soon as the artist's portrait of the dead man was faxed, he'd take it and Linda's photos of the flute player, and he'd drive upriver to Two Falls, Maddie's home base. He thought about Todd Welch. Todd could drive him. Time for a little talk with Deputy Welch.

Meanwhile, he had to find out more about Emil Strohmeyer's heirs. He also needed to stretch his legs, so he decided to walk around to the courthouse for a copy of the old man's will.

It wasn't that simple, of course. Outside his office, the big room buzzed with activity. Old Howell, the desk sergeant, and Jane Schmidt, the 911 day dispatcher, sat as the foci of a double spiral with deputies' desks arrayed around them, some occupied. Phones rang and keyboards clacked. A chest-high counter kept the public at bay. A row of molded plastic chairs provided a resting place for the weary, in this case a depressed-looking Hispanic kid who, Rob recalled, was looking to delay the court appearance for his second DUI. At the other end of the row, a sad woman in a faded sweatsuit waited patiently for something.

Rob stopped by two desks for a word on ongoing cases, then made his escape before Howell could disengage from the debate he was having with a red-faced tourist. Reese liked to chew the fat.

Outside, the wind whipped but the rain had eased up. It was not, strictly speaking, necessary for Rob to go outside and walk around to the front entrance of the courthouse, but he didn't like the slow plod through the corridors of the county jail, slow because of security checks. Besides, the courthouse was worth looking at.

Erected in 1910, the Art Nouveau structure had become a place of pilgrimage for architecture students. It was a monument to pride, good taste, and corruption, an unbeatable combination. A lot of timber and railroad money had flowed through Latouche County in the years before World War I.

He climbed the left wing of the imposing double stairway that led up to the front entrance and stopped at the top for a look south. Marigolds rotted in marble urns atop the newel posts. Below lay the wet roofs of the Klalo business district. Beyond the town, sheets of oncoming rain blew up the Gorge, revealing and concealing the dark slopes of the ravine. The river snaked between them, sullen gray.

At the end of the last Ice Age, the pent-up waters of Lake Missoula in far-off Montana had broken through their ice dam, scoured the flatlands of eastern Washington into steep-sided coulees, then driven through fields of congealed lava four hundred feet deep in their westering rush. There had been people living in the area, Rob was sure of that whatever old textbooks said, and some of them had survived the repeated devastating floods. Their grandchildren told the stories and created the enigmatic drawings chipped into solid basalt. The petroglyphs spoke of human survival. Worth looking at. Worth thinking about.

He entered the heavy double door and stepped into the rotunda below the stained glass dome. It was like standing beneath a giant Tiffany lamp. Heavy doors—glass and imported Philippine mahogany, as if local materials were inadequate to express the architect's pride—opened on the central circle. He entered one marked RECORDS in brass letters. Time for a look at Strohmeyer history.

SHORTLY after dawn, which was coming later in these northern latitudes, Marybeth Jackman called Meg and suggested lunch at Rosa's Cantina.

Meg was a snob about Mexican food, but she agreed at once. If rumors were flying up and down Old Cedar Street, they were probably also flying around the library. "Why don't you bring

Annie Baldwin, too?" she suggested, infusing her voice with faux enthusiasm. "I met her brother."

Marybeth sounded doubtful. Annie was driving the bookmobile in the east county that afternoon.

"I'd like to get to know her. Bring her along for an early lunch—eleven-thirty."

"I'll ask," Marybeth said, her voice cool.

She probably wants a scoop, Meg reflected, hanging up. She hoped the refried beans at Rosa's Cantina didn't come from a can.

They didn't. Rosa's was a large cut above Taco Bell, the *pico de gallo* so fresh the peppers had barely had time to suffuse the salsa. Guitar music played softly. Meg ordered a nice seafood and rice dish on the lunch special, Annie chose a chicken enchilada, and Marybeth a salad.

Annie seemed a little overwhelmed to be eating with supervisors, but Meg got her talking about her bookmobile patrons—lots of housebound people, elderly people who no longer drove and mothers of small children. Several children had a passion for dinosaurs. One tiny woman with large glasses read everything there was to read on naval battles of the Napoleonic Wars. A man from Two Falls was obsessed with books about edible plants.

Meg was impressed with Annie's willingness to cater to their interests, and with her encyclopedic knowledge of the many roads that led up into the hills. Meg said complimentary things about Annie's husband's automotive genius with the bookmobile, and Annie bridled and said oh that Jake, but Meg thought she was pleased.

Marybeth listened with a polite smile and poked at her taco salad.

Just when Meg was beginning to believe she might escape without having to talk about the Body in the Garage, Marybeth said, "Have they solved your murder yet?"

"I don't think so."

"Tell us about it!" Annie burst out. "Jake won't say a word. Just that a city cop found a dead man buried in the floor of your garage."

Meg speared her last tiny scallop. "Well, I'd left the doors open to air the place out and Rob Neill saw a dog in there, digging away." She gave them what she'd told Darcy, omitting the petroglyph, but hyping the comedy when it came to the house search. They drank it up. Marybeth looked almost animated.

"And that's all I know," Meg admitted.

"Convenient having a deputy next door," Marybeth offered. Meg thought the remark was not satirical.

Annie said, "I like Rob. I was a year ahead of him in school. He was small for his age, weedy, must have grown six inches after he left. Everybody knew he was real smart. You could've knocked me over with a feather when he left all that in California and came home."

Meg's ears pricked. "All that?"

"Oh, you know, computers. He was in on some big stuff in the early days of the Internet, before Microsoft took over everything. I guess his marriage went down the drain, so he sold out early and moved north. That's one version of things, anyway. He took real good care of Mrs. Guthrie when she got sick."

"Congestive heart failure," Marybeth offered.

"I wondered," Meg murmured. "I admired her."

"We all did. After she retired as head librarian, she stayed on the library board. It was a darned good thing, too, what with those witch hunters wanting to burn all the books except the Bible and typing manuals." Marybeth's pale cheeks flushed.

"Witch hunters?" Meg ventured.

Annie gave a snort of laughter. "They wanted Snow White off the shelves. Can you believe it? Now they're after Harry Potter."

"But Hazel Guthrie showed us how to deal with them." Marybeth shoved her salad away.

"It's a splendid policy," Meg said. "So Rob Neill took care of her. Literally?"

Marybeth said, "He's not a nurse and anyway she wasn't confined to her bed. She just needed trained help. He hired good care-givers and kept a close eye on them."

Annie's face darkened. "You have to do that." Personal experience there. "He lived at his cabin up at Tyee Lake, but he spent time with his grandma almost every day, Jake said. Even in the middle of a big case. She lived ten years after she was diagnosed, and she was still on the library board when she died."

"She was pretty sick, though, the last year," Marybeth murmured. "Missed meetings or had to leave early. Nobody even considered asking her to resign. Rob did move into town, into her house, that last year."

"And Mrs. Guthrie died two years ago?"

Annie nodded. "Rob's been there three years now, but he still has the cabin up at Tyee. Took his daughter there in August. Nice kid, a real California girl."

"What on earth do you mean?" Meg asked, wondering if her Lucy was a California girl. She kept her voice humorous, but it was not a stereotype she liked.

Annie blushed but stuck to her guns. "It's just that she looks like she's been, I dunno, waxed and polished?"

Meg had to laugh. Marybeth regarded the two of them with incomprehension. Marybeth had a degree in Library Science from the University of Washington, whereas Annie had only a high school diploma and a couple of extension classes, but Annie was obviously brighter where it counted.

A blond server, who looked uncomfortable in a vaguely Mexican costume, intruded to ask whether they wanted dessert or coffee. There was, she said, deep-fried ice cream. Meg said no thanks. Annie looked tempted.

Marybeth glanced at her watch. "Just bring us the bill, please."

"My treat," Meg said. "No, I insist." She smiled at the waitress. "One check."

"Thanks," Annie said. "Oops, I gotta go. See you." And she whisked from the small restaurant almost at a run.

"She's punctual," Marybeth murmured, as if that were Annie's solitary virtue.

"Hmmm. Ah, tell me, Marybeth, what do you know about the Tichnors, the people who owned my house?"

"Not a whole lot. I didn't grow up in Klalo, you know. I moved here from Portland."

"Must have been quite a shock."

Marybeth gave a short, sharp nod. "It was. My ex-husband got transferred. He's a chemist. Then Georgia-Pacific closed the paper mill, and he had to commute to Camas. When we split up, I stayed on. My daughter likes the school, and we have a house."

A nicer house, probably, than a divorced woman could afford in Portland on a librarian's salary. She didn't say that but it was obvious.

Marybeth sighed. "You asked about your house. It belonged to a man named Strohmeyer who had grown children. He left it to his daughter when he died last year."

"Charlotte Tichnor."

"That's the name. Her son's an oncologist in Vancouver, always contributes to Friends of the Library. So does his mother."

The server brought the check and took Meg's Visa card.

"I think there's a daughter, and another son in Portland, something to do with insurance or real estate. I bought a sideboard at the estate sale." She took a last sip of herbal tea and set her cup down. "If you want to know more about local families you could go to the historical society. Mrs. Wirkkala knows everybody. I think she's there on Fridays."

"Thanks." Meg signed the requisite form as Marybeth rose and shrugged into her raincoat.

"Can't think of anything else," she said. "We'll see you next week at the library."

"A week from Monday," Meg corrected, smiling. "Don't rush me. I have a lot of unpacking yet to do. Thanks, Marybeth." She rescued her own damp raingear from the coat rack but almost forgot her umbrella.

Marybeth gave her a small, chilly smile as they headed out into the storm.

 *Chapter 6*

MRS. Wirkkala—call me Helmi—was a fountain of information. A seventyish dumpling with fierce blue eyes, she was delighted to meet the new librarian, and Meg suspected, to hear of Meg's ordeal firsthand.

They sat drinking coffee in Helmi's office in the old Carnegie Library, a sturdy red-brick building like thousands the philanthropist had scattered across the country. In the late 'Fifties, Helmi told Meg, when the book collection and the population had outgrown it, the current library had been erected and the old one turned over to the Latouche County Historical Society. Helmi, a retired high school history teacher, was the unpaid director.

Meg couldn't imagine a better use for the old building. It reeked of history—dark wood, dim lighting, leather-bound tomes. She was glad she wouldn't have to work there.

She obliged Helmi with her well-rehearsed narrative. It was beginning to feel like the ritual retelling of an ancient myth. When the telling was over and Helmi had made appropriate exclamations, Meg explained why she'd sought out someone with a historical perspective.

"I need to know about the people who owned my house, the Strohmeyers."

Helmi gave an impish grin. "A fine old family. Charlotte Tichnor's grandfather was a bootlegger."

"My goodness."

Helmi poured coffee. "I went to high school with Charlotte. She was a real queen bee. You know the type—head cheerleader, homecoming queen, president of the honor society. She was a good student but an awful snob."

"Stuck up?"

"She smiled graciously on the peasants. If you wanted to Be Somebody, though, you had to wear the right clothes, date the jerks on the basketball team, and hang out at the right drugstore after school. Charlotte made sure of that. Finnish girls in homemade skirts didn't cut the mustard." The twinkle reappeared. "I used to remind myself that our Char was the moonshiner's grandbaby."

"Prohibition." Meg slapped her forehead. "The compartment in the garage. I should have thought of that as a possibility at least. The garage is more recent than the house." The house had been built in 1904. "Did Old Strohmeyer get away with it?"

"My dear, he was a local hero. What do you know about Temperance?"

"Uh, Carry Nation?"

Helmi looked at her with pity. "I did my thesis on the Women's Christian Temperance Union. It was the first great women's movement."

"Wait a minute, what about suffrage?"

"That appealed to women with an education. Temperance was *popular*."

"With women."

"Exactly. The Volstead Amendment—Prohibition—was the great triumph of the WCTU."

"Some triumph."

Helmi took a judicious sip of coffee. "Prohibition was a direct consequence of women getting the vote in 1920."

"Why does that make me cringe?"

"Because it was a very bad thing for this country. Organized crime is the spawn of Prohibition, on the one hand. On the other, you have our obsession with other people's vices—drinking and smoking and having sex in the backseat of a car, blasphemy, doing drugs and dancing and reading books about witches, listening to rock music with the volume turned up. Our first impulse is prohibition."

Meg had to laugh. "Do you write pop history?"

"Sometimes I squeeze out an article for our quarterly. Mostly I just watch."

"So it's all women's fault?"

"I wouldn't say that. A lot of the blame lies with Baptist and Methodist preachers, and all of them were men."

"And all of *them* opposed woman suffrage." Meg knew a lot about the suffrage movement.

"There were exceptions."

"The Quakers," Meg conceded. "Other than the Quakers, every single Christian church organization in this country opposed giving women the vote."

"They certainly did to begin with. At any rate, preachers played an important role in the Temperance Movement. I studied the WCTU of Clark County. It was never big here in Latouche County. Too many Catholics."

"Catholics?"

Helmi pushed a plate of gingersnaps at Meg. "Think about it. Myself, I was raised by parents who departed from the Evangelical Lutheran tradition, which may be even more puritanical than the Methodists but was ethnic Scandinavian. The Catholics around here are ethnic German like the Strohmeyers, and nowadays Hispanic. Elsewhere they were Italian or Irish, for the most part. In Clark County, right next door, they were French Canadian. All ethnic."

"Ethnics were excluded from the WCTU?"

"Socially excluded. Catholics were excluded. By and large, black people were excluded. Indians weren't even considered. It was an all-white Protestant movement, like the Know-Nothings and the Ku Klux Klan."

Meg stared. "You're not saying the membership overlapped, I hope."

"Not at all. Separate spheres. The women put on their best hats and went out to ice cream socials."

"And the men took a fortifying sip of White Lightning, and rode out to lynch rabbis, priests, and black men?"

Helmi smiled. "Some of the men. It's not accidental that the Klan was big in that period, especially in Oregon. Washington is less WASPish. Always has been."

"I'm getting dizzy."

Helmi laughed. "It's complicated. I'm just trying to explain why a nice law-abiding German Catholic man like Otto Strohmeyer took to bootlegging alcohol. Gin, in his case."

"His culture was under attack by women and WASPs. I see that."

"You do but our Charlotte didn't. Charlotte thirsted after respectability."

"She wanted to be a Methodist lady?"

Helmi dipped a gingersnap into her coffee. "A WASP."

"I guess that makes sense," Meg said through a mouthful of cookie. The homemade gingersnaps were delicious.

"World War Two did something for Charlotte's character, too. Her father, Emil, had trouble finding work in the 'Thirties. He'd trained as a carpenter, but the Depression hit this town hard. When the Kaiser Shipyard started up in Vancouver, he moved the whole family there. Charlotte went to grade school and junior high in Vancouver, and it gave her larger social ideas."

"I guess the war changed a lot of people."

Helmi nodded. "And helped secularize society. The preachers lost influence. For a while."

"But the Strohmeyers were Catholics."

"Not when they came back to Klalo. By that time they were Episcopalians, very respectable, very WASP."

Meg turned over what she knew of the population shifts during World War II. Long Beach had had a shipyard, and there were the big aircraft factories. "The Strohmeyers wouldn't have been respectable in Vancouver. It's an old town. They would have been considered migrant workers."

Helmi beamed at her as if she were a bright first grader. "In Vancouver, Charlotte baby-sat for an Old Family. She internalized their notions."

"What then?"

Helmi shrugged. "The war ended. Otto died. When people started building houses again, Emil brought his wife and kids home. He built a lot of the ranch-style houses in town, so he was pretty well fixed. He sent Peter, his oldest boy, to college. The second son, Jimmy, went into the army out of high school and never amounted to much." Her round face clouded. "I had a crush on Jimmy."

"What happened to him?"

"Oh, nothing dramatic. He died in Las Vegas ten years ago. Three marriages, no kids. He had a drinking problem, which is a nice irony. Charlotte was the baby and got whatever she wanted. What she wanted was out."

"The real estate agent said she lives in Seattle."

Helmi nodded. "The big time. She went to nursing school at one of the hospitals up there and snared a surgeon. I don't think she ever worked as a nurse after she married Ethan Tichnor. Devoted herself to charities and social climbing."

"Did she succeed?"

Helmi smiled. "Pretty much. She's on the board of half a dozen worthy causes. She belongs to the best clubs. Her husband's dead now, but her children turned out well. They managed to survive going to the best schools."

"And her father left her his house?"

"That's right."

"I guess I don't see what all that has to do with bootlegging."

"As long as she lived here, someone like me would remind her that her grandfather was a moonshiner. Charlotte left Klalo. She never came home."

"Ever?"

"I'm exaggerating for dramatic effect. She made brief ritual appearances. She sent her kids to their grandparents every summer for a month. And she wasn't stingy. Her mother had a long, lingering bout with cancer that must have soaked up a lot of Emil's savings. Charlotte was generous with her checkbook."

"But not with her time. I see."

Helmi toyed with a gingersnap. "I hope I'm not indulging in spite. I liked Emil Strohmeyer. He used to drop in and swap stories. He was proud of Charlotte, proud of the boys, too."

"Why didn't *they* come home to take care of him?"

Helmi's eyes widened. She even blushed. "That's a very good question. Maybe I'm too hard on Charlotte."

Meg said tactfully, "What about grandchildren, do they live around here?"

"Peter has two married daughters in Montana. He taught in Montana, retired to Arizona."

"And the Tichnors?"

"There are two of them in the area. Vance in Portland and Ethan, Junior in Vancouver. Ethan's a big wheel in the medical society. Vance has a real estate agency in Clackamas County."

"Where's that?"

"South of Portland, southeast. I think the boys did visit Emil—

they went fly fishing with him when he could still get around. Carol runs an antiques shop in Port Townsend up on Puget Sound. She oversaw the prep work when Charlotte sold the house, so she was down here more than usual this spring and summer."

"Then I probably ought to talk to her."

"I expect Rob Neill will do that."

"You're right," Meg murmured. It crossed her mind to ask about Hazel Guthrie, too, but she didn't have a good reason to dig, so she suppressed the impulse. "It's just that I'm curious." She rose. "Thanks, Helmi. May I come back for a look at your collection?"

"Any time."

Meg had promised herself she would not enter the Latouche County Regional Library until the day she was scheduled to take over. Still, it couldn't hurt to drive past now and then. She chugged up the main drag and turned onto the tree-lined street, a cul-de-sac, that led to the Klalo branch library. Her headquarters. She'd forgotten how ugly it was.

A symphony of aluminum and concrete, the structure that replaced Carnegie's sturdy red-brick building had been erected at the nadir of public architecture. Prince Charles would see it and abdicate. Thinking, with affection, of Rob's grandmother, Meg parked a moment across from her new workplace and contemplated its sheer hideousness. Hazel Guthrie and her library board had probably found it wonderfully modern. Well, it was a blot on the landscape, but it looked cared-for—scrubbed and polished, embraced by mature rhododendrons that would show a riot of color in May.

A native dogwood three stories high shaded the curved entrance drive. Meg had been told the blossoms were white, not pink, and that Hazel had made the demented architect site the building so as not to damage the tree. Meg wished she had known her predecessor.

She drove home through the wet streets in a thoughtful mood. Helmi Wirkkala's revelations made her uneasy. There had been real malice in the historian's comments on Charlotte Tichnor, so the question was whether Helmi's hostility was justified. The Tichnors hardly seemed the sort to loot artifacts—or to commit murder. Who did that leave? The looters had had to know about the storage space in the garage. That left the neighbors.

Rob Neill's pickup sat in the driveway that led up to the ginger-bread house. On impulse, Meg hoisted her umbrella and dashed up to the handsome front door. The beveled glass window in the door was obscured by a lace curtain. The rain-lashed porch was wide and generous. She knocked and rang the doorbell but nobody answered.

So she trudged down the drive to her own house and went back to unpacking. Helmi's take on the WCTU and the KKK bothered Meg. She wasn't sure she agreed with the historian's assessment, but it did make her wonder whether small-town life was going to be all that wonderful.

WHILE he waited for Todd Welch to show up, Rob started calling Strohmeyer heirs. Carol Tichnor was still incommunicado, but he got through to Peter Strohmeyer on the first ring.

Thayer had brought Rob a photocopy of Emil Strohmeyer's obituary and half a dozen uninteresting clippings of "Social News Notes" from the newspaper. A quick foray on the Internet produced a telephone number for a Peter Strohmeyer in Flagstaff, Arizona. Rob dialed. How many Peter Strohmeyers could there be? Dozens, he thought gloomily, but an elderly female voice said hello.

He identified himself and asked to speak to her husband. "Pete," she called, not bothering to cover the receiver. "It's for you, Pete." Shuffling, murmuring.

"This is Pete Strohmeyer." The voice was a vigorous tenor. "What can I do for you? Is it about the murder?"

"You heard." It was the right Strohmeyer.

"My niece called yesterday. She was pretty upset. I figured you'd get in touch some time. How can I help?"

Rob rolled his eyes. "Tell your niece to return her phone calls."

Peter Strohmeyer laughed. "I expect she's just trying to get her mother to face reality. Charlotte is difficult sometimes. Carol can't very well act without permission."

"Why is that?"

"Well, Lieutenant, she's dependent on her mother to maintain her lifestyle. I like that word, lifestyle. Carol is used to the best of everything, but her shop in Port Townsend isn't a gold mine. So Charlotte calls the tune."

"I see." Rob pulled his notepad closer. "I'd like some background information, Mr. Strohmeyer. I have a copy of your father's will. He left everything to Mrs. Tichnor. Were you estranged from him?"

Strohmeyer laughed again. "No, not at all. He was a great old guy, my dad. We got along just fine."

Rob waited.

"About ten years before he died, Dad deeded over his property on Tyee Lake to me. He said he might as well save me the inheritance tax. That was after my brother, Jim, died. I got the land, and Charlotte was going to get the house in town. It was a fair division of property."

"Okay, I can see that. So you're a Latouche County property holder?" He wasn't on the tax rolls.

"Nope. When Dad died, I sold the property to my nephews. I'm settled down here in Arizona, I've got some medical problems, and I don't travel much. I didn't feel right selling that trout stream, though, while Dad was still alive. He was some kind of fisherman. I gave the boys a good price because I wanted the land to stay in the family."

Rob considered the Strohmeyer legend. "Where on Tyee?" He had a cabin on the lake. He stood up and turned to the large county map that occupied pride of place on the wall behind his desk.

Strohmeyer gave him details of the sale and the plat numbers. Not on the lake itself. Fifteen acres on the banks of Beaver Creek, prime steelhead country. Rob went back to the desk and looked at his notes. "So Dr. Tichnor bought ten acres and his brother took what was left?"

Strohmeyer chuckled. "I figure Vance got the best place for a lodge—right where Grandpa built the old still. Ethan took the timbered hillside, wants to conserve the old growth. He's a vocal opponent of clear-cutting."

"I see. Thank you, sir. Now what can you tell me about the storage cavity in the garage floor?"

Strohmeyer launched into an account of his grandfather's antics, punctuated by chuckles, that coincided with what Carol Tichnor had said. He sounded like a happy man. Rob wished him well and eventually hung up.

He logged back onto the phone directory and found numbers for Dr. Tichnor and his brother, Vance. He had left a message for the oncologist and was about to dial Vance Tichnor's business number when Todd Welch knocked at the door and stuck his head in.

Rob waved him in and hung up.

"You want me to drive you to Two Falls, sir?"

"Sit down," Rob said. "We need to talk first."

Todd sat and twiddled his thumbs. His uniform looked as if it had just been removed from a dry cleaner's bag.

There was no point beating around the bush. Rob described Chief Thomas's phone call. "So she knew about the petroglyph. When I suggested she might have heard about it from you, she didn't deny it."

Todd mumbled something. His ears were red. He looked like his mother, with dark eyes and hair, but he had his Anglo father's height and fair complexion.

"You told your mother?" Rob kept his voice even.

Todd Welch squirmed in the chair opposite him, the hot seat. "Yeah, and she called Aunt Maddie."

"Outsiders," Rob murmured, watching the kid.

"They're family!"

"Let me clarify my point. When it comes to talking about an ongoing investigation by the Latouche County Sheriff's Department, anyone outside the department is an outsider. Got that?"

"Yeah." He sounded sullen.

"Outsiders—mother, girlfriend, auntie in Two Falls."

"The guys told me you found a petroglyph, a broken piece of The Dancers. Aunt Maddie had to know. She's the chief. Mom is tight with her sister. It was natural for her to call my aunt with the news."

Rob sighed. "*I* understand. The sheriff may not."

Todd squirmed and looked miserable.

Rob didn't reassure him, though he decided not to tell McCormick about the lapse. Todd was a rookie.

"That all, sir?" Todd rose.

"Yeah. Just keep your mouth shut and try not to do it again." Rob shuffled through the papers on his desk, looking for the photographs Linda had taken of the petroglyph. He found them under a lab report. He thumbed open the file folder he intended to take to Two Falls. It already held the artist's portrait of the victim. He started to insert the photos.

Todd gave a gasp. He leaned across the desk. "What's that?"

"That's what Vancouver thinks our man looked like." Rob hesitated, then handed Todd the faxed sheet. "Do you recognize him?" It was a young face, almost a boy's. Todd had not been part of the crew that unearthed the corpse. He'd come on duty when Dave Meuler went off, so he hadn't had a look at the body.

Todd sank back onto his chair as if his legs wouldn't hold him. "Eddy. I think it's my cousin, Eddy Redfern."

Rob's mind raced. He drew a long breath. "I'm sorry, Todd, but I have to ask. Are you sure?"

"I...no." Todd held the sheet to the light of Rob's halogen reading lamp. "I think it's Eddy." His voice shook. "It's a bad picture. Oh, Jesus." He dropped the drawing and covered his face with shaking hands.

Rob rescued the paper before it slipped to the floor. Pity and confusion kept him silent for a long while. When he thought the deputy had had time to compose himself, he stood up and shoved the phone console forward.

Todd's hands dropped. His pupils were dilated.

A chill was running up and down Rob's spine. "Will you call your aunt? Isn't Redfern her husband's name?"

As was the family custom, Madeline Thomas had kept her maiden name after marriage. The Thomases had supplied the Klalos with many chiefs and other prominent elders. Madeline was the first woman to be elected principal chief of all three bands, though there had been female chiefs of the local groups before white contact, unusual among Northwest tribes. Her husband, whom Rob had found easier to deal with than his wife, was a fisherman. Redfern used traditional methods, including the notorious gill net. Rob didn't remember whether or not they had children.

Todd chewed his lip. "Yes, my uncle's Jack Redfern, but Eddy's not their son. He's Leon Redfern's second son. Leon is Uncle Jack's brother." He stopped, cleared his throat. "Eddy is...was four years younger than me." He spoke in jerks as if his mind was not in gear. "Real smart. He was a student at Portland State, wanted to be an accountant, to keep the books for the tribe. They're going to start a casino."

"So I heard." The casino was a pipe dream so far, but stranger things had happened. There were two small casinos in Clark County and a big one south of Olympia. Sheriff McCormick shied away from the idea like a spooked stallion. Law enforcement problems in the county, not to mention traffic, would double the day a casino opened.

Rob could see the difficulties, but a well-managed casino could fund health care and scholarships, and jobs would open up in a depressed economy. It might be a good idea. He didn't know. He did know that if the homicide victim was Eddy Redfern, he needed to have a long talk with the principal chief of the Klalos.

He said gently, "Will you call Chief Thomas and tell her you think the victim is your cousin?"

"But you said—"

"This is different. Your aunt needs to know, and she should hear about it from you. Give her my sympathy and ask her if we can see her in about an hour."

Todd nodded, mute.

"If she wants me to break the news to Eddy Redfern's parents, I'll do it first." That was a duty Rob did not relish, but it was a duty.

"I'll ask her. I think Uncle Jack will want to be the one to tell his brother. Is that okay?"

"They should do whatever seems right to them. Take as much time as you need, Todd. I'll go tell the sheriff."

And he did. When Mack heard the news, he was not a happy politician.

 *Chapter 7*

TODD rapped on the passenger window. "She's ready."

Rob extricated himself and his laptop from the shotgun seat and stepped out of the patrol car into gusting rain. He'd been sitting in the car for a good half hour, waiting for Madeline Thomas to put all her defenses in place. It was cold, and the windows had steamed up.

While he waited, he'd been doing electronic busywork and trying to decide how to approach Maddie. The last time he had seen her had been at his grandmother's memorial service two years earlier.

The chief had spoken her piece in full ceremonial costume before the assembled mourners, thrusting herself center-stage, making political hay. He had heard her platitudes through a fog of rage. Not the most useful frame of mind for diplomacy. He suppressed the image. Like Sheriff McCormick, Maddie could no more help being a politician than a skunk could help being a polecat.

Todd pulled the visor of his hat down over his eyes. "Uh, Uncle Leon's pretty upset."

"Upset how?" A gust of rain hit Rob's face. "Better lock the car."

"Aw."

"Lock it." Stealing a patrol car would appeal to the adolescent sense of humor. There were lots of kids in Two Falls.

Todd shrugged and obeyed.

Rob tucked the laptop under his jacket. There was plenty of room. He wasn't armed. "Upset as in grieving or as in wanting to kill me?"

"I dunno. He's had a couple of beers."

"Great."

"He's not a drunk," Todd protested. "He's upset."

Rob nodded. So was Todd upset. So, for that matter, was Robert Guthrie Neill. He didn't want to think how upset Madeline Thomas would be.

He headed for the house. They had parked on the street. Wet gravel crunched underfoot.

Madeline and Jack lived in a double-wide mobile home with a view of the larger of the cascades for which Two Falls was named. The Choteau River tumbled past the village to its confluence with the Columbia.

When Bonneville Dam went in, in 1938, the Choteau band of the Klalos had been relocated to a secondary fishing camp. Unimaginative government housing lay below Maddie's house, along with newer mobile homes, most of them double-wide.

Todd had caught up and was leading him not to the conventional front door but around the side on a path composed of cedar cross-sections set in gravel. The well-groomed walkway led to an annex. The addition was taller than the house, with clerestories and a central skylight rather than ordinary windows. It was roofed with the same practical gray metal as the mobile home, but cedar shakes covered the walls. A cedar lintel surmounted the door, and a carved pediment depicting the chinook salmon, totem of the Thomas clan, gleamed in the rain. The figure had been painted recently.

Todd knocked at the door and opened it without waiting for a response. He ushered Rob into a reception room that was doing its best to look like the interior of a miniature longhouse without the inconveniences.

Museum-quality masks, beaver pelts, button blankets, nets, drums, and ceremonial rattles hung on walls faced with raw cedar. Good use had been made throughout of cedar, fir, and alder. A table by the door exhibited pine-needle baskets. The industrial carpet, a matte brown tweed, looked rather like rammed earth. A convincing gas-powered fire burnt in the center of the floor. Benches, each with a long flat cushion covered in trading blanket fabric, lined the walls. The scent of cedar permeated the whole empty space.

Empty? What was Maddie playing at? Rob strode to the nearest bench, divested himself of his laptop and wet jacket, and turned back to the fire at the center of the room. It radiated satisfying warmth.

Wait, he told himself. And listen.

Todd shifted from foot to foot. "She meets with the tribal council in here."

Rob nodded, head bent, hands out to the fire. Rain drummed on the skylight.

"I'll go find her, okay?"

"Sure."

After an interminable wait, a door opened at the far end of the room and Maddie entered with her husband. Both of them wore plaid wool shirts and jeans, Maddie a beaded headband. They were stocky people, not very tall, but Maddie had solid presence. Todd straggled in after them and shut the door. Leon Redfern did not appear.

"Lieutenant Neill." Maddie inclined her head regally.

"Chief Thomas."

"You remember my husband, Jack?"

Rob extended his hand and Jack shook it. "How are you, Jack? I'm sorry for your trouble."

"Ah, thanks. My brother...he's not so good. Trying to reach Lila up in Umatilla." Jack's seamed face creased with misery.

"Lila?"

"That's his wife." He cleared his throat. "Eddy's mother. She's Nez Perce, visiting her sister up on the rez. They was hunting today."

"I see," Rob murmured. He was trying not to imagine the horror awaiting the poor woman.

Madeline took a step toward him. "How sure are you?"

"Todd made the identification from an artist's drawing, so it's not absolute."

"It's Eddy." Todd hung his head and scuffled his feet. "I'm sorry, Aunt Maddie."

She closed her eyes and took a long breath.

Here it comes, Rob thought. Before she could speak, he said, "I checked missing persons for six counties, including Multnomah and Clark." Portland was in Multnomah County, Vancouver in Clark. "Nobody listed Edward or Eddy Redfern, not in the last ten weeks."

"Leon didn't want to report the boy missing," Jack said heavily. "We been looking for him."

Rob walked over to the bench and retrieved his tape recorder from his damp jacket. "I ought to record this."

Maddie's face set but she didn't say anything.

"Do I have your permission, Chief Thomas?"

"Yes." She squeezed the syllable out. "I suppose you'll use it against us."

He kept exasperation from his voice with an effort. "I want it for my protection, ma'am. And for yours. There should be no misunderstanding about what we say."

She grimaced. "Oh, go ahead."

That took awhile. He gave his name, the date, place, and time, and the names of those present. Eventually he'd have to interrogate Maddie, Jack, and the parents individually, but for now he was just trying to understand how young Eddy Redfern could disappear without anyone saying a word about it to the authorities. He showed both of them the artist's reconstruction and Jack groaned.

Maddie said, "It's not a good likeness."

Rob didn't explain why it wasn't. Chief Thomas blinked back tears.

Rob turned back to Jack, who had sunk onto one of the benches. "You were saying, Mr. Redfern, that Eddy's family were aware that he was missing."

"Well, he didn't get in touch. He said he was off checking something out and not to expect him to show up at the powwow. That was in August. You know kids, they have their own lives these days."

And their own deaths. Rob said nothing.

Jack gulped. "When Eddy didn't come home for the Labor Day picnic we always have, his folks started to worry. Lila talked with his roommates in Portland. He lived in a house with four other students in the Hawthorne district, rode his bike to the college to save gas."

"To Portland State University."

"Yeah. Summer school let out second week in August. They, his roommates, said he left the last week of classes, before exams started, told them he'd finished early. His grades was okay, so that must be the truth. He said he was going to a big swap meet, and then up to The Dalles."

"The Dalles?"

"He has friends on the Fish Commission," Madeline said. "He worked for them two summers as an intern."

"Did he show up there?"

She shook her head.

Jack said, "The girl he hung out with there told Lila that Eddy called her from Portland, said he'd be up later. But he never came."

The timing sounded right. Rob got Jack to give him the girl-friend's name.

Jack didn't know the phone number. "She works for the fisheries people."

"Okay, we can trace her." Rob sat beside Jack with the tape recorder between them.

Maddie stalked over. "Trace her? She hasn't done anything wrong!"

Rob mustered patience. "Find her. Talk to her. Eddy may have said something to her about the swap meet or whatever else he was doing, something that will help us identify his killer. Why a swap meet?"

Silence. Jack and Madeline stared at each other. Todd sneezed. "Sorry."

Madeline said, "He hung out at the big swap meets because he was looking for things that were stolen from us."

"From Lauder Point?"

"A lot of the young ones did it."

"Not me," Todd interjected.

"I wouldn't let Todd," she said with the hint of a sneer. "Didn't want to get him fired."

But Todd knew about it. Rob said, "Let me understand you. You were conducting an investigation, looking for the looted objects, and using your young people as agents?"

"We have a right to do that."

He stared at her.

Madeline's eyes dropped. "They just went to the swap meets and antiques shows." She sat down on the next bench over and gazed into the fire.

"How young?" The hair on the back of Rob's neck prickled.

"No kids under eighteen. Just the ones out of high school, and only if they wanted to and had time. I told them to be careful and not to...to confront any of the dealers. Just to report anything to me that might be part of the missing cache. And to give me the dealers' names."

"And?"

"I didn't think anything would come of it. They like doing it," she burst out. "It makes them feel part of the Klalo people. They've been looking ten years now, different kids every year, never found anything. A few dealers were selling looted stuff, but it wasn't ours. I gave their names to the fisheries people Eddy worked for."

But not to me, Rob reflected. He didn't say anything. Chief Thomas sounded defensive.

"The laws have changed a lot in the last ten years," he ventured, keeping his voice neutral.

"Oh, you noticed?"

He said through his teeth, "I attended three workshops on the changes—two at my own expense. I have a filing cabinet full of cases, legal opinions, and articles from archaeological journals. I noticed."

She made a dismissive noise and turned her face away.

"Paused at four fifty-two." He hit the Pause button. He needed to think, not emote. He walked to the other end of the room and looked at the display of pine-needle baskets. Beautiful work. Some of the baskets must have been very old, but one tiny perfect thing looked as if it had been made last week. He wished his daughter, Willow, could see it.

Artifacts such as the baskets, not to mention the ceremonial objects hanging from the walls, now fetched thousands of dollars at auction. Museums and private collectors had created a market that transformed pothunters into thieves, even grave robbers.

An Oregon man was on trial for looting a burial site in Nevada that dated back several thousand years B.C. In Washington, archaeologists and tribal leaders were at loggerheads over proposed scientific examination of one ancient skeleton. Sacred sites throughout the region had been vandalized. There had been no human remains anywhere in Lauder Point County Park, fortunately. The new laws, actually old laws with new teeth, were an attempt to deal with the situation.

When he thought he had his temper under control, Rob went back to where Todd was hovering over his aunt and uncle. They had been speaking in low voices and broke off at his approach.

Maddie started to say something, but Rob held up his hand. "Let me say my piece. If I haven't offered apologies for failing to find the sacred objects stolen from Lauder Point, I offer them now. There's no reason for you to believe I take the theft seriously after all this time. You're bound to judge by results."

Jack said, "Well, now..."

Maddie shifted on the bench. Todd was staring at him.

Rob kept his voice even. "I'm sorry to offend you with questions, but we do have a homicide. A valuable member of your community has been killed. Finding out who committed this outrage will be easier if you cooperate—"

The door to the main house flew open and a thinner, shorter version of Jack Redfern burst in. "I talked to her. She knows." He broke off, sobbing, and wiped his eyes on his sleeve. "She wants to kill you, Maddie. Hell, she wants to kill *me.*"

Todd and Jack spoke simultaneously. Todd took Leon Redfern's arm and helped him to a seat near his brother. Jack patted his shoulder.

Rob stood still and watched them. When he glanced at Madeline Thomas, she ducked her head, breaking eye contact, as if she were ashamed. So she should be. She hadn't thought anything would come of it. In spite of himself, Rob felt a twinge of sympathy for the stubborn woman.

When Leon seemed calmer, Rob introduced himself and shook hands. He showed Redfern the artist's version of his son's face and waited for the bereaved man to compose himself.

To his surprise, Todd intervened. He gave Leon a brief hug, went to the basket table, and took a big cylindrical tin and a shallow glass vessel from a drawer Rob hadn't noticed. The tin held French cigarettes.

Rob had quit smoking when his daughter was born, and he didn't miss the habit, but he took a cigarette when Todd passed them out. The vessel was an ashtray of the sort found in wealthy households in the 1950s. Jack lit his brother's cigarette with an old Zippo lighter that was probably also a collector's item. Then he passed the lighter around.

Rob managed not to cough when he lit up.

They smoked, Rob and Todd standing, the others sitting. Everyone was silent. The ashtray on Jack Redfern's knee took on a ceremonial presence. Tobacco was a sacred plant to most Native American cultures. This ritual struck Rob as parody—as the room itself was a parody of a longhouse—but the effect was genuine.

Outside, the wind soughed. Rain spattered the plastic skylight. Smoke wreathed and hung in a blue cloud. Leon Redfern calmed and collected himself almost visibly. Maddie's shoulders slumped. Jack smoked and patted his brother's arm, rocking a little on the bench.

As for Rob, the short, filterless cigarette made him queasy and lightheaded, but the nicotine kicked in. He could feel his vision sharpening. His pulse accelerated.

Todd gave a cough and stubbed out his smoke. The others followed suit, Rob with relief. His mouth tasted sour.

Leon Redfern spoke to him directly. "I want you to find my son's killer."

"I'll do my best. Will you tell me about Eddy?"

Leon closed his eyes, opened them, blinking. "He was smart, that kid. And he played good basketball. Made the varsity his sophomore year, shortest one on the team, but he could jump." And he went on, halting to sob as his loss caught up with him. He persisted, dogged, as if he wanted Eddy's life on record. He didn't object when Rob turned on the tape machine.

Rob didn't interrupt. He listened hard. He could tell that Todd was listening, too, and Madeline. Jack sat with one hand on his brother's arm.

When Rob asked Leon the name of his son's dentist, Leon told him, and broke down again.

Madeline said in a low voice, "Did you have to?"

Rob nodded.

There was a long pause. "I have a name for you."

Their eyes locked. "The name of a looter?"

She nodded slowly. "William Meek. From Montana. Nickname Billy or Digger." Her mouth twisted in a grimace. "He's one of those skinheads, keeps dropping out of sight."

"A white supremacist?"

"Aryan Nation," Todd chimed in. "They were recruiting in the high school when I was there. The Aryans came from west-central Asia, didn't they?"

"I believe so."

"We used to say they should go back to the arya they came from." He gave a slight smile. "Bad joke."

"But not a bad idea." Rob smiled, too. He turned back to Madeline. "I'm obliged to you, Chief Thomas. Did you report Meek to the Fish Commission for pothunting?"

"Yes. His name came up three different times with questionable stuff, mostly arrowheads. She, the investigator, said they checked him out, but they could never catch him with the goods on him. She's been keeping an eye out for him."

Rob said, "His name is in the system, then. If he took part in a skinhead demonstration there may be fingerprints. I'll get onto it."

Leon blew his nose on a blue spotted handkerchief. "Will I... Where have they got my boy?"

Rob explained as tactfully as he could about the autopsy and the morgue. "If the dentist's records match, sir, you won't have to make the trip to Vancouver."

Leon looked shocked. "We want to see him, Lila and me. When she gets here, she'll want to see Eddy."

Rob looked at Todd, who swallowed hard and shook his head, no. "Okay," Rob said, "let us know when you want to go and a deputy will escort you."

There wasn't much else to say. Leon seemed even more shocked that the body wouldn't be released at once and retreated into silent misery. Rob showed Maddie a photo of the broken petroglyph. When she identified it as part of The Dancers, she sounded almost indifferent.

As Madeline walked them to the outer door, Rob said, "We'll have to talk to the young people."

"They're scattered all over the place."

"The ones who are here," Rob insisted. "Can you assemble them tomorrow evening? I want Todd and his partner to question them. You gave me one name. We need all the names, and we need their impressions of Meek and the other dealers, everything they can remember."

Maddie was silent. She pulled the door open and stood for

a moment looking out into the rainy darkness. The sun was setting far down the Gorge, turning the river to steel. The hills nearby loomed black. "Yes, okay. Todd and Jake. I know Jake. And I can give them the list of names we sent to the Fish Commission."

Rob said, "Or to me. Now."

He could see from the set of her jaw that he was pushing her, so he didn't insist.

Rob drove the car back along the winding road to Klalo with Todd beside him taking notes on the laptop. Time for a crash course in techniques of interrogation.

"What if I goof it up tomorrow?" Todd wailed at one point.

Rob squirted detergent on the streaming windshield and peered at the wet road. "You won't. You took a class at Clark. Besides, you know the kids. They'll talk to you."

"I'm related to most of them." Todd didn't sound as if the thought made him happy. "Look, sir, I know I should have told you or somebody what the chief was doing, except her investigation started way before I joined the department. Jeez, it started when I was in high school. I stopped taking it seriously years ago."

Rob was silent. He hit a long puddle and the tires hydroplaned. He gripped the wheel and steered with extreme delicacy until the treads bit into the asphalt again.

By rights he ought to tear another strip off Todd's hide, but he didn't feel up to it.

"Chief Thomas doesn't trust me." He swerved around a dead possum. "She and I have clashed in the past, and we probably will in the future." And next time you'd better have your loyalties sorted. He didn't say that. He felt another spasm of anger at Maddie for putting Todd in a vise.

When Todd didn't say anything, Rob added, "You'll have to watch yourself tomorrow. I'll give you exactly what you can tell your cousins and their friends about the investigation—or the sheriff will. Not much, I'm afraid."

"I'll be careful."

Rob said, "That business with the cigarettes was smart, Todd, and kind. I was glad you were there." He glanced sideways but couldn't read the kid's expression.

Red and white lights like a demented Christmas tree signaled a slow truck ahead. Rob eased off on the accelerator and put his mind to driving the narrow highway.

Towser interrupted Meg's trip to the garbage can.

There was no garbage disposal in the sink, so she had two days' worth of peelings, coffee grounds, and assorted grunge to get rid of. She pulled on a rain jacket, flipped the hood up, and made a dash through the dark for the big plastic can. She had set it just outside the crime scene tape at the front edge of the garage. Apparently Towser had been lurking. He leapt on her with a joyous woof.

Meg shrieked and dropped her sack. "No, no. Down, boy. Good dog, down!"

He snuffled at the plastic bag. Fortunately she had not been eating T-bone steak.

She squatted. "Drop it, you pestilential beast."

Towser tugged at one end of the bag and woofed. A good game. Light from a passing car shone on his gleaming brown hide and big brown eyes. He was grinning at her.

"Towser, sit!"

He sat, grinning, bag hanging from his muzzle. Vegetable peelings and coffee grounds cascaded onto her sneakers. She yanked and he yanked back. She heard a car door slam in the distance.

"Cut it out, damn it. Down!" She was half gasping, half laughing. "Come on, Towser. Good boy. Give me the sack, you moron. No, down."

Miraculously, he dropped the bag and nosed around her. As she bent to scoop up the garbage, he gave an exuberant bounce, landed on her back, and knocked her flat.

Face down in wet garbage, Meg fought for air. Words of antique origin wheezed out in the sheeting rain. Towser was licking her ear.

"Towser, sit!"

Meg struggled to her feet and turned.

Rob Neill, one hand clamped on the dog's collar, was scowling at her. Rain dripped from his hair and the end of his nose. "You okay?"

Wordless, she nodded.

"I'll take him home."

She found her tongue. "I'm coming with you."

The frown eased. "As you are?"

She looked down at the front of her jacket. Had she really used that much tomato sauce? "As I am," she said grimly. "This has to stop."

He shrugged. "Your choice. Heel, boy." The dog trotted along beside him, and so did Meg. She was wet through and smelled like garbage.

The Brandstetter house was a one-story brick affair built in the 1950s, probably, Meg reflected, by Emil Strohmeyer. Someone had added an ill-considered front deck. Though lights were on, no one answered Rob's brisk knock and the SUV was gone from the driveway. Towser sat on the deck and looked around. Meg stood behind him, feeling foolish.

"She's in there," Rob muttered and banged on the door with his fist. "Come on, Tammy, open up."

Towser gave an interrogatory woof and licked his hand. Rob scratched between his ears.

"Maybe she's in the bathroom," Meg ventured. She hoped nobody else in the neighborhood was watching.

Rob stared at the door. After a long pause, he hammered again, and this time Meg heard noises inside. The bolt slid with a thunk, and the door opened a crack.

"What do you want?" It was half moan, half wail.

Rob said, "Are you okay, Tammy? C'mon, it's just me."

The door inched open. A woman stood there, hair tumbled, bathrobe gaping over a stained flannel nightgown, though it was not yet nine o'clock. She was holding an ice bag to her face.

"What happened?"

She gave a half sob. "I bumped into a door, okay?"

"If he hit you ..."

"Nobody hit me. Go away." The door started to close.

Rob said, "You'll have to take the dog. He knocked Ms. McLean down just now. Let him into the backyard."

"I can't. Hal said he'd have Towser put down if he pooped out there again. I can't."

"Listen to me, Tammy. You need help, you need somebody to stay with you. Call your son."

"He's in Portland. He doesn't have a car." She was crying. Her nose ran and she wiped it on her sleeve. "I can't put Towser in the yard."

"Let me call Linda Ramos."

"No, no cops! I bumped into a fucking door. Let me have the fucking dog. He can poop in the house."

After a moment, Rob stepped aside and Towser leapt through the opening.

"I know you· mean well, Rob." Tammy Brandstetter sniffed hard. "Just go away, okay? I'm all right." And she slammed the door.

Rob was swearing softly.

Meg said, "She needs help."

"Yeah, she does, but she won't ask for it, and her husband is a goddamn county commissioner." He sounded too tired to be angry. He climbed down the steps and started back. Meg followed.

On impulse, she said, "Eat dinner with me."

"What?"

"I know I'm not an appetizing object at the moment. Give me twenty minutes to clean up. I keep cooking for two, I'm bored with my own company, and I have a nice shepherd's pie in the oven."

"Ah, thanks just the same but—"

"Come on," she wheedled. "I promise not to ask you a single embarrassing question about the investigation."

He stopped and looked at her.

"Well, you're not *supposed* to talk about it, are you?"

A reluctant smile tugged at his mouth. "You should see yourself."

"I was named for Saint Margaret, the queen of Scotland," she said with dignity. "Think about that."

He laughed and walked on. "And I was named for my grandfather who was named for Robert the Bruce."

"Try, try again," she murmured, trotting along.

"Real shepherd's pie?"

"With mashed potatoes."

They ate in the kitchen.

 *Chapter 8*

SIX o'clock Saturday morning, when the alarm went off, Rob did not at first recognize what the sound was, the demoralizing consequence of a good dinner, amusing conversation, and a couple of glasses of a nice merlot. She'd kept her word: no questions. He and Meg—impossible to think of her as the librarian or even Ms. McLean—had mostly swapped daughter tales. When she told him Annie Baldwin's comment on California girls, he'd been startled into unrestrained laughter. Willow did look waxed because, by God, she was. He liked Meg McLean quite a lot by the time he walked home.

I am forty-four years old, he reflected. Gina moved to Portland almost a year ago, and I missed her for maybe two weeks. Crusty bachelorhood suits me. Why am I thinking with my prick at this stage of the game? He grinned at the ceiling. On the other hand …

On the other hand, Ms. McLean was a witness, not very material but a witness nonetheless, in a case under investigation. With an almost tangible jolt, the previous day's mood of gloom and urgency slammed back in place. The snooze alarm started its annoying bleeps, so he smacked it hard and got up. By the time he had showered and dressed, his mind was more or less on the task at hand.

He meant to roust the Brandstetters out of bed with no preliminary courtesies. He thought about Tammy's bruised face and obvious terror. There had been no sign of Hal's SUV when he and Meg had taken Towser to the house last evening, so the commissioner must have gone off before they got there, after the quarrel with Tammy, if there had been a quarrel. What had triggered the fight? Towser? Somehow Rob doubted that, though living with the beast had to be a strain on any marriage.

Hal had been elected to the county board two years before, so Rob had had time to digest the man's peculiar political ideas, but his personality was still a puzzle. Brandstetter seemed to thrive on hostility. Bashing his wife, if he had, had probably cheered him up, but why had he needed cheering up?

Speculation, Rob reflected, strapping on the shoulder holster and yanking his windbreaker over the slight bulge of his hand-gun. It seemed to him that speculation was all he had done since Eddy Redfern's body had been discovered. He needed facts, not scenarios.

He also needed coffee.

Before heading downstairs he ducked into his office and read his e-mail. It was mostly spam, pushing Kevlar body armor or brilliant high-tech investment opportunities. Nothing so far on the skinhead, William Meek, but it was Saturday morning. He logged off, replaced the battery and tape in his recorder, and slipped it and his recharged cell phone into his jacket pockets. He hesitated a moment, then called Dispatch.

Jane Schmidt was not yet on duty, so he talked briefly to Teresa Morales, the night dispatcher, and longer to Earl Minetti, who was starting the day early.

Earl was in a cranky mood. He grunted when Rob explained his own daybreak mission to interrogate the Brandstetters. Earl had found nothing noteworthy on the walls of Meg's garage the day before and that rankled. He meant to sift every inch of the garage floor and was prepared to be boring about it. More power to you, Rob thought, signing off.

He considered calling Dave Meuler, too, but Dave was off-duty, having put in eight days in a row and an all-nighter without extra compensation. The city budget was in dire straits. Dave's report on his interviews in the neighborhood would be waiting at the office. As would the results of Linda Ramos's real estate inquiries.

Outside, it was still night, though the rain had let up. The Brandstetter house lay in darkness. So did Meg's. Rob wondered which shaded window was her bedroom.

Cut it out, he told himself, and picked up his pace. His joints were rusty from all the sitting he'd been doing. He crossed the street and walked on the uneven concrete of a sidewalk that had been poured in 1923. Quiet on that side, too, though Mrs. Iverson's kitchen light shone. He stumbled on a crack and caught himself. Clumsy. Time for a session with Takeo Johnson, but his martial arts partner was off at a conference. Back Monday. Maybe a swim? Could go for a run. It wasn't raining.

"Hi, Rob, what'll it be this morning?" Marge Barnes beamed at him from the brightly lit take-out window of the espresso stand.

"How you doing? How's Benny?" He listened to Marge's worries about her twenty-year-old slacker son while he scanned the menu. Then he ordered what he usually ordered, a double-strength espresso, hold the whipped cream. He didn't like the stuff sprayed from a can. It tasted like shaving cream.

"Slow this morning," he murmured when the first swallow of caffeine brought him into focus.

"It usually is on Saturdays." Marge settled onto her tall stool for a good yack. "I like it quiet. I just wish old Brandstetter would stop staring at me."

Rob glanced over his shoulder at the darkened Brandstetter house. Someone was sitting, half-concealed by an overgrown rhododendron, in one of the heavy wooden deck chairs. Rob turned all the way around and looked. The wood was stained dark and the bulk hunched there was dark, except for the pale blur of face and hands. "He do that often?"

"First time."

Rob squinted. It wasn't raining but the chair had to be damp.

Marge said, "They must be fighting again. I hope she locked him out."

Rob sipped and set his Styrofoam cup on the ledge that thrust from the take-out window. "When did he come out?"

Marge swiped at the spotless ledge with a cleaning cloth. "I dunno. I think he was sitting there when I came on at six, but I didn't notice right away."

Alarm bells clanged. "I'll just go say hello."

"Your coffee?"

"Keep it for me." He was vibrating like a plucked guitar string, but he made himself stand for a moment with his eyes closed. He patted the gun—in place. Good. He opened his eyes.

Hal's mud-spattered SUV, a steel blue Wrangler with bloated

wheels, stood in the driveway, top in place. At three hundred pounds, Hal didn't hunt afoot, but he liked to bounce over the defenseless landscape like the god of internal combustion engines. He kept an old thirty-ought-six in the back, bragged about it.

Halfway across the street, Rob stopped again. It was Hal, sure enough. He was staring. His gaze did not shift.

"Brandstetter," Rob called, keeping his voice low. He didn't want to wake the neighbors unnecessarily.

No response, not a twitch.

By the time he reached the deck, Rob was thinking crime scene. "Hal," he called, "Hal, wake up, you fucking idiot," but he was pretty sure the man was dead.

All right, he thought. Call it in. He didn't want to disturb the surface of the deck but he had to be sure. He knelt for a moment, tipping his head and squinting. Shoe prints showed under the smooth layer of condensation. He avoided the steps, climbed up on the deck at midpoint, and edged around to the left, looping wide.

He came up on Commissioner Brandstetter's chair from the left. The scraggly rhododendron at the edge of the deck blocked the street light, but Rob could see better than he wanted to. The right side of Hal's head was a dark, jagged mass. Exit wound. His hands gripped the arm rests in what looked like cadaveric spasm. Blood and brain had spattered the wooden decking.

Rob stood far enough away not to step in the spatter and called Teresa Morales on his cell phone. He spoke in tones whose calmness surprised him. The adrenaline was in full flow. What about Tammy? Where was she? Did she know about this obscenity? Had she snapped, finally, and killed her husband when he came rolling up in the middle of the night? When *had* Hal returned?

"That's a four-nineteen?" Teresa sounded flustered. "You sure?"

"Yes." He reached out and touched the stiff right hand. Ice cold. The jacket sleeve was soaked with dew. "I need backup. Wife's probably in the house." Not to mention a large, anxious dog. He heard Towser barking. He stared down at the huge body while he and Teresa talked, quiet, half in code. When she grasped what he needed, Rob signed off.

He could hear background commotion in the office, then silence. "Okay. Ten-four," Teresa said.

He retraced his steps along the edge of the deck and walked across the lawn to the sidewalk.

"What's happening?" Marge called from across the street.

He waved a vague arm at her and waited.

Blue and white lights whirled—the city car, one of the rookies. The driver's-side window was open. "What's up?"

Rob leaned on the car roof and bent down to explain and to reassure the officer that he'd already called in his deputies. Joshua Myron, that was his name, looked relieved and maybe disappointed.

Marge Barnes had thrown a jacket over her shoulders and was watching from the drive-in lane. Rob went over to her.

He explained what he'd found and her eyes widened. She was groping for her cell phone. "Look, Marge, I know you want to call your friends and let them know all about it, but it's not a good idea. We don't know what went on yet, or where Tammy is."

"D'you think there might be shooting? More shooting?"

"I hope not, but go back inside, just to be safe. I'll send someone over to take your statement when we know more."

She gulped and nodded, pocketing the phone. "You want your coffee? Dumb question. Be careful, hear?"

He nodded and turned back. He was worried about Tammy. She had been in a volatile state of mind, God knew. Spousal murder followed by suicide was one of the commoner domestic calls. But he didn't think that was what had happened here.

It was still hard to see, though the east was growing brighter. Officer Myron sat in his car talking to somebody, Chief Hug probably. The lights flashed.

Rob walked back across the wet lawn to the edge of the deck. He could make out the entry wound on Hal's left temple. It looked like a contact wound.

Tammy might have shot her husband but she wouldn't have *executed* him. The whole setup was too neat for a domestic blow-up. It looked as if Hal had sat down for a chat with a friend, not expecting trouble, and been shot where he sat. The empty chair on Hal's left was pulled around slightly. Have to cordon off the whole front of the house, the drive, and the SUV.

Meanwhile, Tammy. Towser was still barking, but the sound was perfunctory. Rob gestured to Myron to break off his call. The paramedics should be coming any time now, and the county car. Linda Ramos and Thayer Jones had the night shift. He glanced at his watch—6:42.

"We gonna break down the door?" Myron unhitched the seat belt and emerged from his car.

"I hope not. Wait, there's the ambulance." The boxy white van swung around the far corner by Rob's house with its red lights flashing. Rob had specified no sirens. The county car followed the medics, almost riding the rear bumper. They pulled up and the blue-clad medics jumped out.

"Okay, Josh, I want you to block off the street. Marge's early customers will be showing up any time now and we don't need more civilians on the scene." Good thing it was Saturday. Week-days they lined up around the block.

The kid nodded. He looked disappointed.

It took awhile to sort things out. The paramedics were not hap-py to be kept from the victim, and they were right to question him. With some head wounds life continued, but what did they imagine they could do for a man who had been sitting outside for at least an hour, probably all night, with half his head shot away? Rob described the corpse. They went back, grumbling, and sat in the ambulance to await the medical examiner.

Rob detailed Thayer to tape off the entire front of the house in-cluding the driveway and garage, and to assist Myron with crowd control after that. Thayer didn't grumble. He was an old hand at crime scenes.

Rob looked at Linda. She was not an old hand. "I'm going around the garage to see if I can get at the back door to the house." He gestured. "I don't want to compromise the evidence here."

She nodded, big-eyed. She was in uniform, very trim. He was glad she wasn't wearing her glasses. Contact lenses were safer.

"I want you with me when I go in. I need to locate Tammy Brandstetter. I don't think she's the perpetrator, but I've been wrong before."

"Okay." She touched her holster.

"Got a crowbar?"

"What?"

"Just kidding." He turned to Thayer and explained his intentions. Thayer nodded. He looked bored but would be awake to the first sign of trouble.

The back gate was no trouble at all. It was closed but not locked, typical of the neighborhood, of the whole damned county. Some people didn't even lock their houses.

Rob and Linda entered the yard, and Linda closed the gate behind them. With her trailing, he walked up to the back of the dark, silent house and knocked on the door, announcing their presence. No response. He pounded harder and rang the bell. Towser set up an enthusiastic clamor.

"That's the big dog, right?"

"Yeah. He's a cupcake but he doesn't know his strength."

"I don't like dogs."

"Take it easy, Ramos." He pounded on the door again, and Towser bounced so high Rob could see his bright eyes. The dog leapt at the door and scratched.

"Jesus Maria."

"Let me deal with him. I think we'd better break in. Truncheon?"

She handed him the baton the uniforms carried. The window in the door smashed at the first blow. Covering his hand with the cuff of his jacket, Rob reached through, slid the bolt back, and opened the door using the inside knob.

Towser slid past Linda, knocking her against the jamb, and erupted into the backyard. Rob closed the door.

"*Por Dios.*"

"He needs to pee. Good thing you closed the gate. Let's hope his paws aren't cut." Rob stood for a long moment, head cocked, listening. Nothing. Linda's drawn gun pointed at the ceiling.

"Police," he shouted. "Tammy. Tammy Brandstetter, c'mon, Tammy. It's just Rob Neill. I need to talk to you."

No response. Skin crawling, Rob crunched glass as he crossed the small entryway and walked slowly through the kitchen. It smelled like dog and old food. The hall beyond was black. He thought the living room lay to the left, bedrooms to the right. He flipped the hall light on with his sleeve over his hand, blinked against the brightness, and called again. This time he thought he heard a moan.

Linda said, "Was that a sound?"

They listened, but the noise was not repeated. Rob walked right. The first door, open, showed an office with a desk that overflowed with papers. A computer console sat on the desk and a light showed on the power strip. The first door on the left revealed an empty bathroom. The second was the master bedroom. Tammy lay without moving across the rumpled covers of a king-sized bed.

Rob said, "Tammy, it's Rob. I'm going to turn the light on. Are you all right?"

The body stirred.

"Hey, wake up." He flipped the light on and the room came into sharp focus. It was a mess. Clothes, dirty and clean, strewed all the flat surfaces and scattered over the old shag rug. When he moved toward the bed the reek of vodka and something citrus was sharp enough to stun an ox. Relief flooded through him. She was just drunk.

Relief was followed by a familiar stab of revulsion and anger. In the last year of her life, his mother had drunk a lot and hung out with other drunks. She had died riding with a drunk driver.

"Come on, Tammy," he said briskly. "Wake up. Linda, go get one of the medics. Tell him we have an intoxicated female, unconscious. Tammy, dammit, you need to wake up."

She stirred and moaned a little but she didn't open her eyes. The left was swollen shut and the skin around it gleamed a ripe purple. Better get them to look at her injuries. He checked her pulse, which was slow and steady. Her skin was warm to his touch. He left her lying there.

He found Towser's leash on the kitchen counter, took it out to the backyard, and secured the dog to a metal fence post. The paramedics, happy to have something to do, carted Tammy off on a gurney they wheeled to the back door. Rob thought they hadn't contaminated the area too much. The dog cried a little. Tammy remained comatose.

He sent Linda off with the ambulance, because somebody had to talk to Tammy as soon as she could string two words together. She was, at least technically, his primary suspect. Then he went back to the ridgeback and told him he was a good dog.

With a full food dish in front of him and a bowl of water,

Towser settled down peacefully enough in the yard, but something would have to be done about him if the hospital insisted on keeping Tammy overnight. The son. Rob ducked back into the kitchen, found the phone book with a Portland number for the boy scribbled on the cover.

Around front, Thayer had taped off the appropriate area. Neighbors were waking up all along the street. Some came out to look. Their coffee steamed on the fall air. Marge was talking away on her cell phone. Rob didn't blame her. Josh had cut off all her customers, so she didn't have anything else to do. He didn't see Meg McLean.

It wasn't until then that the political consequences of Brandstetter's death struck him. Jesus, the sheriff. He decided he couldn't take it for granted that Teresa had called Mack, so he phoned the sheriff himself. Mack sounded stunned and almost as mournful as if he hadn't detested Hal. He promised to come right over.

Just what I need, Rob thought without gratitude. He was standing by the county car, watching the scene. Myron had moved the city car so it blocked the corner. Thayer and the rookie were conferring under the street light. Beside Rob the radio squawked. It was Earl and he was incensed.

"Yeah, Brandstetter's been shot," Rob agreed. "And yes, I'll need you and everybody else you can get your hands on. I have a job for you first." He read off the Portland phone number. "Call the Portland police ASAP and have them contact Tom Brandstetter. They can break the news if they're feeling generous. His mother's in the hospital. I need to talk to Tom. Have them ask him to call me." He read off his cell phone number, squinting. For some reason, he could never remember the number.

When he had soothed Earl down, he went back to the espresso stand and ordered another coffee. Marge gave him one on the house.

 *Chapter 9*

"ARE you Margaret McLean?"

Dust cloth in hand, Meg stared at the woman standing on her porch. Blond, middle-aged and fighting it, a total stranger. A reporter? It was a blessing of small-town life that the house was not yet under media siege. In LA there would have been at least three video teams in the street outside. The press was bound to catch on some time.

Meg admitted who she was.

"I'm Carol Tichnor," the woman said. "You bought the house from my mother."

"I see." Meg didn't.

"What's going on?" The woman gestured to her left.

"I don't know for sure. My neighbor said Mrs. Brandstetter down the street shot her husband."

Darcy had banged on Meg's door at seven-thirty with the appalling news. Perhaps because she had not yet drunk a full cup of coffee, Meg leapt to the conclusion that returning the dog to its owner the previous night had triggered the shooting.

Guilt had kept her pent up in the house ever since. She had glimpsed Rob a couple of times in the distance, but she hadn't wanted to go out and harass him, not just to satisfy her curiosity, not even to ease her conscience. Darcy was long gone.

"My God, bodies all over the place," the woman on the porch was saying. "Klalo's turning into a regular abattoir. May I come in? It's cold."

"Yes, of course. I'm sorry, I'm a bit distracted." Meg opened the door and ushered her unexpected guest into the hall. "Excuse the mess. I'm still unpacking."

It was chilly out. There was no rain, but an icy breeze blew from the east, a feature of the microclimate. On her spring visit, Meg was told that the wind funneled through the Gorge from the west or the east. From the west it was wet and ocean-cool. From the east, it was cold in winter, hot in summer, always dry. Wind surfers loved it. People had even been known to build high-tech windmills in the area, though the presence of Bonneville Dam made alternative methods of producing electricity seem redundant.

Meg took the woman into the living room, removed a sheer shadow-panel on a rod from the love seat, and offered coffee. The sofa was covered with a brocade swag, also on a rod, and the armchair held a plastic tray with assorted nails, screws, staples, a tack hammer, and a screwdriver. A stepladder stood in front of the bay window. The woman looked around with a critical air.

It was almost lunch time, but Meg had no intention of feeding anyone who left her with a dead body in the garage. She doubted that Carol Tichnor was the murderer. All the same, the contract for the house had specified full disclosure. At that point in Meg's reflections, her sense of humor caught up with her, and she relieved her guest of her camel's-hair coat.

When they were seated with a tray of steaming mugs, sugar, and cream on the coffee table before them, Meg said, "I'm happy to meet you, Ms. Tichnor—"

"Please, it's Carol. May I call you Margaret?"

"Meg. As I said, lovely to meet you, Carol, but why?" It had not escaped Meg's attention that she was treating Carol with far more formal hospitality than she had shown Darcy. Such are class distinctions. "Why?" she repeated.

Carol grimaced. "I'm under orders from my mother to find out what's happening. The neighbors at home said we had a cop-car outside the house for more than half an hour yesterday. I drove down from Seattle last night. This morning I couldn't reach the deputy who called me. The dispatcher said he was down here, but he's out by the other house, the Brandstetter place, and the officer wouldn't let me past the crime scene tape. So I thought I'd ask you."

"Good luck," Meg said ruefully. "I probably know less than the average passerby." She gave a brief account of finding the petroglyph and the ensuing melodrama, wondering whether she shouldn't just record the story and press Play when somebody asked. "I believe they've identified the victim." Rob had told her that much the night before.

"Who?"

"I don't know. It's not yet official. Maybe they're still contacting family members." Time to shift gears. "Will you tell me why nobody mentioned the storage compartment in the garage floor? I felt awfully stupid."

Carol shifted on the love seat as if it were uncomfortable. "It was a joke to everybody in the family but my mother. Great-grandpa Otto's stash. We should have nailed the lid down." She described the old man's bootlegging activities as if she'd told the tale many times for comic effect, but her heart wasn't in the telling.

"Your mother disapproved?"

She sighed. "My mother disapproves of anything even remotely tacky. Her grandfather was her ultimate humiliation, though her father made her wince, too. I think she married my father because he was correct and colorless. I loved Dad but he was not an interesting man. Total workaholic. He treated everything as work. It killed him."

Meg thought of her own stern, humorless father who had not been pleased to acknowledge a "bastard granddaughter." His term. Meg and her father had come to a parting of the ways. That still hurt. "She wanted him to be dull?"

"She wanted him to be correct," Carol said. "My brother Ethan is like him, though Eth at least enjoys music and once smoked a joint. Vance and I were a great trial to my parents. He cleaned up his act when he married. Have you met Vance?"

"No."

"Charming is the word." She gave a small, reminiscent smile. "He's a very good salesman. Makes a bundle selling overpriced houses in Lake Oswego and spends it all on the Good Life. He collects wine, used to open a five-hundred-dollar bottle with a weekday dinner sometimes, just to say he could. Moira put a stop to that with one lift of her eyebrow. She's rather like Mother." That seemed to surprise her. She took a brooding sip of lukewarm coffee. "Didn't somebody once say all boys marry their mothers?"

Sophocles? Meg suppressed the thought.

Carol gave herself a small shake. "Vance can charm the birds out of the trees. Has he dropped by?"

"No."

"Earlier this week, he said something about visiting the old place on his way to that lodge he's building up on the lake."

"Maybe he came before I got here Tuesday. I look forward to meeting him." The doorbell rang. Meg rose and went to answer it.

It was Rob. Worried, she thought, and who should blame him? His shoulders in the gray windbreaker hunched against the wind. It ruffled his hair and stung color across his cheekbones. "Is Carol Tichnor here?"

"I was just getting acquainted with her. Would you like a cup of coffee?"

He shuddered. "I OD'd on double-shot espresso. You heard about Brandstetter?"

"I heard that Tammy shot him."

He frowned. "We have no idea who shot him."

Meg drew a long breath. "My God, what a relief."

"Relief?"

"Yes, I thought perhaps having the dog in the house drove her over the edge. I felt guilty."

"That may be what happened, but I doubt it."

"Come in. You're running up my propane bill."

He followed her into the living room and exchanged courtesies with Carol, who addressed him as Lieutenant Neill and apologized with a little too much gracious humility for not returning his telephone calls.

He, in turn, treated her with steely deference. He asked her for an interview that afternoon. It was plain that interview was a euphemism for interrogation.

"I have business with the realty office, but I guess I can manage it. Four o'clock? I'm staying at the Red Hat. They do a decent margarita." She batted her lashes at him.

"At my office in the courthouse annex." He gave terse directions. He also suggested that she arrange for her brothers to meet with him.

"Good heavens, Lieutenant, when? It's a long drive up here and they're busy men."

"So am I a busy man," he retorted. "This is a homicide investigation, Ms. Tichnor. I want to see them in person as soon as possible."

"But Ethan's a doctor!"

"He can tell his patients he's going to Mazatlán," Rob snarled. "Tomorrow. It's Sunday."

"I'll try."

"Thank you. I have to go. I'm waiting for a search warrant." He hadn't sat down, and he made for the door with a curt nod to Meg as he left.

"So that's Robert Neill," Ms. Tichnor purred. "What an attractive man."

Meg stared at her. Maybe she was into bondage.

THE warrant might not have been necessary. It was a murder scene. However, the killing had happened outside the house. Considering the political ramifications of Brandstetter's death, Rob preferred to play it safe.

He intended to read every scrap of paper in the frowsty office. He also wanted Forensics to do a thorough examination of the SUV and the garage. Hal was bound to have had a gun collection. Rob wasn't about to wait for Tammy to sober up long enough to give permission.

While he waited for Earl to bring the warrant, Rob had deployed the skeletal Crime Scene Team to see what they could get from the footprints on the steps and the deck. He wasn't hopeful of results because the wind was drying everything rapidly, but Jake Sorenson thought he'd got one footprint that wasn't Brandstetter's. It was at that juncture that Rob went in search of Carol Tichnor. He was already having trouble keeping the two cases going at once—and keeping them separate in his mind.

Shortly after he got back, Linda Ramos showed up. She had delegated the "death-watch" chair at the hospital to Jeff Fong after Earl called Jeff to duty from his son's soccer game. Jeff would not be happy.

Rob was happy. He needed Linda. He set her to photographing the exterior of the SUV as soon as she and Jake had finished the steps. When Earl arrived with the warrant, having chased down Judge Meyer at the supermarket, Rob turned examination of the deck and SUV over to him.

Rob donned protective gear, and Linda and Jake followed him inside for a fast but hopefully thorough take on the office. The rest of the house could wait. After the initial forensic chores were done, he sent Jake back outside and began to organize the real search of Brandstetter's office. It was not a large room, but Hal had crammed it with books and pamphlets and heaps of paper, mostly printouts. The computer loomed. A large poster of Jesse Ventura in full wrestling costume hung over the desk. The edges of the poster curled.

Rob and Linda were deciding on a division of labor when Tom Brandstetter called on the cell phone. Rob backed away from his territory, the desk. Fingerprints smeared the flat surfaces. They'd used the iodine gun. He covered the receiver. "I need to take this now, Linda. You might as well get started on the file cabinet."

"Right."

He stepped into the empty hall, peeling the thin latex glove from his right hand. "Hello, Tom. Did the Portland police explain what happened here?"

Tom's voice came across quiet, detached. "Yes."

"I'm sorry."

"I'm not."

Rob could think of nothing to say to that.

The boy said, "They told me my mother is in the hospital. Was he beating on her again?"

Rob described what he'd observed of Tammy the night before and suggested, with ponderous delicacy, that she had used vodka to deaden the pain.

"She does that." Same detached voice. "I guess I'd better come."

In the office, Linda said something in Spanish.

Rob said, "She needs you, Tommy, and so does Towser."

The boy gave a laugh that was half a sob, the first sign of emotion he had displayed. "Poor old guy. I couldn't take him to Portland with me."

"Rob!" Linda called.

He waved an arm in the direction of the office and wound down his conversation. Tom said he had enough money to take the commuter shuttle home. The bus got into Klalo around five on Saturday. Rob doubted that the Crime Scene Unit would be done with the house by then. He supposed he could put Tom up in his guest room. But not Towser. He didn't say that. When he and Tom had finished the conversation, he clicked the cell phone off to give the battery a rest.

"Find something?" He pulled the latex glove back on.

Linda was all but bouncing in the doorway. "You got to look at this, Rob!" She pulled him into the room and led him to the desk. On a clear patch of surface she had laid a brown leather wallet.

Rob took a pencil from a tray on the desk and used it to flip the wallet open. An Oregon driver's license lay exposed, address in Portland. It had been issued to Edward Leon Redfern.

Rob felt as if someone had socked him in the kidneys. He cleared his throat. "Where did you find it, in the file cabinet?"

"Stuffed down behind a bunch of folders."

He continued to stare down at the hopeful young face. Linda shifted beside him. He spared her a glance. "Good work, Deputy."

Her teeth gleamed in a smile. "It's a link, huh?"

"It is." It was more than that. It was damn near an explanation. All kinds of random data clicked into place, like a slot machine running a winner, three cherries in a row. Rob felt a surge of anger at Brandstetter so strong the air took on a red haze.

But Brandstetter was dead, too. Shit. He took the right glove off again, pulled out his cell phone, switched the power back on, and used the speed dial to reach the sheriff, who was going to shit bricks and hit the fan, probably in reverse order.

MEG went to dinner with Carol Tichnor. Carol was paying. She hated to dine alone, she had said as she extended the invitation in Meg's chaotic living room. Meg wasn't sure why she agreed. She didn't like Carol.

"Vulgar curiosity, my dear," she told herself as she parked the Accord outside the Red Hat's rustic restaurant.

It was seven and dark. Carol sat at the bar with an empty margarita glass on the high counter in front of her. A stuffed elk head stared balefully down on a scene of subdued chatter. There was no sawdust on the floor. Handsome people dressed for the weekend by Norm Thompson clustered in twos and fours around rustic tables. They were waiting to be called into the restaurant. Meg was glad she'd taken the trouble to put on a cowl-necked cashmere top over velour pants.

She ordered Scotch-rocks and perched on the high stool next to Carol. She hated high stools. Her feet swung like a six-year-old's at a soiree. "How's it going?"

Carol gave a short laugh. "Great, considering I spent two fucking hours repeating myself."

"I take it Lieutenant Neill showed up to question you. He was pretty busy this afternoon."

"Not too busy to waste my time." She brooded. The bartender set a fresh margarita in front of her, removed the empty, and placed Meg's drink on a small cardboard coaster decorated with a red hunting hat. "And he didn't tell me a damn thing."

Meg took a swallow. Not Laphroaig.

"He just kept on and on about the keys. I don't see the point."

Meg thought the point was obvious.

"And he wanted to know about my business."

"Your antiques shop?"

Carol drank and licked salt from her lips. "How do you know... oh, good old Darcy."

"She's a bit intrusive."

Carol dismissed Darcy with a wiggle of her fingers. "I specialize in needlework, not Indian junk."

The flute player was hardly junk. Meg said, "Quilts?"

"Some. Mostly white-on-white embroidery and appliqué-work. Old lace."

"Must be interesting. Where do you find your stock?"

That was good for ten minutes on the joys of business travel. Carol traveled a lot, mostly in the South and Northeast, occasionally in Belgium and France. They finished their drinks. Melting ice had rendered the whisky innocuous. Carol ordered another margarita.

"Tichnor, party of two." The hostess bearing menus.

Carol made a face at the bartender, canceling her drink, and they rose. Meg slid off the stool with a thud.

The dining room faced the river but it was too dark to see much. When they had ordered, baked turbot for Meg, planked salmon for Carol, and Carol had approved the wine, a local shiraz-merlot blend that tasted surprisingly good, Carol said, "Ethan's in a snit. He'll miss his Sunday afternoon symphony concert."

"You contacted your brothers?"

"Deputy Dawg did. He got through to Ethan and left a message for Vance. I think Vance and Moira went to Salishan for the weekend."

It was plain that Rob's attractiveness had worn off where Carol was concerned. He cracked the whip one too many times, Meg reflected, amused.

The waitress brought warm herb bread and a mesclun salad dressed with a subtle vinaigrette.

At that point, Carol made an effort to play the gracious hostess. She asked Meg why she had moved to Klalo. Carol was enough of a Northwesterner to assume that Meg wanted to leave the Los Angeles Basin, but too much of a city girl to understand the call of the wild.

Meg was beginning to wonder about it herself. She made an effort to explain why she'd taken the job. Despite her summers in Klalo, Carol didn't remember who Hazel Guthrie was until Meg reminded her.

"Oh, the woman in the gingerbread house. Her husband was a pharmacist, I think. They had a little kid."

"No, Robert Neill is her grandson."

Carol digested that. "So she was a librarian?"

Meg said yes but didn't bother with further details.

They talked, mostly about Carol's ex-husband, an insurance executive with a taste for trophy blondes. The turbot was delicious. Carol poked at the salmon and drank another glass of wine. The party at the next table sang happy birthday to an elderly lady. Everyone laughed. Carol wrinkled her nose.

When Meg's description of the library met with palpable boredom, she diverted the conversation to other matters. She found Carol heavy going. The woman was either preoccupied or self-absorbed. She was also three sheets to the wind by the time they reached the last sip of shiraz.

Meg declined dessert and asked for decaf. Carol ordered a brandy. The waitress brought both, along with the tab, which was probably extortionate. Meg didn't offer to split the check. Carol scrawled her room number on it.

"Hey, it's my big sister." A tall, fleshy man with razor-cut blond hair beamed down at them. He wore a khaki jacket with lots of pockets over a ragg pullover and tan pants with zips and tabs. Hunter chic?

"Vance, honey." Carol lurched to her feet, sloshing brandy.

Vance Tichnor kissed his sister's cheek and she sank back onto her chair. He pulled one out for himself.

"And who is your lovely guest?"

Ew, Meg thought. She allowed herself to be introduced.

There was a moment when Vance Tichnor's blue, blue eyes looked her over, flicked, and dismissed her as not worthy of effort. She was at the age when women experience that look, so she caught it.

However, Vance ordered a brandy and turned the charm on. It almost worked. Unlike his sister, he knew of Meg's job and said appropriate things. He spoke with becoming affection of his dead grandfather, waxed nostalgic about summers in the old house, amused her with tales of the bathrooms' eccentricities, and described the elaborate lodge he was building on the banks of Beaver Creek.

Meg sipped cold decaf. "I know people fish at Lake Tyee in summer. What do they do this time of year?"

Vance's eyes crinkled in a fetching smile. "Hunt. And later, when the snows come, there's cross-country skiing. I have five acres to play around with. I may put in a toboggan run."

Meg had once fallen off a pair of skis at Lake Tahoe. "A toboggan run. Like sledding?"

He laughed indulgently.

Meg wondered whether he had filed an environmental impact statement. "What happened to the still?" Oops, she thought. A Scotch and two glasses of wine and I run amok.

The laugh segued to a smile that sobered her. "Ah, the famous still. Long gone, I'm afraid. The copper probably went into scrap drives during World War Two."

"Very patriotic," Meg said cordially. She rose and extended her hand. "It was good to meet you, Mr. Tichnor. Your lodge sounds impressive. Thanks, Carol. Nice dinner."

Carol turned back to her brother and her brandy.

Meg drove home with care. A DUI would be a bad idea at the start of one's career in a small town. A patrol car sat in front of the Brandstetter house, dark, engine running. The yellow tape around the driveway and the front deck flapped in the wind. She reversed directions, using Rob's driveway because hers was still taped off, and parked in front of her own house. Her headlights caught Rob, Towser on a leash, and a thin young man coming back on the sidewalk across the street.

They crossed over when she killed the engine and waited while she got out of the car. She locked the door and fumbled for her house key. "Good to see Towser on a leash."

The dog gave a bounce and woofed at her. "Down, boy," the young man said. He was short and thin with a nose stud and dark cropped hair.

Rob was holding an unlit flashlight and wearing a heavier jacket than the windbreaker he'd worn that afternoon. "Meg, this is Tammy's son, Tom. He's staying with me until they release his mother from the hospital."

Meg said, "Hello, Tom. I'm sorry about your father."

"Hi. Emil used to take me fishing. You bought a great house." Tom had a light tenor and sad eyes. He resembled neither parent. Perhaps he was a changeling.

"I think so, too." She turned to Rob. "I ate dinner with Carol at the Red Hat. She said you couldn't reach Vance Tichnor this afternoon because he was off some place with his wife."

"Salishan. It's a resort at the coast."

"He showed up alone about forty-five minutes ago."

Rob frowned.

"I got the impression she was expecting him."

 *Chapter 10*

I suppose that hound is sleeping in your guest room." Meg poured Rob a stiff Scotch. She was drinking herb tea herself, having gone past her usual limit. Strange, she felt wide awake, though it was after eleven.

"Back porch." He looked sheepish as well as tired. He'd seen that her light was still on when he returned from his unscheduled detour to the Red Hat. "Short of sending Towser to a kennel, I couldn't think what else to do."

"What's wrong with a kennel?"

Both eyebrows went up. "Consider the size of that animal. Picture him sick and covered with fleas."

Meg shuddered. "I get the point." She didn't exactly. Fleas or no fleas, Towser wasn't Rob's responsibility. Nor was young Tom. "Is the kid sleeping on the porch?"

He grinned. "I offered Tom, not Towser, the guest room, but he wanted a sleeping bag on the porch with the dog. Fortunately, the back porch is enclosed and not much colder than a meat locker." His eyes narrowed. "There's a space heater somewhere…"

Before he could dash off on another rescue mission, Meg said, "Did you interrogate the Tichnor siblings?"

He swallowed Scotch, savoring it. "Carol passed out. I talked to Vance."

"And?"

He took another sip of Scotch and set the glass down. "I ought to go home before I fall down."

"I think I'm entitled to know who has keys to my garage. That's what you were asking him about, wasn't it?"

He stood up. "I can't talk about the investigation. You know that, Meg. Goddamn."

"So swear me in as a reserve deputy."

Dead silence for the space of three breaths. He said something rude.

She looked at him over the rim of her mug. "Hey."

He sank back onto his chair.

"This is a very small town," she said.

"It's bigger than Two Falls."

"Small." She swallowed tea. "And it's a small department."

"And your point is?" He was watching her, eyes shadowed.

"Tell me about your boss."

The frown between his brows deepened. "McCormick? I like him."

She waited.

"He's up for re-election. He's going to want quick and easy answers."

"A cover-up?"

"No," he said patiently. "I like Mack. He's a good man. He wouldn't do anything dishonest, but he's bound to worry if I don't come up with solutions before Election Day. That means he'll *want* to think simple. He'll convince himself that he's just using Occam's razor."

"And he has the power to stop the investigation?"

Rob made a circle on the surface of the kitchen table with his whisky glass. "He has the power to cut off the funds, and he can take me off the case, though I don't think he'd do that unless I goofed up big-time."

"*Is* there a simple solution?"

He shut his eyes, opened them, stared at her. "Raise your right hand."

"What?"

"Repeat after me..."

When she had sworn to uphold the Constitution of the State of Washington and ordinances of Latouche County she had never read, she murmured, "Feckless Meg."

"Surely not."

"I'm a creature of impulse." Such as the time she found herself pregnant at twenty-three outside the bounds of matrimony. "Will that oath hold water?"

"Unless somebody challenges it, and they won't. I'll enter your name on the reserve roster tomorrow."

"I was kidding!"

They exchanged a long look, long and somber.

Rob ran his finger over the rim of the whisky glass. "You're intelligent, detached, and observant. You're also in the clear for the crucial weeks of August, according to your former co-workers." A fugitive smile quirked his mouth. "And you have special skills I intend to call on at no expense to the county."

"Skills?"

"You're a librarian."

"No lie."

"As you said, it's a small town and a small department." He shoved the glass away. "I need help, Meg. I also need somebody to let me know when I'm crazy."

She thought about that and, ultimately, believed it. "Then tell me about the case. Who had keys to my garage?"

"Realtors. Dennis Wheeler."

"Darcy's Dennis?" Her voice squeaked.

He said wryly, "That's the sum total of what I got out of Vance Tichnor. I think he's jealous. Emil was fond of Dennis. Wheeler used to drive the old man out to Beaver Creek for a couple of hours of fishing when he got so he couldn't drive himself."

"Innocent." Meg breathed a sigh of relief.

"Maybe, maybe not. Dennis's political opinions are slightly to the right of the late commissioner's."

"I gathered that. Is it relevant?"

"Maybe."

Meg turned things over in her mind. "There were other garage keys?"

"There was a lockbox outside the house. Linda says all the Tichnor keys were in that."

"Oh, of course. I remember now. The agent who showed me around had to punch in a code to open the box. It was a multiple listing. You said Linda. Who's she?"

"The deputy who told you about the body in the garage."

"The one with the iodine gun. She and Jake searched the house."

"Right. The realtor's keys remained in the lockbox in those weeks before the deal closed." He rubbed the back of his neck. "*You* don't have a key to the garage's back door. Dennis has both, according to Vance. So your back door key is still missing. You're sure you never had it?"

"Yes." She spoke with greater assurance than she felt.

"The locks weren't changed and they weren't forced."

"Okay. Key still missing. That answers one question. Now tell me about your simple solution."

He reached for the glass, swallowed the last of his Scotch, and shook his head, no, when she offered more. "Mack has Brandstetter killing the man buried in the garage, and Tammy killing Brandstetter. He wants me to prepare a case against Tammy."

"Will you?"

"I'll look into it, certainly. I won't know much until I talk to her tomorrow, and maybe not then. Brandstetter died intestate. This is a community-property state. She inherits. That and a history of abuse—Tom described it—and the fight they probably had yesterday make a strong circumstantial case, but I don't think a jury would convict without something solider in the way of evidence. Say, his blood on her nightie, the weapon in her makeup case. Deputy Fong did a GRT and it showed negative for gunpowder residue. And she was probably out cold at the crucial time."

"So you don't think she did it?"

"No, and I don't think Tom did, though his motive is as strong as Tammy's. Hal was shot at very close range, and there's no sign that he resisted. You met Hal. Does that sound likely, even with Tammy pulling the trigger?"

"No."

"He didn't trust many people. Whoever was with him was someone he did trust." He shook his head. "With his life."

Meg shivered.

"He was killed after eleven, when the espresso stand closed, but before three, according to the ME." He rubbed his face. "Whoever it was had spent some time with Hal that evening. Someone parked a car behind the SUV."

"To get something?"

"Who knows? The two of them probably sat there on the deck and talked for a while. Then his good buddy, whoever it was, stood up, put a gun to Hal's temple, and shot him."

Meg's stomach clenched. "What about witnesses? Weren't there any insomniacs on Old Cedar Street?"

"Two people remember hearing a car backfire but they're foggy about the time. You told Jake *you* didn't see or hear anything."

"I slept without twitching for nine hours."

"Enviable." He yawned. "I didn't notice anything either. Neither did the Brownings nor the Wheelers, according to Deputy Jones. Mrs. Iverson across the street thinks she saw a car leave around three—she'd got up to use the bathroom—but she's pretty deaf. She didn't hear anything. The house between the Wheelers and the Brandstetters is a rental, empty at this point. I have high hopes of Kayla Graves and the wind surfers. They were off somewhere all day, though, so they'll have to be questioned."

"Tomorrow."

"Right." Rob yawned again and stretched. "Thanks, Deputy." He started to rise.

"Wait just a damned minute. What about the body in the garage? What about my petroglyph?"

He frowned and sat down once more. It was awhile before he answered her. "Brandstetter or somebody associated with him murdered a college student named Eddy Redfern, Todd Welch's cousin."

"Oh, no." She called up Todd's round rosy face, his charming air of certainty about life and the Republican Party. "Oh, poor Todd."

"It was hard on him. He made the identification." Rob rubbed his neck. "Eddy was looking for the Lauder Point artifacts, according to his friends and family in Two Falls. Jake and Todd verified that this afternoon. I spoke with Chief Thomas myself yesterday."

"Chief Thomas?"

"Eddy was a Klalo." He gave her a thumbnail biography of the principal chief of the Klalos, including his unfortunate relationship with her. "She sent those kids out without police support to find the missing artifacts."

"She gave them her distrust of authority? I see."

"I don't, quite. If the kid had common sense, he would not have confronted the thieves all by himself. I need to know more about Eddy. I also need to know whether Brandstetter masterminded the original theft, and why, and who helped him. I don't see Hal hoisting petroglyphs into the pickup that hauled the loot away from Lauder Point, though he wasn't so fat ten years ago."

"But he was an elected official!"

"Give me a break. We live in the Tropic of Greed. If power company executives and their government lackeys didn't object to looting the state of California, what was there to stop a simple Libertarian commissioner like Hal from looting a county park? In any case, he was just the proprietor of a service station at the time of the theft, not an official."

"You're depressing me."

He gave a wry smile. "Bring on the Prozac. How many law enforcement officers can claim two unsolved wrongful deaths in their front yards?"

"Is it a question of ego for you?" That was risky. Meg waited for him to blow up.

His eyes narrowed and his mouth compressed. After a moment, he shrugged. "A question of competence, anyway. I thought I knew what I was doing."

"Well, you do." She almost reached over to pat his hand, he looked so depressed, but she thought better of it. "You just need more information. For instance, why haven't the other artifacts surfaced, where are they, and where have they been all this time? Do you think all of them were kept in the garage? That might implicate Mr. Strohmeyer."

His mouth relaxed in a half smile. "See, I need your input. Those are some of the questions that keep pushing me away from Mack's simple solution. It's possible, even probable, that the Lauder Point collection was broken up and sold in separate lots. I don't think the petroglyphs have been put on the open market, though, so the odds are either that Brandstetter sold them privately or kept them himself."

"Where did he keep them, in my garage?"

"I doubt it. That was more likely a temporary storage space after Strohmeyer's death. Or after he became bedridden in the last year of his life."

Meg got up, poured herself a cup of cold tea from the pot, and nuked it in the microwave. "Do you think the sale of the house took Brandstetter by surprise?"

"It may have. He may have expected it to go on sitting empty indefinitely. Sometimes that happens when an elderly person dies. It did sit empty. The will wasn't proved until the end of June."

She sat, cupping her hands around the hot mug. "Three years ago, I inherited a house in Brentwood. It took a year and a half before I had a clear title to it." Her father had contested the will. The house had belonged to his only sister. Aunt Margaret's bequest, woman to woman, had boosted Meg's spirits in ways she was only beginning to understand, but that was not really Rob Neill's business.

"I inherited three years ago, but I only sold the house this April," she said.

He nodded, as if she had explained a puzzle. "So you thought about it for a while."

"It's a nice house in a good neighborhood." About half a mile from the Getty Museum. "I thought about living in it and commuting to work. Then I got this job offer. Selling the house meant I could afford to accept it and still send Lucy to Stanford." Her aunt had had the house built in the 1950s for $30,000, an ordinary three-bedroom ranch house. It sold for a million and a half. Meg still couldn't believe her luck. Of course, there had been taxes, and tuition and fees at Stanford were outrageous.

"But you did think about it." Rob rubbed the spot between his eyebrows. "Most people who inherit a nice property would, but Charlotte Tichnor didn't think twice. She sold the house as soon as she could. She had people in to plan the garage sales, and a crew to fix the house up, by the first of July. Lots of coming and going."

Meg sipped tea. "If the petroglyphs were hidden in the garage, then there's a chance the thieves couldn't get at the compartment in July without calling attention to themselves."

Rob apparently agreed. "The fact that the loot was moved in early August, when most people around here were out of town or otherwise occupied, argues for Brandstetter's active supervision."

"Somebody had to know the neighborhood well?"

"Exactly." He wriggled his shoulders as if they were sore. "I don't see Brandstetter spending ten years of his life gloating over a private gallery of native art. If their house is evidence, neither Hal nor Tammy had an aesthetic bone in their bodies. I think Hal, or Hal and his accomplice, sold the loot to a collector, I hope to a local collector. They say Germans get off on pre-Columbian art. I don't want to think of those petroglyphs somewhere in Düsseldorf."

"Shall I see what I can do about finding private collections of artifacts?"

"I have a list, but it's pretty skimpy." His gray eyes met hers. "Are you free tomorrow, Meg?"

"Yes." Except for the small matter of unpacking her belongings.

"There are stacks of printed material in Hal's office. Will you sort the books for us and see if you spot anything that bears on the case? Cases. Jesus." He dragged both hands down his face. "I'm beat. I'd better grab some sleep while I can. I have to interview Tammy tomorrow and soothe the sheriff."

Besides running two investigations. "Okay, I'll do your sorting for you, and I'll go on the Internet to look for collectors. Sir."

He smiled at that, yawned hugely, and left.

EARL Minetti was already at the Brandstetter house by the time Rob showed up Sunday morning, and Earl fairly quivered with ambition. The team wasn't due in until nine.

Rob had walked the dog, then hardened his heart and rousted Tom from the sleeping bag, pointed out coffee and cereal, and abandoned the kid to his own devices. When Rob left the house, the shower was running. It was 6:45.

He called the sheriff and had a long talk, checked his e-mail, and reviewed his notes. Then he went out to look the site over.

He found Earl in Brandstetter's office.

"Finished with the rest of the house?" Rob asked in what he hoped was a noncombative tone of voice.

"Pretty much." Earl wore coveralls and latex gloves. "Thayer's done a gun inventory out in the garage, but he's not finished yet. There's a lot of crap here, too. It'll take some organizing."

Rob and Linda had organized the office search the day before. Rob suspected Earl knew that. "I intend to go through the rest of the desk today."

"Why should you do it? You have enough on your plate." Earl gave him a gentle, patronizing smile. "The trouble with you, Rob, is, you don't delegate."

"I'm glad you said that." Rob returned the smile. "I arranged to have Ms. McLean examine the print material."

"What!"

"Swore her in as a reserve deputy." Rob began to feel downright cheerful about his wacko impulse.

"She's a witness."

"Technically."

"She's a fucking suspect!"

"No, Earl, she's not. Solid alibis for the whole month of August, no motive, no connection with Brandstetter or Eddy Redfern. She'd never heard of Redfern."

"I don't like it. Why bring in a civilian?"

"We need help. She's a professional librarian, trained to deal with print material. She could probably check out the computer, too, but I'll handle that." Rob mentioned Hal's computer because computers were Earl's weak point. He could boot up and follow directions, but he had no confidence and very limited experience outside the conventional police databases.

Earl's mouth twisted. "What did McCormick say?"

The sheriff had taken a good deal of persuading. "No problem," Rob said.

Earl made a skeptical noise in his throat.

"The price is right," Rob murmured.

"Hell."

"She'll sort the books and printouts and look for patterns. I was waiting until I talked to Tammy. Some of what's stacked in here may be hers. Still, if you're at loose ends you can move the print stuff to the dining room table. That'll give Linda and me a little elbow room."

"Linda!"

"Do you want to pull Ramos off the job?"

Earl opened his mouth.

"Might be bad for your team's morale, Earl. She's the one who found Redfern's wallet." Whoever checked the files would have found the wallet, but Linda deserved some kind of reward. "Credit where credit is due," Rob said piously.

Earl knew when to give in. He looked crestfallen.

It occurred to Rob that the morale problem might lie with Earl. He could be an asshole, but he was a well-trained technical expert and a reasonably effective sergeant. He had already intimated that he felt left out.

Time to mend a fence. "How about a cup of Marge's coffee? We need to talk."

"Well..."

"Is the living room usable?"

"Yeah. Finished that yesterday. There's a few things I want to look at in the master bedroom, but the office is the main problem."

"Right." Rob led the way down the hall. Earl shed his protective gear on the living room sofa and they went for coffee.

Back in the living room, Rob took Earl through the evidence they had in both cases. Earl had high hopes of the Brandstetter garage with all those guns. When he heard that Dennis Wheeler had keys to Meg's garage, he was fired up and ready to get a warrant to search Wheeler's house and garage. They talked that over, as well as Rob's impending interview with Tammy Brandstetter.

Rob thought a judge would refuse to issue a warrant for the Wheeler house, but it wouldn't hurt to try. Eddy Redfern was an Indian. Dennis had been known to make racist cracks about Indians, not to mention blacks, Jews, Mexicans, feminists, and gays, with the occasional jab at dumb Swedes. Rob thought Dennis got his opinions from talk radio. Maybe they ran deeper than that.

"You're talking to Tammy this morning?"

"Yeah. Mack made a ceremonial visit to her last night. He figured he owed it to the commissioner's widow. He told her about Hal." If she didn't already know.

"I bet that's a relief to you." Earl sounded almost congenial.

"He wasn't sure she took it in," Rob said wryly. "I'd better get over there. They're releasing her this morning. Can she use her car?"

She could, but Earl didn't want anyone messing around in the garage, so he backed the rusty Toyota out himself and parked it in front of the house. He gave Rob the keys and Tammy's handbag, which he'd found in the bedroom. No sign of a handgun in Tammy's domain, apparently. Certainly not in her purse. That was good to know.

 *Chapter 11*

WILLIAM ("Digger") Meek had been booked in Montana for simple assault the previous April. He had since disappeared from sight. The Kalispell detective who phoned Rob said Meek's girlfriend had refused to file charges.

They talked awhile. Meek was a known associate of half a dozen white supremacy groups, but not a mover and shaker. He had once had the shit beaten out of him by a Colville tribal leader who heard him boast of grave robbing. Nobody involved in that episode, not even Meek, had been willing to file charges. He had spent six months in jail for an earlier assault. In his younger days, he had been fined repeatedly for possession of amphetamines. He was forty-nine years old. The Kalispell detective was sending fingerprints and an old photograph.

Some of these details Rob already knew, but he was glad to have confirmation. The connection with Lauder Point was tenuous, though, no more nor less than Chief Thomas's word. The Fish Commission investigator had sent an e-mail confirming that they hadn't been able to prove anything against Meek.

Rob brooded about the pothunter as he rode to the hospital with Tom in Tammy's car. What was needed was a connection between Meek and Harold Brandstetter. Maybe Tammy would give it to him.

He waited for Linda Ramos outside the two-bed room while Tammy shed a few audible tears behind the privacy curtain and Tom said nothing much. Busy care-givers stalked the halls, some pushing carts laden with sinister containers or stacked linens. The reek of disinfectant hung on the air. Rob hated hospitals.

When Linda showed up, she looked tired. "My Mickey threw up all night." Mickey was her five-year-old son, Miguel.

"Good God, have you taken him to the doctor?"

She gave him the pitying smile of an experienced mother. Mickey was on the road to recovery in the care of his *abuela*, she said, but *she* was exhausted. Not surprising. Besides dealing with a sick child, she had just moved over to the day shift.

Rob commiserated. He also filled her in on the latest developments. When she heard about Dennis Wheeler's keys, she scowled. When she heard that Meg was busy sorting papers and books in a quasi-official role, she laughed aloud. "I like her. She was too polite to ask dumb questions while we searched the house." She gestured toward the hospital ward. "What about this one?"

Rob glanced at his watch. "We give her five minutes, then we wring her dry." He handed Linda the recorder. "Always assuming she doesn't demand a lawyer."

"The son is here?"

"Our dog-sitter," Rob assured her.

Linda grinned.

Tom came out almost at once, said hello to Linda, and told them his mother was getting dressed. He'd brought her clothes and makeup.

"Is she okay?" Rob asked.

Tom made a face. "I guess so. It's hard to tell. She wants me to stay in Klalo for a while."

"Can you do that?"

He shrugged. "My boss won't like it, but it's not as if I've got a high-end job."

"You going to college?" Linda asked.

He flushed. "I'm taking a class at the Culinary Institute. I want to be a chef."

Linda gaped.

Rob said, "Good idea." He tried to imagine how Hal would have reacted to a son who devoted himself to the perfect soufflé. Maybe that was the point. Maybe Hal had reacted and Tom had left.

When Tammy was finally ready to receive them, Rob wondered if he'd been wise to wait. She was composed and almost confident. The shiner gleamed purple beneath a coat of pink makeup base. He sent Tom off to wait in the hospital cafeteria.

He introduced Linda, who set up the recorder on the formica top of the bedside table, pulled a chair from beside the unten-anted bed, and took out her notebook. She always made useful notes on visceral responses—eye dilation, clenched muscles, color rising and falling. She also indicated which questions she thought ought to be repeated.

Rob remained standing as he went through the preliminaries. When he read Tammy the Miranda Warning, she said she didn't want a lawyer.

She was sitting in the "death-watch" chair with the pale light of day shining on her from the side. She wore pull-on pants and a flowered top. Her dim brown hair was neatly combed, but she needed a haircut. She kept her hands folded on her lap.

"I'm sorry to have to question you, Tammy."

She inclined her head, self-possessed, forgiving.

"Tell me about Friday. When did you go to work?"

Her eyes widened, or the good one did. He'd surprised her. He was ready to bet she had meant to tell him she couldn't remember anything.

After a moment's hesitation, she said, "I have a four-day week. Hal wanted it that way. On Fridays, I shop for the next week at Safeway and the bakery."

"And the liquor store?"

Her jaw set. "And the liquor store. Three fifths of vodka, two jugs of Collins mix, and a bottle of Jim Beam. Want the receipt? I have it here." She tapped her handbag. "Hal always checked the liquor store receipt."

"I'll take your word for it." And the clerk's word. "Did you come straight home?"

"Yes."

"Was Hal there?"

"He'd got up. He wanted lunch." She snorted. "Two Hungry Man dinners and a quart of chocolate chip mint ice cream. Same thing every day. He was easy to shop for."

"What happened then?"

"I made myself a sandwich and a drink—vodka Collins. Then I stuck the dishes in the washer and set up for dinner. I laundered some clothes."

"Where was Hal?"

"In his office. He had DSL and spent a lot of time on the Internet." She shut her eyes briefly, opened them, and said, "We were going out after dinner to the Timberland Tavern. I called my friend Betty Krause to see if she and her husband would be there. I don't like the Timberland on Friday and Saturday. It's too rowdy. Betty wasn't in, so I left a message. Hal hates, uh, hated Betty. When I hung up he started in on me."

Rob waited.

"He slapped me around." She touched her black eye and went on, toneless, "I made myself another drink. When I worked up the courage, I said I didn't want to go out, that I'd stay at home and watch a movie on the DVD. He slapped me around some more, but we were interrupted."

Rob waited. He half sat on the second bed. Outside, an orderly pushed a metal cart heaped with soiled linens. The P.A. system called a doctor in hospital code.

Tammy shot Rob a sideways look out of the good eye. "Somebody called on the cell phone."

"Who?" He kept his voice unemphatic with an effort.

She shrugged. "No idea. A man. Hal went into his office and didn't come out."

"What time was that?"

She shrugged again. "Midafternoon. I fixed the pot roast and had another drink."

"When did he leave?"

"I dunno. I was pretty foggy by then. I served dinner around six-thirty. He hogged it down, as usual, and then he complained about it, as usual, and somewhere in there he gave me a black eye. Oh, yeah, that was after he went into the backyard to check on the weather. He got a faceful of rain and stepped on a dog turd."

Linda shifted in her seat and made a note.

"He yelled at me to walk the dog. Then he left."

"In the SUV?"

"Of course in the SUV. Hal weighed three hundred and twenty-two pounds. You think he could fit into my Toyota? I shoved Towser out the front door, climbed into my night clothes, and got some ice for my eye and the vodka bottle. You know the rest."

"The timing's confusing me. When did he leave?" Rob stood again, walked to the foot of the bed, and turned back.

"I wasn't looking at the clock."

"After dark?"

"Yes."

"Did he say where he was going?"

"He may have. I wasn't listening." She bit her lip. "Portland. He said something about driving to Portland."

"Where in Portland?" It was an hour-and-a-half drive to reach Portland Airport, another half hour to downtown. If Hal had left before eight... "Where?" he repeated.

"I don't know." She drew a long, shaky breath. "After you showed up with Towser and the short woman, I dived into the bottle. I don't remember anything after that. I was drunk, so sue me."

"You were beyond drunk." Rob could've bitten his tongue. The censorious tone was not useful. And not fair.

"I think Sheriff McCormick came by here last night, but I was still pretty muzzy. Is Hal really dead?"

"Yes."

"Thank you, Jesus."

Rob rolled his eyes at Linda. "Are you sure you don't want a lawyer, Tammy?"

"Absolutely. I didn't kill Hal, but I'd like to give the man who did a big, spitty kiss."

"The man? What man?"

She shrugged. "Man, woman, whoever."

Rob decided to come back to that later. "Tell me about Hal's friends."

"Hal didn't have friends, he had toadies. Sycophants." She smiled a gentle smile. "Hey, yesterday I couldn't have pronounced sycophant."

"His associates, then."

"Hal was a bully. That's a funny word, bully. Bully for you. It sounds sort of harmless." Her hands began working, clenching the loose fabric of her tunic.

"He could be intimidating." As soon as he made the banal remark Rob wished he hadn't. The woman had been beaten routinely.

However, she went on, her face as serene as if he had not spoken, "A bully is not just intimidating. A bully enjoys watching intimidated people crawl to him. A bully gets off on hurting people. A bully has no soul." She leaned toward him, very earnest, hands pleating the fabric. "This country is run by the bullies, of the bullies, for the bullies. Listen to our so-called foreign policy. Look at the mentality of business leaders. Listen to rap lyrics. Watch a football game."

"You didn't agree with Hal's political ideas?"

"He had slogans, not ideas." Her lip curled and she leaned back in the chair. "And all the wannabe bullies clubbed together to make him a county commissioner. I got drunk for a week after that election."

"As I recall, he had strong backing in the Sport Fishermen's Association."

She nodded. "And the gun clubs and the loggers and every tavern between here and The Dalles, plus the preachers who were disappointed when the world didn't end on January first of that year, and at least two talk show hosts. You want me to name names?"

"Yes."

She did. They discussed Hal's supporters, but there were no surprises. The board of county commissioners was nonpartisan. Neither major political party had endorsed Hal, nor had the unions.

Commissioners were paid only a token salary, so they had independent sources of income or they didn't run. They tended to be lawyers or real estate developers. Some fools had seen Brandstetter's unexpected victory as a refreshing change. It was a change, all right.

When she wound down, he said, "Where did Hal get his money?"

"For the campaign?"

"For that and in general."

"He got some funds from right-wing action groups for travel and advertising. The gas station's in a good place for tourists, so it's profitable. He paid a manager to run it but stayed in the black, and then there was my income."

A nurse's aide stuck her head in the room, said oops, and withdrew. Linda flipped a page in her notebook.

Rob said, "You're a freelance bookkeeper?"

"I'm a good bookkeeper. I have clients here and in Two Falls. Hal was always pushing me to take on more." She gave a sharp, unamused laugh. "I kept the books for half the small businesses in town, but Hal wouldn't let me look at our finances. He gave me a fucking allowance. I don't even know if he had life insurance. Probably not. He thought he was immortal."

Rob remembered Hal's computer, still to be accessed. "What did he use, Quicken?"

"Yes. Password 'Perot.'"

Rob suppressed a grin. "As in H. Ross?"

"He thought I didn't know it. The sucker wrote his passwords down, kept them in the family Bible, the one in German that he couldn't read. Not that he wanted to. At least he wasn't religious." She said that dispassionately, as if Hal's religious sentiments would have been another blow but not a serious one.

Though Rob would have figured the passwords out eventually, knowing them would speed things up. "You didn't access his computer at all?" He found that hard to believe.

"I showed him how to use the computer when he first got it." Her voice took on a ragged edge. "After that, I didn't enter the room. He told me if I did, he'd kill Tommy. He would have, too." Her hands twisted.

Linda drew a breath.

Rob turned the revelation over in his mind. It was sickening but plausible. It also gave Tammy a strong maternal motive for murder, stronger than self-defense.

Linda shifted again on her chair, jotted another note. In the hall, two people held a brief conversation and the P.A. system crackled with code.

"I use a laptop for business," Tammy was saying in dull, mechanical tones. "I sit at the kitchen table when I have to bring my work home."

Rob nodded and stopped the recorder. He flipped the cassette over, reinserted it, and pressed Record. "Did Hal have other sources of income?"

"Sometimes he was flush. I never figured that out. He gambled, mostly poker, and he used to cackle about ways to cheat the IRS. He hated income tax. That's why we live here." Washington has no state income tax. Oregon does.

"Any other sources of money?"

Tammy's forehead creased with concentration. "There were the swap meets. He liked swap meets. He bought and sold guns for cash. And vintage cars, through the station."

Bingo. "Did he do any pothunting?"

"Like digging up Indian burial grounds? No. He had friends who did when he was a kid, and his father collected arrowheads. Hal got those when the old man died."

"You're sure he didn't go out prospecting for pots?"

"Can you imagine Hal hiking?"

"With difficulty."

She gave a small snort of laughter, genuine this time. "Hal could talk sports like nobody's business, but he never did anything to keep in shape after he left school."

He'd been the star center of the Klalo High School football team, if Rob remembered correctly.

Tammy said, "I was hoping he'd have a heart attack." The P.A. system paged Dr. Rowland.

Rob rubbed the spot between his eyebrows where a headache threatened. "Did Hal know any pothunters?"

"One of his cronies made money selling arrowheads and thunder eggs, but I haven't seen him around lately."

Rob held his breath.

She shook her head. "I can't think of his name. Bill something."

Rob opened his mouth to say William Meek, closed it with a snap, and waited. No leading of witnesses. When she didn't say anything more, he ventured, cautious, "Did the man have a nickname?"

"Besides Bill? I don't think so. God, that must've been ten years ago, before Hal got respectable. They used to sit in the backyard with a case of beer and chant politically incorrect names for all the people they hated, which was anybody not male and not white. All women were cunts and bitches except for the few who were feminazis."

"Do you remember what Bill looked like?"

"Scrawny and short. I'd recognize him but he's hard to describe—hair-colored hair, mean little eyes. He wore jeans with a big cowboy buckle." She shook her head again.

Rob decided to wait until the Kalispell photograph arrived before he pressed her, but he began to feel optimistic. Two nurses walked past the room in jocular conversation. A phone rang three times.

Rob shifted gears. "Did Hal associate with Dennis Wheeler?"

"Dennis? One of the toadies. Dennis thought Hal was some kind of prophet." Tammy frowned. "I haven't seen him hanging around much in the past year, though. Maybe Darcy straightened him out. Dennis is a blowhard, but she calls the tune. Lucky Darcy," she added, bitter.

"What about the other neighbors?"

She shook her head, no. "The girls across the street thought Hal was funny at first, but that didn't last long. He despised women, and they must've caught on. The Iversons next door to them are Democrats, real liberal. They once had a Kerry sign in their yard. Hal snuck out and knocked it down a couple of times, but Mrs. Iverson put it back up. She keeps calling Animal Control when Towser runs loose."

"That has to stop, Tammy."

She looked down at her clasped hands. "I know. Tommy will exercise him on the leash. I can't anymore, he's too strong for me. I would've kept him in the yard, but Hal enjoyed letting Towser out into the street, stirring people up, especially Jim Browning. Jim's a retired Marine, you know, and Hal tried to recruit him." Her mouth quirked. "Jim told him to fuck off."

Rob glanced at his watch. Ten-thirty. The doctor would be showing up soon. "Okay, Tammy. Let's go through it again."

She made a face but didn't resist. He let Linda ask the questions while he considered what he'd learned. The phone call was crucial. They had found Hal's cell phone in his coat pocket. There would be a record of that phone call and others. Rob wanted to get on it, and on the trip to Portland. Where in Portland? The city sprawled. He wished he didn't have to interview the Tichnors that afternoon.

When Linda came to a pause, he said, "Did Hal know Emil Strohmeyer's grandsons, Tammy?"

Tammy looked bewildered. "Well, yeah, both of us knew them. We hung out together summers when we were little kids, a bunch of us. Carol, too. I guess you were too young to join in. Hal grew up in the house we live in now. I lived over on Alder. We played kick the can."

Rob had not come to live with his grandparents until he was nine. Hal, Tammy, and the three Tichnors would have been in high school by then, maybe college. Odd that neither Vance nor Carol had said anything about Hal's death.

"When did they stop spending their summers in Klalo?"

"I don't know, Rob. Puberty, probably. I started picking strawberries summers when I was twelve, and I did a lot of baby-sitting, so I wasn't around all that much. Hal worked for his dad."

"Doing what?"

"His father owned the old Phillips gas station downtown. He sold it when Hal was in high school, and they built the new station out on Highway 14. Hal always worked for his dad."

"Hal wasn't drafted?"

"No, flat feet."

"Lucky." Rob's father was killed in Vietnam the year Rob turned eight. He supposed he ought to check out the Tichnor brothers' draft status in that era. Vance had probably had a lucky draw at the lottery. Ethan, who was older, would have had an academic exemption.

Linda had resumed her questions. Rob listened critically. She was good, more empathetic than he was. Being a mother herself, she pursued Hal's threat to kill Tom. By the time Tammy's doctor appeared to release her, Linda had established strong motives for both Tammy and young Tom.

Hal had conducted a reign of terror. It was hard not to believe he got what he deserved, which was a rotten way to think about a murder victim in the course of an investigation. If the sheriff insisted on mounting a case against Tammy, somebody from the DA's office would have to interview her doctor. Rob suspected she had been incapable well before midnight.

They took their leave of Tammy after advising her they'd be seeing her again. She planned to spend the night at the Red Hat. Did he mind keeping Tom and Towser? He said no, wondering what he'd let himself in for. He trusted that Earl would finish with the Brandstetter house soon.

Linda had driven a county car and offered Rob a ride to the courthouse.

"It's almost lunch time," he said as they made their way down the long hospital corridor. "Go check on Mickey. I'll walk. I need to stretch my legs."

"Okay, I'll make you a copy of the interview after lunch and write up a statement for Tammy to sign."

"Good. I ought to tell Tom his mother is free to go. See you later." He headed downstairs to the cafeteria where he found Tom drooping over bad coffee and an old issue of *Willamette Week*. The place bustled with care-givers in colorful polyester uniforms and glum relatives of patients. The noise level was high.

Too high for Rob. He gave Tom the good word and left by the side entrance. Outside the air smelled delectably fresh. A light breeze blew from the east. He threaded his way among the back streets and through blocks of old houses that separated the courthouse from the newer hospital.

When he got to Birch Street there wasn't much traffic. It was Sunday. He walked along the row of elaborate Victorian houses, thinking about questions he needed to ask Ethan and Vance Tichnor and their sister. The wind had picked up. A plastic grocery bag fluttered against someone's privet hedge.

Carol had said nothing at all about Hal's death, yet according to Tammy they had been childhood playfellows. Kick the can was quite a bond. Rob had been good at kick the can, being small and sneaky. Most childhood games favored the large and straightforward.

"Rob! Robert Neill!"

He stopped and focused on the elderly woman in a track suit who had stepped through a neat gate in the hedge. He felt a twinge of dismay. "Mrs. Crookshank, how are you?"

She touched his arm with a liver-spotted hand. "Very well, thanks. You're looking good, Robert. I hear you've been busy."

He made a polite noise of agreement. Mrs. Crookshank had been his fourth-grade teacher, a reasonably sympathetic woman. Because he couldn't very well tell her to piss off, he asked after her daughter and diverted her from current events. Maxine Crookshank was a San Francisco investment banker, a source of mystery to her mother, so she chatted about her fiftyish child for several minutes and Rob half listened. He had nothing against Maxine.

He heard the truck accelerate behind them and turned. When it lurched toward them on the wrong side of the street, he shoved Mrs. Crookshank through the open gate, wrapped his arms around her, and rolled until he ended up on top of her on the lawn with his ears ringing.

She was saying something indignant.

"What?" Stupid.

"Was that a gunshot?"

"Yes." Several gunshots.

"Get off, you're hurting me. Rob, are you all right?"

"Stay down." He shoved himself up, pulling his gun from the shoulder holster, and staggered to the gate, but the truck had vanished. Doors opened on both sides of the street. Heads poked out.

He shook his own head to clear it. Dumb bastard. He shoved the gun back in place and reached into his jacket pocket for his cell phone. He couldn't focus, but he punched 911 anyway and got Jane.

As his tinny voice relayed information about the shots and the truck to the dispatcher, he made his way back to Mrs. Crookshank. A green Datsun pickup, he said. Small. Older. Dirty. Washington plates, something starting with BE, driving erratically.

His former teacher still sprawled on the lawn. She stared up at him. The frame of her glasses had bent and the glasses hung from her left ear.

He knelt beside her and lifted the glasses off gently. "Are you all right?"

"No, I don't know. My back. You're bleeding, Robert."

"I am?"

The phone squawked.

"All over your face."

He touched his forehead and his hand came away red. "No shit."

Jane said, "What's going on?"

"Uh, I'm not sure. Cut my head, I guess."

"That's a four-twenty-two? Shall I send an ambulance? Rob?"

He collected his wits. "Yes, they need to check out Mrs. Crookshank. I had to shove her down and she says her back hurts."

"But you're okay?"

"Jesus, Jane, I don't know. I think so. Send the paramedics and a patrol car. And tell them to find the fucking pickup." He signed off, thrust the phone into his pocket, and sat on the damp grass beside the elderly woman.

"You shouldn't use bad language." Her mouth quivered.

He smiled at her. "I know. I'm sorry."

 *Chapter 12*

HAROLD Brandstetter had had a tight focus—or a narrow mind—so his books were a disappointment to one who had cut her teeth on the Library of Congress Subject Heading Index.

Meg noticed the German-language Bible right away. It was an anomaly among the ranks of military histories, right-wing rants, conspiracy theories, pop biographies of political hacks, and how-to books on wilderness survival and bomb building. The fiction, all paperback, consisted of paranoid thrillers of the Tom Clancy ilk.

Hal had claimed to be a Libertarian, but Meg saw no evidence that he had studied John Stuart Mill or any of the classic theorists of small government. Or even Ayn Rand. Of course, that didn't mean much. He'd probably looked at the more recent proponents. Meg had met a born-again Christian who had never read St. Matthew.

Hal did have an assortment of handbooks that dealt with evaluation and pricing of antiques, including coins, guns, and cars, and one or two university press paperbacks on Indian artifacts. None of the books except the Bible had intrinsic value. Whatever his preoccupations, Harold Brandstetter had not been a book collector. But he had been a gun collector, predictably, with stacks of gun magazines, and he had been interested in the idea of collecting.

Meg flipped through the Bible, no easy task wearing latex gloves, and noted a number of lists and yellowed clippings. Most of them had been stuffed between the opening pages and were worth a closer look. She set the tome with its dark gothic type aside, with a Post-it that said "Important."

When she was satisfied with her book categories, which didn't take long, she began sorting printouts onto the bare surface of the dining room table. She could hear noises from the office and the master bedroom down the hall. Earl Minetti and Jeff Fong were completing the forensic work.

Although Meg had seen Minetti directing the Crime Scene crew in her garage, and he must have seen her, he had introduced himself to her with some formality. He also introduced a slim young Chinese American who wore sweats beneath the protective coverall. Fong had round metal-rimmed glasses. He smiled at her. Minetti was less welcoming but minded his manners.

They had left her almost at once and gone off about their own business. A vacuum cleaner whirred and stopped. Every once in awhile, a cell phone would ring and she would hear a low male voice. Otherwise the house was silent. It smelled of dog and could have done with a good dusting.

Meg took a little tour. The decor was retro without being fashionable, as if the Brandstetters had inherited the furnishings and never changed them. A depressing oil painting of a sherbet pink mountain hung in the living room. The sofa was brown plush with a matching armchair. A huge white leather recliner, not of the period, sat in front of the big-screen television with VCR and DVD players docked beneath it. She saw no evidence of interest in music, no CDs or tapes. The carpet was beige shag *avec* dog hair.

In the dining room, a dim color print of dead birds and a shotgun hung over the sideboard. The table and chairs looked as if they hadn't been used in years. Perhaps they hadn't. The chrome-legged breakfast table in the kitchen showed signs of heavy use. She gathered that the Brandstetters did not entertain.

There were no family pictures in sight, but dozens of photographs showed Hal's truculent red face next to one politician or another. These photo ops had been carefully framed, then hung without much sense of spacing, too low or too high, in the hall, the dining room, and the living room.

The housekeeping was just good enough not to be slatternly. Tammy Brandstetter must have vacuumed and dusted once a month, and at a guess, cleaned out the clutter once a week. She had left no mark of personality on the public rooms of the house. Nothing showed her interests apart from the dog, a large exception in every sense.

Towser was a presence: dog scent, dog hair, a well-chewed raw-hide toy on the living room carpet, scratch marks on the doors, dog dishes in the sink. Meg wondered if Hal had been afraid of Towser, and if so, why he had tolerated the ridgeback. Perhaps Hal had been afraid to be afraid.

She was sorting the printouts by subject matter and website, a no-brainer, so she let her mind wander as her hands worked. If, as seemed probable, Hal had been in on the Lauder Point theft, he had not stolen the artifacts because he found them interesting for their own sake. Neither he nor his wife collected art. But somebody did.

What kind of person collected things? Until she inherited the Brentwood house, Meg had never had the means to acquire a collection, and she doubted that she had the temperament, either. She would not have collected books—too much like work.

She enjoyed reading, and she knew enough to admire a well-designed, well-bound volume, but book collectors' obsession wasn't reading. She had known collectors with mint-crisp first editions who bought cheap paperback versions of their treasures *if* they wanted to read them.

To amass a true book collection you needed reasons other than love of the written word. Some book collectors were motivated by greed. If they were shrewd and knowledgeable, they could make good money on first editions of writers like Stephen King. Others wanted to impress. On her one trip abroad, Meg had visited the Chester Beatty Library in Dublin, a dazzling personal collection of medieval manuscripts. It said a lot about Beatty's taste and expertise as well as his wealth. Impressive.

Some collectors were scholars who wanted to lay their hands on everything ever published about Dutch sailing vessels or Civil War weapons, or whatever. Some were antiquarians with no interest in anything published after a given date. Some were just accumulators. They liked books, and the books piled up, but they never culled them. Meg was fond of accumulators, but she wouldn't have wanted to live with the book dust at home *and* at work. A by-product of decaying glue and paper, it is obnoxious enough to be classified as an allergen.

She was sorting with a will. Halfway through, she came across a bibliography, a thick printout of sources that dealt with the looting of archaeological sites. It focused on the impact of looting on scholarship and on the victimized cultures. One of the articles listed was called "Killing the Past," a crisp summary of the consequences.

Meg had not only visited the Beatty collection in Dublin, on the same trip she had also made a pilgrimage to the British Museum. At that time, the book collection was still housed in the huge museum in Great Russell Street. She had viewed the Lindisfarne Gospel and the Gutenberg Bible with suitable awe. Then, with an hour to kill, she had strolled through the wing housing the Elgin Marbles.

Early in the nineteenth century, Lord Elgin had sailed to Athens, hired local workmen, and crated up all the Periclean sculpture he could find on the Acropolis. He had sailed back to London with his booty, and the swag had later been given to the British Museum. It remained a bone of contention between the British and the Greeks.

True, the works he appropriated had been lying unvalued in the dirt when Elgin removed them. True, air pollution in present-day Athens was so appalling, the acids would probably destroy the art. Equally true, the works were Greek, not English, part of the heritage of Greece, and they belonged in Athens, the city that had offered them as a tribute to the goddess of wisdom. Both sides made other points, but that was the gist of the argument.

A mostly neutral observer, Meg had found the well-conceived display of the Elgin Marbles disorienting. In London, their meaning changed. The sculptures became not a tribute to Athena but the trophies of a nineteenth-century aristocrat. A Scot, as Lord Byron had pointed out in his scathing satire on the subject, not an Englishman. They were, however, displayed in London, not in Edinburgh.

And the moral of the story? Was Lord Elgin a looter? Were the modern equivalents of Lord Elgin, the great museums and galleries, looters, too? They spent unimaginable wealth on pots, masks, temple friezes, rock art. And low-life scum like Hal Brandstetter often brought them the goods.

And what about the archaeologists themselves, the scholars who studied pots and masks and rock drawings *in situ?* It seemed to Meg that, just by looking at the artifacts, they focused the minds of collectors and thieves on what they studied, so they became part of the mentality without wanting to.

Meg browsed through the titles listed in the bibliography on looting. She had a lot of experience with bibliographies, and this one was a winner—well organized, deep, clearly annotated, a pleasure to behold. Apparently, Hal had thought so, too. He had highlighted the articles that dealt with collectors of Native American artifacts.

Meg was getting a headache. She backed off a couple of steps and stared at the heaps of sorted paper. Collectors. What about them? Her Aunt Margaret, the one who left her the house, had collected thimbles. It was hard to imagine anyone killing in the course of thimble-theft.

"Time out for lunch?" Earl Minetti stood in the hall and eyed her work. "I want to lock up."

"Good idea. Do you like chili?"

"Uh, sure."

"I made a big pot overnight. It should be fairly tasty by this time, and the two of you are welcome to join me." Meg was still into therapeutic cookery. "Three of you," she added. "Jake's out in the garage, isn't he?"

Minetti nodded. He looked wary, as if he wondered why she was being so generous.

No such thing as a free lunch? Meg led the way to her kitchen. She would feed them there where it was comfortable. The dining table was heaped with boxes.

Jake made himself at home while the other two had a look at the ground floor of the house and Meg dished up.

"Hey, Meg, you're a cop," he said, grinning.

She smiled back. "Not really. I'm a consulting expert. Sounds more expensive."

He laughed. "Something I can do?"

"Put out the silverware and glasses." She cut bread, glad she'd had the wit to thaw another loaf that morning.

He fumbled in her flatware drawer and came up with the right cutlery.

"How's Todd?"

He made a face. "Torn in two. His mom and Maddie Thomas keep calling him, wanting to know what's happening, and he can't tell them. Not that there's anything to tell. I wish they'd lay off." He plunked down knives and big spoons all around. Who needed forks?

"The young man who was killed—"

"Todd's cousin, Eddy. Todd's sick about that. I guess I would be, too. I hope we stick it to the bastard who killed him." He rummaged in the cupboard, found glasses, and set one at each place.

"You don't think it was Brandstetter?"

He eyed her with the same wariness she had seen in Minetti, and for that matter, in Rob Neill.

"Never mind, Jake. I have my own ideas, but they're just ideas. You guys will sort it out eventually. Why don't you go round up the other two?" She started ladling chili into the big soup bowls she had bought when Lucy started bringing home boyfriends.

The chili passed muster if the silence that fell as the men ate was an indication. Meg thought it tasted okay, though she probably should have chopped another *poblano* into it. It was chili definitely *con carne*. Somewhere she had a nice recipe for vegetarian chili. To a man, the deputies drank milk. Meg was not a great drinker of milk herself and had been nipping at a half gallon since her first shopping expedition. Gone in one fell gulp.

A cell phone rang. Minetti wiped his trim little mustache with a paper napkin and said, "Minetti, yeah. At Ms. McLean's eating lunch. What?"

Meg wagged the ladle at Jeff. "More?"

He held out his bowl. "I haven't tasted chili that good since I left California. The folks up here don't have a clue."

"My God, they did what?"

Everybody looked at Minetti. He had turned pale. "Right away, Jane. Ten-four." He set the phone down. "Somebody in a green pickup just shot Rob Neill."

Men shouted. The ladle clattered in the tureen. Meg couldn't get her breath.

At last she heard Minetti saying, "The ambulance is on its way. Jeff, you keep on with the house. Jake, we need the patrol car. We're looking for an older Datsun pickup with Washington plates. Green, she said."

Jake was on his feet. "He saw the shooter?"

Minetti shoved his chair back and stood, too. "I guess so. Some old lady was talking with Rob when it happened. I think she was hit, too."

Jeff said, "Just a fucking minute, Earl—"

Minetti turned. "No. Somebody has to keep after Brandstetter's killer. You can finish the house. You know what to do. I'll call you when I get better information."

Jeff's mouth set but he nodded. "House key?"

Minetti dug in his jacket pocket and threw the key to Jeff. "We're out of here. Thanks, Meg."

"Yeah," the other two chorused. "Thanks."

Meg got up in a daze and turned the burner off under the pot of chili. Jeff trailed the others, disconsolate.

"Hold on," she blurted. "I'm coming with you."

"But I don't—"

"It's perfectly all right," she said firmly. "I need to finish sorting the printouts and take some notes. You can supervise me." And she walked out on the dirty dishes.

When she returned to the fusty Brandstetter dining room, though, Meg couldn't remember what the piles of paper meant. Her hands shook.

Calm down, she told herself. There's nothing you can do about Rob, so do what you can. You had an idea. She sat on one of the chairs, closed her eyes, and trembled. Jeff was banging around in the master bedroom.

She hoped Rob wasn't badly injured or God forbid dead. It sounded as if he wasn't dead. Yet.

Collectors, that was it. Something about collectors, their peculiar psychology. J. Paul Getty. When he left his enormous fortune to the museum bearing his name, curators around the world shook in their boots. The Getty Museum could outbid them all. The core and genesis of the Getty was the old man's personal collection.

Personal collection, personal obsession. Rob, God willing, should be looking for a compulsive personality, a wealthy compulsive. Somebody with taste and intensity.

That might do as a general observation. What about specifics? The collector wanted not books nor Greek statues but Indian artifacts, probably just from the Gorge. The Lauder Point collection had not been famous. Someone had had to know enough about it to value it. That was too mild. To lust after it, and, once he possessed it, to keep it so well hidden that no word of its whereabouts leaked out.

He. She had used the masculine pronoun. Why not she? Carol Tichnor? Her mother? From what Helmi Wirkkala had said, Charlotte Tichnor fit the profile better than her daughter. Meg began to imagine a scenario in which the lady spun a web of chicanery from Seattle, using as agents her father's neighbors and her own children, especially her daughter, whom she could bully. Charlotte's web.

I'm a pushover for literary allusions, Meg reflected, and with a lurch of nausea, I wish I could bounce that one off Rob's head. She gritted her teeth and forced her mind back into the frame of logic.

Charlotte had been something of a figure in Seattle society. The logical course was to search the archives of the *Seattle Times.* Brandstetter's computer. Meg had jumped to her feet and was halfway to the office before it occurred to her that she shouldn't mess with Hal's computer.

She drifted back and picked up the blank notebook she had brought and not yet used. Time to plod. She ripped off the annoying latex gloves, took out her pen, jotted "Seattle papers/Charlotte," and then began to write up what she had done and why. It took awhile. Listing the website addresses Hal had used was blessedly mind-numbing. Then there was the question of collectors.

"Coffee?"

Meg jumped. "You startled me."

"Sorry," Jeff said. "I can't concentrate. That doesn't seem to be your problem."

She took a good look at his face. "I could do with a latte."

He handed her a cup. "Single, whipped cream."

Meg didn't like whipped cream but she took it. She must have been concentrating if she hadn't heard him leave the house. She had been lost in her thoughts about the psychology of collectors.

They went into the living room. Jeff paced and sipped his through the lid. Meg sat on the sofa and watched him.

"Any word?"

"I think they found the Datsun pickup."

"I meant about Rob."

"No. I called the hospital, which is not a good idea, and they gave me the usual runaround. I should know better. My wife's a physician's assistant."

"Do they have the shooter in custody?"

"No, and Earl is pretty sure the truck was stolen. It was found unlocked in the Safeway parking lot."

"Frustrating."

He plopped onto the armchair. "Yeah."

Meg took a sip of latte and licked whipped cream from her lip. "How long have you worked for the department?"

"Eight months." He shot her a semi-hostile look. "I suppose you're going to ask why a nice Chinese boy like me didn't study medicine."

"Didn't you?"

"No." A reluctant smile curved his mouth. "Though my mother did indicate that she thought I should. Vigorously. For years."

Meg smiled. "It's hard for parents not to interfere. I thought my daughter should be a belly dancer, but she prefers physics."

Jeff sighed. "I'm a refugee from Silicon Valley. Systems analyst. When the bottom dropped out, we moved north to be near my wife's family. Keiko got the job here, so I looked around for something to do."

"Keiko. That's not a Chinese name, is it?"

"Japanese. Another disappointment for my mother. Keiko's father is Nisei, spent some time in the internment camp in Ontario when he was a kid. He runs a big nursery south of Portland."

"Do you have children?"

"A son. He's six and into soccer." His face clouded again. "I was watching him play yesterday when the sheriff called me in."

"Do you like being a policeman?"

"I don't like being yanked away from my family." He cleared his throat. "But I do like working for Rob Neill. Jesus, I hope he's okay."

Meg found herself clearing her throat, too. "I can't say I know Rob very well. So he's a good boss?"

"Yeah. He's evenhanded and smart. Not real sociable, you know, but he can be funnier than hell when he wants to be. The thing is, when he hired me, he didn't ask me whether I was thinking of opening a restaurant."

"What?"

"He didn't make insulting assumptions," Jeff explained. "He looked at the test scores and asked me whether I'd ever fired a gun. I said no, but I was a pretty good wrestler in high school. So he took me to the gym, tossed me over his shoulder a couple of times, and said he thought I'd do. I had to take courses in marksmanship and gun safety, but he let me work part-time while I was training. I needed the money."

The cell phone rang. "Fong," he said. "Yeah. Really? Okay!" He listened for a while, thanked the caller, and signed off. "Rob's all right and so is the lady who was with him."

Meg found she couldn't speak.

Jeff was grinning like a maniac. "He was scheduled to interview Dr. Tichnor at two, and he made it to the appointment. I do not envy the good doctor."

 *Chapter 13*

ROB kept Dr. Tichnor waiting almost half an hour. He hoped the delay, though it wasn't deliberate, would put Tichnor on edge, but Sheriff McCormick's infallible political sense led him to show up before two o'clock and greet the oncologist as he arrived.

Mack and Ethan Tichnor were good buddies by the time Rob got there. Against medical orders, he had showered in the department washroom, and he was wearing crumpled clothes from his locker, including a T-shirt that advised people to visit Powell's City of Books. He'd stuffed what he had on at the time of the shooting into an evidence bag.

Mack had made free of Rob's office and was sitting behind the desk. "Here he is, Ethan. Rob, have you met Dr. Tichnor?" Mack rose and walked around the desk, taking Rob's elbow and practically shoving him into Tichnor's arms.

They shook hands. Rob wondered whether Tichnor had contributed to the sheriff's campaign fund.

The doctor said, "I see you've been in the wars. Did they ice that bruise?" Aside from the twelve stitches in his scalp, Rob had a ripe contusion across his left cheekbone, assorted muscles ached, and his right kneecap was turning black-and-blue.

"I'm okay," he muttered, annoyed and embarrassed. "Did Linda report in, Mack? Ah, there she is."

Linda stood in the doorway. She clutched the recorder and notebook to the bosom of her uniform and stared at Rob with unnerving intensity.

Mack said, "Well now, I'll let you three deal with this sad business. I'll take the press conference alone tonight, Rob. You'd look like hell on TV."

"Thanks." That was a relief. McCormick had been dealing with reporters one by one, but the story was now complex enough to interest the Portland media. Rob thought Mack would turn the opportunity into campaign gold.

The sheriff was shaking Dr. Tichnor's hand. "Good talking to you, Ethan. Let's get together one of these days for a little jazz."

Jazz? Rob watched his boss disengage. As far as he knew, McCormick's interest in music began and ended with Elvis Presley. Apparently Mack had said the right thing, though. Tichnor was smiling when the sheriff finally left.

Rob introduced Linda. "If you'll sit down, sir, we can get started." He motioned to Linda to take up her station.

Tichnor sat in the chair opposite Rob's and tweaked his trousers. He was wearing slacks and a pullover as if they were an exotic costume. Rob suspected a suit and tie were more his speed.

"I hope I can help." A solid, graying man without his brother's easy manners, the doctor had a voice that was light for his size. "I was shocked to hear of Harold Brandstetter's death. I remember him well from our summers here. I was two years ahead of him, and Vance, my brother, was two years younger. Hal was Carol's age."

"I hear he played football."

Tichnor said ruefully, "So did I. Very badly. Vance was the star in our family. And Carol, of course, was a cheerleader. They have the bounce, I have the brains." He offered this mild joke with a tentative smile. "It's a good thing football wasn't emphasized in our school the way it was in Klalo." They had attended an elite private school in Seattle. It surprised Rob to hear they played football at all, instead of, say, polo.

"What did you think of Brandstetter?"

Dr. Tichnor frowned. "He wasn't my sort, Lieutenant. Vance thought he was terrific, but that was probably just childish hero-worship. I think they still fished together once in awhile. You can ask Vance."

"I'll do that. Neither your sister nor Vance mentioned knowing Brandstetter when I talked with them yesterday."

"That's strange. Maybe they hadn't heard about the murder." Tichnor shifted in the chair, twitched the knees of his trousers again. "I thought we were here to talk about the body you found in my grandfather's garage."

Rob was silent for a moment, then took the gamble. "There may be a connection."

"Between that killing and Brandstetter's?" Tichnor's voice choked off. He rubbed the bridge of his nose, cleared his throat. "That's bad news. And your...experience this morning, the shooting in Birch Street?"

Rob waited.

"Perhaps some madman..." Tichnor's voice trailed. He straightened in the chair. "One reads news stories of serial killers, of course."

"I doubt that those were serial killings, Doctor." Rob was feeling his way. Abruptly, he switched tactics. "Where were you between about seven P.M. Friday and seven yesterday morning? For the record, sir."

Tichnor's eyes widened. "I...good heavens, in Vancouver. I live in Vancouver. My wife and I had dinner at Bacchus with friends. We went home before ten and went to bed. I got up around six and did my exercises, swam a few laps in our pool. We have an indoor pool. Marilyn has back problems and swimming helps." He bit his lip. "I fixed myself breakfast and called the hospital. Marilyn woke around eight. We had coffee together."

"Do you share a bedroom?"

Tichnor blushed. "I suppose you have to ask. Yes. We sleep together, and she's a light sleeper."

"Thank you. And again, for the record, where were you the first two weeks of August? Your grandfather's house had just been sold."

"In and out of town." Tichnor began to sound annoyed. "And by town I mean Vancouver. Before that, in June, we stayed here at the Red Hat for two days, while my wife went through the family furniture and china to see if she wanted anything. Mother told us to take what we liked. We had attended my grandfather's funeral, of course. Now he's gone, we never come up here."

"Did you have keys to your grandfather's house?"

"Carol was staying there at the time. She let us in."

"Have you ever had keys to the house or garage?"

"No."

"Do you use a cellular telephone?"

"A cell phone?" Tichnor blinked. "Yes."

"The number?"

He rattled it off without hesitation, still looking bewildered.

Rob stood up. His muscles were more than stiff. He walked to the window of his office and looked out at the parking lot. "I talked with your uncle in Arizona."

"Uncle Pete? Good God, about what?"

Rob turned back and met the man's anxious eyes. "He said he sold you and your brother property on Tyee Lake. I believe your brother is building on his five acres. Mr. Strohmeyer said you bought ten."

"Yes, of course. He wanted us to keep the land in the family. I'm not an outdoorsman, Lieutenant. I always brought a book when Grandpa took us fishing, but I do appreciate the beauty of the countryside."

Rob lowered himself into the chair. "Your uncle said you want to preserve the old-growth timber on your land."

"I certainly intend to."

"Is your brother sympathetic to that idea?"

Tichnor's mouth tightened. "Vance deals in real estate. He'd oppose a clear cut, because it would lower the value of housing in the area."

"But he's building a large structure on the site of your great-grandfather's still?"

"He's building a vulgar palace," Tichnor grated. "He must have taken out half the trees on the property, and his earth movers have churned mud into that pristine trout stream. Pshaw!"

Reference to the still hadn't produced a reaction, but the trees had. Rob found that interesting. "I take it you don't approve of development in that area."

"No, I do not. Have you seen what's going on up there, Lieutenant? Tyee is turning into Lake Tahoe North. Jet skis on the lake! Convenience stores! Time-share condos! It was one of the most tranquil places in the Northwest. It was unique. Now it's interchangeable with half the resorts in the country. Next thing you know they'll put in an outlet mall."

"And your brother will be able to take advantage of the rise in real estate values?"

"The developers ought to be shot, and the county commissioners along with them!" Tichnor sputtered. He took out a white cotton handkerchief and touched his upper lip. "I beg your pardon. That was intemperate. Brandstetter was a commissioner, wasn't he?"

"Yes. I sympathize," Rob said wryly. "I have a cabin up there." There were very few "cabins" left at the lake.

"A cabin?" He sounded surprised, then his eyes narrowed. "The Guthrie cabin? I thought you looked familiar. You're Robert Guthrie's grandson, aren't you?"

Rob nodded.

"You look like your grandfather."

"So I've been told." About five thousand times in the past twelve years. By Mrs. Crookshank, among others. Rob flashed on the elderly woman's wide, frightened eyes as they rode to the hospital in the ambulance. She'd held his hand tight the whole way.

Mrs. Crookshank might have checked out all right medically, but she was going to have nightmares. The shooter's bullets had drilled holes in her front window. He reminded himself to phone her daughter Maxine.

Tichnor's voice took on reminiscent softness. "I liked Mr. Guthrie. He knew I wanted to be a doctor like my father, so he used to talk with me about new pharmaceuticals when I stopped by the soda fountain. He knew all the old drugs, too. He had a great collection of mortars and pestles. And of old remedies. Did he show them to you?"

Rob smiled. "Lydia Pinkham's Tonic? Sure."

"It was mostly alcohol." Tichnor sighed. "A fine man. Tell me he didn't die of cancer."

"Heart attack."

"Good," the oncologist said fiercely. The intensity faded. "I'm sorry."

"Don't be. I have to agree with you." If he had to die then.

"Well, well, Robert Guthrie's grandson. That makes me feel my age. Listen, Robert, about my brother. We've had our differences but we both enjoyed our time in Klalo. This killing in Grandpa's garage, it's a violation of memory."

"And a violation of Edward Redfern's civil rights." Rob heard Linda suck in her breath.

Tichnor tugged at the neck of his sweater. "Was that the victim's name? Who was he?"

"A college student. A member of the Klalo tribe, the Two Falls band. He was studying accounting at PSU. A promising kid. Does that ring a bell?"

"My mother said some tramp had been killed in a brawl and buried in the garage."

Rob didn't dignify Charlotte's theory with a comment.

"This Redfern was an Indian?"

"Klalo," Rob repeated. "A nephew of the principal chief. I think he was being groomed for a position of leadership in the tribal council."

Tichnor seemed puzzled.

Rob looked at Linda. She was scribbling like crazy. Impatience pushed at him. He had played it cautious too long. "We have reason to believe that Edward Redfern was investigating an old theft. Ten years ago thieves made off with a number of Klalo artifacts from Lauder Point County Park. They included three major petroglyphs."

"I remember reading about it in *The Oregonian*."

Rob rotated his left shoulder. "Redfern told friends he was following a lead. We found a fragment from one of the petroglyphs near where the body was buried. The inference is that the rock art was stowed in your great-grandfather's bootleg cache at some point, and that Redfern came across it."

Tichnor had taken out the handkerchief again. Sweat gleamed on his forehead.

Rob rubbed his aching elbow. His knee throbbed in sympathy. "These stolen petroglyphs were not just art, though the law would classify them as stolen art. They were numinous objects."

Tichnor stared at him.

"Objects of religious veneration. What looks like simple theft to the law is sacrilege to the Klalos."

"But that's terrible, terrible." He was almost whispering.

"It's not nice," Rob agreed. "No nicer than desecrating a cathedral."

"And you believe this young man accosted the thieves as they were moving the artifacts?"

"We think the thieves, or the collector who bought the artifacts from them, killed Redfern to prevent him from exposing their activities. The killing appears to have been spur-of-the-moment, though it will be classified as homicide if it was done in the course of a felony."

"And we still have the death penalty."

"We do."

"I oppose the death penalty."

Rob said, "You may be right, sir, but this murderer has to be stopped. Now. If you know anything, anything at all, that would clarify why your grandfather's garage was used, please don't hesitate to tell me."

The telephone rang. Rob lifted the receiver. "Neill."

"Vance Tichnor is here, Rob. Sort of impatient."

"Thanks, Reese. Keep him cool." He hung up, muttering imprecations under his breath. Great timing. "Well, Dr. Tichnor?"

But the oncologist had had a chance to master his feelings. "I'm sorry, Lieutenant. It's a terrible thing. I haven't the faintest idea why this young man's body was buried in the garage. I hope with all my heart that you bring the killers to justice."

That sounded like a farewell address. Rob knew when to fold a hand. He let Tichnor go.

When the door closed behind him, Linda said, "I wanted to ask him some more questions!"

Rob said, "Me, too."

"He knows something."

Rob smiled at her indignation. "We'll have to have another round with him. Meanwhile, let's take a look at his brother. Hey, how's Mickey?"

"Mickey is good." Her mouth quivered. "Rob, I have to say it. If I'd driven you here from the hospital, that madman wouldn't have had a chance to shoot at you."

"I disagree." He held her gaze, unsmiling. "I think he was waiting outside the hospital. When you left without me, he waited a bit, then went hunting."

"Hunting?"

"He drove along the direct route to the courthouse. When I strolled onto Birch Street he spotted me and accelerated. He was improvising." Birch Street led straight to the courthouse. He added drily, "If things had gone the way he wanted them to in the first place, he would have been shooting from a stationary vehicle. We might both be dead."

"Jesus Maria."

"Exactly." He picked up the phone. "Okay, Reese, you can send the great man in. Did the brothers punch each other out in passing?"

Reese chuckled.

As Rob hung up, he glanced at Linda. Her warm brown skin had taken on a gray tinge. "We both had a close call."

"I guess so." She sounded scared. Good.

Vance Tichnor stormed past Sergeant Howell, slammed himself into the chair his brother had vacated, and didn't bother to shake hands. High dudgeon, Rob reflected. That was an expression he'd always wanted to use. He decided to save it for Meg.

"I've had it with you clowns," Vance shouted.

Linda was inserting a fresh tape into the recorder. Rob intoned the usual details of time and place as Tichnor continued to rant.

"...and you kept me waiting forty-five fucking minutes while my mealy-mouthed brother sat in here and poured poison into your ears."

Rob said, "Good afternoon, Mr. Tichnor."

"What the hell happened to your face?"

"I ran into a door. Do you use a cell phone, sir?"

"What the fuck? Yes, of course. I'm a businessman."

"Number?"

"I have two goddamn cell phones."

"I'd like the numbers. I have the ones for your home and office."

Mouth sulky, Tichnor complied. "I don't understand why you're wasting my time like this."

Rob said, "I'm conducting a murder investigation, Mr. Tichnor. It's not necessary for you to understand. All you have to do is co-operate. Or call your lawyer."

Tichnor huffed.

"Tell me about your lodge at Tyee Lake."

"I have a right to build on my own property. I've had title to the land since last spring."

"This is a National Scenic Area. Did you clear your plans with the feds?"

"Tyee Lake is not within their jurisdiction!"

"Just asking," Rob said mildly. "How about with the county?"

"Yes." Tichnor's eyes shifted.

"How far along is the construction?"

"It will be finished by the first of November."

"Fast work. I suppose you'll use your lodge to entertain clients."

"That's right. It's a retreat, a business investment."

"What kind of car do you drive?"

"What?" He gaped, clearly surprised by the change of subject.

"Car. Vehicle."

"I have four 'vehicles.'" Tichnor's lip curled. "Not counting my wife's BMW."

Rob waited.

After a fulminating pause, Tichnor described a new Ford Windstar, a 1964 E-type Jaguar, a Dodge Ram, and a restored 1959 Cadillac DeVille with a continental kit. All four were registered in Oregon. He knew the license numbers.

"Impressive." Rob winced as a muscle in his shoulder went into spasm. He rotated the joint very gingerly.

"I have an image to maintain."

"Where were you from seven Friday evening until seven yesterday morning?"

Tichnor blinked. "At home."

"Address in Lake Oswego?"

"Yes."

"Corroboration?"

"What?"

"Can someone corroborate where you were?"

"My wife attended the opera. I don't like all that caterwauling myself, so I stayed home and watched a DVD."

"Servants? Children?"

"No kids. No live-in servants. What the fuck?"

"Murder, sir. Harold Brandstetter was shot some time Friday night or Saturday morning." Rob wiggled his shoulder and the spasm eased.

"I don't see what that has to do with me. I barely knew Brandstetter."

"That's not what your brother told me." Rob flexed his sore knee. His shoulder twinged.

"Fuck Ethan." Vance took a long, steadying breath, and said in tones of sweet reason, "I knew Hal when we were kids. That's a long time ago."

"And haven't seen him since?"

Tichnor gave him a pitying smile. "Of course I've seen him. We went fishing once in awhile. But Hal wasn't exactly the kind of guy I'd take home to Mother."

Interesting expression. "Farted a lot, did he? Used indelicate language? Drank his beer from the can?"

"He was a rough diamond."

"Cut the shit, Tichnor. You just told me you got planning permission from the county for the casino you're building up on Tyee Lake."

"Casino!"

"I was alluding to the style of architecture. Are you telling me you didn't mention the lodge? Hal was a fucking county commissioner." Tichnor's language was catching.

"Okay, so we talked it over."

Rob waited. The stitches in his scalp were starting to itch and his cheek throbbed.

Tichnor's face underwent a transformation that was interesting to watch. The high–blood pressure color faded. The scowl lines softened.

He gave a hearty salesman's laugh. "Hell, you got me. Yeah, we talked it over. I must have seen Hal four or five times this spring and summer, just talking things over. And I went out for steelhead with him at the end of September. The thing is, my wife didn't like Hal, so we didn't socialize. We weren't friends in that sense. How's Tammy doing, the widow? I ought to send her some flowers."

Rob didn't comment. "What're you driving today?"

"What *is* this?"

"What were you driving between eleven and twelve-thirty?"

"The Windstar."

"Do you own a gun?"

"I have a cabinet of guns, most of them old. I bought some from Hal. He used to deal in secondhand guns. Three years ago, he found a Winchester rifle for me, a real antique, and a German Luger the year before. Last fall I bought a handgun, a .22 with a pearl-handled grip."

"Are they registered?"

"I have a collector's permit in Oregon."

"Do you own a .357 magnum revolver, double action?" Brandstetter had been shot by a weapon of that caliber.

"What...no." He bit off the negative, bristling.

"Would you object to taking a Gunpowder Residue Test?"

"Yes, by God, I would object. I didn't kill Hal."

"So you said." It was interesting that Vance assumed the GRT was for the Brandstetter shooting, not the drive-by.

"Why don't you take a look at the wife?" he went on, heated. "I understand they had marital difficulties. She's unstable."

Rob didn't comment. "Do you know Dennis Wheeler?"

"Who?"

"Neighbor of Hal's, young guy."

"Oh, yeah. He has a set of keys for the house. I told you that."

"Edward Redfern?"

"No." No visible reaction.

"How about William Meek?"

"No, and there are ten thousand other county residents I don't know either, so don't run their names by me." He was turning purple again.

"Where are your keys to your grandfather's garage?"

"Shit, Neill. You asked me that last night. I don't have keys to the garage. I never had keys to the garage."

"Just thought I'd ask," Rob said soothingly. "Linda, do you have questions for Mr. Tichnor?"

"Yes, sir. About county land-use regulations. How many bathrooms are there in that lodge you're building up on Tyee Lake?"

"Six," Tichnor snapped.

"Septic tank or sewer?"

"Septic. There's no sewer line in that area."

"What about access roads?"

"What about them?" He was almost shouting again. "I told you I talked with Brandstetter. That doesn't mean there was anything off-color about my plans. They meet the county's criteria a hundred percent. Hal just sped things up for me."

"Will you reconsider the GRT, sir?"

Silence. Tichnor gave a reluctant nod. "Okay."

"Thank you, sir," Linda said. "The technician will administer the test as you leave. Do you drive a pickup?"

"No. Yes, sometimes. Dodge Ram."

"What color?"

"Red."

She took him through everything again. By the time she finished he was speaking through clenched teeth, but she didn't trip him up. He was a nasty customer, but sharp.

At five Rob decided to let Vance Tichnor go. Linda ducked out to see to the Gunpowder Residue Test.

It was almost time for the departmental meeting Rob had scheduled and he wanted to take a painkiller before it started. He wondered whether he ought to assign Earl Minetti to sit through the press conference in case the sheriff needed help with facts. Not a bad idea. Earl would like a chance to shine on television.

 *Chapter 14*

"OH, it's you." Darcy smoothed her hair and glanced up and down the street. She was standing in her front doorway in answer to Meg's knock. "I thought it was that reporter." She wore fresh lipstick.

"Reporter?" Meg echoed.

"The guy from *The Oregonian.* He wants to interview us." Darcy stepped back. "Come in out of the wind."

Meg entered directly into a room that stretched the width of the Craftsman house with a lounge on the right and a dining area on the left. A pass-through with a handsome plaster arch led from the dining room into a bright kitchen. A narrower arch led back toward the bedrooms.

There was lots of dark wood in the main room, the floor was polished oak with braided rugs, and everything had been done up in decorator-magazine country, wrong for the architectural style. The house smelled as if the Sunday roast was well under way. A computer game with lots of zapping and clanging was just audible from a back room.

"I won't stay," Meg said. "I dropped by to ask for the keys to my house and garage. I believe Dennis has a set."

Darcy looked relieved that Meg wasn't expecting to be regaled with coffee. "Keys. I'll ask him for them. Have a seat." She disappeared through the hall arch.

Meg removed a small metal car from the nearest chair and sat. A tattered copy of *The Poky Little Puppy* on an end table was the only other evidence of a child in the unnaturally tidy room. Darcy's color scheme was mostly ivory with indigo and off-pink patterns, lots of patterns. She favored gingham and spotty wallpaper with stylized tulips. The lace curtains displayed elaborately worked chevrons and stars.

When Darcy reentered, followed by a sullen hunk with an Elvis mouth, Meg was relieved. The decor made her dizzy. The computer continued to zap aliens.

She rose. "You must be Dennis."

"Yeah. Darcy says you want Old Strohmeyer's keys." Elvis ignored her out-thrust hand.

She let it fall. "My keys, actually."

"How the hell did you know about them? *She* never asked me for them."

"She?"

"The old lady. Charlotte Tichnor. Who told you I had a set of keys?"

It was only then that Meg remembered she wasn't supposed to know about Dennis's keys. Rob had told her about them under seal of the confessional.

"Hmmm, now who was it?" She mimed bafflement while her mind raced in circles. "Somebody mentioned those keys just the other day." Yesterday.

"Carol Tichnor, I bet." Darcy smoothed her hair.

Kind of Darcy to rescue me, Meg thought. She gave Dennis a big smile. "Carol took me to dinner at the Red Hat. Wasn't that sweet of her? We talked."

Dumb bitch. Dennis didn't say that aloud, or Meg, who was feeling dumb, might have taken umbrage. Afterwards, it occurred to her that he meant Carol.

He dug in a pocket of his Dockers, came up with a key chain, and thrust it at her. The chain had a plastic Day-Glo tab on the end with a large black *S* in Gothic script, S for Strohmeyer.

Meg counted the keys. "Which of them opens the back door of the garage?"

He touched one that was brighter than the others. "He, Emil, changed that lock a couple of months before he died."

"I see. Thank you."

The doorbell rang. Darcy gave a little jiggle and ran a dampened finger over her eyebrows. Dennis shrugged his massive shoulders.

"See you later," Meg fluted. She slid out the front door past a young man in jeans who was laden with a tape recorder and a digital camera.

"Hey, aren't you...?"

Meg fled. When she reached the sanctuary of her kitchen and looked out the window, she spotted a video crew filming her backyard from the alley. The camera bore the logo of one of the Portland television stations. She drew what curtains she could, threw the keys into her junk drawer, and hunkered down to wait out the siege. She had meant to drive to the grocery store.

Media assault was bound to happen. Two whole days of homicide investigation without journalists thrusting themselves onto the scene constituted some kind of rural miracle. That didn't make the prospect of urban notoriety welcome, however brief it might be.

After she had put her notes into the computer and made printouts, Meg salvaged the leftover chili. Since she'd made a lot, she was able to scrape four portions into microwaveable containers. She stuck them into the freezer beside the leftover shepherd's pie and vegetable soup. They'd come in handy when she started work. *Work.* She wondered whether she ought to call Marybeth Jackman and decided to let sleeping assistants lie. It was Sunday.

Meg didn't feel restful. She was still jangling with relief that Rob Neill had survived what sounded like a drive-by shooting. It was such a Los Angeles event, she almost felt guilty, as if she had brought a plague of violence north with her. And she was having emotional avoidance symptoms. She liked Rob a lot. She hoped that the depth of her distress hadn't made that too obvious to Jeff. Now that she knew Rob was all right, she didn't want to consider why she had been more shaken than she had a right to be.

Margaret the Magnificent was beginning to look a lot like her old impulsive self, so she tried chanting one of the mantras she had selected to combat fecklessness. "'And keep you in the rear of your affection,'" she intoned, "'out of the shot and danger of desire.'" It had to work.

She was glad Lucy didn't call.

She made herself an omelette for dinner and settled in for an evening of unpacking. When she stuck her head out the side door around seven, the camera crew had gone and she didn't see the reporter's car either, so she wandered out for a breath of fresh air.

She bumped into Tom and Towser in front of her garage. Towser consented to have his head scratched and didn't even leap on her. He did grin.

"How's your mom?"

"Fine. Hiding out in her motel room. We had a room service meal." Tom made a face.

"What a shame. Tell her she owes it to your education to feed you dinner in the dining room."

He was a solemn young man but he smiled at that. "Yeah." The smile faded. "You hear about the shooting?"

"I heard that somebody fired shots at Rob."

"He had to have twelve stitches." Tom shivered.

Meg felt a frisson of alarm. Jeff had said Rob was all right. "Is he home? I need to talk to him."

"No, he had some work to do on Dad's computer." Tom gestured down the street. "The sheriff's holding a press conference at the courthouse right about now."

"So that's where the journalists went."

"Rob's hiding. He says they'll get bored after a day or two." Towser woofed. "Okay, boy. Ms. McLean, do you think Mom should have Towser put down?"

"What! Of course not." The dog might be a nuisance, but he didn't deserve the death penalty.

Tom patted Towser's square brown head. "The thing is, she's afraid she won't have enough money to stay in the house, and I can't take him to Portland. No pets in my apartment house. You wouldn't want to adopt him, would you? He likes you." A definite wheedle.

"I...no, absolutely not."

"Rob can't because his schedule's too erratic."

"Mine, too," Meg lied. If anything, her schedule was going to be too predictable. Inspiration struck. "Your father had a valuable gun collection, right?"

"Yeah."

"Sell it and use the money to support Towser in style. Your mother can hire a dog walker for him."

Tommy looked at her, wide-eyed, then laughed aloud. "Yes! That's brilliant, Meg. Dad would hate it."

Meg was feeling sententious. "Things work out, Tom. I know

you don't believe that now, but it's true." And keep you in the rear of your affection. Towser woofed and gave a small bounce of agreement.

When Tom went on his way, Meg returned to her house and started in on the boxes stacked on the dining room table. She had finished clearing that room out, and was flattening cartons with an eye to baling them, when a knock came at the kitchen door. She glanced at her watch. After ten.

It was Rob, shivering in the risen wind.

"Come in. You look like death," she said frankly.

"I've been told that already."

"I like the outfit."

He glanced down at the knee-shot jeans and the T-shirt that peeked out from a mungy gray zippered sweatshirt. "Be grateful it's not covered with gore."

Her throat closed. She cleared it. "Would you like a drink?"

"I would like a complete anesthetic." Wincing, he sat down at the table. "But a finger of Scotch will do. I need to talk to you."

"Me, too, or vice versa, but first things first." She got out the Scotch and poured two moderate dollops. "Tom said you were working on the computer."

"Yes. Thanks for setting the German Bible aside. Hal's passwords were in it."

"Heavens, in code like numerology?"

"A straightforward list tucked between the pedigree of a remote cousin and a reminder to send the garnet earrings to Tante Anna." He rolled a sip of Scotch on his tongue.

"That must have made things easier."

"It did. I got financial data the IRS would be happy to have and some interesting phone numbers. Hal's e-mail was overflowing. He must have corresponded with every paranoid freak in the country. We may even have to interview some of them. And I found out where he went Friday evening."

Meg leaned forward. "Where?"

"Portland Airport. I accessed his credit card records. He tanked up the SUV at an airport station. I called and talked to the attendant. Unfortunately, Hal was alone at the time or I might have a description of the killer."

"Somebody flew in and killed him?"

He swallowed Scotch, frowning. "I don't know. Maybe. It's confusing." He looked at her. "I ought to fire you."

Meg had been expecting that. She took a judicious swallow of her own Scotch. "Sorry. Fire me and I sue the county."

"Meg..."

She met his eyes for a long moment. He looked gaunt and bruised and very tired. "You're feeling guilty about the poor lady you were talking to when the man shot at you, and you want to take it out on me. No way."

He lowered his eyes. "I seem to have made myself a target. I'd rather not do that to anyone else. Mrs. Crookshank was bad enough."

"That's a great name."

"She was my fourth-grade teacher." He traced the rim of his glass. "She's okay and she forgave me, but we must have been quite a sight." He described Mrs. Crookshank's adventure in sufficiently comic terms to provoke a smile, but Meg thought he was forcing the humor.

"So you rolled across the lawn in your fourth-grade teacher's embrace? That's funny, all right, but you must have one hell of a headache." She tapped her skull. On his, a shaven strip showed ugly black stitches.

"It's just sore. I bet you think I was shot."

"You weren't?"

He touched his head. "I ripped my scalp open on one of those underground lawn sprinklers they used to install in the nineteen-fifties. You know, the kind with the round metal cap that sticks up into the lawn and makes the mower clank. Bled all over the place."

Startled, she met his eyes. They both laughed. "Oh, dear, I'm sure your head hurts, but it *is* a little anticlimactic, isn't it?"

"Anticlimactic is good."

"And Mrs. Crookshank is all right?"

He grimaced. "She's grateful. I saved her life, or so she thinks. She told me my father would be proud of me."

"Would he?"

"How would I know?" His brows snapped together. "How the hell would she know? He's been dead since nineteen sixty-eight and she never met him." He took a hasty sip of Scotch. "Sorry. It always burns me when people do that phony channeling act."

"Did she do it to you in the fourth grade?"

He was silent.

Meg swallowed whisky. "How old were you when your father died?"

"Eight. He was killed during the Tet Offensive. February. My mother and I were living here with my grandparents. I don't remember the rest of the third grade. We moved up to the cabin on Tyee Lake when school let out, and my mother started drinking. I guess she didn't know how to be a widow." There was no sarcasm in the last comment, just sadness.

"It must have been terribly hard for her."

"I can see that now. Then I was angry, angry and scared. I didn't know what to do."

Meg shivered.

"By the time I got to the fourth grade, I was a walking ball of fury. I kept picking fights with kids who were bigger than I was, which was practically everybody in my class. I was a trial to Old Lady Crookshank."

"And you dislike her—"

He interrupted. "I don't dislike her, Meg. She tried to be sympathetic and failed. Anybody would have. When I see her, though..."

"It throws you back into that state of mind?"

He sighed. "That's it, and I can't avoid her. She was a friend of my grandmother's."

"I'm sorry," Meg said softly. "Your mother died, too?"

"One of her drinking buddies drove off the River Road in a sleet storm almost exactly a year after Dad died. They were both killed." He shivered and took a gulp of Scotch. "Jesus, I have not had a good day. I ought to go."

"Well, at least you didn't apologize."

"What?"

"Nothing. Tell me about your father. Do you remember him?"

He rubbed his shoulder and took a sip of whisky. "He was a nice guy, funny, a Chicago Irishman with red hair and freckles. The name was originally O'Neill. By the time he volunteered for a tour in the combat zone, he was a staff sergeant. He told my mother it would be safe but boring. He'd spend his time at brigade headquarters in Saigon typing forms in triplicate."

"And it would have been safe enough, I suppose, if headquarters hadn't come under rocket attack?"

He glanced up from his drink. "You know about that? Most people don't."

"I read a little about it. He volunteered? He must have been career military."

"A lifer," he agreed. He rubbed the side of his face, winced, and dropped the hand. "My mother met him in Tacoma when he was stationed at Fort Lewis. Grandma sent her to Pacific Lutheran, which is a good, quiet liberal arts college. I guess Gran was hoping Mom would settle down, but she was a party girl and probably rebelling against all those books."

"It was the beginning of that era of rebellion."

"Not at PLU," he retorted. "They, my grandparents, kept expecting her to do well in school and she never did. She was their only child. She eloped with Dad, and I came along seven or eight months later. He was almost thirty and she was nineteen."

Meg was thinking about her father, who had been in his thirties when she was born. "Did you get along with him?"

"Sure. We enjoyed each other." He took a thoughtful sip. "He could see I was going to be small for my age. I guess he showed up at some first-grade fiesta and spotted that I was the runt. So he started teaching me judo."

"Wow," Meg said feebly. Judo sounded like a recipe for disaster to her. "He taught you to fight?"

"No, he taught me how not to get picked on."

"Oh. I guess that would be a problem for a little boy. I was small, too, and I stayed that way." She smiled at him. "Unlike you. For girls, being small can be an asset, the Gidget syndrome. Did your father teach you when to fight and when not to?"

"He was strong on avoiding fights, used humor to defuse tension. He didn't teach me that. I observed it."

"You admired him, didn't you? I wish I could feel that way about my father. Not that he was Hal Brandstetter. I feel so sorry for Tommy."

"Me, too. I had a great dad and I was damned angry when he died, but I think I would have been all right if my mother had known which way was up. Fortunately, I spent a lot of time with my grandparents that last year of her life. They were terribly grieved when she died, but they made the effort to help me deal with it. We had a bumpy road for a couple of years, though, and fourth grade was the worst."

"If Hazel Guthrie had feet of clay, don't tell me."

"She kept me busy." He rubbed his arm again and rotated the shoulder. "She could be a bit overwhelming, but I didn't rebel against her until high school. Gran was great on board games— Scrabble and things like that. And she fed me science fiction, so I learned to like books. She also gave me my first computer."

"Let me guess. Radio Shack?"

"A TRS80 Model I. Great machine. I made it sit up and bark."

"Was your grandfather into computers, too?"

He gave a reminiscent grin. "Lord, no, he even distrusted electronic calculators."

"What did he use at the drugstore, an abacus?"

"Cash register. The kind with a bell."

"I remember those."

He sipped Scotch, raising the glass in a half salute. "Grandpa was quiet, a birder and a fly fisherman, and he used to take me canoeing on the lake. The best thing he did for me in that period, though, was to enroll me in the karate school. He was no fighter himself, but something had to be done about my temper. He knew I would associate martial arts with my father and work at it. I did, too. I never tried for a black belt, but I liked the discipline right from the first, the calmness, being in the moment."

Meg made a mental note to read up on karate. The fashion these days was for tae kwan do and tai chi, but karate had a long and honorable history. She liked the idea of a small boy being taught to contain his belligerence in a ceremonial and effective way.

For a while they sat silent, thinking separate thoughts, then Rob finished his drink and shoved the chair back. "Thanks. I'd better take myself off before KATU-TV decides we're trysting in the kitchen."

Not a bad idea, trysting. Meg stood up. "Wait. I have a report for you."

"Already?"

"I'm fast and cheap." Lordy, like an airport whore, Meg thought. Keep you in the *rear* of your affection. She ran from the room, returning in better order with a printout of her notes. "Here. I also had a couple of ideas."

He groaned theatrically.

"Oh, shut up. What about Charlotte Tichnor as the collector, the mastermind? She has the profile of an obsessive."

"Kind of long-distance."

"Say she uses her children to do the work."

"It's a thought."

She eyed him suspiciously but his face was grave. "The thing is, Brandstetter wasn't the collector, though he may have been the thief. He wasn't interested in any kind of art, and he had no sympathy for anyone else's culture."

"I agree. A person of taste and refinement, that's the kind of suspect I need. Carol?"

Meg shook her head and repeated Carol's offhand remark about Indian junk. "She was too looped to con me. She's intense enough about needlework, but I don't think she'd kill for an antimacassar. And if she wouldn't kill for needlework, she certainly wouldn't kill for rock art."

"What about her brother?"

"Vance?" She visualized the high-colored face, the confident swagger. "I don't know. He has a glittering surface."

"Maybe surface is all there is."

She frowned. "Maybe. He's one of those people who are always onstage. I had no sense of what he was really thinking or what his interests are other than making money and showing off."

"He collects guns and cars."

Meg made a face. "What's the doctor like?"

Rob described Ethan Tichnor's indignation over the felled trees on his brother's property.

"So he has intensity? Carol said he was boring."

"Boredom is in the mind of the beholder or something. I thought *she* was boring, not that I've seen much of her. She was role-playing, too, when I talked with her here *and* in the official interview."

"She's a born tool, you know. Her mother uses her. I suspect her husband did. Why not the perpetrator?"

Rob yawned. "Ouch. Face hurts when I do that. You said you had ideas, plural."

"Oh. Well, about Edward Redfern. You've been assuming he was onto the thieves, that he tailed Brandstetter here."

"Yes."

"What if he was pursuing the collector instead? What if he thought he was safe and Brandstetter surprised him?"

His eyes widened. After a moment, he said, "You may have something. I need to think about what that would mean." He tapped the printout. "Thanks, again. Good night, Meg. I'll fire you if things heat up again around here, but you do good work." He cocked his head. "And your ideas aren't half-bad either."

She decided to make a clean breast of things. "Uh, speaking of ideas, I sort of goofed. I asked Dennis Wheeler for his set of keys."

He went still, frowning.

She scrabbled in the junk drawer, found the keychain with its Day-Glo tab, and handed it over. "I'm sorry. That was stupid."

"Did you try it? The back door key."

"No."

"Let's see if it works."

It didn't.

Rob took the keys and the printout with him, and Meg went back inside. She almost wished he had reproached her.

 *Chapter 15*

DAVE Meuler did good interviews. Chief Hug had let him come back on duty. Rob decided to borrow him and asked Dave to interview all the residents living on Old Cedar Street and in the three houses behind Brandstetter's, looking for witnesses to the killing. Some of the interviews would duplicate Thayer's hasty survey of Sunday afternoon. It was hard to believe there weren't eyewitnesses to the shooting, but what bothered Rob most, on reflection, was all the noise.

Two shots fired from a .357 must have made a loud report. True, people in the area were used to hearing gunfire in October. It was hunting season. But not in town and not in the small hours of the morning. There had been the sound of the killer's vehicle, too, coming and going, doors closing, voices maybe, and the dog.

Rob couldn't imagine Towser snoozing through a commotion like the shots that had killed his master. The dog didn't yap. His voice was low-pitched, but it could reach a considerable volume. Tammy had been unconscious and Mrs. Iverson was deaf, but the wind surfers should not have been insensible, and they had been at home by that time.

"Shall I start with the Brownings?" Dave flicked lint from his navy blue uniform sleeve.

"Listen, Dave, I'm not trying to horn in, but I'm going to see if I can catch Kayla Graves."

"Hot stuff," Dave said appreciatively. Kayla had quite a reputation.

Rob clucked his tongue. "Come with me. Those kids are more likely to have noticed something than the Brownings."

"Okay. Which of us is the Good Cop?"

Rob had to laugh. "You. I look like a villain."

"Wait till the bruise turns green. You'll look like Algae Man."

The red Mustang was missing. Kayla was on night duty at the nursing home. She usually had breakfast/dinner at Mona's after she came off her shift, but she was due back at any moment, or so Tiffany said.

It was Tiffany's day off. She blinked at them sleepily when they rang, and led them toward the kitchen. She wore boxer shorts and a T-shirt that extolled her favorite sport. Her Lhasa Apso sniffed at the two of them without much curiosity when they stepped into the hall, then stumped off. It was a fat, somnolent creature.

"Um, coffee?" Tiffany offered.

Rob declined. Dave accepted instant colored water and dosed it with sugar and creamer. They sat at a sticky-looking table.

Tiffany punctuated her account of her roommates' whereabouts with yawns. Lisa had breakfasted early and left to receive a shipment of new boards at the shop.

While they set up the recorder and Dave recited the time, date, and persons present, Tiffany drank half her coffee. It seemed to revive her. "It's about Old Brandstetter, right? Somebody did the world a favor." She yawned again. She had perfect teeth.

Dave said, "The killing happened between midnight and five Saturday morning."

She wrinkled her nose. "Bad luck. We partied until eleven on Friday. Kevin and I went to bed then. I don't know about the others for sure, but they probably hung it up around then, too. We were all going out on the river early Saturday. Except Kayla. She doesn't surf after the end of September."

"Who's Kevin?"

"Friend of mine from Portland. Kevin Dykstra." She spelled the name for him. "Want his phone number?"

"Yes."

She screwed up her face, shook her head, and went off. Eventually she returned with her purse and a bathrobe. She shrugged into the robe and began digging in her handbag. "Ha, found it." She brandished an address book and read off a number. "That's his cell phone."

"Have you talked with him since Saturday?"

"No. We're not, like, engaged or anything. He's a grad student, a bit young for me." She dimpled. Rob thought she couldn't be thirty.

"So you had a few beers?" Dave prompted.

"Quite a few," she admitted. "That's probably why I woke up when the dog started barking. Bladder overload."

Dave said, "Did you hear shots?"

She frowned, pensive. "Uh-uh. No shots, not consciously anyway. I heard the dog. He barked for quite a while."

"Did you see anything?"

"My bedroom's in the back. I peeked out the front hall window." She pointed upward. "I didn't see anything and the dog was, like, calming down, so I used the toilet and went back to bed. It was cold in the hall. I went right back to sleep. Kevin didn't move."

Rob said, "Did you hear anything other than the dog?"

"No, sorry." Outside, a car door slammed. She cocked her head. "That's Kayla. Maybe she can do better than me."

Dave took her through some of his questions again while they waited for Kayla, but Tiffany stuck to the same story. No hesitations, no contradictions. She was probably telling everything she knew.

Kayla dragged in, handbag over her shoulder, coat open over a neat rose-pink uniform. She looked her age, which was thirty-one.

Her eyes brightened when she saw she had visitors. "Hey, cops in the kitchen, sounds like a great TV series. How're ya doing, Rob?"

Dave shot Rob a look, and he felt his neck go warm. "Fine, Kayla. Do you know Officer David Meuler? City force. We're looking for witnesses to the Brandstetter killing Friday night." Saturday morning, actually.

She tossed her coat and bag on the counter and sat beside Rob. "Friday. Hmm. My night off. We boogied awhile, didn't we, Tiff? Polished off a case, which is not terrible for six people. I had a couple of beers and too many potato chips. My, uh, date drank maybe six beers. He fell asleep as soon as we crawled into bed." From her tone of voice, Rob gathered that the date would not be crawling into Kayla's bed again any time soon. She gave them a name Rob didn't recognize and a local phone number.

Dave said, "Do you remember hearing anything, say, between two and three?"

"About two-thirty. I probably heard the gunshot without, you know, *hearing* it, but I would have just rolled over and gone back to sleep if the dog hadn't made such a racket."

Good old Towser. Rob said, "Did you go to the window?"

She nodded. "I lay there a few minutes, but when Towser kept barking I got up and went to see what was going on. My room's at the front. I saw a car pulling away, as if it had just backed out of the driveway. He had his lights off. I thought that was weird. He tapped the brake once when he got to the corner, then turned south."

"You said he. Did you see the driver?"

"Nope, could have been anybody, male or female."

"Could you see Hal?"

"No, there are bushes screening part of the deck. I looked for a while but I didn't see anything else. I heard he was shot sitting in one of the deck chairs."

"Yes."

She was silent a moment, eyes dark with weariness. "I almost got dressed and went over, because the dog barked and barked, but I was too tired. Would I have been able to do something for Brandstetter if I had?"

"No," Rob said without hesitation. Among her many positive attributes, Kayla was an excellent nurse.

She gave him a small smile. "Thanks."

Dave pushed the recorder a millimeter closer to her. "You said you saw a car."

She made a face. "Yes, but I'm nearsighted and wasn't wearing my contacts. I think it was more like a van than a car, and sort of gray or light blue, but I have no idea of the make and I couldn't see the license plate numbers. No, wait a minute." She closed her eyes. "The red brake light came on. May have been an Oregon plate or a vanity plate, something like that. I have the impression of letters rather than numbers. Does that help?"

Rob let out the breath he had been holding. "Yes, thanks. It helps a lot."

She looked almost alarmed. "I wouldn't recognize it if I saw it again."

"It's okay, Kayla. You've narrowed the field for us. Is it too much to hope for that you looked at your watch?"

"Bedside clock said two thirty-seven," she replied. "I could see that. It has oversize numbers."

"Outstanding." Dave gave her a huge smile. "Can we go through it again?"

"Okay." She suppressed a yawn. "But make it snappy. I'm winding down now and I need my sleep."

In the rehash, Kayla decided that the van was probably fairly new. The corners were rounded, not boxy. She gave them the name of Lisa's squeeze, a kid from Troutdale. She thought he hadn't spent the night. Other than that she added nothing, but she said the Lhasa Apso had given a couple of yips out of sympathy for Towser. As she climbed back into bed, she had heard Tiffany flush the toilet.

Kayla agreed to sign a statement as soon as Dave printed it up. They thanked her again and left, Dave to pursue the Brownings and the Iversons, Rob to do some departmental paperwork at his office, and afterwards, to look deeper into Hal's computer. The interview had vindicated Rob's opinion of Towser as well as of Kayla.

He was stiff, sore, and irritable after a night of predictable nightmares. The stiffness bothered him. He had thought he was in better shape. Middle age.

He walked to the courthouse, which helped ease the stiffness but not the paranoia. He had to avoid whirling and diving into the bushes whenever a car came up behind him. At his office, the paperwork blotted up an hour. He read the lab report on Eddy Redfern's clothes and on the soils taken from Meg's garage. There were some puzzles, minor, he thought. It would be awhile before results came through on the Brandstetter house.

Reality intruded in the form of pending cases. He made reassignments. Earl would be testifying in court on Tuesday. Linda and Jeff were looking at Hal's tax and financial records in official sources, but one of them was going to have to drop out and work on an ongoing problem of trespass in the north county near Tyee Lake. Rob wished he could go out to the lake himself. He needed to put the cabin in order for the winter.

His mind drifted to Meg's insight into Eddy Redfern. Maybe Redfern *had* found the collector. Rob played around with that, then gave some thought to Dennis Wheeler's keys. Meg looked charming when she felt guilty. That must have saved her bacon more than once when she was a child.

He walked back, less stiff and less jumpy. Outside his house, he bumped into a lurking *Seattle Post-Intelligencer* reporter and said innocuous things. The video crew had gone home. At the Brandstetter house, he looked at the phone numbers garnered from all the interviews, the ones from Hal's cell phone, and the computer records of Hal's telephone charges. There were three matches: Dennis Wheeler, Vance Tichnor, and Charlotte Tichnor. Rob damped down the stir of excitement. There could be innocent explanations, but the matches were interesting.

The cell phone had kept a record of the last five calls, the earliest to a number in Portland listed to some woman. That number also recurred on the billing list. The next to last was a Spokane number. One of the flights into PDX Friday evening originated in Missoula with an hour's layover in Spokane on the way to Portland.

Hal had called a Montana number seven times in the previous four months, but that number was also registered to a woman. Rob e-mailed the Kalispell Police Department for the name of William Meek's girlfriend, the one who had dropped assault charges.

Earl came by at one with sandwiches and big news.

"We got a match?" The fingerprints from Montana. Rob took a large bite of pastrami on rye. They were sitting at the Brandstetter kitchen table. "William Meek?"

"Yeah, two matches," Earl crowed. "The lab says Meek rode in the SUV. Good prints, so they're recent. *And* the sucker drove the Datsun pickup."

"No lie?" Rob chewed.

Earl was too full of enthusiasm to eat. "You know the GRT showed positive for the truck. Now we have prints. We've got him, Rob. I have to say I thought he was a long shot. You were right." That was generous-minded.

Rob thanked him gravely. "Maddie Thomas did the legwork, or her kids did." He thought of Eddy Redfern without joy. There was no evidence that Meek had killed Eddy.

"Time for a warrant?" Earl looked eager and hopeful.

He meant an arrest order.

"For the drive-by shooting anyway. That'll give us enough to hold him."

"I'll get right on it."

Rob smiled. "Eat your sandwich."

Earl was in a blissful frame of mind. He had answered two questions on camera at the sheriff's press conference. He pontificated about that between bites. Rob let him. Then they sifted the evidence in both cases again, looking for patterns they could use in a case against Meek.

As far as Rob was concerned, arrows still pointed to the Tichnors, Dr. Ethan excepted, and even he was concealing something. And it was time for another look at Dennis Wheeler, too. But Meek was a bird in the hand. Almost in the hand. Maybe he'd gone back to Kalispell.

While Earl set the warrant request in motion and stepped up the search for Meek, Rob made phone calls. Carol Tichnor was still registered at the Red Hat. Vance had stayed one night and checked out. Rob called Vance's home and left a message for Mrs. Tichnor to call him. She had disliked Hal Brandstetter, clearly a woman of discernment. Rob retrieved the name of the woman Hal had called repeatedly, too, but it didn't mean anything to him. He sent in a query to Multnomah and Clackamas counties.

He also tried Seattle. Apparently, Charlotte was still in British Columbia, but the lodge at Harrison Hot Springs reported that she had checked out. A name came through from Kalispell; Rob left a message for Meek's girlfriend, Monica Peltz, to call him as soon as possible.

Earl was due at the autopsy in Vancouver. That left Rob to wind up forensic examination of the Brandstetter house. He had Jeff crate up the papers and electronic copies of the computer records. The discs and papers went to the courthouse, to the evidence room. Meg's handiwork, the print sources, he transferred to Hal's desk, neat stacks neatly labeled.

The garage was a disappointment. Rob had thought they might find something in there to indicate Brandstetter's role in the Lauder Point case, but nothing conclusive showed up. The trail was too cold. He checked the gun collection one last time, while Jake had the SUV hauled to the compound for a closer look. Neither in the garage nor in the house was there physical evidence, other than the wallet, of Brandstetter's role in the murder of Edward Redfern. None of Hal's keys fit the locks on Meg's garage, either.

Some time that afternoon, Tom had taken Towser out for a long run and returned him to the fenced yard. Rob paid a visit. The big ridgeback snuffled his hand affectionately and fetched a stick with galumphing enthusiasm when Rob threw it for him. Rob was scratching the right place on his head and telling him he was a fine, public-spirited hound when Meg showed up at the fence, looking good.

"Hi," she said. "How goes the battle?"

He told her about William Meek and was startled to discover he hadn't told her of the man earlier. He explained the upcoming arrest. She extended congratulations, but Rob thought she was disappointed he wasn't going to arrest Charlotte Tichnor. Towser snuffled. Rob scratched.

"You're all duded up," he observed.

Meg blushed. "I thought the press would be out in force, and I wasn't going to be caught in my grubbies two days running. I'm just headed to the grocery store. Can I get something for you?"

He considered. "A couple of steaks and some salad greens? I'll cook dinner for you."

"You don't have to."

"My turn. You can critique my renovation of Hazel Guthrie's kitchen. The rest of the place is a mess."

"Tom—"

"Tom and his mother are moving home tonight. She's over at her sister's right now waiting."

"Okay, well, great."

"You don't like steak?"

"Sure I do. What kind?"

"New York cut. I like mine on the small side but don't let that cramp your style." He dug out his wallet and handed her two twenties. "I have wine. And chanterelles. The mushrooms were great this year. Get something for dessert, too." He didn't have much of a sweet tooth so he left that vague.

She beamed like the rising sun. "Chanterelles. Wow."

"It's chanterelle country."

"Are you sure you have time for this?"

"Well, shit, I need to celebrate, right?" He also needed to call McCormick with the joyful news. And McCormick ought to call Chief Thomas.

Meg was looking at him with a doubtful expression. Smart lady. Rob had doubts, too.

"I'm tired of eating Cheerios. I'll make time." He checked his watch. "Around seven?" It was five. Tammy was expecting to have access to the house at six.

Meg jogged off and Rob went back to the garage.

At six-ten, as Rob was turning the house keys over to Tammy and her son, Dispatch called with a complaint from the campground on River Road.

River Road didn't run along the Columbia, despite the name. It followed the course of Beaver Creek from Tyee Lake to the Kapuya, a minor tributary of the Columbia. The campground was private and new. It catered to tourists in the summer and hunters in the fall. So far the manager had run a trouble-free establishment, and that was a good thing. So Rob told the dispatcher to send Jake and Todd to investigate. Then he went home, changed into jeans and a pullover, not quite grubby, and started thawing stuff. When Meg appeared with the steaks and salad makings, he had even cleared and set the kitchen table. Hazel's dining room was covered with drop cloths.

He set the steaks to warm up in a marinade and took Meg on a tour of the house. He thought she liked it and was glad she could see past the drop cloths and stepladders and half-peeled wallpaper. The *pièce de résistance* was the turret room. Like many fancy Victorian houses of its era, the old place had a turret. It was the one room besides the kitchen that he had finished fixing up.

"It was my room when I was a kid. Now it's Willow's. She picked out the furniture in August."

"It's great, like something out of an English novel."

He smiled. "It is now. When I had it, it was something out of a spaceship." He led her back downstairs. "She's going to spend Christmas vacation with me this year, so I wanted to have it done for her."

"I guess I ought to fix a room for Lucy, though I'm not sure she'll come north. She says she has a job lined up."

"Jobs are good."

"Yes, but I'll miss her."

"You can take Willow shopping if you like," he said generously.

She laughed. "Such a deal."

Steak, chanterelles (thawed and sautéed in butter and white wine), green beans with a touch of garlic, twice-baked potatoes (thawed and heated), and a salad of the mixed greens Meg had selected. Not an exercise in gourmet cookery but a good meal. He enjoyed it and liked Meg's enjoyment. His ex-wife had always picked at her food.

"This is only the second time I've eaten chanterelle mushrooms." Meg speared a last morsel. "They're so expensive in LA."

"Not cheap here either. I have mushroom-picking friends. Chanterelles are a bitch to clean but they're worth it. More wine?"

"Half a glass. Thanks. Are you sure this Meek person is the murderer?"

He poured. "I'm sure he attempted murder. Mrs. Crookshank will be pleased."

"And the sheriff will be pleased?"

"You got it." His cell phone rang.

"Don't mind me," Meg said generously.

He stood up and went out into the hall. He could have talked in front of Meg but it didn't seem hospitable.

"Yeah, Neill."

Teresa Morales said, "Jake says they have an apparent suicide at the campground."

"Okay. Does he need the Crime Scene crew?"

She cleared her throat. "The thing is, he says the victim may be your wanted man."

"William Meek?"

"He's not sure, Rob."

"Head shot?"

"Yes."

The steak churned in Rob's stomach. "Tell him to secure the site and wait. I'm coming out. Call Earl. Better send Linda, too."

"She's on days."

"Shit. Jeff?"

"Yes, he's on call. He won't be happy."

"Neither am I," Rob said and signed off.

 *Chapter 16*

MEG did the dishes. She left Rob's change on the counter and took the dessert home. An ice cream torte it was, with lots of dark chocolate curls. She stuck it in the freezer alongside the leftover chili. Then she took a bath, went to bed early, and thought serious thoughts, mostly about Rob.

Lust was all very well, expressed or suppressed, and chanterelles had their charm, but a real attachment was something else. She wasn't ready for it. She didn't want complications. "And I like my own house," she told herself, hugging the duvet.

Not that she disliked the gingerbread house, a grand house on a grand scale. A Beverly Hills designer of opulent spaces would have found the kitchen disappointing, but Meg liked it. A pantry slid out from the cabinet by the refrigerator.

She nuzzled the pillow and her mind drifted. The stove and water heater were gas-powered like hers. Why? Should be electric. The town sat practically atop Bonneville Dam. Ah, power outages. Not a good thought.

The kitchen. Meg's eye for color was not exact, and she was apt to be suckered by trends, so she'd been stuck with a lot of hunter green in her own decorating adventures. The most striking thing about the kitchen, apart from the fact that it was obviously Rob's and not Hazel's, was the color palette, like something from a landscape of Provence. It should have looked incongruous in the Pacific Northwest, but didn't. It just looked cheerful. Rob didn't strike her as a cheerful personality. Small puzzle.

After awhile Meg fell asleep and didn't dream, or if she did the images faded away.

*

THAT afternoon, Rob had seen to it that the sheriff called Madeline Thomas with the news of William Meek's impending arrest, so his first thought when the dispatch call came was to have Mack phone the chief with word of Meek's probable death. Rob and the sheriff talked it over as Rob drove, one-handed, along the winding River Road. It was supposed to rain again before morning.

According to McCormick, Chief Thomas had taken the prospective arrest in without comment. Saving her big guns. The suicide dimmed Mack's elation to quiet satisfaction. He considered the two cases closed.

They were not closed. The loot was still missing. And there were other loose ends. Rob pointed them out and signed off. He didn't like to drive and talk on the phone.

When he turned his pickup into the campground, he could see the revolving light of the patrol car, straight ahead and some distance away toward the river side of the camp. But a knot of people had gathered at the office to the right, a blockhouse he thought also contained the showers and restrooms usual in a well-designed setup. Since it was the beginning of the week, fewer campers and RVs dotted the grounds than would have been the case on Friday or Saturday. Apart from the patrol car, no other vehicle was close to what he took to be Meek's campsite.

Jake, in uniform, strode from the clump of men with his hand held up. When he recognized the pickup, he let his hand fall and stepped aside, waiting. "Hi, Rob. You made good time."

"Jeff not here yet?" Rob's muscles protested as he twisted to get out of the pickup. He grimaced and wriggled his shoulders.

"No. His wife's on duty at the hospital. He'll come when the sitter gets there."

Rob looked around. "Who are all these people?"

"Campers. Hunters, mostly. I figured you'd want to talk to them."

"And to the manager. When did it happen?"

"God knows. A while ago. Listen, about Todd—"

"Something wrong with him?"

Jake drew a long breath. He didn't look wonderful himself, and Rob was reminded of how young *he* was. "He's hiding out in the car. Won't talk."

"Won't or can't?"

Jake shrugged. "He found the body. It's pretty ugly."

"Are you sure it's Meek?"

"Driver's license in his wallet. Right build."

"Okay, good man. Take Todd a Coke or something while I have a word with the manager. What's his name?"

"Chuck Bellew. I went to high school with him. Lives here with his girlfriend and her kid. Hey, there's Jeff's car." A small gray Toyota pulled in beside Rob's pickup.

"That's a relief. I'll need somebody to baby-sit the hordes here while you tend to Todd."

"I could help Jeff with the witnesses."

Rob met Jake's troubled eyes. "I think it's more important to give your partner a little support. He's a rookie. You've been around for a while."

Jake nodded, eyes downcast.

Rob touched his arm. "Is there a Coke machine?"

"Yeah. By the shower room."

"Okay. Pump some sugar into Todd and have a talk. I'll send Jeff for the two of you when it's time to question these people. Earl and Thayer should get here with the Crime Scene van pretty soon."

"The van's on its way."

Rob nodded and headed toward the blockhouse. A heavy young man in sweats came out of the manager's office to meet him.

Rob introduced himself and shook hands.

"Look, Mr. Neill, er, Lieutenant, can't these people go back to their campers?"

"I'd like to speak to them first, Mr. Bellew. And I need to talk to you at some length."

"Me?" His eyes widened. "I don't...didn't even know the guy."

Rob raised his hand. "In a minute, Bellew. Jeff?"

Jeff Fong came to his elbow. "You called?"

"Sorry to drag you out tonight. We need to take names and addresses here. Got your notebook?" He meant the notebook computer.

Jeff nodded. "In my car."

"Good." Rob drew a breath and used his Shakespearean-actor voice. "People, listen up."

The murmur of discontented hunters gradually stilled.

Rob looked them over in silence. Eleven, all men, most in their late twenties or early thirties, two older men who looked as if they had been hunting since Lewis and Clark. As the silence extended, they began to shuffle their feet and murmur.

Rob told them his name and introduced Jeff. "You probably know there's been an accident here, a shooting. You're all potential witnesses, so I'll need your names and permanent addresses. Deputy Fong will take that information down now." He turned to Bellew. "Got a desk or a table and a couple of chairs we can use?"

Bellew jerked his head. "In the office."

"Okay, thanks." Rob raised his voice again. "When you've given the deputy your name in the office here, you can go back to your poker games...."

The tension eased into chuckles.

"But don't leave the campground until one of the deputies has taken a statement from you, okay? And go easy on the beer. Thanks. Jeff?"

He stuck around until Jeff had herded them into a line outside the office. They would see him one by one, and they jostled a bit lining up, but the jostling was good-natured. When it was clear they were going to cooperate, Rob turned back to Bellew. "Where can we talk privately?"

Bellew jabbed the air with his finger. "I live in that trailer." A new single-wide sat across from the office. "Wendy's putting the kid to bed. Kitchen table okay?"

"Fine."

"I can't be gone long. The office is supposed to be manned until ten." It was nine-fifteen.

"Jeff won't take much time."

"Okay," Bellew grumbled, "but I got one reserved spot left. Guy's supposed to show up any minute." He led the way to his house.

The mobile home was cluttered with the toys of a preschooler but smelled clean. Noises from the bedroom end of things indicated that a child was taking a bath. The design of the place was small-scale but efficient. Everything seemed to be within arm's reach. Rob put his tape recorder on the kitchen table and sat down. Bellew sat opposite him, looking resigned.

"Deputy Sorenson probably told you—"

"Guy blew his brains out," Bellew interrupted. "Ate his gun."

Or appeared to. Rob nodded and intoned the usual information as he turned the recorder on. Bellew gave his name and address, then said, "I think I heard the gunshot."

"You don't know?"

"It's hunting season, man. Things go boom."

"When?"

"Late last night, around midnight. I was watching TV with Wendy. I got up to go see about it, honest, but she thought it was just a backfire or a liquored-up hunter off across the river. Sound carries funny on the river. Nobody called or nothing."

"Okay. Did you hear a car leave?"

"No. Had the DVD on. We watched *Terminator II* again."

"Right. So when did you investigate and why?"

"I make the rounds. I walked around the trailer, must have been six o'clock this afternoon, and saw that the window on the far side was smashed. Nobody answered my knock, so I went back to the office and called 911."

"Ten after six."

"Yeah. The dispatcher said the guys would be out as soon as they dealt with a wreck on County Road Eight in Two Falls. I had dinner, left Wendy at the desk, and walked back over to the trailer, must've been seven-thirty. The more I thought about the window the more it bothered me. It looked like it was smashed *out*."

Rob waited, silent, watching the round, good-natured face. The child in the bath gave a happy shriek amid sounds of splashing.

Bellew rubbed his nose. "I tried the door. It stuck, see, and I thought it was locked. I jiggled it and got it open and looked in. Well, fuck me, the guy was dead. I could see that as soon as I stuck my head in the door. I backed out and ran for the office." His face creased and he gave a sheepish grin. "After I tossed my cookies."

"So you called it in again?"

"Yeah, she, the lady on the phone line told me Jake Sorenson and Deputy Welch were on their way. I know Jake. They got here about eight-fifteen."

"Must've been some wreck in Two Falls."

Bellew shrugged. "Jake said it was a mess. DUI with an under-age driver in his dad's truck. No injuries but they had to wait for the kid's old man to show up. Kid totaled the truck. Lots of paper-work, I guess."

Rob made a face. "I guess. So, when they got here, Jake and Deputy Welch inspected the site and called for assistance?"

"Yeah, Jake said Welch threw up, too. I didn't go back there with them. I got a delicate stomach."

"Okay. I appreciate your frankness, Mr. Bellew. When did the victim check in?"

"I dunno. The trailer belongs to Akers Construction. Somebody must have lent him the key. I noticed the car Saturday morning and went over to give the guy the once-over. He didn't appreciate me waking him up."

"You had words?"

"Nothing serious. Little guy about five-five. Banty rooster, my mom would say. He come over and registered at the desk."

"What name did he give?"

"William Meek. Showed me his I.D. Montana driver's license. Said Old Man Akers let him use the trailer whenever he was in town. Maybe so. Akers didn't move the trailer down from Tyee Lake until September, and *I'd* never seen Meek before. His car had Oregon plates. He said it was a rental."

"So Meek was here over the weekend. Did he say why he was in town?"

"Hunting. I didn't see a gun, rifle, I mean." He grimaced. "I saw the handgun all right. Hey, there's my customer. Gotta go sign the man in."

Rob logged out and turned the recorder off. The vehicle outside turned out to be the Crime Scene van with Thayer Jones at the wheel.

Earl got out of the passenger side as Rob and Bellew approached. He didn't looked pleased. "Doc's on the way."

"That's good. This could be difficult."

"Suicide, huh?"

"Could be, or could be murder rigged to look like suicide. We need to be careful."

Earl bristled. "Aren't we always?"

"Just a heads-up, Earl," Rob murmured. "Want to bet it's not the gun that killed Brandstetter?"

"Ten bucks the other way."

"No takers," Jeff said at his elbow. "I got the population sorted, Rob, and had them tell me which campsite they're at."

"Good idea. Jake can help you with the interviews. Let me know when the ME gets here. He's going to be sarcastic as hell, three trips up the Gorge in five days."

"Hey, he gets paid for it."

The ME was a special consultant paid by the job. He made more on one call than the deputies on salary made in a week, so Jeff's sourness was probably justified. On the other hand the rate of questionable deaths in Latouche County was not high. The previous year there had been only two homicides.

"I need to finish with you, Mr. Bellew," Rob called as the manager headed to his office.

"It'll have to be in there." Bellew jerked his thumb toward the blockhouse and ducked into the office.

Earl and Thayer gave Jeff a lift to Meek's campsite in the van. They would do some preliminary work on the scene while they waited for the medical examiner.

Rob followed Bellew into the over-bright office with his mind on Todd Welch. He started the tape again but had trouble picking up the thread of the interview. "So Meek checked in with you Saturday morning?"

Bellew nodded. "Yeah, around nine."

"The car doesn't look like a rental." Rob was sitting by the manager's desk behind the check-in counter.

"Could be Rent-a-Wreck," Bellew offered, leaning back with the creak in his big office chair.

"True. We'll check the registration. You said you didn't know him."

"Saw him once. Alive, that is. Didn't talk to him after that."

"But you saw him come and go?"

"I don't clock the folks in and out, Lieutenant. I think he was gone most of Saturday and Sunday. Didn't see him alive on Monday either. I noticed the car was in place Sunday evening when I was checking a couple of guys in. That'd be around seven-thirty."

Rob probed the matter of timing until Bellew started to get testy, then decided to drop it. With luck one of the campers would have noticed Meek's movements. The hunter who had reserved a place showed up, so Rob closed the interview and went out to see to his crew. And to check up on Todd.

The ME was still forty-five minutes down the road. At least he had called in. Thayer was doing things with a vacuum cleaner and Earl had the camera out, so Rob stayed out of their hair after he'd taken a quick look at the corpse. Earl said Jeff and Jake had gone off to start interviewing the poker players. Nobody mentioned Todd.

Rob went over to the patrol car. His stomach was churning, and not from the sight of the dead man. Meek looked the way anyone would in the circumstances, blood and brains everywhere. Rob doubted that the ME would be able to say whether the man had killed himself or been killed.

Todd was sitting in the passenger seat with the engine off. The windows had steamed up.

Rob got in on the driver's side. He didn't look at Todd. "Tell me about it."

No reply. Rob waited.

Todd rubbed his nose on his sleeve. "You seen him?"

"Meek? Yes."

Another silence. "I vomited."

Rob let that pass without comment.

Todd covered his face with both hands, pulling them down slowly. "Shit, I give up. I quit."

"Okay, but I still want to hear about it."

"Didn't you hear me, asshole? I resign!" His fist pounded the dash. "I don't want to be a fucking cop anymore."

Rob shot a glance sideways.

Tears were streaming down Todd's face. He wiped them away with his hand. "I apologize, sir. I shouldn't be calling you names. I'm just so goddamn *mad* I don't know what I'm saying." He grabbed a tissue from the box on the dash and blew his nose.

He was such a nice kid, Rob thought sadly. Imagine apologizing.

"I wanted to kill the sucker and there he was dead. It's not fair. He killed Eddy, my little cousin Eddy that I taught to shoot baskets. I wanted to see the bastard suffer, only somebody beat me to it. And that's not right."

Rob drew a long breath that was mostly relief. Todd's paralysis began to make sense. At least he was talking. "What's not right?"

"Feeling like that. Wanting to kill. I'm supposed to be a professional."

Rob let him talk. He rambled. He was angry and sick, frightened, disappointed in himself, and full of unmerited shame. It was an old, old tale, but it needed to be told.

When Todd wound down, Rob said, in as matter-of-fact a tone as he could master, "You need to take some leave, Todd, but quitting seems extreme. You're a good deputy."

"Shit!"

"Think you're the first cop who wanted to kill a suspect? Be real. You wanted to kill Meek, but you didn't."

"No, but—"

"You said somebody beat you to it. Nope. Clear case of suicide." He watched Todd.

Todd's eyes narrowed, his fists clenched. "No! No, I'm sorry, I don't buy it. Somebody shot him, like somebody shot Hal Brandstetter."

"The sheriff thinks it's suicide."

"Convenient." Sarcasm rang heavy in Todd's voice. "I suppose Meek killed Eddy and Brandstetter and tried to kill you, then got a conscience. Give me a break."

"I find it hard to swallow myself. We'll see what the ME says."

"Well, ask him how that window got smashed. I suppose Meek shot it out and then whirled around, sat down, and bit the barrel? That doesn't make any kind of sense."

Rob chuckled.

"What the fuck?"

"Listen to yourself. You were in that trailer maybe sixty seconds, but you were observing, and now you're trying to make sense of the evidence." He met Todd's indignant glare and smiled.

After a solemn moment, the deputy's mouth eased in a sheepish grin. "Okay, okay. I may have nonprofessional instincts, but I didn't say I was dumb."

Rob dug in his pocket and came up with the keys to his pickup. "My truck's parked by the blockhouse. Drive yourself home and do whatever you do to unwind. I'll see you tomorrow morning."

"But Jake—"

"He'll understand. I'm going to keep him busy here most of the night anyway. You all right?"

Todd took a long, shuddering breath. "Probably not, but I'm better than I was."

"And call your aunt."

"Really?"

"Yes. She'll expect you to call. The sheriff's already talked to her."

Todd opened the door.

"And Todd."

"Yeah?"

"Go easy on the theorizing. At least with civilians."

"Okay. Thanks." He trotted off, resilient as a puppy.

Rob felt a hundred years old. The window might have been hit by a fragment of bullet or bone flying out from the suicide shot. Todd's "theory" would take some proving.

 *Chapter 17*

MARGARET McLean, please," said the caller, as if Meg had a personal secretary at home. Meg didn't know whether to be flattered or annoyed. The voice was crisp, female, and elderly.

"Speaking."

"Ah, Mrs. McLean, this is Charlotte Tichnor. My daughter gave me your number."

"How do you do?" Meg's heartbeat accelerated. She didn't bother to correct Charlotte's error.

"I must apologize, first of all, for not telling you of the compartment in the garage. I suppose every family has its skeletons."

But few have resident corpses. Meg said nothing. Her mind was working fast for nine o'clock in the morning. She had been playing solitaire with her computer. She backed out of the game.

Charlotte sighed. "However, that is water under the bridge. Do you have any idea where Carol is? She has not telephoned me in several days."

What can I say to this woman that won't spook her? "She was staying at the Red Hat Motel. I ate dinner with her." Lord, when was it? After Brandstetter's death. Events had been happening so fast, Meg had lost track of time. "Saturday evening."

"I keep leaving messages," Charlotte said plaintively, "but she doesn't call."

"Perhaps I could go over there this morning."

"Would you? That's very kind."

"No problem." Meg picked up her coffee cup left-handed and made for the kitchen. "Ah, I've been meaning to write you a note, Mrs. Tichnor. I believe you've been a strong supporter of the library for many years."

Charlotte made a polite, deprecatory noise.

"I wanted to thank you for your generous help, and to float an idea past you. From time to time, we set up special exhibits to draw people into the library and give them a taste of culture." Ew. Meg poured herself a cup of thick black coffee.

"Yes?"

"I was wondering whether you would lend us specimens from one of your fine collections." The *Seattle Times* archives had been informative. "The netsuke, perhaps. Not the whole collection, of course. A sampling."

Charlotte gave a gentle, patronizing laugh. "Oh, my dear, I'm afraid not. I never let the netsuke out of my sight—in a manner of speaking, of course. They're kept in a room constructed to display them to advantage and to provide maximum security. They're very valuable. And I only show them to close friends." Not quite true. She had showed them to the Japanese consul. Hence the news story Meg had dug from the archives.

"Mmmm." Meg tried to sound sad but understanding.

"I'm afraid the facilities at your little library would be inadequate. My insurance—"

Not so little. Meg gave a mournful sigh. "Perhaps not the netsuke then. What a shame. Does collecting run in the family, Mrs. Tichnor? I know your son, Dr. Ethan, is also a very kind patron of the library."

"Ethan?" Charlotte's laugh tinkled like sleigh bells. "The only thing Ethan and Marilyn collect is music. Jazz," she added with evident disdain. "And classical, of course. Marilyn is fond of Renaissance consorts. You would hardly want to display a cabinet of discs."

Oh, why not, Meg thought, flashing on ancient wind-up phonographs and wax records. Or a jukebox full of 45s. "I know that Carol is an expert on needlework."

"White-on-white embroidery." Apparently Carol's obsession met with her mother's approval.

"Does Vance have a special interest also?"

"You've met my son?" Charlotte's voice changed.

"Yes, the evening I dined with Carol. A charming man."

"I thought he was at the Oregon coast," Charlotte interrupted.

"Handsome blond man, fifty-ish, hearty laugh. He told me about the lodge he's building on Lake Tyee."

"Tyee Lake," Charlotte corrected, still sharp. "Yes, he's building a house on the family land." She didn't mention the still.

"I know he collects guns," Meg interposed, "but guns would hardly be suitable for a library exhibit." Talk about a security problem. "Perhaps he collects other things as well. Paintings?" Pots, arrowheads, rock art.

"You'll have to ask Vance. He has many interests. I wouldn't call him a collector, however. Vance is a showman. And he has a short attention span."

"Oh?"

"He acquires half a dozen items—first-rate, of course, enough to impress his friends and clients—then turns to something else." She gave another tinkling laugh. "As a child he collected comic books, if you can imagine it. I soon put an end to *that*. Vulgar things."

"I believe collectors pay quite high prices for early comic books," Meg ventured.

"They may. People also watch mud-wrestling. But not people of taste and discernment."

"No doubt you're right." Meg took a swallow of coffee and made a face.

"Vance changed his major three times at Santa Barbara. He wanted to be an anthropologist, of all things. I must go, my dear. If you find Carol, please tell her to call me at once. I am concerned about this murder."

"Which one?" Meg blurted.

A silence followed. "There's been another?"

Meg explained about Hal Brandstetter. "A neighbor. No doubt you knew him."

"I knew the parents to speak to." Charlotte's voice dripped icicles. "I don't remember the son. Good day, Mrs. McLean." And she hung up.

Interesting, Meg thought. She poured her coffee down the sink and walked outdoors. It was raining. She looked to be sure that Rob's pickup was still missing from the usual parking spot on his driveway, then scuttled back to her warm kitchen.

The least Rob could do was call. She had no idea why he had had to leave so abruptly the evening before, and her curiosity was eating at her. She had his cell phone number, but she hesitated to phone in the middle of what must be a hot investigation. Back to FreeCell. Nine o'clock was *way* too early to call on Carol Tichnor.

Once at the computer, however, she found she was too impatient to play Patience. What she needed was a mental workout. She logged onto the Internet, Google search this time. She went back to the Lauder Point website and verified the nature of the collection. Rock art, spear- and arrowheads, querns, button blankets, pineneedle baskets, a carrying board for an infant, a bentwood box, two elkhide drums, and a lovely knife with an obsidian blade. There was a black-and-white photograph of the knife. The county offered a thousand-dollar reward for information leading to recovery of the stolen goods, not a large reward considering their probable current value.

Okay, she thought. That's what we're searching for. Now let's have another look at Brandstetter's bibliography. She thought of it that way, though it was emphatically not Hal's work. She did a search by subject, and by keywords, one by one, and printed a couple of articles.

Then she did the search again on Google, limiting the time line to recent articles. That was when she found the odd item on pesticides. In the 'Forties and 'Fifties, organic artifacts stored in museums had frequently been dusted with DDT to prevent insect damage. Many of the artifacts had since been repatriated to the appropriate tribes, and authorities were becoming concerned about DDT contamination. They had issued health warnings. Since the article came from the University of Arizona, Meg thought it would be credible, even in a court of law.

She printed it up, and just for good measure, found another item, an advertisement, that touted an easy method to detect contamination by DDT. It was a long shot. If the loot had been stored improperly for ten years, the odds were that the organic artifacts had been damaged and disposed of. All the same, she picked up the phone and called around until she found a Portland outlet that sold the detection kit.

The process sounded simple enough, though chemistry was not Meg's strong point. The shop promised to ship it to her overnight, and her Visa took another hit. Well, she would save the receipt, and the county could reimburse her if anything came of it. She decided to test dirt from the storage compartment. According to the company blurb, the test should not take more than an hour.

Meanwhile, Carol. Meg called the Red Hat. Carol was still in residence but she didn't answer the phone. Meg left a message and changed from sweats to resort clothes. Charlotte was probably right to be concerned. It was odd that Carol had not called her mother with news of Brandstetter's death, especially now that the sheriff's department was linking the two cases publicly.

When she got into the Accord, Meg switched on the radio. It was tuned to the NPR station, which was doing a fund-raiser at boring length, so she fiddled with the dial. The local country station came in loud and clear.

The windshield wipers swished in time to a Bonnie Raitt ballad. So what was she going to say to Carol apart from Call Mama? Though she felt some pity for Carol with such a mother, Meg's dislike had grown in the intervening time. Carol was not an appealing human being, and her interests seemed entirely self-focused. Okay, she was from Seattle. How about them Mariners?

The news came on. A dead man had been found at the River Road Campground. "Sheriff McCormick indicated that the victim, William Meek, an apparent suicide, had been a prime suspect in the murder of Commissioner Harold Brandstetter. A warrant had also been sworn out for his arrest in the drive-by shooting in Klalo on Sunday."

The Accord swerved and Meg clutched the wheel. The language of the news report was hedged with "allegedly" and "probably," but it was clear that Rob's boss believed the Meek suicide was the answer to Latouche County's crime wave, including the murder of Edward Redfern. She wondered whether Rob agreed.

The news story said nothing of the Lauder Point theft, and the announcer went on to a salmon-fishing controversy followed by three commercials in rapid succession. The weather forecast was melancholy. As Meg pulled into the Red Hat parking lot, the D.J. was already leading up to Charley Pride. She switched the engine off and sat for a minute or two, thinking about William Meek's death and its implications with regard to the missing artifacts.

She didn't get very far. The DDT business still interested her. She guessed it would interest Rob, too, even now. The apparent resolution of the Brandstetter murder would take some of the media pressure off the sheriff's department. Maybe Rob would have time off. That was a good thought.

At the desk, Meg asked for Carol Tichnor. No answer from Carol's room. Meg had turned away and was heading toward the exit when Carol walked out of the corridor that led from the restaurant.

Meg hailed her.

Carol stared as if to say who is this woman. "Uh, hello."

"I came to let you know your mother wants you to call her. She telephoned me at home."

Carol's face went still as a mask. After a blank moment, she said, "Thanks. I will. Nice to see you again."

"I hope your brother's well. Your mother thought he was at the coast."

"And you told her otherwise?" Carol bit her lip.

Meg widened her eyes. "I had no idea his presence in Klalo was a secret. Is he staying here, too?"

Carol shrugged. "I haven't seen him since Saturday. See you, Meg." And she whisked off through a door labeled ROOMS 101–129 / POOL / LAUNDRY.

By the time Meg got back to the Accord, her hair was soaked. Dolly Parton was singing about a letter written on a blue piece of paper. Dolly sounded down.

ROB was sitting in his office in the courthouse annex, yawning over paperwork, when Moira Tichnor called him.

She identified herself as Vance Tichnor's wife, and Rob went blank. His hands scrabbled through the papers on the desk surface. He had questions for this woman, but what were they? He'd had two hours of sleep and his head felt like wet pumice.

"Uh, thanks for calling, Mrs. Tichnor."

"My pleasure." She had a sultry voice. "Are you the dishy detective I saw on television the other night?"

Rob's sense of humor stirred to life. "Sorry, no. You're thinking of my sergeant, Earl Minetti. I'll pass the compliment on to him." Take that, Earl.

She gurgled. "By all means. What can I do for you?"

"I had a couple of questions for you in connection with the murder of Edward Redfern."

"That's the Indian boy who was found in the garage? I really don't know anything about it, Lieutenant."

"I'm sure you don't, Mrs. Tichnor." He pulled a scribbled sheet of paper toward him and squinted at it. Bifocal time. "First of all, can you confirm that your husband was at home Friday evening? From seven P.M. Friday until seven Saturday morning."

"Oh, well, I'm sure he was. I went to the opera with a dear friend from Mills. Lovely production. We had a few drinks afterwards at the Benson. It was late when I got home, so I tiptoed in like a good mouse and went straight to bed. Sleepy time. I didn't wake up until ten-thirty or eleven Saturday."

"And you and your husband don't share a bedroom?"

"No. He snores." She sounded amused. "He has his bedroom. I have mine. Our dressing rooms adjoin. I heard his DVD player still going strong when I came in."

"I see." He held the paper to the light. "Do you know a woman by the name of Phyllis Holton?"

Silence. At last she said in a taut voice, "Phyllis is one of Vance's sales staff. A realtor. She's worked for him for years."

Rob digested that.

"May I ask how her name came up?"

Rob took a gamble. "Harold Brandstetter called the number frequently in the last month or so. Commissioner Brandstetter was killed early Saturday morning."

"The bastard!" Mrs. Tichnor no longer sounded sultry. She was one angry woman.

Rob said, cautious, "Are you referring to Hal Brandstetter?"

"That fat idiot? No, you fool, I mean Vance. Brandstetter probably used Phyllis to relay messages to my charming husband. I warned Vance I'd divorce him if he resumed his affair with Phyllis. She was his mistress all through his first marriage, but I don't stand for that kind of treatment. I value my health. God knows who else she sleeps with. I warned Vance in no uncertain terms, and he promised me he'd break off with her. Well, obviously he didn't. Tell him from me he can meet my lawyer any time."

"Mrs. Tichnor?" She had hung up.

Rob dialed her number.

"What?" Moira Tichnor half screamed.

"Mrs. Tichnor, I'm sorry to upset you, but I'd like to clarify this relationship. Ms. Holton is—"

"The bitch who is humping my husband."

"Do not hang up, ma'am, unless you'd like a lengthy personal visit from the Clackamas County Sheriff's Department." He could hear her breathing. "Thank you. Now, what can you tell me of your husband's involvement with Harold Brandstetter?"

"They were childhood friends." She sounded sullen but calmer. "Hal was filth, literally greasy. He ran a gas station, of all things." She gave a short, unamused laugh. "Really, when I married him five years ago, I thought Vance was more fastidious. Silly me."

Rob waited.

"Mostly they went fishing together, male-bonding stuff. Hal bored and disgusted me, and I have nothing in common with little Tammy Faye, or whatever the wife's name is. When Vance decided to build on the Tyee Lake property, I was afraid he'd tangle himself in deeper with that loser, and that's what he did. He swore he was just making sure he'd get the necessary building permits from the county, but it was more than that."

"More?"

"It was as if Brandstetter had something on him. We were supposed to go to Salishan Thursday. Vance promised me we'd go, then something came up in Klalo, I assumed a call from Hal or the builders. Vance took off in the Windstar. Just left me a note."

"What time did your husband come home?"

She was still for a moment, then said in a cold, flat voice, "I used my season ticket at the opera Friday night. I don't know what Vance was doing in your godforsaken county. I wish I'd never heard of Latouche County."

"Tell me about Vance's guns."

"Guns? What about them?" She sounded frightened.

"I understand he's a collector."

"Collector? Ha! Vance is a magpie. He has a small gun collection and two vintage cars and a lot of expensive wine. That's showing off. His knowledge, even of guns, is shallower than a saucer. When we remodeled last year, I made him get rid of most of the junk."

"When last year?"

"Early spring. Vance doesn't collect. He just uses things to impress people. And sometimes," she added with great bitterness, "he uses people to impress people. He used me. I see that now."

Rob said, "Tell me about the house on Tyee Lake. Have you seen it?"

She sniffled and gave a watery laugh. "God, yes, in all stages of construction. I told you Vance likes to show off. It's a big house. Lots of windows and bathrooms."

"Which contractor did he use?"

"Uh, Akers? Yeah, I remember thinking it was a good name for a developer. Acres and acres."

Rob drew a long, long breath. All right. "How far along is the project?"

"They were installing carpets last week."

Almost finished. Damnation. He was hoping the lodge was still in the dirt-and-squalor stage. "Mr. Tichnor is not registered at the Red Hat Motel. Could he be staying at his new place?"

"Probably," Moira Tichnor said with weary indifference. "Or he may be snuggled up with lovely Phyllis."

"Do you know her street address?"

"Just a minute."

He listened to rustling silence. She came back on the line with an address in West Linn. Close to Lake Oswego, lower rents. He thanked her and wound down. She sounded subdued now, anger spent. She was probably calculating marital debits and credits, and trying to decide whether it was time to cash in.

His cell phone rang. "Neill."

"Hello, Rob. It's Meg."

"Jesus, I forgot to call you. I'm sorry."

"It's okay. I hear you had a suicide to attend to."

"Was it on the news?"

"Radio. Listen, Rob, Charlotte Tichnor called me." Meg's voice warmed as she reported her revelations. She was clearly still on Charlotte's trail, though she had targeted Vance Tichnor as well. Not to mention Carol.

Rob made appreciative noises. What Meg said was interesting, but Mack was going to pull the plug on further investigation any moment. That took the bloom off the rose.

She ventured a cautious question about Meek's death, so Rob told her about Todd's emotional crisis.

"Oh, poor Todd. Are you sure he's all right?"

"I stopped by his apartment this morning. He was eating a breakfast pizza with pepperoni."

Meg laughed.

"I think he'll survive." He added, "It's hard on him, though. I told him to take a couple of days off."

"What about Chief Thomas?"

Rob groaned. "Look, Meg, I need to get back to work. Can I drop by later?"

"Sure. I've got our dessert in the freezer."

"Cold comfort food?"

He liked her laughter, the right music on a blue day. He hesitated, lost for a moment in a pleasant reverie, then shook his head to clear it and rang off.

Phyllis Holton. He found the number for Tichnor Realty and dialed it. The woman who answered put him through to Ms. Holton without a quibble. Rob identified himself.

"Latouche County? I suppose this is something to do with Mr. Tichnor's property up there. How can I help you?" The voice was professionally pleasant.

"I'm calling in connection with the murder of Harold Brandstetter, Ms. Holton."

"It's Mrs. I'm a widow."

"Thank you. When we examined Brandstetter's telephone records, your home number came up repeatedly."

Silence. Mrs. Holton cleared her throat. "I met Commissioner Brandstetter only the one time. He called to leave messages for my employer, Vance Tichnor."

"I see. What was the nature of the messages?"

"I'm not sure that's your business."

Rob said, "I'm conducting a homicide investigation, ma'am. Anything Harold Brandstetter did in the last twenty-four hours of his life is my business. He called your home. Why was that, Mrs. Holton? Mr. Tichnor informed me with some heat that he's a businessman and has not one but two cell phones. With message service, I imagine. Why would Brandstetter call your home?"

Again, a hesitation. "Both Vance and Brandstetter were a little paranoid about cell phones—"

"Hal called from a cell phone."

"I suppose he thought he'd be able to catch Vance at my place," the woman said wearily.

"Is that usual in the real estate business?"

"There's no need to be sarcastic, Lieutenant. Vance and I are old friends. Why am I engaging in euphemism? Anyone who knows us will tell you that Vance and I are lovers. We have been for many years."

"So his wife suggested."

"Ah, poor Moira." She sounded rueful rather than catty. "Our Moira is a little childish, I'm afraid. She's twenty years younger than Vance. A trophy wife. I suppose you know the expression."

"It has wended its way upriver."

She laughed. "She's expensively slim and expensively educated and expensively clothed. She looks great on public occasions. Mama approves of her taste."

"I see," Rob murmured by way of encouragement.

"Thick as a plank," Phyllis Holton said without evident rancor. "Moira may well have been in love with Vance when they married. God knows he's an attractive man, and I know he lusted after her. I don't want to suggest there was no emotional attachment, but I'm afraid they bore each other. She doesn't get his jokes, and he doesn't like opera. What can I say? She'll take him to the cleaners one of these days, and he'll deserve it. When he wants comfort, he comes to me."

"Then you know him very well. What can you tell me about his collection of Native American art?"

"His—" She broke off, coughing. "Sorry, frog in my throat. I don't know what art you're talking about. Vance is a compulsive collector. I suppose at some point he may have collected pots or arrowheads, but, if so, he moved on to other things. Right now he's buying a vintage Daimler."

So much for that gamble. Rob thanked Mrs. Holton and hung up.

There was no serious doubt in his mind that Vance Tichnor had acquired the Lauder Point artifacts, perhaps even commissioned the theft. Probably at a later time, he had stored at least some of them in his grandfather's garage. There was no way Rob could see of implicating him in the murder, however, and no way to be sure that the loot had been taken to his new lodge.

Tichnor was influential. The speed with which his plans had been approved by the county commissioners, commissioners other than Brandstetter, indicated that Rob would have to walk warily. He did not yet have grounds for a search warrant, and Mack was about to close the case.

Frustrated, Rob shoved his chair back and stood up. Time for another visit to the courthouse. The plans for Tichnor's lodge would be on file—and the names and telephone numbers of the principal contractors. He'd already spoken to Akers about the trailer at the campground. Akers claimed not to know William Meek. He had given a key to Hal Brandstetter, whose politics he admired.

 *Chapter 18*

ROB showed up at the happy hour, though he didn't look happy. He presented Meg with a bottle of Laphroaig. She wondered whether single-malt Scotch went with chocolate ice cream, but she didn't hesitate to pour.

Though her living room was more or less in order, they sat in the kitchen anyway. She was making soup again. It was soup weather.

The Scotch rolled on Meg's tongue and slid down her throat to the nerve endings along her spine, radiating a gentle Caledonian warmth as it went. "Good stuff."

"It is. My grandfather prescribed a tablespoon of whisky in a glass of hot water for most ailments including the pangs of puppy love."

"Wise man." The lid of the soup kettle rattled.

Rob cocked an eyebrow. "What's that? Smells good."

"Split pea soup with ham hocks. Do you want to stay for dinner?"

He opened his mouth as if to say no, looked at her, and grinned. "You have to stop feeding people. Jeff told me about the killer chili. Did you ever want to be a chef?"

"Of course I did. Do you know what good chefs make in Southern California?"

"More than good librarians?"

"You got it." She took another exquisite sip.

"What kind of chef?"

She looked at him. "Vegan. Stop stalling. I want to hear about the investigation."

He clenched his eyes shut and opened them. "It's a sorry mess. Maybe I don't want to talk about it."

"Too bad. I do."

"You're a hard woman."

A hard woman? A hard man is good to find. She almost said it out loud, caught herself, and blushed.

A slow grin touched Rob's mouth, as if he had read her mind, but he refrained from comment. He was flushed, too, she noticed. They both looked away and the lid rattled.

"Uh, all right." Rob's amusement leaked from him like straw from an effigy. He looked tired. The bruise on his cheekbone was turning green and sliding south. "The investigation. I'll give you the sheriff's version first. William Meek and Hal Brandstetter did the Lauder Point job ten years ago. Hal stored the loot in Emil Strohmeyer's garage with the old man's permission. Never mind that we haven't found the lost key in there with the rest of Hal's keys. He sold some of the swag and used the money to establish himself as a public figure."

"Just like that?"

Rob grimaced. "It took awhile. Meek went back to Montana and did Montana things, like drilling with militia groups and beating up his girlfriends."

"I think you're traducing a great state."

"Probably. I'm not traducing Meek, though. He was nasty. Hal and Meek kept in touch. In August, Hal decided to move the rest of the artifacts from the garage because you were coming."

"Considerate."

"He was a sweet guy."

"What about the murder?"

"Eddy Redfern had tailed Hal to the garage from a big swap meet at the Pacific International Exposition Center in Portland. We know Hal attended the meet, and Eddy told his friends he was going to. Eddy surprised Hal and Meek while they were moving the petroglyphs. Hence your fragment of The Dancers."

"He surprised them and they killed him? Just like that?" Meg swallowed Scotch.

Rob nodded. "Hal or Meek, we don't know which but the sheriff likes Meek, bashed Eddy's head with a crowbar they tossed in the river later. They left Eddy lying in the garage overnight. They tried to bury him the next day, but rigor had set in and they couldn't fit the lid over the cavity with his body in it."

"Ew."

"So they dug up the area behind the garage and used the dirt to conceal their victim, leaving the lid propped against the back door."

"And then?"

"Meek went back to Montana and Hal went on with his life, voting no when the commissioners met, loosing Towser on the general public, and battering Tammy."

"And then?" Meg repeated, relentless.

He made a face at her and took a sip of Scotch. "You drove up from California, opened the garage, Towser found the corpse, and the jig was up."

She smiled. "Do people say that?"

"I doubt it. I'm trying not to be sarcastic, but I'm only human."

"Go on."

"Hal panicked and called Meek, who flew down from Montana Friday. They got together for a heart-to-heart on Hal's deck, quarreled, and Meek shot his good buddy with a .357 magnum double-action revolver, which he just happened to have in his jacket pocket despite having come straight from the airport. Somehow he had also acquired a newish van, which he then drove away from Brandstetter's house with the lights off."

"No kidding?"

"Someone did. Towser barked. Kayla Graves, who lives across the street, heard the dog and looked out in time to see the van leave. She thinks it had Oregon plates. She didn't see Hal's body because of the big rhododendron at that end of the deck. Towser shut up and Kayla went back to bed with her boyfriend, who didn't waken on account of drinking too much beer."

"True?"

"That part's true. On Sunday, having dumped the mythical van somewhere, Meek stole a Datsun pickup. He lurked outside the hospital waiting for me to come out."

"Why?"

His mouth twisted. "Because I was such a threat to his well-being, of course. When I left by the side door, he trailed along Birch Street, spotted me talking to Mrs. Crookshank, sped up, and fired shots at the two of us. I cleverly avoided being hit by rolling over the lawn sprinkler. Meek abandoned the pickup in the Safeway lot, where he had parked his rented Subaru."

"What Subaru? I thought he was driving a van."

"Maybe he had two cars. The van has evaporated. We know he rented the Subaru at the airport branch of Rent-a-Wreck, even though Hal met him. Meek drove it out to the River Road Campground, where he had been staying since he shot Hal."

"What?"

"Before the legendary quarrel, Hal gave him the key to Akers's small travel trailer, which is parked at the campground."

"Huh."

"So there Meek was, camped with a passel of hunters. He brooded about his failure to kill me and Mrs. Crookshank over three cups of coffee and a Twinkie, became disconsolate, and shot himself in the face with the aforementioned .357, also shooting out the window of the trailer. Am I leaving anything out?"

"That's too dumb for words."

"My humble opinion, too. I conveyed it to Sheriff McCormick, in somewhat more tactful terms, and will take a day of well-earned comp time tomorrow while we wait for the autopsy results. Mack can't close the case until the ME has spoken. My sergeant, Earl Minetti, will be happily occupied doing the paperwork while I drive up to Tyee Lake to winterize my cabin. Do you want to come along?"

"I...sure. You mean that's it?"

He took a hearty swallow of Scotch. "No, I'll poke away at the theft on my own time, the way I have been for ten years, but the official investigation into the murders will be closed."

Meg brooded. She sipped Scotch and got up to stir the soup. "What about the Tichnors?"

"What Tichnors?"

"They're involved. I *know* they are. For God's sake, why are they here?"

"Vance is overseeing the last housekeeping chores before the lodge is finished. Carol is cheering him on."

"Fudgsicles."

"Do people say that?"

Meg didn't even smile. She gave the soup a vicious stir and began pulling bowls and glasses from the cupboard. "Okay, that's the sheriff's version. What about yours?"

"Mine still has a lot of question marks." He got up and helped her set the table. "Do you have crackers?"

"Saltines? Yes."

"I like 'em with split pea soup. I don't know why."

"*De gustibus,*" she said and rummaged in a cupboard for soda crackers.

"No fair. English clichés only. *Chacun à son goût.*"

"Make the salad." Meg turned back to the soup. "*I* will pick apart the sheriff's scenario. Starting with the Lauder Point robbery, which is not the starting point. I can believe Brandstetter and Meek did it, but why? Meek was a pothunter, but he apparently made a living from arrowheads and other items from his own neck of the woods. Brandstetter..."

Rob washed his hands at the sink. "Hal inherited his father's arrowhead collection. Otherwise, *nada.* And he had no taste." He took a package of presorted, premixed greens from the refrigerator and poked some of them into two bowls. "That was easy."

"Onions. Tomatoes."

"Right." The refrigerator door opened again. "Go on."

Meg said, "The question is why two yahoos like Hal and Meek would think of breaking into the county park building at all. They had to have a client who was willing to pay them to take the risk."

"Some risk."

"I've been reading about pothunters." Meg took a spoonful of soup, blew on it, and tasted it. "Yum."

"And?" He had found her French knife and was slicing green onions rapidly.

Meg admired his technique. "Don't cut your fingers off."

"No chance." He divided the onion slices between the two bowls.

"Good phrase. Most pothunters take no chances. Their quarry, so to speak, is way out in the tules."

"The what?"

"Cut it out. You lived in California for a while. Out in the woolly wilderness with nobody around to interrupt them or question them. County parks, on the other hand, are patrolled at least some of the time, and are often full of nonlarcenous citizens. Why take the risk?"

"Money."

"Right. Somebody whose name both of us know paid Hal and Meek to steal the artifacts."

"Vance Tichnor," Rob said gloomily.

"I still favor Charlotte but she seems less and less likely. Vance. He's swimming in money. He collects only high-quality stuff. He once took anthropology classes."

"Right."

"His mother said so. She also said he's impatient. He wouldn't want to chug along collecting one little item at a time. Buying the whole shooting match would suit his temperament. Also, he knew Hal Brandstetter, and what Hal would and would not do."

Rob was hunting tomatoes. He found one in Meg's vegetable crisper. "This is not a tomato. It's a simulacrum made of Styrofoam dyed pink."

"I know. Set it on the window ledge to ripen and forget tomatoes. There's oil and vinegar here." She tapped a cupboard door.

He took the condiments from the cupboard and began dressing the salad without instruction, olive oil first, then balsamic vinegar. He found her supply of hulled sunflower seeds and sprinkled them over the bowls. Meg approved. She began ladling soup. She had already cut bread. Analysis languished while they sat down and addressed their meal.

"Charlotte Tichnor has a notable collection of netsuke," Meg murmured. She speared a bit of lettuce. "Only the best. She keeps them in a special room with special security and only shows them to close friends."

"Hmmm." He crumbled a soda cracker into his soup.

"Vance wouldn't have been able to display his goodies."

"Of course he would. To select friends and clients, the kind who wouldn't ask inconvenient questions. He would get a kick out of the risk of exposure, and it wouldn't have been very large."

"How so?"

Meg stirred the soup in her bowl. "Once the furor over the robbery died down, most people would forget the details, if they ever registered. Only police officers, archaeologists, and Native Americans from the area would continue to care—"

"And they aren't the kind of people Vance hangs out with?" He spooned soup, sounding thoughtful. "His clients have to be business executives, corporate lawyers, dope dealers. The cheapest house he sold last year racked up three-quarters of a million dollars. His friends, with notable exceptions like Hal Brandstetter, would be drawn from the same circles."

"Lawyers and MBAs." Meg nodded.

"Bean-counters," Rob said, crushing another cracker. "Anthropologists, archaeologists, and art historians are noted for their poverty. They would not be clients. So Vance could show his loot privately to a few friends at a time, and brag about the great deal he got at a swap meet. All without serious fear of exposure."

"Corporate executives collect art as an investment," Meg offered. "They think of it that way, most of them. And Vance would gain prestige points for his taste."

"From those with pretensions to taste, like his wife." He grinned, started to say something else, and apparently changed his mind.

Meg scowled. "I'll lay any odds you like he showed the petroglyphs to his mother."

"I defer to your superior knowledge. I still haven't spoken to the lady."

"She made my blood run cold." Meg jabbed her salad. "Do you know she made Vance get rid of his comic book collection when he was small? I bet she made him burn them." She chewed vigorously.

Rob clucked his tongue. "This is great soup. Can I have more?"

"Help yourself."

"I will." And he did. "I forgot lunch."

Meg buttered a piece of bread. "Okay, so Vance paid Hal and his pothunting friend to steal the collection, and that was that for a while. Everybody was happy."

Rob was eating with fierce concentration.

"What destabilized the situation?" Meg chewed artisan bread. Excellent texture. She'd have to buy more. "That's what I don't understand."

"His wife made him clean out his junk."

"What?"

"Spring of last year. A year and a half ago. Emil Strohmeyer was ailing. I think Vance moved the collection to the garage while he waited for the old man to die."

Meg shivered. "That's so cold."

"His wife told me he uses people, and I can believe it. If you're right about his urge to show off his collection to the select few, his showplace at the lake will include some kind of vault or secure display area for the loot."

"How do you know that?"

"I don't know it. I'm speculating. Huge houses at Tyee and other scenic spots have always struck me as strange. People who can afford them don't live in them. They use them maybe twice a year for a couple of weeks."

"And the houses sit idle the rest of the time?"

"Some do. Some involve time-shares. People buy a week or two, and bring their families or friends for a good time. The owner hires a cleaning service. Other places are owned by corporations for the use of clients and upper-level executives. Some are essentially small hotels."

"Hotels?"

"Guest houses. I suspect Vance was moving in that direction. He could advertise the amenities back East, or in Japan or Germany, supply fishing and hunting guides, cater the food. I looked up the plans. There are four suites in one wing with an apartment in the other for a manager. Professional kitchen and pantry. Storage rooms, sauna, spa for eight, wet bar in the 'great room.' Entertainment center with all the bells and whistles in a less formal lounge."

"The only thing lacking would be willing maidens," Meg said sourly. She laid her spoon down. "And he could hire those, no doubt."

Rob shrugged. "Wonderful what money can do. If his clientele were foreigners, a gallery displaying the artifacts would be a real drawing card."

"Then I hope the baskets and drums were liberally dusted with DDT," Meg said with venom.

Rob stared. "I don't follow."

"Gosh, I didn't tell you. Let me show you." She jumped up and ran from the room, returning with the printout of the article on DDT contamination. Excitement made her voice rise. "They've sent out health warnings!"

Soup forgotten, Rob read the article from start to finish, set it down, and looked at her. "Do you know what you have here?"

"A clue?"

He was silent for quite a while. Then he got up, walked around the table, pulled her to her feet, and kissed her on the mouth. He tasted of soup and Scotch.

"Hey!"

"I beg your pardon. I was overcome."

They stood staring into each other's eyes, sexual enthusiasm flashing like heat lightning all around them. At last, Meg said, softly, "Rats, I was saving that up."

"What?" His mouth twitched at the corners.

Reluctantly, very reluctantly, Feckless Meg smiled at him. "Upstairs, *mon ami*. I don't do kitchens."

 *Chapter 19*

A telephone rang upstairs. Faintly. It was not Meg's phone. She was sloshing in the downstairs tub, enjoying the overall tingle that came of a good sexual romp. Two years it had been since the last time, and well worth the wait.

She climbed out of the tub and toweled herself off. It was, incredibly, only eight P.M.

The phone stopped ringing.

She took her time dressing in the rose-patterned caftan she had brought down. She felt energized and wide awake. Rob, on the other hand, had fallen asleep as if poleaxed—with a smile on his lips. She contemplated that sad fact. He had had perhaps two hours of sleep since their steak dinner the night before, so it wouldn't be fair to indulge in feminist resentment. Still, he might have squeezed out a word or two of postcoital conversation.

Dressed but damp around the edges, she strolled into the kitchen and started a pot of coffee. Upstairs, the shower switched on. Meg inspected the ice cream torte and decided to leave it in its icy nest next to the chili.

She had finished washing the dishes by the time Rob straggled downstairs. His hair was wet, his clothes were crumpled, and he looked sheepish.

"How about them Mariners?" Meg said amiably.

He laughed. "I'm sorry. That was gauche."

"Coffee?"

"Thanks. Obviously I need it."

"Ice cream?"

He rubbed one shoulder. "Why not? Mind if I listen to the message that woke me up?"

"Feel free."

He had the tact not to leave the room when he pressed the Play button on his cell phone.

"Rob, it's Jake. Jake Sorenson. Will you call me? I'm at home." Jake sounded worried. He gave the number.

"It's not going to go away," Rob muttered. He set the phone on the table and walked around to where Meg was slicing ice cream torte with her French knife. "Hey."

"Is it about Todd?" She set the knife on the counter and turned.

"I don't know." His eyes were dark. He bent and kissed her on the forehead. "I'm sorry. You're a lovely woman and a great humanitarian."

"Call Jake," Meg said gently.

While he placed the call, she poured two cups of coffee. His side of the conversation was calm and not informative.

He said, "Phone Ginger again, and don't worry. He's probably just driving around. Yes, I know, Jake. We have to wait." The phone squawked. "Yes. Call me again when you've talked to her." He set the phone down.

"So?" Meg sat down and took a swallow of coffee.

"Jake's worried because Todd has gone off somewhere."

"Are *you* worried?"

"There are half a dozen harmless possibilities, but yes, I'm worried." He was frowning down at the ice cream as if it might contain DDT. "He was very, very angry."

"Jake?"

"Todd. He wanted to kill Meek himself."

"Because of his cousin?"

"Yes. Todd found Meek's body." He glanced at her, frowning. "It was a headshot. Ugly. Todd threw up. For a kid with a lot of pride, losing control would be hard enough. Then Jake found Meek's wallet and told Todd Meek was suspected of killing his cousin. A jolt from the opposite direction. It tied Todd in knots. He couldn't move." He poked at the ice cream, gave up, and drank coffee.

Meg said, "I'm so sorry for him. He won't, uh, harm himself, will he?"

"I don't think so. It would take longer for him to get to that point." He grimaced. "He's more likely to go off half-cocked into a fire fight."

"Like his cousin?"

Rob was silent.

"What are you going to do?"

"What the hell can I do?" He set his coffee cup down and it slopped. "Sorry. I'm frustrated. With civilians, there's a twenty-four-hour waiting period before we act on a missing person report. I can alert the dispatcher, though. I'd better do that now." He stood up and this time took the phone into the hall.

Meg ate a bite of ice cream that tasted like cold straw. Ridiculous. She got up and went for the Scotch. When Rob returned she said, "A tablespoon in hot water?"

His mouth relaxed. "Better make it a straight shot. Do you mind talking about the DDT article?"

"I don't mind. Let's take it into the living room." She poured careful measures of Laphroaig into two glasses. Then she stuck the ice cream dishes in the freezer.

Meg was edgy. She thought Rob was, too. He sat in her easy chair, the better to avoid a cuddle. She sat opposite, on the love seat. "So," she said. "DDT."

He took a swallow of Scotch, eyes closed. "There were traces of DDT in the soils sample from your garage."

Meg groaned.

He blinked at her. "What?"

"I just paid an enormous sum to have a contamination kit shipped here overnight."

He smiled. "Not a bad idea. You can give me the receipt. I'll have Earl come over in the morning to retest, just to make sure."

"I guess it makes a difference?"

"It gives me semi-solid evidence the loot was here." He drew a long breath and exhaled slowly. "With the fragment of petroglyph, it will give me grounds to ask for a search warrant."

"To search Vance Tichnor's lodge?"

"Yes."

Meg brooded. "You said semi-solid evidence."

"It's conceivable that old Strohmeyer routinely used DDT in his garage."

"Oh, no," Meg wailed.

"Hey, don't give up. I'm trying to think like a Tichnor lawyer. Tomorrow I'm going to ask the parks director whether they ever used DDT on the exhibit. If they did, that will sway at least one judge I can think of."

"It's all politics, isn't it?"

"So I've been told." He sounded almost cheerful. "Now, come up with a way I can demand a pound of flesh from Vance Tichnor, and we're home free."

"A pound of flesh? Oh, fatty tissue. DDT accumulates in fatty tissue."

"Right. According to this." He tapped her printout. "If he's been handling the organic artifacts repeatedly, there should be a fairly high level of contamination."

"He looks as healthy as a horse."

He tapped the printout again. "Unless you're allergic to it, DDT doesn't cause obvious symptoms in people."

"It just accumulates. In fat cells. How about testing Towser?"

His eyes narrowed. "Now there's an interesting thought. No, I won't have to test him. I'll have the lab recheck the results on your corpse." When she stifled a gasp, he gave her an apologetic look. "If the dirt in that hole is contaminated, then Redfern's body will show traces. He lay in the ground two months."

"What about the petroglyph?"

"I need to talk to the parks people. I need to know whether they used DDT and *how* they used it. If they sprayed each organic piece separately, then the petroglyphs, being inorganic, won't show much in the way of contamination. But maybe they fogged everything in sight."

The cell phone rang again. Rob answered without hesitation. "Yeah, Jake. Okay. Yes, in the morning. I'll call Chief Thomas, too. Yes. Talk to you tomorrow." He set the cell phone on the arm of the chair, leaned back, and closed his eyes.

Meg stared at him, bewildered.

After two minutes that seemed much longer, he sat up and smiled at her. "Do you have deputy clothes? Your outfit makes you look like a peach melba."

Meg blushed. That was the whole idea. Good enough to eat. "Deputy clothes? Something unisex and severe?"

"Jeans and a jacket. I need to talk to some people tonight, two of them women, and I don't want to roust Linda Ramos out."

"You actually intend to treat me like a cop?"

A slow smile touched his eyes. "Only temporarily, believe me." He stood up. "I'm going home to get a recorder." He picked up the cell phone. "And to change the batteries in this damned thing. It's fading on me. Can you be ready to go in twenty minutes?"

"Uh, sure. Better brush your teeth."

He cocked an eyebrow. "Ah, the Scotch. You're right."

He took more like half an hour. Meg waited in the kitchen once she had changed into pants and a blazer. She had brushed her own teeth, thriftily rescued their whisky glasses and covered them with plastic wrap, the better to prevent evaporation. She had found a pen and notebook, organized her purse, and had saved the remains of the split pea soup to the freezer by the time Rob got back. Not that she was impatient.

He knocked at the side door and entered. "Ready?"

"Who are we interrogating?"

He clucked his tongue. "Such a word." He seemed in high spirits. "Dennis. Tammy. Carol. In that order."

Meg dried her hands and fumbled the keys from her purse. "Okay, let's go. Want to bet Dennis is playing computer games while Darcy reads to their son?"

"No takers."

But it was Darcy who answered the door. She blinked at them.

"Just a neighborly call," Rob said affably. "I need to talk to Dennis."

"Uh, okay. He's with Cody. Hi, Meg."

Meg smiled and didn't explain her presence.

"Uh, I'll get Dennis." Darcy vanished from sight.

Rob set the recorder on a doily on the nearest end table and they waited, side by side on the sofa but not touching. Rumbles from the bedroom area indicated that Dennis was not best pleased. A child's voice piped, high and querulous.

At last Dennis deigned to appear, wearing sweats and a hostile expression. "What d'you want, and why is *she* here?" He caught sight of the recorder.

Rob said, "I thought you might prefer to talk here, Dennis. Ms. McLean was sworn in as a reserve deputy several days ago. She's going to operate the recorder. Meg?"

Breathing a prayer to the gods of media, Meg pressed Record. The machine began to whirr.

Rob gave the date, adding, "It's eight forty-seven P.M. Present are Dennis Wheeler, Deputy Margaret McLean, and myself, Robert Neill." He finished the rigamarole with stately relish as Dennis began to sweat.

"Do I need a lawyer?"

Rob shrugged. "If you want one. I just have a few questions for you about the house keys you returned to Ms. McLean."

"Oh, them."

"And about your relationship with the late Commissioner Brandstetter."

"Relationship!" Dennis huffed. He remained standing, as if sitting would be a confession of weakness.

"Friendship," Rob amended, mouth twitching.

"So I liked Hal, so what?"

"No problem."

"I been working out of town most of the time since school started. Didn't see much of him." He crossed his arms and shifted from one foot to the other.

"Okay. Where were you the first two weeks of August?"

Dennis repeated the story Darcy had told of Cody's first trip to Disneyland and the engine that overheated in Ukiah. By the time he wound down, his arms had dropped to his sides.

"Dates?"

Dennis screwed up his face and came up with exact dates.

"Did you see Brandstetter immediately before and after your trip?"

"Well, yeah, but just to talk to on the street. He walked the dog evenings. Darcy made me warn him about letting the ridgeback run loose. He didn't like that."

"And?"

"And that's it."

"Okay. I understand you shared Brandstetter's political ideas."

"I thought it was time for the gov'ment to pay some attention to real Americans, yeah. Want to make something of it?"

"No, just interested. Did you contribute to his campaign fund?"

"A hundred bucks. It was deductible. My tax man said it was okay." His voice rose and he took a step forward.

"Hey, Dennis, I don't work for the IRS."

"Yeah, well. It's a free country. Or was." Dennis rubbed the back of his neck. He was red in the face and looked absurdly young. The donation was probably his first political act, a sad thought.

"Now, about the keys," Rob said.

"Old Strohmeyer gave them to me! He *asked* me to keep a set in case he got locked out. He was always forgetting his keys those last years."

"And you didn't give them to Mrs. Tichnor at any time?"

"No, never talked to her."

Rob frowned. "What about her son?"

"The doctor?" Dennis looked wary.

"Vance. The real estate dealer. The one with the pearl gray Windstar with Oregon plates."

"Uh, no." Dennis glanced at Meg, looked away, fidgeted.

Meg said, "You told me Mr. Strohmeyer had the lock changed on the back door of the garage. That key is newer than the others."

"Sure, yeah. He changed it awhile before he died."

"Did he say why?"

"Um, kids were fooling around, getting in."

"The lock hasn't been changed," Rob said with the absolute authority of one who has looked at everything through a forensic lens. "Not in years. Come on, Dennis, give. What's with the key? It doesn't open the back door."

"It doesn't?"

"No."

"Shit. They told me—" He broke off. He rubbed his face, let his hands fall. "Okay, so I lied. Carol asked me for the keys, the whole set, couple of days before we took off for California. She returned them the next day, except for the back door key. Said she'd lost it. When we got back from California, there was an envelope in the mailbox with a new key. The note said she'd copied the real estate folks' key and not to tell anybody about the missing one. I didn't try it out, honest."

"What's the story about Strohmeyer replacing the lock?"

He rubbed his thick neck. "Hell, I just made that up when Mrs. McLean asked why the key looked different. I didn't mean nothing by it. I thought the key would work and she'd never know." He sounded aggrieved. "I didn't want to get Carol into trouble. Dumb bitch."

"So the back door key has been missing from your set since before you went to California?"

He stuck his jaw out. "I said so, didn't I?"

"You didn't lend it to Hal Brandstetter at any point?"

"Hal?" He looked bewildered. "Why would I do that? It was Strohmeyer's key. Hal never had nothing to do with Strohmeyer. The old man was a goddamn pinko liberal. Hell, he was a stinking *socialist.*"

"I thought you went fishing with Mr. Strohmeyer," Meg interposed.

Dennis glowered at her. "Well, yeah, he knew where to go, all the good holes. He was okay about fishing. But he was always talking about unions, said he was a member of the carpenters' union, never hired nothing but union labor. He told me I ought to join the machinists' union. I don't believe in that shit. I told him so. He cackled some song, something stupid about bloodstained banners." Dennis heaved a sigh. "What the hell, he wasn't a bad old guy. He just liked to push my buttons."

Meg was hastily reviewing what little she knew of union anthems, but she couldn't get past "Solidarity Forever" and "Union Maid."

Rob said, "Hal never fished with Strohmeyer?"

"No."

"But he did fish with Vance Tichnor." Rob, offhand.

Dennis nodded. "We went together, the three of us, and fished the Kapuya when the steelhead was running. I missed out this year, though. I was working down in south Portland."

Rob leaned forward, not so casual. "Vance barely recognized your name when I talked to him."

"He...what?" Dennis shook his head like a horse with a pesky fly. His eyes were dark with anger and hurt. "He's full of shit. We must've fished together half a dozen times the last three years."

Rob eased his shoulders against the back of the sofa. "Did Vance quarrel with Hal over politics?"

"No. He just said his granddad was old-fashioned. Vance never talked about nothing but land deals."

That had to be a disappointing answer. Meg glanced at Rob out of the corner of her eye.

He smiled and stood up. "Thanks, Dennis. I'll bring a printed statement around for you to sign."

"That's it?"

"For now. Unless there's something you'd like to add."

Dennis's eyes shifted. "Well, you know, the night Hal was shot."

"Yes?"

"Around two-thirty. I woke up and took a piss. Heard the dog barking."

"Okay. Thanks. Did you look out?"

"Well, yeah. There was this van in the driveway, behind the SUV, you know? There's bushes and shit, so I couldn't see it real clear."

Meg held her breath.

"Yes?"

"I saw the van leave. The lights was out, but the guy tapped his brake at the corner and turned left. The van had Oregon plates."

Rob exhaled a long, slow breath. "Was it Tichnor's van?"

"Naw. I dunno. Didn't recognize it."

Rob looked at him and he flushed a darker shade of red but he didn't say anything.

Rob said drily, "Thank you, Dennis. Do you remember the number of the van?"

"No. I just thought it was weird. The dog shut up after awhile and I went back to bed."

"How's your eyesight?"

"Twenty–ten, both eyes."

"Okay, let's be sure about this." Rob sat down and took him through everything again, rapidly. Dennis's native belligerence had returned by the time Meg turned off the recorder. She and Rob left. Dennis had remained standing the whole time.

 *Chapter 20*

WHEN Rob rang the Brandstetter doorbell, Towser woofed. Meg could hear the television playing. Tammy answered the door with the dog at her side.

She smiled at them. "Hi, c'mon in. Tom's watching a horror flick." Towser bounced. As Meg and Rob entered, the dog kissed both of them.

Laughing, Tammy calmed him and led them toward the kitchen. Tom waved a preoccupied hand as they passed. Something was decomposing on the screen to heavy melodrama from a full orchestra. If Brandstetter had been her father, Meg supposed she would have found horror soothing, too.

The kitchen was tidy and almost clean. Tammy offered coffee, tea, bourbon, or vodka. They declined everything. Towser took a couple of loud laps at his water bowl, sniffed their legs, and retired to a dog pillow where he watched them with bright brown eyes.

"So it's not a social call?" Tammy's black eye was fading. She'd had her hair cut. She smelled of shampoo, and faintly, of vodka, but she wasn't drunk.

Rob said, "Your doctor is giving you an alibi, Tammy. You're not a suspect in Hal's death."

She burst into tears and sank down on a chair at the kitchen table. Meg patted her shoulder and gave Rob an inquiring look. He made a soothing gesture. Let her cry.

While Tammy sobbed and Meg made comforting noises, Rob set up the recorder.

Eventually, Tammy blew her nose on a wad of Kleenex and composed herself. "Sorry. It's just the relief. Uh, Ms. McLean?"

"Meg."

"Thanks. Tommy told me your idea about the gun collection. I've already had two calls from gun freaks in the area wanting to buy. Ghouls."

"Soak 'em," Rob said. "You're selling?"

"When I can."

"Shouldn't be a problem. Community property."

Tammy sniffed happily. "That's what my lawyer said." She explained Meg's dog-walking scheme and Rob laughed.

"Brilliant. He's a great dog, Tammy, and you'll want him around when Tom goes back to Portland."

Her face clouded. "Yes. Tom missed an evening class."

"It'll be okay," Meg murmured, hoping so.

Rob said, "You're probably wondering why Meg is here."

"Tom said she was working for the department."

"Yes, she sorted Hal's books and magazines for us."

"Bunch of junk."

"Will you keep them awhile? I don't think we'll need them, but it's better to be safe than sorry."

"Okay, but I'm turning that office into a sewing room."

Meg pulled out a chrome-legged chair and sat next to Tammy. "It sounds as if you're making plans."

"Yes." Tammy gave Meg a watery smile and scooted her chair sideways so they could see each other's faces. She dabbed at her eyes. "I can plan now. It feels strange. My bookkeeping clients have been really kind. I used to think they hired me because Hal intimidated them, but they haven't fired me."

"That's great."

"You do a good job." Rob sat across from the two women and pulled the recorder to him. "Can we ask you a few questions about last August, Tammy?"

"August?"

"Yes, July and August, after the Strohmeyer house went on the market."

"Oh, yeah, the other murder." She shook her head. "I keep forgetting about it, what with Hal's death and everything. What can I tell you?" Her hand clutched the wad of tissue. "I have to say I was probably drunk most of the time. I drank myself to sleep."

"Well, that's bad news, but I just need a general idea of what was going on in the neighborhood, at least to begin with." Rob started the machine and intoned the usual information. "Why don't you tell me who was here and who went off on vacation, starting around the end of July?"

"Dennis and Darcy took Cody to California. I remember that." And she went on. She had noticed a lot for a woman who spent extended periods in a stupor. Nothing she said was very startling, however, and Rob seemed to be keeping the conversation in placid channels.

Tammy accounted for the Iversons, the wind surfers and their resounding rap, the Brownings, who spent a week at the beach, and Rob's pretty daughter, Willow. Tammy had seen Meg once, probably the day Meg made the offer for the house. The espresso stand across the street had done a land-office business the whole time, which annoyed Hal. Tommy hadn't come home. Rob didn't ask about the Tichnors, and Tammy didn't mention them.

Meg listened and let her mind drift. If they were going to interview Carol, they ought to get on the stick. Carol spent a lot of time in a stupor, too. It was half past nine.

At last Rob said, "Did you notice Carol Tichnor's car in the neighborhood?"

"After the SOLD sign went up? No, but I was working an inventory of that bead shop that went out of business down on Alder. So I wasn't here much in daytime the first week of August. The weird thing is, I don't remember seeing Bill Meek at all."

Rob cocked an eyebrow. He didn't say anything but his eyes were intent on Tammy's face.

Tammy gave an apologetic smile. "I heard on the radio that you think Bill killed Hal. Is that true?"

"The sheriff is convinced," Rob said neutrally.

Tammy must not have picked up on Rob's doubt. "Good, I can believe it. Bill was a rattlesnake. I remembered his last name after you left the hospital Sunday. I meant to call you. Did he really commit suicide?"

"Mack thinks so."

"Too soon to tell, huh?" Tammy wasn't slow.

"You were saying you didn't see him in the early part of August."

"Mind you, that doesn't mean he wasn't here in town. Bill never stayed with us. He used to drink with Hal, but he never stayed the night. He was a real loner. Mostly he camped at the lake, and Hal rendezvoused with him at the Timberland when they had some deal going. The bartenders out there might've seen him."

"Yes, we're asking around."

Tammy nodded. "I was surprised to see Vance Tichnor."

In the pause that followed, Meg looked at Rob.

His face was blank and he sat very still. "You saw Vance with your husband?" He kept his voice casual.

"Yes. I assumed it had something to do with his grandfather's property, but I didn't talk to him. He showed up a couple of times in that van of his."

"When?"

She gave a helpless shrug. "Early August. I think he and Hal talked on the deck, but I don't really know. I was drinking." Her voice rose.

"It's okay, Tammy." Rob stood up. "I just wanted to jog your memory a little. If you think of anything else about that time period, anything at all, let me know."

"It was funny about Hal and Vance."

Meg's finger poised on the Pause button.

Tammy went on, "We wouldn't see Vance for months, years, sometimes. Then he'd hang around, all friendly like he wanted to sell us something. I remember he was in and out a lot a year ago last spring. Maybe it was natural. His grandfather was pretty sick by then."

Rob sat down again and Meg waited, hands in her lap. Rob was watching Tammy's face.

"Vance had a different van then, or a pickup with a camper shell. Hal helped him move stuff into Emil's garage." She gave a derisive snort. "Or so Hal said. Hal and Dennis Wheeler. Couple of bulls in a china shop."

Rob swore. Softly, gently, comprehensively.

"What?"

Rob smiled at her. "Keep talking, lady. I'm interested."

But there wasn't much more to tell, apparently. Tammy looked alarmed and confused, and Meg didn't blame her. Rob hadn't said anything about the earlier period. He was interested in August, wasn't he?

When they left, finally, at ten minutes of ten, Meg said, "What was that about?"

Rob laughed. "Moira Tichnor decided to clean house a year ago last spring, remember?"

"Gosh, the loot. Vance moved it then." That made sense. "Won't Brandstetter's body show an accumulation of DDT?" Not to mention Dennis Wheeler.

"We shall see. I want to talk to Dennis again, maybe in a dungeon with thumbscrews."

Meg was driving the two of them in the Accord. She didn't like riding in pickups. She always had to climb up into them. Rob's was full-size. The parking lot of the Red Hat was half-empty. Rob let Meg carry the recorder, the better to look professional. Carol was not going to buy her impersonation of a police officer.

Rob strode up to the desk and showed the clerk his identification. The kid—he had a stud in one nostril and spiky puce hair—came around and used his card to let them into the right corridor. Rob walked straight down the long, long hall and banged on the door of Room 123. Meg had to scurry to keep up.

As if she had been expecting someone, Carol opened the door at once and not on the chain. Alarm chased disappointment across her well-preserved features. She fixed on Meg. "What the hell?"

Meg smiled but said nothing.

"I need to ask some more questions," Rob announced, stepping toward Carol.

She held her ground. "It isn't convenient."

"Neither is your family's obstruction. Let us in, Ms. Tichnor."

"What about her?"

"Meg is here because I want a witness. She's a reserve deputy."

"Scared of me, Robbie?"

"Cautious," Rob said coldly. "Very, very cautious."

Carol shrugged. "Come in. I have nothing to hide."

"I'm delighted to hear that. Meg?" He indicated an armchair by a handsome cherrywood table. The room was large and well appointed as motel rooms went.

Meg sat and set up the recorder. "Now?"

"Yes."

She pressed Record and Rob rattled off the requisite information.

Carol sank onto the foot of the bed. She wore a robe of some plush fabric, blue with stylized flowers embroidered at the yoke and wristbands. Her slippers had matching flowers. A scent, vaguely familiar, hung on the air. It made Meg want to sneeze, but a lot of perfumes did that.

Rob remained standing, though there were three other chairs. "We retrieved Dennis Wheeler's keys."

"Keys again." Carol pouted in an exaggerated way but Meg thought she was worried. "Keys to Grandpa's house?"

"My house," Meg said. "I'm a little peeved, Carol. First there was the secret cache in the garage. No disclosure. Now I find that a man I don't know has a complete set of keys to my house and garage. Still no disclosure. How would you feel?"

Carol blinked. "Oh, come on."

"You come on. I am suffering acute mental distress." Meg didn't look at Rob and kept her face straight with an effort. God did not mean her to sound like a lawyer, and she would sooner embrace a cobra than sue anyone. Carol didn't need to know that.

"I'm sorry," Carol muttered. "I forgot Dennis had a set of keys."

Rob took over. "Short-term memory problems, Ms. Tichnor? Wheeler said you borrowed those keys the first week of August."

Carol's hands clenched on her plush lap. "He's lying."

"I don't think so. And he was off in California when the murder occurred. He's not a suspect."

"I am?"

"Yes. *You've* lied to me repeatedly." The implication was that Dennis hadn't. But Rob didn't say that, probably because it wasn't true.

Silence. Carol ran a hand through her artfully tumbled curls. "Well, okay, I borrowed the keys, but I gave them back right away."

"Except for the key to the back door of the garage."

"I lost it and made a copy."

"No, Ms. Tichnor. The key you gave Dennis doesn't work in the lock. I tried it."

"Maybe it's a bad copy."

"It's not a copy." Rob was pacing. "Where are the two missing keys? The back door key is also missing from the set the realtor gave Ms. McLean. A little puzzle. An intriguing little puzzle."

"What can I say?"

He stopped in front of her and stood looking down. "The truth would be refreshing."

"I don't know what happened to them. And I don't see why it's such a big deal." She was whining.

Rob turned his back, fetched a chair, and sat facing her. "Don't pretend to be stupid. The body of a murder victim was found in the garage. The doors were locked. Neither lock was forced. Not in August, not ever. Whoever locked the garage knew what was in it."

"Well, I don't have either key. Why don't you go away? I've told you everything I know."

He leaned forward, fists on his knees. "Where's your brother?"

"On duty at the Vancouver hospital, the Southwest Washington whatever-they-call-it. Used to be Saint Joseph."

"Your brother Vance."

"At home with his wife?"

"No."

"Then I don't know."

"Have you seen Vance or talked to him since Saturday?"

"Uh, he called me Sunday after you interviewed him, said he was going out to look at his lodge."

"Has he called you from there?"

"No. He hasn't called me since Sunday."

Rob leaned back, skepticism in every lineament. "Why did you come down from Seattle, Ms. Tichnor?"

"My mother told me to." Carol jumped to her feet and went to the chest of drawers that doubled as a sideboard. An ice bucket, a bottle of lime mixer, and a fifth of gin reposed on the shiny surface beside a plastic tray of paper-wrapped tumblers. She ripped the paper off one glass, threw in an ice cube, and poured herself a drink. Gin and a splash of mixer. She took a swallow and tossed her hair back. "When Mother says jump, I jump."

Rob let that ride. "Going back to Vance. We're looking for

him. We've been looking for him since Monday in connection with another death. If he calls you again, tell him to come in voluntarily."

"Another death? But that was..." She bit her lip.

"Was what?"

"Do you mean the suicide out at that campground? What could that possibly have to do with my brother Vance?"

"That's what we'd like to ask him," Rob said blandly. "Now, about your own movements in August."

"I came down to check out the house and take some papers back to Seattle for my mother." She gave dates in early August with the air of one repeating herself. "You can't imagine *I* had anything to do with the killing."

"Why not?" He cocked his head, eyes measuring. "You look fairly fit. I imagine you play tennis or golf. It doesn't take a lot of strength to bash a man's head in with a metal rod."

She took a gulp of gin. "Except that I don't go around doing that kind of thing. Metal rod?"

"A crowbar, maybe. A tire iron. Some kind of prying tool. What you might use to open the cache in the garage."

She clutched her drink with both hands. "I did not enter Grandpa's garage after the house sold."

Rob went on, as if she hadn't spoken, "It was a panic killing, probably. The body was left there in the garage a good twelve hours, then stuffed into the cavity with dirt shoveled over it. I don't see you doing that. But panicking? Sure. That's exactly the kind of thing you'd do, Ms. Tichnor. Panic and call your brother for help. Where was he? At home? Did you call him to rescue you?"

"No, no. You've got it...I didn't enter the garage." She finished her drink and went to the phone. "I'm calling my lawyer. Get out."

"*You* didn't enter the garage. Did Vance? Maybe it was Vance who panicked."

"Get out," she screamed. "Now. Both of you."

"Or you'll call the cops?" Rob walked over to the cherrywood table. "Interview terminated at ten thirty-eight." He hit the Stop button. "Maybe you're wise to call a lawyer, Ms. Tichnor. You were keeping something in the garage, something you had to protect. Edward Redfern was killed because he found out what it was. If your brother calls, tell him to come in to my office. If he won't, tell him from me we'll bring him in."

He looked at Meg and jerked his head. Let's go. She stood up, expelling a long breath.

Carol was tapping out a phone number. She listened impatiently, pressed another. "This is Carol Tichnor. I need to talk to Oliver right now. It's ten-thirty Tuesday night. He knows where I am." She hung up.

Someone scratched at the door.

Rob, with Meg at his heels, swung the door wide. "Well, I'm damned, it's Mike Calhoun. How you doing, Mike?"

A chunky man in full resort regalia gaped at him. "Neill? What the hell? Carol, honey, you okay?"

"Get out," Carol said through her teeth. "All of you. Get out. Leave me alone."

The chunky man beat a fast retreat down the hall.

When Rob and Meg got back into the Accord, she said, "Weren't you a little hard on Carol?"

He fastened the seat belt. "Hard? No. She's an accessory to murder. I should have taken her down to the courthouse for a six-hour session without the drink tray handy. I'm too tired for that tonight. Tomorrow."

Meg started the engine and the inevitable windshield wipers. When she had backed around and driven from the lot, she said, "I'm sorry. I was out of line."

"To question me? Nonsense." He sounded preoccupied.

She drove for a while, mind turning over the three interviews.

Rob said, "I'm a maverick, as it happens, doing short interviews. It's standard procedure to go over everything at least twice. You almost always catch something the second time around."

"I see. Did they help?"

"The interviews? Of course. With Carol, you know, I was just stirring the sludge with a long stick. I want her to have nightmares." He chuckled. "I'll bet we gave old Mike a nightmare or two."

"Who is he?"

"Local Romeo. He's married to a nice grade-school teacher, but he's been romancing guests at the Red Hat since it opened."

"Just worked his way around to Carol?"

"Or vice versa. They seem well suited."

"Is that a catty remark?" She glanced at him.

He was grinning. "Probably. Mike was president of my senior class in high school. Most likely to succeed. Dated the cheer-leaders."

"It's been downhill from there?"

"Something like that."

"Maybe children should be protected from social success in high school."

"Willow is doomed." He touched her hand, the gear-shifting one. "How are you, Meg?"

"Full of energy and confusion. Thanks for trusting me with the tape recorder." She pulled into his driveway, backed around, and drove forward to her usual parking spot. "You ought to go home and get some sleep. I saved your Scotch, by the way."

He was silent for a moment. She was afraid she'd offended him by suggesting he needed rest more than sex, but he turned, smil-ing in the dim light. "Why don't I come in, drink a toast to your bright eyes, and then go home?"

"Okay. But you'll have to let me know what's happening to-morrow or I'll perish of anxiety. I take it we're not going to win-terize your cabin at Tyee Lake."

"We'll see. First thing in the morning, I'm going to pry a search warrant out of Judge Meyer."

Meg led him into the kitchen and took the glasses out of the cupboard without turning on the overhead light. It was too bright. She removed the plastic wrap.

Rob took his glass. "At least you didn't stick it in the refriger-ator."

"I'm not a barbarian. *Sláinte.*" She raised her glass.

He touched it with his. "Cheers."

"What about Todd?" The whisky went down hot.

He grimaced and took another swallow. "I can't call Chief Thomas at this hour." It was after eleven.

"Do you think she knows where he is?" She set her glass on the counter.

"She'd better not," he said grimly and finished his drink. He took her face in his hands, which were cold from the chill outside and from the glass, and kissed her with slow deliberation, tasting of Scotch. "To be continued?"

Meg nodded. Her mouth tingled. She didn't smile at him, but she saw him out.

 *Chapter 21*

AT nine Wednesday morning, Rob walked to his office. He had taken muffins and lattes to Meg's around six-thirty—and apologized again. She was a forgiving woman.

When he called Jake from home after seven, the deputy told him Todd was still missing. That triggered a round of fruitless phone calls to Todd's friends and relatives. His mother sounded worried. Rob couldn't reassure her. He called Judge Meyer's office, too, and left a message on the machine that he'd be asking for a search warrant.

He called Vance Tichnor's cell phones and left messages. He called Ethan Tichnor's numbers and rejected calling Carol. Moira Tichnor wasn't answering. Neither was Phyllis Holton. Rob began to feel as if his phone were attached to his ear, so he took a hike to the courthouse.

The walk lasted about twenty minutes. Time to reflect. Time to figure out a strategy for dealing with the principal chief of the Klalos. When Rob reached the department, his mind was so focused on Madeline Thomas, he almost walked past her husband, Jack Redfern, without seeing him.

Jack sat in one of the plastic chairs outside the bullpen with Sergeant Howell looking down on him from the booking desk. When Rob appeared, Jack got up in stages like a much older man and started the ceremonial warm-up.

Rob greeted him gravely and with relief. Given a choice of dealing with Jack or Jack's formidable wife, he would take three Jacks any day. They shook hands. Rob stopped only to ask Reese to hold his calls and send in some coffee. Then he led Jack into his office.

They spent time, as was polite, discussing the weather and

the steelhead run. At last, Rob thought it was safe to venture a question.

"I have a missing deputy, Jack. Your nephew, Todd Welch. Does Maddie know where he is?"

Jack looked sheepish and rubbed the back of his neck. "Well, hey, she talked to him."

"Yes. I told him to call her after William Meek's body was discovered."

Jack was silent. Rob waited. The office intern, a high school boy, brought bad canteen coffee. Rob considered asking him for a pack of cigarettes, but that would have caused a major scandal. The boy left.

"Maddie went off," Jack said when he had sugared his coffee and taken a sip.

Rob waited.

Jack swallowed coffee and grimaced. "I'm worried."

"Me, too." Went off where? When?

Jack shot Rob a look he couldn't interpret. Another silence.

At last, Jack sighed. "Lila's making war."

Rob groped in his memory. "Your sister-in-law?"

"Eddy's mother," Jack said heavily. "Feel like I'm living in a combat zone."

When Rob didn't comment, he added, "You gotta know, Madeline is a leader but she's never been Lila's chief. Lila don't understand. She's Nez Perce and not real traditional. She says Maddie stole her son from her. It wasn't like that."

Rob thought Lila was probably on the right track.

Maybe Jack read his mind. "Madeline can't help it. She has that power over people. She never told Eddy anything she didn't tell the others."

"Searching for the artifacts in Emil Strohmeyer's garage was his idea?"

Jack's jaw set in a stubborn line. "She never sent Eddy on no secret mission."

"Are you sure?"

"Maddie told me she didn't. She don't lie. Not Maddie."

Except to herself, Rob thought sadly.

"But Lila keeps at her. And now she's gone, Madeline, I mean. She was gone when I got up this morning."

Rob said, "Gone. I'm trying to understand. Do you mean she's gone off to think about what happened or she's gone off to do something?"

Jack scrubbed his face with his hands. "Off to do something. She meditated. She's *been* meditating since we found out about Eddy. This time, though, I think she had her a vision. You know what I'm talking about? Damn." He started to rise.

Rob said, "I've been studying."

Jack sank back on his chair.

"She was asking for a sign?"

"Yeah." He said something in Klalo, shook his head, looked at Rob. "You're not laughing?"

"No. It's not a laughing matter." In the silence that followed he could hear Jack breathing. At last Rob made himself take the gamble. "I'm about to ask Judge Meyer for a warrant to search Vance Tichnor's property on Tyee Lake for the Klalo artifacts that were taken from Lauder Point. Do you know any reason I shouldn't go in there with a team of armed deputies?"

Jack stared at him. "How'd you know?"

Rob said, "You've got to be open with me, Jack. That's a dangerous man."

"There's an old burial ground up there."

"Show me." Rob got up and went to the map of Latouche County on the wall behind his desk.

Jack stood up in stages again. A lot of fishermen developed rheumatism. He walked to the map and stood looking at it. "It's up on the hill. I can't show you exactly. That wouldn't be right."

"Okay. Here's the boundary between Vance's land and his brother Ethan's hillside. It follows the creek."

"Yeah. The burial ground's on Ethan's property, looks down on Vance's." He didn't touch the map.

Rob did. "Vance's new house sits here in this meadow."

"Camas meadow," Jack interrupted with an edge of anger.

Rob waited. At one point, the camas bulb had been a staple food in the area. Women passed knowledge of good camas meadows from mother to daughter, as they also did of huckleberry patches and the stretches of forest floor where chanterelle mushrooms grew. The harvests were intelligent.

Jack walked back to his chair and lowered himself into it. "Old

Man Strohmeyer was careful where he put his still, and he always let the women gather camas. And Emil, he was okay, too, and his son, Pete."

"But not Vance." Rob sat, too.

"Bastard brought in bulldozers. He didn't even ask. When Maddie talked to him, he offered to *pay*."

"He missed the point?"

"Damn right. So she's been watching him."

It was one of Rob's deeper convictions that the universe operated on irony. Madeline had been watching Vance Tichnor. For her own reasons.

Rob said with care, "I think Tichnor paid Meek and Brandstetter to steal the Lauder Point artifacts."

Jack shot him a sidelong glance. Enigmatic.

"Did Madeline have Vance in mind as the collector when she was sending her young people out to find the artifacts?"

"She never said."

Rob held onto his temper with an effort.

"Not at first. Not ten years ago."

"That's a relief." And it was. So much so that Rob felt almost lightheaded. There was no point bawling out Jack Redfern for concealing information. "When did she start to suspect him?"

"August, for sure."

"When Eddy disappeared?"

"Before that. It was something one of the construction crew said about the house."

"A vault?"

"There's a place in the house where he could hide stuff. She looked up the plans."

"So did I," Rob said grimly. But not until yesterday.

"And there's a security system going in. One of them big electronic webs with lasers and shit."

"It's not in place yet?"

Jack shook his head. "Todd has a cousin on the finishing crew, one of the Welch boys." Not a Klalo.

A spy, though. Another spy. "Madeline ought to be in charge of Homeland Security."

Jack laughed aloud, subsiding into wheezes and wiping his eyes. Rob's cell phone rang.

"Robert Neill," he said, watching Jack master his amusement.

"Ethan Tichnor returning your call." The doctor's voice rang higher and lighter even than it had during the interview. "You said it was urgent."

"Yes. Very urgent." Rob covered the mouthpiece. "Please excuse the phone call, Jack. It's Dr. Tichnor."

Jack nodded, still grinning, as Rob rose and walked from the room. He ducked into the empty office Earl and Thayer shared. Earl was waiting at Meg's for the testing kit to arrive, and Thayer was taking another look at the disturbed area behind the garage for something to do while they waited.

"Right, Doctor," Rob said. "I'm about to search Vance's house at Tyee Lake for the Lauder Point loot. I'll have to trust you not to warn him."

"That's—"

"Will you listen? What do you know about DDT?"

A startled exclamation from the other end assured him he had Tichnor's attention.

When Rob had paraphrased Meg's article, Ethan said heavily, "Then Vance will show a level of DDT consistent with exposure to the organic items?"

"If he's been handling them over the years, yes."

"In the fatty tissues." Tichnor sighed.

"I need your help, sir."

"He's my brother."

"Yes, sir, he is. And you could hang up right now, phone him, phone your mother, phone your lawyer. But don't you think it's time to bring a halt to Vance's obsession? He may have killed three men to protect his hoard. That's sick. You're a doctor. Surely you'll agree that your brother needs help."

A long silence. "You say three men?"

"Edward Redfern, Harold Brandstetter, William Meek. I think Eddy Redfern surprised Vance, and that the first killing was almost accidental, but the deaths of Brandstetter and Meek were carefully executed, and executed is the right word."

Tichnor said something under his breath.

"What's that?"

"You have no proof."

Rob gritted his teeth. "I have enough proof for a warrant to search for the stolen items. As for the murders, I don't have sufficient evidence yet to ask the judge for a Probable Cause to Arrest order, but I do have some proof. More will come in. Vance used his van, the Windstar, the night he shot Brandstetter. It was seen in Brandstetter's driveway by at least two people at half past two in the morning."

He heard Tichnor inhale sharply.

"Your brother is no genius, Dr. Tichnor." Thank God for that. "He's already slipped up a couple of times. Hiring Meek to take a potshot at me is just one example."

"Now wait—"

"Please hear me out. I want you to come out to the lake with me and talk your brother into surrendering. If you won't try that, I'll have to take a team of deputies into his compound. There are construction workers in there. It could be dangerous to them and to us. And dangerous to Vance. Will you give it a try?"

Tichnor said sadly, "He showed me the dagger."

Rob held his breath.

"You've got to understand. Vance never grew up. He was always looking for approval."

"From your mother?"

"At first. Latterly, from anyone he respected. Maybe a year after the Lauder Point theft, he showed me a ceremonial knife with an obsidian blade. The bone handle was inlaid with mother-of-pearl. I admired it, of course I did. It was beautiful. He never would tell me where he got it, just looked mysterious. Protecting his sources, he said. I didn't think about Lauder Point. The news stories had all talked about the petroglyphs."

That was true. They hadn't gone into much detail about the organic artifacts either. Another nice irony.

Tichnor said, "It wasn't until after I talked to you Sunday that I looked up the Lauder Point case. I saw a picture of the dagger on the website."

Rob had scanned that photo with his own hands.

"So then I knew." Ethan sounded as if he might burst into tears.

Rob thought Tichnor was sincere but there was no guarantee. "Will you come out and talk to him?"

Another pause. "Yes. I'm on my way."

"Please don't call your mother, sir, or your sister."

Tichnor gave a shaky laugh. "Believe me, they're the last people I want to talk to. Carol and I were supposed to keep Vance out of trouble."

Carol? Rob swore silently.

As if he had read Rob's disbelief, Tichnor said, "Carol used to be able to wind Vance around her little finger, but lately the roles have been reversed. I'm afraid my mother doesn't understand the extent of Carol's drinking problem."

"But Vance does?"

"Yes. He manipulates Carol. I try to protect her. I'm coming now because I have to protect her from Vance."

"She knows too much for her own safety?"

"I fear so," said Ethan Tichnor. "I'll meet you at your office within two hours."

Rob said thanks to a dead telephone. He asked Reese Howell to send Dave Meuler to the Red Hat to check on Carol. Just in case.

When he returned to his office, Jack was looking at his map of the county.

Rob apologized for the interruption and explained.

"That doctor's going to try to get his brother to surrender?"

"Yes."

Jack heaved a huge sigh. Of relief, Rob thought. "That's good. I don't want Maddie caught in a fire fight."

"And Todd?"

"Not Todd either."

"Is he out there with the construction crew?"

"Taking his cousin's place. They don't look much alike, to my way of thinking, but Todd told Maddie he didn't think Tichnor would notice."

Probably not. Which didn't mean Todd was safe. He was armed, probably, and in a reckless frame of mind.

Rob said, "Okay. I need to get that search warrant and organize my team. Backup," he added when Jack started to protest. "Are you game, Jack? I want you to take Dr. Tichnor and me out there. Show us where Maddie is. I'm assuming she's on the hillside that looks down on Vance's house. I need to speak to her."

"I didn't talk to her this morning."

"So you said. Is that where she goes?"

Jack nodded. "I been there with her couple of times."

"I'm not asking you to show me exactly where the burial ground is, and I'll keep my mouth shut about it."

"What about the doctor?"

"He won't know it's there if we don't tell him."

Jack looked doubtful.

"He's not a outdoorsman," Rob said, using Tichnor's own expression. "He wants to leave that hillside alone. No logging, no ski trails, no building. He told me that."

"Yeah, for how long?"

One day at a time. "It's his property for now. Don't look for trouble."

"I'm a peaceful man," Jack said.

"Except about gill-netting?"

He grinned. "Hey, I'm peaceful about that, too. I just dip that old net peacefully into the water."

Rob smiled and stood to shake hands. He suggested that Jack fuel up on breakfast or whatever and get his raingear, if they were going out to the lake. The weather was momentarily decent but a front was coming in from the west.

By the time Rob had dropped by Judge Meyer's office and warned the sheriff and soothed his ruffled feathers, Dave had called from the Red Hat. Carol had not checked out of the motel, but her car was missing from the lot. Rob thought she must have driven out to Tyee Lake to confront Vance.

He picked up the phone and dialed the cell phone number for Akers Construction. The old man answered.

Rob identified himself. "Mr. Akers, I have to warn you that I'm going to execute a search warrant on Vance Tichnor this afternoon."

Matt Akers gave a startled squawk.

Rob took a breath. "I want you to take your men off that site as soon as possible.

Another squawk, this time indignant.

"Yes, sir, I understand. Tell Vance you have an emergency at some other building site, that you'll be back in the morning. Tell him whatever you think will work, but don't warn him I'm coming."

"Why the hell not? He's a friend of mine."

"Harold Brandstetter was a friend of yours, too."

Akers cleared his throat. "Hal was a fine man, fine."

"I'm taking Vance in for questioning in Hal's death."

Akers gasped. "What about that Meek guy? McCormick said that Meek killed Hal."

"He said it was possible, Mr. Akers. I have reason to believe Vance Tichnor killed your friend. By this afternoon, I'll have an arrest order from Judge Meyer to bring him in as a material witness. Is that the kind of trouble you want to mess with, sir?"

"I...Hal? You're not bullshitting me, are you, Neill, because if you are—"

"No, sir. I think Vance Tichnor is a triple murderer."

"Triple?"

"Edward Redfern, Harold Brandstetter, William Meek." The list of names had begun to sound like a litany.

"Oh, God, okay. I'll call my foreman."

"Will you tell me when your men have left the site? I don't want anyone to get hurt."

The subdued contractor assured Rob that he would call.

When Rob hung up, he was sweating. The phone rang again. Earl, reporting in, happy as a clam. Not only had he verified a high level of DDT in Meg's garage, but Thayer had found a key buried a couple of feet down in the dirt behind the garage. It opened the back door lock. Thayer was real sorry he hadn't found it the first time he searched. He hadn't thought he'd have to dig that deep.

Rob congratulated his sergeant and asked to speak to Meg, but Earl said she had gone off somewhere in her car.

 *Chapter 22*

MEG did not enjoy being patronized by Earl Minetti. When the DDT test kit arrived at ten-thirty, courtesy of FedEx, he took it and the receipt and told her to get lost. He was politer than that, but Meg grasped his meaning.

Paranoia raised its ugly head. Was Minetti's attitude a message from Rob? Meg considered phoning in a protest, but Rob had said he was going to ask for a search warrant that morning. Getting a warrant probably took time. She would wait and protest over a glass of Scotch. Let Minetti do the test and get his hands dirty.

Meanwhile, it was time to leave the house, time to escape. She was unlocking the Accord for a run to the grocery store when she spotted Towser with Tom Brandstetter in tow. She waited on the sidewalk, greeted Towser, submitted to having her hand licked, and asked Tom how his mother was.

"Uh, fine." Tom looked sleepy.

Towser bounced.

"Full of piss and vinegar, isn't he?"

"Piss, anyway." Tom looked at her from shy dark eyes.

Meg laughed. "Want to go for a ride?"

"Sure. Can Towser come, too?"

"Well…"

"I'll go get his car rug to protect the back seat. He likes riding around."

"He may, but does he restrain himself? I want to drive out to Tyee Lake." Until she said it, she didn't know that was what she wanted. Rob had promised her a trip to Tyee Lake. "I've never been there, but I understand the road winds. I don't want Towser to jump me while I'm driving."

"He'd never do that, Meg." Tom sounded so earnest Meg half

believed him. "And there's a place by the lake where I could let him have a run."

"A field with an eight-foot-high chain-link fence?"

Tom laughed. "You're a funny lady. Naw, it's just an area they were thinking about turning into a park." His face darkened. "That was two years ago. Some dumbshit contractor's probably built condos on it since I was up there last time."

"No leash law at the lake?"

"It's unincorporated."

"Let's go look it over. Is there a café out there?"

He made a face. "Greasy spoon."

"I don't feel up to making a picnic. Besides, it's cold. Let's drive up, give Towser a run, and choke down a hamburger."

"I guess I could do that." His mouth quirked.

Meg smiled at him. She thought his sense of humor was going to save his life. "Go get his majesty's rug while I find my rain jacket." And the cell phone. Meg never drove farther than the grocery store without her cell phone, the better to summon AAA when the car broke down.

"Sun's shining."

"If there is one thing I've learned about the weather around here, it's that rain is coming. Ten minutes?"

"Okay." Tom trotted off with Towser at his heels.

River Road made Meg glad she wasn't driving a twenty-five-foot moving van. The road—a county highway—followed the Kapuya, a jolly little river that twindled its way downhill and turned at every obstacle in its course. A few miles out of Klalo, on Beaver Creek, they passed a big campground that must have been the site of William Meek's death. Meg shivered.

The basalt cliffs along the river were brilliant with fall leaves in bronze and red and the intense yellow of maples, but Meg had no time to appreciate their beauty. She clung to the wheel and navigated the eighty-five-degree curves at twenty-five miles an hour. In one brief straight stretch, a pickup full of hunters passed her doing fifty. The hoot of its horn faded around the next bend.

"Want me to drive?" Tom offered.

"Shhh. I'm concentrating."

In the back seat Towser gave a happy little yip.

"What?"

"He saw a deer," Tom explained. "He's got great eyesight. He's a sight hound."

"A sight hound?"

"He's bred to hunt by sighting his prey instead of tracing a scent. So he yipped when he saw the deer."

Jesus, what if a deer ran across the road? Meg gritted her teeth and clung to the wheel. Basalt gave way to glacial boulders and crumbling hills of gravel thick with trees. The road wound. Just as she thought things were going to get better, Tom said, "That's the turnoff."

"Up there?" A narrower road headed up a bluff. Signaling, she turned left under the nose of an affronted log truck. The car shifted down and labored up the switchbacks. They came out at last on what Tom said was prairie.

Meg didn't know from prairies. Scrubby conifers dotted pastures thick with grass. There were driveways and mailboxes, five or six at a time. She saw houses. Most were double-wide mobile homes, but some more ambitious structures had been built in a style she recognized as Displaced Californian. The road wandered but the curves were gentler. She spotted horses, and in one high-fenced pasture, a herd of llamas.

Latouche County was very large and mostly empty. She wondered how so few deputies could keep track of so many square miles. The Forces of Evil (name your brand) could hide an army between Klalo and Tyee Lake.

The road began to climb again into real forest, following the course of a stream that shouted prime trout fishing. The trees at the very top had a dusting of snow. Every once in awhile a narrow road led off into the dark woods. Fir, Meg thought. Maybe spruce. Something with short needles. The undergrowth flared red.

"I'm glad you're with me," she murmured.

Tom said, "Hey."

"Otherwise I'd never find my way home."

Tom laughed. Towser gave a happy snort. He was behaving well, but the car was going to smell doggy.

The approach to Tyee Lake was heralded first by a sign with an arrow that said three miles, then by gated entrances to what had to be elaborate compounds. A heavy dump truck full of debris pulled out from the open gate of the third driveway on the right. A parade of pickups and small cars full of men in hard hats followed the truck.

Meg waited.

"That's the road to Vance Tichnor's lodge," Tom said.

"How do you know?"

"Sign says Tichnor's Lodge."

"Ah." Meg followed the last of the pickups in stately procession along the road to the lake.

After a mile or so, the dense forest opened and she saw patches of green lawn in front of modern houses with lots of glass, heavy stone chimneys, and three-car garages. Most had roofs of tile or enameled metal on which leaves and drifts of brown needles had accumulated. She turned a last corner and there it was, Tyee Lake.

Blue, blue water in a deep green setting. Wooden piers stuck out into the lake. Most of the boats were small and battened down for the winter. Patches of reed and narrow stony beaches ringed the shore. Two rowboats drifted in mid-lake, so still their occupants' fishing rods cast straight-line shadows on the water. She could barely make out houses on the opposite shore, the lake was so wide. Meg gave a sigh of pure bliss.

Rob had spent one miserable summer here as a child, yet he still came back. He had brought his daughter back. Meg could see why.

"So where's this park area?"

"Keep driving," Tom said. "Over there, beyond the Tenas Klootchman Café."

"Our greasy spoon?"

"That's it. The name's Chinook jargon. You can park in that lot on the lake side and I'll let Towser loose for a run."

"Won't he eat the ducks?"

"No, or if he does it will be a merciful death. He's really quick."

Meg glanced at Tom. He gave her a wide grin. She parked with care, thinking, insofar as she was thinking at all, that Tom Brandstetter would grow up to be a charming man when he got past the nose stud.

As long as Meg didn't have to control Towser, it was fun to see him greet the wilderness. He bounced off toward the lake with

Tom in tow. Meg stood on the gravel and watched. Then she surveyed the "park."

Someone had mowed the weeds, and a weather-beaten picnic table slumped by the water. The parking lot had been graveled, but the paths were strictly grass and mud. Meg picked her way to the table and sat down. Towser and Tom had disappeared into a clump of trees to her left. To her right, a man rowed a boat out from a dock with slow, elegant strokes. He wore a red-and-black plaid shirt and his boat was a faded red. If she had been a painter she would have reached for her brushes.

She wondered which of the houses along the shore was Rob's cabin. The Guthrie cabin. Not that elaborate place with the cantilevered deck. Not the two-story gray job with the long narrow windows, nor the misplaced Colonial with its smug backside to the lake. The next house, small with unpainted cedar shakes, was possible. She thought it was old enough. Someone had painted the shutters dark green. It fronted the lake, and she thought she saw the curve of a canoe peeking around the far corner.

At that point, Tom returned with Towser still on the leash, so she asked where the cabin was.

Tom pointed in the other direction. "That one. About halfway along beyond the A-frame with the big lawn."

"Ah. Time for lunch?"

"Sure. I'll put Towser in the car and let him off the leash after we've eaten, okay?"

Meg handed him the keys.

The greasy spoon did a not-bad hamburger and outstanding real potato french fries with the skin on. The coffee was horrible. Tom drank a root beer. She asked him about his culinary ambitions, and he was still talking when they went back outside.

It was only half past one. The sky had clouded over, turning the water gray. A sharp little wind blew from the southwest. At least, Meg thought so. She had lost her sense of direction on the drive up. Tom released Towser, and the ridgeback took off along the lake in great leaping bounds, woofing for joy. Ducks scattered.

Meg locked the Accord and watched for a while, smiling, then drifted back to her table. Tom followed the dog with the leash in his hand, but he was in no hurry. Neither was Meg. She decided to take a long look at Rob's cabin.

It was far off for good observation, but it looked snug, small and snug. White clapboard siding, silvery cedar shakes on the roof, a chimney. A screened porch faced the water. A propane tank crouched below one window. There was a small, square dock suitable for swimming or tying up canoes. Something, perhaps a wind vane, whirled atop one of the piers. Rob's cabin was dwarfed by the A-frame and the vast three-story palace beyond it. Once upon a time the cabin had stood by itself and looked almost like a house.

It was beginning to snow. A few flakes drifted on the rising wind. Meg forgot the cabin. Snow! Enchanted, she watched for a good five minutes as the tiny white flakes whirled and thickened. Her cheeks burned with cold. Then she remembered the road back. Good God. She stood. "Tom!"

"Meg?" said a voice behind her.

She turned.

Carol Tichnor stood on the grass, hands in the pockets of her inappropriate camel's-hair coat. She had tucked an Hermès scarf into the neck and she was wearing white wool pants. Wind ruffled her hair. Her eyes glittered.

Meg stared. "Hi. Did you drive out to see your brother?"

"You have to help me." Carol spoke in a low intense voice as if she were afraid of being overheard, which was foolish because the nearest person was Tom at the far end of the park with the bouncing ridgeback. Tom had found a stick. He threw it in Meg's direction and Towser leapt after it.

"Tom, we have to go," Meg called. She turned to Carol. "Help you? I don't understand."

"I want your car." Same low, intense tone.

Meg gaped. "Something wrong with your BMW?"

"Give me your keys."

"You have to be kidding." She took a step past Carol in the direction of the parking lot and fingered the keys in her jacket. The BMW sat on the far side of her Accord.

"No. I'm not kidding." Carol pulled a small handgun from the right pocket of her coat. She had turned to follow Meg, her back to the lake.

Meg froze in place. "Are you out of your mind? Put that thing away."

"I need your car. They have Vance's road blocked off. Three patrol cars, at least. I drove past them. The cops have to know my car. So I need yours. Give me the keys."

"In your dreams." Meg backed away, stumbling slightly on the rough grass surface.

"The keys." Carol jabbed the barrel of the gun toward Meg's car.

"Look, Carol, at worst you're an accessory—"

Carol gave a snort of derisive laughter. "Ms. Detective. I killed that Indian. He was in the garage, harassing Vance, making accusations. I was bringing Vance the crowbar from his van. I just raised it up and hit the Indian on the head. Hard. It was like he was a snake or something. I couldn't stop hitting him. I killed him, and Rob Neill knows. You were there. You heard him. He said I panicked. I didn't panic, not then. Then I was cool. Afterwards, we, Vance and I, we both panicked."

"Why are you telling me this?"

"Because I'm going to kill you." She raised the gun.

"Wow, Meg, what's going on?" Tom was maybe fifty yards away with the dog bouncing beside him.

"No, go back, Tommy. Help! Get help!" Meg thought that was what she shouted, but she couldn't be sure because all of a sudden things were happening.

Carol whirled, saw the approaching hound, and fired.

Towser gave a yelp. Meg shouted. Carol turned back. She was raising the gun again when the enraged ridgeback tore into her. Towser had covered the gap in four curving leaps. Carol stumbled, screaming, and the gun flew.

"Stop!" Meg screeched. "Tom, you've got to stop him." She grabbed for Towser's collar and he snarled at her, shaking his head. He was rending Carol's right leg above the knee, twisting and silent. As Carol screamed and flailed out, Meg heard something snap.

"Leave it," Tom shouted. "Leave it! No bite! Towser, come!" He yanked at the dog's collar. Towser snarled. Bright arterial blood spurted.

"Get water," Tom panted as the dog twisted. When Meg didn't comply, he repeated the command. "Water!"

Meg glanced wildly around. She spotted a rusty bait tin at the water's edge and ran for it. When she returned to the heaving mass, Tom shouted, "Throw it on him. No bite, Towser. Leave it!"

Meg sloshed icy water over the animal's head. Then she ducked in and grabbed for the thrashing woman, who was still screaming.

"He'll kill her. Oh, God." Meg pulled at Carol. The tan coat and the white wool pants showed splotches of scarlet. "Lie still, Carol. You're bleeding." Carol thrashed.

"Hey, what's going on?" The heavy woman who owned the café puffed across the road. She wore an apron with a wide ruffle over jeans and a T-shirt.

Tom snapped the leash to Towser's collar and pulled him off. The wet hound snarled, baring his fangs. Meg saw a long weal on his shoulder muscle. The bullet had hit him.

Blood spurted from Carol's thigh. Meg squished at the wound with both hands. Carol moaned.

"Give me your apron," Meg shouted at the proprietor of the Tenas Klootchman. "She's bleeding to death."

The woman was no fool. She whipped off her apron and tore off the ties with hamlike hands. "Let me at her. I'll make a tourniquet. Goddamn dog oughta be put down."

"No!" Tom wailed.

"She shot him," Meg said grimly. "He saved my life. Can we tie it here? He went for her thigh."

Carol's sobbing subsided into ominous silence. Meg thought she had passed out, and no wonder. There was blood everywhere and it was bright red.

Between the two of them, Meg and the café owner rigged a tourniquet. Meg thought it was working. At least there were no more spurts. The woman, her nametag said Patsy, was sitting splay-legged on the grass with her fists clenched on the tourniquet tie. Blood smeared her thick forearms.

"Patsy?"

"Yeah, call 911."

"Right. Tom?"

"You can't put Towser down. He was defending himself!"

"Yes, I know." Meg dug in her pocket for the keys and handed them to the sobbing boy. "Put him in the car, Tom."

"He's hurt. She shot him."

"Yes. I'll take him to the vet as soon as I can, but we have to get medical help for Carol now. Okay, Tom?"

He wiped his nose on his sleeve and pulled the dog closer. Towser growled. "Yeah, all right. Shall I bring you the phone?" Meg's phone was in the car.

"Please."

Patsy touched the unconscious woman's neck. "She has a pulse."

Meg said, "You're a jewel, Patsy. How do you know? I can never find a pulse, myself."

The woman gave a shaky laugh. "I took a course."

"Well, it paid off." Meg yanked off her jacket. "I guess we should keep her as warm as possible."

"Yeah. Man, I didn't need this."

"Me either."

Their breath hung on the air a moment, then blew away in wisps.

Tom ran up with the phone. "I'm going back to Towser."

"Yes, keep him calm. There's a first-aid kit in my glove compartment."

"Right." He disappeared as Meg hit 911 with bloody fingers. Her jeans and jacket were drenched with blood.

It took her awhile to make herself clear to the dispatcher. The phone kept fading in and out, which didn't help. When Meg was sure both an ambulance and a patrol car were on the way she thumbed the power off.

"Jesus," Patsy said. "She confessed to murder?"

Meg drew a long, shaky breath. "Yes, and I'm pretty sure she was telling the truth."

"Who the hell is she?"

Meg started babbling. By the time Jake Sorenson's patrol car screamed up with its lights flashing, Patsy Diefenbach knew more than she probably wanted to know about Tichnor history.

Patsy kept her hands on the tourniquet. Meg shivered beside her and babbled. Snowflakes settled on the grass.

 *Chapter 23*

A T eleven-thirty, the judge signed the search warrant. Meyer raised less of a fuss about the arrest order than Rob expected, and promised to send the paperwork right away. Things were coming together. Dr. Tichnor showed up at the courthouse annex a little past twelve.

Rob went out to meet him at the booking desk.

Tichnor's khaki pants held a crease and his boots shone. He sported a tailored hunting jacket. At least he hadn't come in a three-piece Italian silk suit. "I'm late. I stopped by the Red Hat. Carol's not there."

"I think she's gone out to the lake. I have a car looking for her." Rob had sent Jake Sorenson out to search for Carol's car—and for Todd. Rob didn't mention the missing deputy. No point causing confusion.

Tichnor's face reflected his anxiety. "I'm afraid for my sister."

"Then we need to get going. Is Vance armed?"

"He's a gun nut."

"I know he has a collection, but I thought it was still in Lake Oswego."

The doctor's tension eased a little. "I hope so. He's probably got some kind of handgun in his van, though."

Along with two cell phones he wasn't answering.

Rob ushered Tichnor into his office. "Make yourself comfortable. I'm getting things organized." He explained briefly about Madeline Thomas.

"She's out there on my land?"

"Yes. Watching Vance, according to her husband. Jack is going to show us where she is."

"Good. We'll need a guide." Tichnor ducked his head and his

ears went red as if he were embarrassed. "I've been to the lake, but I haven't walked around that area since I was in my twenties."

"You bought the land sight unseen?" What it was to have money to burn.

"I bought it for the trees, and because Uncle Pete wanted me to. My wife thought I was crazy to invest in land here. She wants to buy a place in Cabo San Lucas. I hate Cabo."

The office phone rang. "Neill."

Reese said, "Judge Meyer sent the warrant and the arrest order by messenger."

"All right. Has Earl come back?"

"Eating lunch in his office. Thayer, too."

Rob glanced at his watch. "Tell them all to assemble in the briefing room. Fifteen minutes."

"Okay."

"Any word from Matt Akers?"

"I was getting to that. He just called. His crew left the site ten minutes ago."

"Did he say anything about Todd Welch?"

"Todd?"

Rob explained Todd's masquerade.

Reese gave an exasperated cluck. "I'll call Akers again."

"Right. Do that. We'll need body armor for the troops, including me, Dr. Tichnor, and Jack Redfern. Oh, and a bullhorn."

Reese squawked.

Rob overrode the objection. "Yeah, I could use the P.A. system in the car, if I could take a car in the back way, but I can't. Get me a bullhorn, just in case."

They discussed weapons. AR15s for the deputies at the gate. Rob didn't like the thought of a shoot-out, but if Vance tried to make a break for it, they'd need to stop him. If, God forbid, Vance had taken Todd hostage, someone might have to shoot Vance. Thayer was a sniper.

And if I don't get the team into place soon, Rob thought, the sucker may drive off with the loot and Todd's dead body in the back of the Windstar.

"Jack Redfern just showed up," Reese said.

"Good, send him in."

Later, on the long drive to the lake, Rob considered the odd coming-together of personalities. On the face of it, Dr. Tichnor and Jack Redfern had nothing in common, but both of them were mild-mannered, humane men who wanted a nonviolent resolution. They got along.

Rob was driving a county car for the first time in a while. The engine ran a little rough. The other cars had gone ahead and were already in place. He thought the deputies understood the game plan.

He had Tichnor beside him. Jack slewed sideways in the back seat, as if riding in the back of a police car didn't suit his dignity. He had probably had rides in the backseats of other patrol cars in connection with gill-netting, so sticking him there along with the Kevlar armor wasn't tactful. Rob needed to talk to Tichnor, though.

"Tell me about Vance."

"He's not stupid."

"I know." They were passing the Hunters' Roost Campground. Rob glimpsed yellow crime scene tape fluttering in the distance.

"Vance is impulsive and, your word, obsessed."

"Why the Lauder Point artifacts? I don't understand that at all."

"That was Grandpa." Tichnor sounded miserable. "He took us to Celilo Falls before The Dalles Dam went in. Then he showed us the artifacts from the drowned sites near Bonneville. He took us out to Lauder Point Park right after the little museum opened."

The road began to twist along the river.

"My grandfather took me to Lauder Point, too. It didn't make me want to steal what was there." As a child, Rob had not been history-minded. Rockets and space probes had interested him more than arrowheads, but he didn't want to say that with Jack in the car.

Tichnor said, "Grandpa collected arrowheads. When we got home from the park, he showed them to us, all laid out on velvet. I remember Vance cut his finger on a piece of obsidian."

"Okay, so he admired his grandfather's collection."

"Grandpa gave it to him. It was his first collection."

"I see." His first, and acquired without effort.

Dr. Tichnor was saying, "Vance did a study project for seventh-grade history, using the arrowheads. He had a real interest. At one point, he wanted to be an anthropologist."

"Did the family discourage him?"

"No. Dad probably pointed out that anthropologists don't make a lot of money, but that wasn't really an issue. If Vance had become a professor at some college, my mother would have been delighted, even if he made peanuts. She would have given him an allowance. It wasn't money."

"So what was it?" Girls? Booze?

Tichnor ruminated. "Vance's grades weren't wonderful. He'd pick something up, then drop it. Changed his major three times. He wound up with a degree in business, but he didn't work at it."

"That doesn't sound obsessive."

"You're right." He eased his seat belt. "The thing is, he knew his grades would never be top of the class or even more than adequate, whatever he studied. He would have had trouble getting admitted to a rigorous graduate program, and he wouldn't have settled for second-rate."

"Not even for the pleasure of studying something he enjoyed?"

"No. Maybe that's a family failing, Lieutenant. I was hung up on grades myself as an undergraduate."

In all likelihood, Vance had looked at his brilliant brother's academic achievements and despaired. Rob said, "But you studied something that continued to interest you?"

"'The fascination of what's difficult.'" Tichnor's hand gripped his seat belt as Rob passed a car. "I should have been a jazz pianist."

"No lie?"

Tichnor gave a short, self-conscious laugh. "We're straying from the subject at hand."

"I appreciate your candor, however."

"I'm trying to figure Vance out. It was probably my mother's netsuke that triggered him off. She'd been collecting them for years. She traveled to Japan a couple of times, took classes at the Henry Art Gallery, paid outrageous prices to dealers. After my father died, she spent a lot of time and money setting up a secure place to show them off."

Rob glanced at him.

His mouth set in a thin line. "She kept on about how important the collection was, and by implication how important she was for having the taste and gumption to preserve a part of the past. It wasn't her past, God knows. I once said why netsuke, why not whiskey decanters, Mother?"

Rob smiled. "And?"

"I thought she was going to disinherit me," Dr. Tichnor said ruefully. "She didn't talk to me for several years. I had to send messages through Carol."

"That's extreme."

"Mother is extreme. Vance is like her in a lot of ways, though he's more affable, at least on the surface. Both of them have a streak of ruthlessness." Tichnor fell silent, probably considering just how ruthless his brother could be.

Rob flashed his lights and passed a county maintenance truck. "Vance's wife seems unimpressed by his collector persona."

"Moira's not very bright about people."

Another silence. They were into the glacial till. Huge boulders thrust from among the trees. The creek twisted around others and the road twisted with it.

Tichnor said, "Vance's first wife, Isabel, shared his enthusiasms and humanized them. I liked her, but it was probably a mistake for them not to have children. For their marriage, I mean, not for the children."

Rob was glad he'd said that.

"Even though the divorce was Vance's idea, it turned out to be a trauma for him. It made Isabel bitter, and I don't blame her. She got their collection of Southwest Indian pottery in the settlement."

Indian pottery. "I presume they acquired the pots through dealers?"

"The pots weren't antique," Tichnor said, "and I'm sure they paid a fair price. Isabel liked several artists—Zuni, I think—and she and Vance even commissioned vases. She taught him about the culture and the techniques. They used to enjoy making buying trips to New Mexico in the winter." He fell silent.

Rob waited. The road kinked and straightened.

"I've been brooding about it. I suspect Vance began to think about the Lauder Point artifacts in the aftermath of the divorce, when he was picking up the pieces."

"How so?" Rob wheeled the car through a long S-bend.

"He would have realized that without Isabel he couldn't trust his own artistic judgment. A lot of their friends sided with Isabel. Most of their social life had centered on those people. Their real social life, I mean, as opposed to the people Vance cultivated as part of his business."

Rob wondered whether Vance classified Phyllis Holton as a real friend or a business friend. "He lost his friends and had trouble replacing them. I think I see what's coming. He needed to impress people, and the means to do it were gone."

"He must have decided to acquire someone else's collection," Tichnor said simply. "It's a logical alternative."

Jack made a rude noise.

Tichnor twisted against the seat belt. "I'm sorry, Jack. I'm just trying to understand my brother's mentality. I don't think that way."

"Yeah," Jack said. Rob thought he sounded skeptical, but Jack was a peaceful man and didn't push it.

"How does Carol come into the story?" Rob overtook a kid driving a purple low-rider.

"I don't know." The doctor sighed. "She was such a pretty girl, a natural blonde with a fashionable figure. Fashionable in that era didn't mean straight up and down. She was perky, too. My friends were crazy for Carol. Being her big brother gave me a lot of prestige."

"In high school?"

"Yes. We attended different colleges."

"Vance, too?"

"He liked California, so he enrolled at UC Santa Barbara."

"Surf and turf," said Rob, who had accumulated enough courses for a degree at Cal Poly without planning to.

"Carol started at Mills, then transferred to Santa Barbara when Vance entered as a freshman. I never understood that. They were close but not joined at the hip, as my granddaughter would say. After Stanford, I went on to med school at the U Dub. Carol married an insurance executive who collected blondes."

"Collected," Rob mused. Funny how the word came up. Carol went out of her way to be collectible, in his opinion. "What was her major?"

"Art history."

Rob frowned. "And she runs an antiques shop that specializes in needlework?"

"That was a late-blooming interest. Post-divorce. In college, she was mainly interested in having a good time. Vance joined in. They thumb-tripped together through Europe one summer." He made a gulping sound as Rob passed two sight-seers in slow-moving cars.

Rob tried to imagine Carol hitchhiking.

"I sound censorious. Carol once accused me of being jealous, but I had a pretty good time myself. I didn't begrudge them their pot parties and rock concerts. Mother was scandalized, though, and she didn't hesitate to enforce her feelings."

"What do you mean enforce?"

"She had the power of the purse."

"Money."

"Yes, partly. Money and disapproval. She set Vance up in business, and she helped Carol sort through the wreckage when the executive dumped her. She now makes Carol a very generous allowance." He tugged at the seat belt. "Mother expects them to be suitably grateful."

"You said Vance never grew up. Sounds as if Carol has problems along those lines, too."

"I suppose she does. But Vance has an edge of aggression. He schemes. Nowadays, he uses Carol to keep in good with Mother. And for other things."

"What things?"

"They *cover* for each other. Always have."

That was vague and Rob meant to pursue it, but the radio crackled. He answered. The dispatcher patched Earl through.

"Uh, we have a situation here."

"Tell me."

"There's a bunch of Indians from Two Falls hanging around the entrance, ten maybe. One of them has a drum, and a couple of them are carrying signs. We're keeping them off the property, and they're not doing anything much yet, but I don't like it."

Rob swore under his breath. "Are they blocking the highway?"

"No, and we won't let them block the access road either."

"What about Tichnor?"

"No movement. His van's still in front of the house."

"Press?"

"Not yet."

"Okay. Keep things quiet." He considered telling Earl to warn the Klalo assembly that Vance was dangerous, but that might just step up the danger if *they* were armed.

"Right."

"I'll be with you—" he checked the time "—in twenty-two minutes."

"Ten-four."

Rob signed off. "I'm going to shoot you, Jack."

Jack chuckled. "I never said Maddie was alone."

Rob switched on the lights and hit the accelerator. A pickup pulled off the road to let him by. At the turnoff to the lake, he had to use the siren on a daydreamer. Fortunately, the road surface was dry, though the sky had begun to cloud over. Snow was forecast at the lake elevation. He covered the distance in seventeen minutes.

When he stopped, lights still flashing, Dr. Tichnor said, "Thank you, Lieutenant. I've always wanted to do that." His eyes shone.

 *Chapter 24*

VANCE Tichnor was in a trap. When the fact sank in, he was going to fight like a wolverine.

Earl had not yet closed the highway. It was too soon. While Jack talked to the Klalos, Rob reconsidered his strategy. Maybe removing the construction crew had been a mistake. Maddie was off on her hillside. Todd was God-knew-where. Vance was in the house. Alone.

The house sat a good half mile back from the highway, almost on the banks of Beaver Creek. Earl had sent Linda into the woods to observe. She'd reported that Vance had gone out on his deck a couple of times, once with a cell phone at his ear, but he hadn't come out to his van. It was just possible he didn't yet know he was in a trap.

Abruptly, Rob made up his mind. He left Jack talking to a young woman who carried a sign that said DESECRATOR and walked over to where Earl was standing.

"Pull the cars back about a hundred yards."

"You crazy?"

"No. You can always shoot out his tires, Earl. I just don't want him to panic when he sees you at the gate. I don't want him to see you at all."

A sedan passed. The driver gawked.

"Close the highway in both directions, but set up your flares out of sight of the gate."

Earl's face brightened.

Something to do at last, Rob thought sardonically. Earl did not like to wait. "I'm going to walk in the back way with Dr. Tichnor, just like I told you. We'll talk to Maddie, then we'll try to talk to Vance. Any word on Todd?"

"No, but that sure was a strange business with Carol."

"What? Something happened?"

"You must've just missed seeing the ambulance on the highway. Jake called from the hospital. It's weird. Carol was attacked by a rabid dog."

Rob gaped.

Earl's eyes betrayed earnest bewilderment.

"I think I want Jake's version." Rob called the dispatcher, and she connected him to Jake.

The deputy was still at the hospital. Rob heard him through twice before grasping the salient facts. One, that Meg was all right. Two, that Carol, who would live but might lose her right leg, had confessed to killing Eddy Redfern. Three, that Towser had attacked her after she made the mistake of shooting him. Ridgebacks are normally good-natured, Towser more than most, but they defend themselves with the utmost vigor.

How Towser and Meg came to be frolicking on the shore of Tyee Lake, Rob did not know. He almost called Meg for an explanation, but decided he didn't need to be distracted from the matter at hand, which had just got more complex. He found the thought of Meg in danger very distracting.

If Carol had killed Eddy Redfern, then the deaths of Brandstetter and Meek looked different. That was the crux of the matter.

Rob signed off, ordering Earl to pull the patrol cars back and block the highway. Then he strode to the car where Ethan Tichnor waited. Jack was talking with Maddie's warriors.

Rob sat in the driver's seat. When he understood what had happened to Carol, the doctor wanted to head straight to the hospital. Not a good idea. They argued. Finally, Rob put Tichnor through to the hospital and let him talk to the surgeons.

While the tide of medical jargon washed through the car, Rob got out and told Jack what he knew. It was a risk, but Rob didn't like the mood of the demonstrators. They were having a powwow good time.

"She killed my nephew?"

"Yes. She's not in any condition to escape, either. You have a legitimate interest in what we do with the artifacts, Jack, but it seems they're contaminated with DDT, so you won't want to handle them without some kind of protection. We're going to tell Maddie, then I'll send the two of you out—"

"DDT?"

Rob explained. "They'll be evidence in a big court case anyway. We'll have to keep them awhile." Quite a while. Years maybe. "There's nothing you can do here."

"I want to talk to Madeline."

"Me, too. Let's go. Tell your crew to take a coffee break or something."

Jack met Rob's eyes with no trace of humor in his own. "What you call artifacts are holy things. These kids are not gonna leave until we know The Dancers is safe."

Rob said quietly, "Isn't that up to Chief Thomas?"

Jack's mouth tightened.

Rob waited.

Jack sighed and his eyes lowered. "Okay, let's go."

After some talk, the demonstrators retreated to their pickups, which Earl had made them leave a good distance from Vance's gate.

Rob retrieved the Kevlar vests from the backseat of the patrol car. "Wrap it up, sir. We need to get going."

Tichnor flapped a hand and went on talking.

Rob tested the bullhorn and hooked it to his belt. He patted his gun, which he would just as soon have left behind, and double-checked that Jack had put his vest on right. Dr. Tichnor got out of the car, looking somber but somewhat reassured. He donned his vest without protest.

Rob ordered Linda Ramos out of the woods and Thayer in. Thayer took his rifle and strict instructions to stay out of sight of the house. Then Rob was ready to go.

He backed the car around, drove to the doctor's access road, a track really, and jolted down it half a mile. At that point it was better to walk, the brush was so thick. Tichnor was full of questions and so was Jack. Rob ignored them, his mind on the man waiting in the huge, empty house. And on Madeline Thomas.

The snow came thicker and had begun to stick, though it wasn't terribly cold out. It would start to get dark soon.

Tichnor wasn't used to hiking. He puffed along behind Jack and Rob, but he didn't complain. Salal, scrub pine, and blackberry briars tangled the track as it sloped gently to the bed of Beaver Creek. Sword ferns thrust up. Their dark fronds were just beginning to curl with frost.

They crossed the stream on a fallen log on hands and knees, Rob somewhat impeded by the bullhorn. Then their way led uphill, and there was no discernible path through the silent woods. Rob let Jack take the lead.

After twenty minutes of heavy going, they emerged in a small clearing from which they could see the back of Vance's lodge, the yard, and the footbridge that crossed Beaver Creek. A yard light lit the van, and another light burned in one of the interior rooms, dimly illuminating the larger room that faced the rear deck. Rob saw no sign of life.

There was no sign of Madeline Thomas either.

Rob and Dr. Tichnor sat on a log while Jack reconnoitered. Tichnor was shivering. Rob gave him his wool hat and that seemed to help.

While they waited, Rob checked in. Thayer was in place. Vance had turned on the yard light as Thayer approached through the woods, scaring him out of three years' growth, but Vance hadn't come out to investigate. At that point, Earl interrupted Thayer's slow commentary.

"Guess who just showed up?"

"Who?" Not Meg, please God.

"Todd Welch."

Rob suppressed a whoop of relief. "No shit? Where has he been?"

"Said he left with the construction crew."

"Let me talk to him."

A crackling sound. Rob was going to skin Todd alive when he saw him, but first things first.

"Yeah, Rob?"

"I'm looking down on Vance's house. Where's the strong room, if I enter from the back?"

"I didn't get into it. Tichnor was giving me a dirty look, so I went on out. That lounge in back gives onto the deck. The secure room is tucked in behind the media center on the left. Door looks like it leads to a closet, but I saw Tichnor come out. The room's bigger than it seems from the outside."

"Okay. Will you go over and talk to the Two Falls contingent? Tell your cousins we're going to start negotiating in a few minutes."

"That it?" He sounded as if he expected a reprimand.

"That's it." For now. "Hand me back to Earl."

Earl wanted to detail all his brilliant arrangements, but Rob could see Jack coming down through the trees, so he signed off. When Jack got close enough to speak to without shouting, Rob stood up.

"Did you find her?"

"No. She was there earlier, though."

"What do you think?"

Jack's eyes were dark with misery. "I think she got impatient and went down to talk to him. I think he captured her. She's in that place. Call that a lodge? Goddamn." He began to cry.

"Hey, take it easy. We're going to talk to him ourselves, and we hold all the cards."

"Not if he has Maddie." Jack wiped his eyes on his sleeve.

Rob unhooked the bullhorn from his belt. "Did you bring your cell phone, Dr. Tichnor?"

Tichnor patted his pockets. "Yes. I turned it off so it wouldn't ring out here and betray our presence."

"Thanks," Rob said gravely. "Is one of Vance's cell phone numbers on the speed dial?"

"Yes. Number seven."

"Good. I'm going to hail him now, and tell him to answer the phone. Then I want you to call him."

"What do I do when he answers?" Tichnor sounded nervous.

Rob didn't answer because he didn't know. His own stomach was doing flip-flops. He was glad he had skipped lunch. "Here goes." He thumbed on the bullhorn and walked out into the open where Tichnor could see him.

"Vance! Vance Tichnor! It's Robert Neill from the sheriff's department. I want to talk to you." He waited, watching snow-flakes whirl like dust motes in the distant yard light. There was no response. No gunshots, either.

Rob raised the bullhorn again. His voice always sounded odd through a microphone. "Tichnor, I know you're in there. I have your brother here." He beckoned to the doctor, who rose slowly and walked to Rob's side. "Here's Ethan, Vance. He has news for you. He's going to dial your cell phone. When it rings, answer it."

Jack said, "Somebody's moving down there."

"Good."

It was so quiet Rob could hear the doctor's cell phone as it dialed the number. The phone rang seven times and a message came on.

"Disconnect," Rob said. He raised the horn again. "Answer the phone, Vance. Carol's in the hospital. Your sister. Ethan needs to talk to you." He thumbed the horn off. "Try it again, sir."

Dr. Tichnor hit the speed-dial number. This time Vance answered on the fourth ring.

"Vance." The doctor cleared his throat. "Carol's been hurt. They think she may have to have her leg amputated. She says...they tell me, she confessed to killing young Redfern. Is that true?"

Vance gabbled something.

"Yes, I know you're in trouble. I'm trying to help."

Rob said, "Hand me the phone, sir."

Tichnor said, "Lieutenant Neill wants to ask you something. You do? Oh, God, Vance, why?" More gabble. He thrust the phone at Rob. "He has Ms. Thomas."

Jack said something sharp.

"Wait," Rob said. He put the phone to his ear.

Vance was swearing.

"Mr. Tichnor, will you confirm that you've taken Chief Thomas prisoner?"

"Chief? What the hell?"

"Madeline Thomas is principal chief of the Klalos. I'm sure she told you that." Not to mention the earlier confrontation over the camas meadow.

"She told me a bunch of crap. I didn't listen. I don't listen to trespassers."

Or look at them, apparently. "I want to know whether or not you have her."

"Yes, I have a hostage, Neill, all trussed up like a turkey, and I intend to use her as soon as it's dark."

Rob waited.

Vance went on, bluff, bragging. "I roughed her up a little but she's all right. Stupid bitch." He sounded like Hal Brandstetter.

Rob said, "The artifacts in your vault, the one hidden behind the media center, belong to the Klalos. You have Chief Thomas, Vance, but she posted a dozen or so people outside your gate waiting for you to come out. And I have patrol cars blocking the highway in both directions. I warn you not to harm Chief Thomas in any way."

The silence crackled. Then Vance said, in something closer to his normal voice, "I won't hurt her unless I have to. I'm going to take my collection and my hostage and drive out of here."

Rob drew a long breath. "I have a more plausible scenario for you."

"What? I suppose you're going to threaten me, fuzz."

"Stop talking like a child. I want you to release Chief Thomas now, unharmed."

Vance cackled. "Not on your life."

Well, yes. "I want you to agree to exchange Chief Thomas for me."

Jack gasped and Dr. Tichnor made a noise of protest.

"Why the hell should I?"

"Because I can talk you through those patrol cars, once Chief Thomas has sent her people home. It's that simple, Vance. Chief Thomas is dangerous to you. You've already offended the Klalos by taking their sacred objects from Lauder Point."

"I didn't steal them." Vance sounded sullen.

"You paid Brandstetter and Meek to steal them. The law doesn't recognize a difference between a crime and the commission of a crime, between theft and hiring a thief to steal. You're a thief." He drew a breath. Better tone it down. "The people waiting out by your gate know you stole the petroglyphs and the knife and the ceremonial drums. I wouldn't give a nickel for your chances while they're out there."

Rob was bluffing. So was Vance. It was a game of blindman's bluff with Maddie Thomas the prize. Rob wondered if he should play the DDT card or save it.

Vance said, "I want to talk to Ethan."

Rob handed Ethan the phone. "Don't let him break contact."

Tichnor nodded, eyes on the ground as if he were embarrassed or ashamed.

Jack took Rob's arm. "Do you think he'll let her go?"

Rob said, "Yes. When he does, I want you and Maddie to walk out to the highway on the track we came in on. Go out and send your young people home. They could get hurt in a shoot-out."

Jack mumbled an assent and let his hand drop.

Dr. Tichnor said something low and angry into the phone.

Rob and Jack looked at him.

The oncologist shook his head. "No, no tricks. I'll let you talk to him." He handed Rob the phone. "He wants to arrange the exchange. I'm sorry, Neill."

Rob said into the phone, "I'm glad you're willing to see things my way, Vance. We'll wait while you untie Chief Thomas. Bring her out so we can see her."

"I'll bring her out with a gun at her head, Neill. I'm not shitting you. I'll kill her. I've killed before."

"Yes," Rob said. "I know you have. But Brandstetter was blackmailing you, wasn't he?"

"He was bleeding me dry!" Vance sounded astonished, almost grateful to be understood. "He threatened Carol. He was an evil man. He deserved to die. So did Meek."

"Chief Thomas doesn't." Rob kept his tone matter-of-fact. "Untie her and bring her out to the deck. Leave the phone on. When I can see she's all right, we'll talk."

"No tricks. I know you have snipers who can shoot the eye out of a squirrel. The minute I hear anything I don't like, the bitch dies."

Rob waited. He could hear breathing on the line.

Then Vance said, "Okay. It'll take a few minutes."

"Do it."

In the blank silence that followed, Jack blew his nose and Dr. Tichnor sat on the log again as if his legs wouldn't hold him up.

Rob felt nothing. He was open to the universe, listening. The wind moaned and a few snowflakes whirled through the cone of light that shone down on the van. His radio crackled.

He keyed it on and spoke low. Earl listened, giving an occasional squawk of protest, but Rob knew he would see the logic of an exchange. He agreed to keep Thayer back from the house. In reserve.

Rob turned the radio off. Suddenly he could hear voices through, but not on, the telephone. Vance must have stuck it in his pocket. He was shouting, and so was Maddie. Oh please, Madeline, just shut up, Rob begged silently. Shut up and for once cooperate.

Perhaps she heard him. The voices stopped. He could hear thumps and brushing noises, as if Vance were bumping into things. A light came on in the lounge. At last, a dark blur appeared at the door that led out onto the deck. After an interminable moment, the door opened. Vance thrust Maddie out ahead of him. Her hands were bound behind her, and he was holding a handgun to her right ear.

He fumbled in his pocket with his left hand and withdrew the phone. "Okay, here she is. What now?"

Rob said, "Untie her hands, Vance. I'll wait."

"Not until I know what's going to happen."

Rob beckoned to Ethan Tichnor, who stood up slowly as if his knees creaked. "When Chief Thomas has spoken to me and I know she's all right, I'll give my gun to your brother. Then I'll walk down with my hands out where you can see them. Chief Thomas will walk across the deck, down the stairs and across the yard. She'll meet me at the footbridge. I'll come over to you when she's on this side of the creek."

"How do I know you don't have hidden weapons?"

Rob said, "Your brother is going to pat me down. I'll hand him the phone when I've spoken to Madeline Thomas. Free her hands."

"I need to cut the rope," Vance muttered. "I'll have to put the phone down."

"Then do it."

If Rob had been standing where Maddie was, he could have taken Vance out in the clumsy interval while Vance wrestled one-handed with a pocket knife. He had slipped the phone into his jacket pocket again. Madeline stood head down, as if dazed. Rob hoped she wasn't.

When her hands were free at last and she held them out, Jack gave a little sob.

Rob said, "Let me talk to her."

Vance handed Maddie the phone.

"I have Jack here, Madeline. Can you hear me?"

"Yes." Her hand fumbled the phone. "My hand's asleep. Tell Jack I love him."

Rob waited.

"I won't let you do this, Lieutenant." Her voice was hoarse from disuse. She cleared her throat.

"Why not? It makes sense."

"Maybe to you. I have a responsibility to my people."

Rob's anger blazed. "What is it with you, Chief? Do you always hog the limelight? There are more lives at stake here than yours. You've already sacrificed one young man to your little project. If Vance Tichnor is cornered out at the gate, he won't hesitate to shoot everything in sight."

"I can't—"

Rob closed his eyes and counted backwards from ten. "I'm sorry. That was out of line. Please, Madeline, just walk out of there and tell your kids to go home."

"You're sure? The Dancers—"

"I'll bring The Dancers out to you."

Silence. Rob heard Vance say something sharp.

"All right." Madeline sounded weary. "I'll do what you say."

Vance took the phone from her. "Satisfied?"

"Yes. Thank you. Can you see me?"

"Yes, but I don't see...ah, there's Ethan. Okay, big brother, disarm the bastard."

Rob handed Dr. Tichnor the telephone and withdrew his handgun from the shoulder holster. The doctor took it with shaking fingers and dropped it into his pocket. His jacket sagged from the weight.

Rob held his arms out. "Tell him you're searching me."

Tichnor complied and Vance said something.

"He asked if you're wearing a bulletproof vest. He wants you to remove it."

"Okay." Rob dropped the Kevlar vest on the weeds at his feet. He felt lighter and colder. He pulled his jacket back in place.

The snow had almost stopped. Patches of white gleamed on the dirt of Vance's yard.

The doctor kept the phone to his ear with his left hand. His right moved lightly over Rob, patting but not prodding. Vance's voice squawked.

"He says you can start walking now. Take care, Robert."

"Yes."

"She's coming," Jack muttered.

Rob picked his way down the uneven slope to the footbridge, careful to keep his hands in sight. When he reached the bridge, he waited for Maddie. She walked as if something hurt.

When she reached him, she said, "I am more sorry than I can say."

"Go send your people home." Rob kept walking. Vance Tichnor loomed. He stood well back, close to the door as if wary of snipers. He kept the gun centered on Rob's face, holding the weapon in both hands. Rob thought it was a .38.

"Come up here, sucker."

Rob climbed the stairs with deliberation, hands out from his sides. Empty hands, he thought. That's good. Tichnor was sweating. As Rob approached the door, Tichnor took a step sideways and Rob felt cold metal touch his ear.

"In the house ahead of me. No tricks."

Rob took his time, eyes narrowed against the light. The lounge was huge and unfurnished except for a couple of plastic outdoor chairs. It had a very high ceiling and the colors were muted. The hardwood floors needed polishing. A huge wall of teak cabinets on the left had to be the media center.

"Sit," Tichnor said. "I'm going to tie you up."

Empty hands, Rob thought. He turned slowly so as not to alarm the other man. "I thought maybe you'd show me the Lauder Point loot first, Vance. I've been looking for it for ten years, after all."

Vance gave a sneering laugh. "Some detective."

"It's supposed to be interesting, especially the petroglyphs." Rob kept his face blank, hands out from his sides, light and empty. He had an impulse to remove his boots, too, as if he were engaged in some kind of mystical martial arts lesson. He held Tichnor's gaze.

Vance laughed, a sharp, uneasy sound, and shrugged. "Sure. Why not?"

"You'll want me to help you move the stuff. The petroglyphs must weigh a lot." They were on the small side, as rock drawings went, but had to be heavy.

Vance thought. "You move them. I hold the gun."

"Whatever. Where is it?"

"Over there." Vance gestured with the gun. Getting careless.

Rob walked slowly across the room and touched the handle of

the "closet" door. It opened with a heavy, soundless swing that indicated its true function. "Where's the light?"

"Left of the door."

Rob felt and touched a switch. The lights came up gradually and he caught his breath.

He was facing something like a shrine. Glass-fronted teak cabinets lit from within displayed the artifacts with an elegance that called attention not to any one piece but to the ensemble. Here, they said, is an important collection.

The three petroglyphs had pride of place, with Tsagiglalal, She Who Watches, in the center, Running Elk to the left, and The Dancers to the right. Even the minor artifacts—baskets, drums, stone pieces—had been arranged with sensitivity. Rob looked hard at The Dancers, off balance without the missing shard. The ritual knife glittered on sky blue velvet.

Rob said, "I'm impressed. A German businessman would be blown away."

"German?"

"You were going to use the lodge to entertain foreign investors, weren't you?"

"Want to make something of it?"

"No. I'll need packing materials. Boxes."

"Out in the kitchen." Vance waved Rob out with the gun barrel. Vance had apparently forgotten about tying Rob up.

When he had retrieved a couple of boxes under Tichnor's suspicious gaze and gone back to the secure room, Rob said, "What first?"

"The small stuff. I removed the seats from the van earlier. You can lay the rock drawings flat in the back, layer them with blankets, and pile the boxes on top."

"Sounds as if you've been thinking."

"If you're going to do it, get a move on. It's turning dark already."

Rob approached the cabinet that held the ceremonial drums. "I guess it won't hurt me to handle these things one time, but I sure wouldn't want to make a habit of it."

"Shut up. What do you mean?"

"They're contaminated with DDT. Didn't you know?"

"I don't believe you!" The gun waved.

Take it slow. "That was what I was trying to warn you about, the first message I left on your cell phone. The parks people used to dust organic artifacts with DDT to prevent insect damage. Must be fifteen years' worth of pesticide on these things. How do I open this?"

"I'll open it." Vance sounded agitated and his movements were jerky.

Rob took a step backwards and waited as Vance wrestled the latch one-handed. The gun moved to cover Rob.

"The feds have sent out health warnings. Lot of medical double-talk. I gather that DDT accumulates from repeated exposure." Rob shook his head. "I don't suppose you have latex gloves in that kitchen."

"I...no. You're shitting me."

"Why would I lie about DDT?" Using the tips of his fingers, Rob removed the first drum from its nest and laid it carefully in the nearest box. "We ought to cover this with newspaper or something."

"I don't have newspaper."

"Wouldn't want to mar the surface. That's elkhide. They scrape it and use elk brains to cure it. How about using cloth? You must have towels or blankets."

"Towels. No. Get out of here. I have to talk to you. What about this DDT?" When Rob turned and looked at him, Vance waved the gun. He was sweating. "Out."

Rob walked very slowly out into the lounge.

"Sit on that chair. That one. Move it."

Rob stood still. "DDT kills small animals. Mice, bats, fish. The effects are slower for people, but over the years... Say, you don't have asthma, do you? Your breathing is kind of harsh."

"Stop it!" Vance screamed. "I want you to sit down!"

Empty hands, empty hands. Rob turned, knees bent. Now. He dropped to the floor, legs slashing. The gun went off as it flew from the other man's hand. Vance fell.

Deaf from the gunshot, Rob scrambled. Tichnor was heavier and taller, but he was carrying excess weight. They rolled across the floor, grappling for control. Rob used his knees. As Rob's elbow connected with his jaw, Vance grunted and sagged onto the oak surface.

Rob twisted Vance's right arm back and pinned the wheezing man belly down on the slick floor. Blood splattered where his chin hit the boards. Rob jerked and heard the joint crack. Vance moaned.

"Lie still!" Rob dug one knee into Tichnor's back and pinned the flailing left arm with his other leg. He could see Vance's .38 where it had slid all the way across the room and come to rest against the base of the media center. Vance heaved, and Rob twisted the arm, yanking up. Then he groped for the radio in his left pocket, thumbed it on, and shouted for help. Vance howled like a dog.

 *Chapter 25*

MEG drove back to Klalo in the dual wake of the ambulance and Jake's patrol car. Tom and Towser cried the whole way. Both of them had a lot to cry about.

Something was going on at Vance Tichnor's access road. Meg thought she glimpsed picketers with signs among the cops and cop-cars, but she didn't dally to find out what was going on. Jake and the ambulance sped south, and Meg followed. Lights flashed, sirens whooped, and nobody messed with them.

They ducked down out of the snow almost at once, but the road was wet with rain. Meg slewed around corners and almost lost control half a dozen times, but all three vehicles reached the hospital safely.

At the emergency room entrance, Meg left Tom and Towser to guard the car and ran over to Jake. He said he was waiting for the doctors to evaluate Carol's condition. He had talked to the sheriff, who intended to charge Carol with the murder of Edward Redfern, and though it probably wouldn't hold up in court, the attempted murder of Margaret McLean, Librarian.

At the scene, Jake had bagged Carol's gun and called a tow truck to bring her car in. The paramedics had found her purse, with identification and insurance card, stuffed into the left pocket of the camel's-hair coat, so Meg didn't see any point in sticking around the hospital. She had no intention of calling Charlotte Tichnor. Let the police inform Carol's mother. Meg hoped never to see or talk to a Tichnor again. She said so, with passion.

Jake agreed to come the next day for her full statement. Out at the lake, he'd recorded preliminary statements from Meg and Patsy while the paramedics worked to stabilize Carol.

"What about the dog?" That was the question uppermost in Meg's mind now the surgeons had charge of Carol.

"She shot him?"

"Yes. I saw it. She told me she was going to shoot me, too. He saved my life. They can't put Towser down. It's not fair!"

Jake said, "I dunno, Meg. Try not to worry about it. The thing is, that dog is dangerous."

"That dog is a hero." Meg was almost in tears herself.

"Hey, nothing's going to happen right now. Take the pooch to the vet and have him checked out. And, uh, maybe you'd better change clothes."

Meg looked down at her hands and arms. They were brown with dried blood. She supposed she was splattered all over. For the first time, it occurred to her to worry about exposure to whatever maladies Carol's blood might carry. She groaned.

Jake read her mind. "They can test you for AIDS and so on later. No hurry."

"Jesus."

"Hey, it's routine these days."

Abruptly, she came to her senses. "I'm dithering. Right. Thank you, Jake, and I hope you find Todd."

"Yeah, me, too. I hope I get out of here in time for the raid."

"Raid?"

"Well, not a raid. Rob's serving Tichnor with a search warrant."

"I knew that. The patrol cars, right?"

"Yeah."

"It went out of my mind, what with Carol and the dog." She stood on tiptoe and gave Jake a swift peck on the cheek. "Good luck. Give my love to Annie."

He grinned. "See you later."

Tom composed himself in time to deal with the vet, so Meg paced the waiting room while pet owners clutched their sick animals and stared at her as if she were Lady Macbeth.

When Tom and Towser came out at last, the veterinarian came with them.

He patted Tom on the arm and scratched Towser's head. "Don't worry, boy, we'll take care of you." He looked at Meg. "This dog will not be put down." He sounded as if he expected her to argue.

"Good." Meg felt a surge of relief that she wouldn't have to mount a crusade. "Let me know what I can do to help. Ready, Tom?"

Tom nodded and clutched at Towser's leash. Meg thought the dog had been tranquilized. A good thing.

She drove home without listening to Tom's report on Towser's medical condition and saw the two of them off in a daze. Then she ran into her house, stuffed all the clothes she had been wearing into a garbage bag, and showered until the hot water ran out.

Between diminishing jolts of adrenaline, she felt so exhausted that she lay down on the sofa and slept. She thrashed through nightmares but never quite surfaced. It was pitch dark out when she did wake up, and the doorbell was ringing.

She stumbled to her feet, ran a hand through her hair, and walked down the dim hall. If it was Darcy Wheeler, Meg was going to send her off with a flea in her ear.

Rob was leaning on the doorbell.

She blinked at him, wordless.

"Are you all right? I phoned and you didn't answer. When they dropped me off, I knocked at the back door and that didn't work either." He took a big breath. "So I came around here. I thought something was wrong."

"What time is it?"

"After ten."

"Come in. I was just taking a nap on the couch." She pulled him down the hall and plunked him onto the sofa. "You look terrible. What happened to your arm?" He was holding his left arm stiffly.

"Cracked my elbow on Vance Tichnor's jaw."

"What! Tell me."

He sank back and she sat beside him, almost but not quite touching.

"Nope," he said. "You first. Jake gave me his version. Why the hell did you drive out there at all?"

"Cabin fever."

"Yeah, but why Tyee? You knew I was going after Vance." He sounded accusatory, as if she had committed some infraction.

Meg bristled. "No, sir, I did not know any such thing. You told me you were getting a search warrant. That's all."

"All!"

"I'm not an experienced police officer. What do I know? If you'd said you were going to take Vance into custody, I'd have stayed out of the way."

"Hmmph."

"I don't know this area, remember? You mentioned your place at the lake, and it sounded interesting. So I loaded Tom and Towser into the Accord and took off."

"But Earl said—"

"Earl. Ha! Earl told me to clear out, to leave the DDT test to the big boys. So I left. I went away. I did what you wanted, I even found your murderer, and now you're bawling me out?"

Rob groaned. "I can always count on good old Earl."

"Then pushing me out wasn't your idea?"

"No."

"Okay, then." Meg frowned. "Earl wants your job."

Rob grinned. "I know. It's fun to watch him." The smile faded. "I worried about you."

She took a good look at him. "Well, I didn't worry about you, but I guess I should have. Tell me everything. No, wait, I'll get the Scotch." She jumped up.

When she got to the kitchen, her stomach informed her that the Tenas Klootchman hamburger was a thing of the distant past, so she fixed a plate of cheese, olives, and crackers, threw in a bowl of Bakersfield almonds, and poured Scotch. Doubles. She carried the tray to the living room.

Rob, who was leaning against the back of the sofa with his eyes closed, opened one eye and burst into laughter.

"What?"

"I was laying this little bet with myself." He wiped his eyes, chuckling.

Meg set the tray down. "And you won?"

"I won. I knew if I looked pitiful enough you couldn't resist feeding me." He pulled her down beside him.

Meg sat but she was still on her dignity. "I'm feeding *me*." She crunched an almond. "I slept through dinner."

He sat up, took a glass, and raised it in salute. "Confusion to our enemies."

"Confusion to Tichnors." She clanked her glass on his, sipped Laphroaig, and grabbed a cracker. When she had laid a slab of

Tillamook sharp cheddar on it, she said, "Now you can tell me. I'm fortified."

He gave her a terse account of his afternoon. By the time he finished she had lost her appetite for cheese and crackers.

"So you charged Vance with murder?" she asked almost at random, because her mind was not on legal details. At some point his arm had circled her shoulders. She leaned against him, feeling the warm thrum of life in him.

"Two counts and theft. He admitted to me that he killed Hal and Meek, but confessions aren't enough these days. The DA thinks the evidence is weak in the Meek case, but he was willing to give it a try. The campground site is still being examined, and Jeff is after witnesses, so who knows what they'll come up with?"

"Who knows?" she echoed, snuggling.

"We think we have a footprint from Brandstetter's deck that matches a pair of boots Earl found at the lodge. That, the gun, and the van make that case stronger. We also charged Vance with possession of stolen goods. And we have a blood sample. If his cholesterol level is as high as I think it is, we should be able to test for DDT without getting a court order."

Meg had to laugh.

"And, of course, we have the artifacts."

She straightened to look at him. "Then Vance is safely in the county jail?"

"Under sedation at the hospital, with Ethan and his lawyers in attendance and a deputy at his door." He constructed a cracker-and-cheese sandwich and ate it with deliberation.

"He should be locked up."

"Hey, he will be." He brushed crumbs and took another sip of whisky. "They'll bring him in tomorrow when the doctors release him. Want to bet he has your garage door key on his key chain? Thayer found the other one."

"Where?"

"Buried behind the garage. He took another look."

Meg snuggled against him.

He gave her shoulders a squeeze. "Further questions, madam?"

"Carol confessed to me that she killed Eddy Redfern." She burrowed in his sweater.

"I know. You could've knocked me over with a feather."

"Cliché number five."

"I'm on a roll. Are you okay, Meg? That must've been hard to deal with."

"I have the feeling I haven't even begun to deal with it." Her voice shook a little. She cleared her throat. "And I'm full of questions. If Carol killed Edward Redfern, why was his wallet in Brandstetter's file cabinet?"

"I gather from what Vance said before the lawyers showed up that he and Carol panicked. They did what Vance has done all along, left it to Hal to do their dirty work."

"So Brandstetter buried Eddy in the garage?"

"Hal and Meek did. It was supposed to be a temporary arrangement, according to Vance, but I suspect Hal liked the idea. It gave him a strong hold over Vance. Hal was blackmailing him, bleeding him dry. Or so Vance said." His voice trailed off. He sounded tired, but he was warm and alive. For now, that was enough.

Time for closure. Meg sat up and took a long, fortifying sip of whisky. "Remember when you swore me in as a deputy?"

He smiled at her. "Sure. A moment of inspiration."

"Among other things, you said you wanted somebody to tell you when you were crazy."

He grinned and pulled her to him. "So I did. Can you hold off doing that for a while?"

Meg kissed him on the mouth. "Not indefinitely."

THE next morning, Sheriff McCormick called a press conference for eleven o'clock. Madeline Thomas held hers at ten.

Mickey Simonson

ABOUT THE AUTHOR

Sheila Simonson is the author of ten novels, six of them mysteries. She taught English and history at the community college level until she retired to write full-time. She has a grown son and lives with her husband in Vancouver, Washington.

Set along the Columbia River Gorge, *Buffalo Bill's Defunct* wrestles, on the local level, with the global problem of the destruction of ancient artifacts. Simonson remembers visiting the salmon fishing sites along the Columbia as a child, before their tragic drowning by the waters of The Dalles Dam. She likes to hear from readers, who can visit her website at http://sheila.simonson. googlepages.com.

MORE MYSTERIES
FROM PERSEVERANCE PRESS
🂡 *For the New Golden Age* 🂡

JON L. BREEN
Eye of God
ISBN 978-1-880284-89-6

TAFFY CANNON
ROXANNE PRESCOTT SERIES
Guns and Roses
*Agatha and Macavity Award
nominee, Best Novel*
ISBN 978-1-880284-34-6

Blood Matters
ISBN 978-1-880284-86-5

Open Season on Lawyers
ISBN 978-1-880284-51-3

Paradise Lost
ISBN 978-1-880284-80-3

LAURA CRUM
GAIL MCCARTHY SERIES
Moonblind
ISBN 978-1-880284-90-2

Chasing Cans
ISBN 978-1-880284-94-0

Going, Gone *(forthcoming)*
ISBN 978-1-880284-98-8

JEANNE M. DAMS
HILDA JOHANSSON SERIES
Crimson Snow
ISBN 978-1-880284-79-7

Indigo Christmas
ISBN 978-1-880284-95-7

KATHY LYNN EMERSON
LADY APPLETON SERIES
**Face Down Below
the Banqueting House**
ISBN 978-1-880284-71-1

**Face Down Beside
St. Anne's Well**
ISBN 978-1-880284-82-7

Face Down O'er the Border
ISBN 978-1-880284-91-9

ELAINE FLINN
MOLLY DOYLE SERIES
Deadly Vintage
ISBN 978-1-880284-87-2

HAL GLATZER
KATY GREEN SERIES
Too Dead To Swing
ISBN 978-1-880284-53-7

A Fugue in Hell's Kitchen
ISBN 978-1-880284-70-4

The Last Full Measure
ISBN 978-1-880284-84-1

PATRICIA GUIVER
DELILAH DOOLITTLE
PET DETECTIVE SERIES
The Beastly Bloodline
ISBN 978-1-880284-69-8

NANCY BAKER JACOBS
Flash Point
ISBN 978-1-880284-56-8

DIANA KILLIAN
POETIC DEATH SERIES
Docketful of Poesy
(forthcoming)
ISBN 978-1-880284-97-1

JANET LAPIERRE
PORT SILVA SERIES
Baby Mine
ISBN 978-1-880284-32-2

Keepers
*Shamus Award nominee,
Best Paperback Original*
ISBN 978-1-880284-44-5

Death Duties
ISBN 978-1-880284-74-2

Family Business
ISBN 978-1-880284-85-8

Run a Crooked Mile
(forthcoming)
ISBN 978-1880284-88-9

VALERIE S. MALMONT
Tori Miracle Series
**Death, Bones, and
Stately Homes**
ISBN 978-1-880284-65-0

DENISE OSBORNE
Feng Shui Series
Evil Intentions
ISBN 978-1-880284-77-3

LEV RAPHAEL
Nick Hoffman Series
Tropic of Murder
ISBN 978-1-880284-68-1

Hot Rocks
ISBN 978-1-880284-83-4

LORA ROBERTS
Bridget Montrose Series
Another Fine Mess
ISBN 978-1-880284-54-4

Sherlock Holmes Series
**The Affair of the
Incognito Tenant**
ISBN 978-1-880284-67-4

REBECCA ROTHENBERG
Botanical Series
The Tumbleweed Murders
(completed by Taffy Cannon)
ISBN 978-1-880284-43-8

SHEILA SIMONSON
Latouche County Series
Buffalo Bill's Defunct
ISBN 978-1-880284-96-4

SHELLEY SINGER
Jake Samson &
Rosie Vicente Series
Royal Flush
ISBN 978-1-880284-33-9

NANCY TESLER
Biofeedback Series
**Slippery Slopes and Other
Deadly Things**
ISBN 978-1-880284-58-2

PENNY WARNER
Connor Westphal Series
Blind Side
ISBN 978-1-880284-42-1

Silence Is Golden
ISBN 978-1-880284-66-7

ERIC WRIGHT
Joe Barley Series
**The Kidnapping
of Rosie Dawn**
*Barry Award, Best Paperback
Original. Edgar, Ellis, and
Anthony Award nominee*
ISBN 978-1-880284-40-7

*REFERENCE/
MYSTERY WRITING*

KATHY LYNN EMERSON
**How To Write Killer
Historical Mysteries:
The Art and Adventure of
Sleuthing Through the Past**
ISBN 978-1-880284-92-6

CAROLYN WHEAT
**How To Write Killer Fiction:
The Funhouse of Mystery &
the Roller Coaster of Suspense**
ISBN 978-1-880284-62-9

Available from your local bookstore or from
Perseverance Press/John Daniel & Co. at (800) 662-8351
or www.danielpublishing.com/perseverance.